RCV 1 3 2007

STL / BAY

12/08

ω

D0443382

Colorado Pickup Man

COLORADO PICKUP MAN

JACQUIE GREENFIELD

FIVE STAR

An imprint of Thomson Gale, a part of The Thomson Corporation

THOMSON

™

GALE

Detroit • New York • San Francisco • New Haven, Conn. • Waterville, Maine • London

W

THOMSON

GALE

Set in 11 pt. Plantin.

LIBRARY OF CONGRESS CATALOGING-IN-PUBLICATION DATA

Greenfield, Jacquie.
    Colorado pickup man / Jacquie Greenfield. — 1st ed.
        p. cm.
    ISBN-13: 978-1-59414-615-2 (hardcover : alk. paper)
    ISBN-10: 1-59414-615-2 (hardcover : alk. paper)
    1. Ranchers—Fiction. I. Title.
PS3607.R4537C66 2007
813'.6—dc22   2007020697

First Edition. First Printing: October 2007.

Published in 2007 in conjunction with Tekno Books.

Printed in the United States of America on permanent paper
10 9 8 7 6 5 4 3 2 1

This book is dedicated to my husband, Doug. You are my best friend and real-life hero. I love you very much.

And to my four children, Jacob, Hannah, Adam, and Amanda, thank you for your heartfelt hugs and enthusiastic support. You are all such a wonderful blessing and I thank God for you every day. Remember, never give up on your dreams.

ACKNOWLEDGMENTS

This book would not have been published without the countless hours of reading and editing by my faithful critique partners. Diane Palmer, you are an angel in every sense of the word. Thank you for all your wonderful advice and your clever drawings in the margins of my manuscripts. They really brought my words to life! Pamela Nissen, you see things in a whole new light and are truly an inspirational writer. Roxanne Rustand, your books have inspired me for years and I only hope I can touch my readers the way you've touched yours. Nancy Nicholson, your countless hours and insight helped shape my book from a jumbled mess of ideas into an organized, thought-out novel.

And to my family and friends, who ask every day how my writing is going and if I'm published yet, I could not have come this far without all of your support and encouragement.

Two can accomplish more than twice as much as one, for the results can be much better. If one falls, the other pulls him up; but if a man falls when he is alone, he is in trouble . . . two can stand back-to-back and conquer.

Ecclesiastes 4: 9–11

CHAPTER ONE

Perspiration trickled from the brim of Debra Walker's cowboy hat. Sitting atop her eight-year-old buckskin mare, she made an impatient shift in the saddle. Blazing heat from the horse's hide seared straight through her jeans into the backsides of her thighs.

The Denver Tri-County Auction Barn seemed as hot as an old wood furnace this Sunday afternoon. Large oscillating fans hummed in vain, trying to circulate the hot and dusty July air.

Debra had been cooped up in a corner horse stall for the past eight hours. She tugged at the collar of her bulky denim work shirt and blotted the moisture beading her forehead and upper lip. Sweat and grime saturated a red tank top she wore beneath her shirt, only intensifying her discomfort.

Beams of late afternoon sunshine filtered through an exit door standing wide open. She was tempted to bolt—ride like the wind into the Rocky Mountain sunset. Disappear to a happier time in her life when she and her father used to camp for days up at Big Bear Pass.

But that was before her parents' divorce, before she'd taken over the ranch . . . before her father had been fatally gored by a steer.

Static crackled over the loudspeakers throughout the enclosed facility. "Lot number eighty-four!"

Debra flinched. Her knuckles whitened as she gripped the leather reins. Loud thuds from horses kicking the walls in the neighboring pens drowned out the heavy pounding of her pulse.

She turned in her saddle and flicked a glance of dread toward the sticker on her mare's hindquarters. *Eighty-four.* Her throat constricted, making it hard to breathe. She felt like she was headed to the gallows for an execution instead of to the auction block to sell her beloved horse, Branded Sunset.

As she sucked in a painful gulp of air, Debra's three cracked ribs were a constant reminder of how she'd failed her father in the end. Pungent aromas of manure, sweaty hides, and sweet oats filled her senses, all bittersweet reminders of what she'd left behind.

Forever, if she had her way.

Flipping her long black braid over her shoulder, she tugged her cowboy hat down to her eyebrows and gave a gentle nudge with the heel of her boot. "Come on, girl. Let's get this over with."

Brandy's hooves clopped noisily on a cracked cement corridor as they plodded toward the auction ring. Rows of wooden pens housed dozens of horses of every breed, size, and color. Several colts skittered nervously, whinnying for their mothers. The less anxious animals shoved their noses into alfalfa-filled hay nets hanging in the corners of their stalls.

Brandy halted in her tracks. Her muscles bunched. Her ears pinned back.

Tied to the outside of a stall, a young palomino colt gave a low warning snort.

Dreading a confrontation between the two horses, Debra gave Brandy a reassuring pat on the neck and urged her horse around the frisky yearling. "Easy, girl," she soothed. "We don't need any trouble today."

A good five hundred head had cycled through the center ring since the sale began three days ago, and with an oversaturated horse market, the auction made for a disorganized, congested livestock barn.

Giving the colt a wide birth, Debra reined Brandy to the other side of the aisle. A big paint stepped into their path. Brandy shied and stepped backwards, bumping into the young palomino.

A sickening thump sounded against Brandy's rump. Brandy gave a shrill whinny and reared back on her hind legs.

Debra gasped and grabbed hold of the saddle horn.

The colt kicked again.

Not to be outdone by such a young stud, Brandy bucked and twisted her body, her rear hooves nailing the colt in the abdomen. With Debra's weakened upper body strength, the abrupt jerk whipped her right out of the saddle.

Rustic posts and beams swirled together in a haze. She clenched her eyes shut, gritted her teeth, and stifled a tormented scream in her throat as she slammed into a wooden fence. When she dropped into a pile of musty hay, prickly straw stabbed her in the butt, straight through her jeans.

The air whooshed plum out of her. But it was her chest that received most of the impact. It felt like she'd inhaled a thousand tiny razor blades as needles of fire radiated clear around her ribcage.

"You okay, ma'am?"

Her eyes stung. The wooden fence she'd slammed into blurred into a bank of fuzzy snow. *Oh, God.* This was it. She was going to die. Right here, right in the middle of a horse barn. She seized an agonizing breath then hung her head between her knees.

"Ma'am?" That same low baritone sounded above her head. "Do you need any help?"

Blood pulsed so loudly between her ears she thought she'd imagined the voice at first. Maybe she was in heaven and this was some kind of an angel here to take her out of her misery.

She blinked hard, her vision slowly clearing as she focused on a pair of fancy lizard-skin cowboy boots. They were large boots; huge, actually. Did angels wear cowboy boots?

A loud whinny penetrated the fog in her head and she realized she wasn't dead. Worse, someone had actually witnessed her untimely and ungraceful dismount. The pain in her ribs suddenly mixed with the humiliation of being unseated by her own horse. Now she wanted to burrow a tunnel right into this pile of straw. Instead, she gave a slight shake of her head to let the man know she didn't need any help.

"Both horses seem to be okay," he said. "There's no marks."

Thank God. Living with the guilt of her father's death these last two months had been hard enough. If anything had happened to Brandy, she'd never forgive herself. Hoping to hide the heated blaze of embarrassment that smothered her face like a hot, heavy saddle blanket, she went to tug her cowboy hat down.

Her hat was gone.

"Looking for this?" the man asked, holding her black Resistol in front of her.

She braced her elbows on her bent knees and managed a breathless "Thanks," then took the hat and shoved it on her head, yanking it clear down to her eyebrows.

"What do you think, J.D.?" a man hollered from behind. "She hung on better than any professional saddle bronc rider. I'd give her an eighty-two."

Another man chimed in, "Nah, she deserves at least an eighty-nine."

Debra cringed. Lifted her hand and waved, acknowledging the harmless gibes coming from the peanut gallery, all the while trying to hide the effects of the scorching heat that seared her chest like a branding iron.

"Give her a break, guys," the first man named J.D. drawled in her defense. "This is a lot of horse for a pretty little gal like this to be handling."

Pretty little gal? If she weren't about to pass out she'd laugh at his comment. At five-eleven-and-a-half, she'd never been described as little. Big-boned, buxom, robust even. But as far as pretty went, the closest any man had come to telling her she was pretty was her father, which in her book didn't count.

Hoping to appear somewhat in control, she flipped her heavy black braid over her shoulder and wiped her sweaty palms on her faded Rocky jeans. With gritted teeth, she pushed up with her legs and stood.

Bad idea. Blood quickly drained from her head. She swayed. A powerful arm wrapped around her waist. The next thing she knew she was pressed firmly against a solid wall of muscle. Searing warmth radiated around her ribcage like a thermal heat wrap.

"Easy, now." A man's voice sounded next to her ear, his mouth so close to her face she could feel the warmth of his breath on her heated skin. "Maybe you ought to have a doctor take a look at you."

"Doctor?" she repeated, not fully comprehending what was happening. Her head floated as if it was filled with helium. She felt her hat slip off as she nestled her cheek against a firm pillow covered with soft denim. Earthy scents of the barn were now mixed with an intoxicating dose of woodsy pine, fresh mint, and the purely masculine scent of a man who'd put in a good day's labor. Had she met up with her father in heaven?

It seemed an eternity since she'd felt his brawny arms wrapped around her, listened to his heart as it beat a loud, comforting cadence in her ear. Maybe the last two months had all been part of a horrible nightmare and she was finally waking up.

Static from the loud speakers crackled in her ears. "Lot number eighty-four! Second call!"

15

Debra gasped, nearly jumping out of her boots. Her eyes flew wide. It was only then she realized her fingers were curled into the denim material of a man's shirt, a shirt stretching across a chest twice as wide as her father's.

Oh, God. This was not a dream, and the man in front of her was definitely not Clyde Walker.

She shoved away, too embarrassed even to look this big cowboy in the eye. "Sorry about that, mister. Guess I landed harder than I thought." Her voice sounded short and breathy. She hunched over at the waist, bracing her hands on her thighs.

"Easy, darlin'," he drawled, keeping a gentle grip on her upper arms. "Maybe you ought to sit down a spell."

"No. I'm okay. Just got a little winded, is all." She used the collar of her denim shirt and dabbed at her lips, hoping to sound more in control. "I'd better get going. I'm on deck, and after waiting around all day, I'd hate to get bumped to the end."

"Tell you what," he said, hunkering down beside her. He had her hat cupped over his knee as he spoke next to her face. "How about I ride your mare into the arena for you? Even the best horses get spooked in an environment like this."

"Thanks, but I can take it from here."

"It's really not a problem," he insisted, splaying his palm across her lower back. "You can stand by the auctioneer in case he has any questions."

She had to grit her teeth. He sounded just like her father now. He'd never wanted her to be involved with the sale of his horses. He'd never wanted her involved with his ranch, *period.* Had hired hands to do all the dirty work. Said a secluded horse ranch was no place for a single young woman to live the rest of her life. Even sent her away to college to pursue a career.

But even four years of college hadn't changed her mind, and she'd been hell-bent on proving her father wrong. She'd been put to the test the day he'd injured his back. For two years prior to his death, she'd worked around the clock, overseeing all the livestock, watching the market, even doing most of the training of the expensive horses herself.

It hadn't been enough.

She hadn't been enough.

A wrenching pain tore through her chest, and it wasn't because of her injured ribs. Now, because of her, Daddy was buried six feet under with his boots on!

"Ma'am?" A large warm hand made a gentle caress over her lower back. "I'd feel a whole lot better if you'd let me get a doctor. My brother's just around the corner."

"No, I'm fine," she said through clenched teeth. "I appreciate your concern, but really, I don't need any help." She may have failed her father miserably in the end, but she was for darn sure gonna handle the sale of her own horse.

"Now don't take this the wrong way," he said, keeping a firm grip on her arm. "But you don't look fine. Maybe you oughta—"

"I said I got it," she snapped, sounding more irritated than she'd intended. Standing to her full height, she turned to face this overbearing cowboy, but instead of looking him in the eyes like she did most men, she had to tip her head back to meet his gaze.

She gulped. Now she understood why he referred to her as a little gal. The guy practically towered over her as he stared down at her from under the brim of a straw Stetson cowboy hat. Dark brown eyes locked with hers, preventing her from even blinking. A brown, trimmed mustache curled around his lips into a nicely shaped beard covering only his square chin, goatee style.

"Pardon me," he drawled, thumbing his hat back on his forehead, openly scanning her from her hat down to her cowboy boots. "You're not so little, now are you?" A toothpick dangled precariously from the corner of his mouth now curled into a lazy grin.

He rubbed his whiskery chin and stepped back a pace, giving her another once over as if *she* were on the auction block. "I was right about one thing. You sure are pretty."

She couldn't seem to get her voice to function; her tongue somehow stuck to the roof of her mouth. Living on a secluded ranch most of her twenty-four years hadn't exactly provided her with a wealth of opportunities to converse with eligible men. Even in college, she'd commuted from the ranch every day, rarely staying after class so she could get home and help her father with the chores.

And after an incident with a ranch hand when she was sixteen, her father had made sure she'd kept her distance from the opposite sex—especially brawny cowboys like this one, whose biceps were bigger than her thighs. Remembering those arms wrapped securely around her waist just moments before, her heart did a little two-step with her stomach.

She caught a whiff of her own body odor and almost cringed. A rank blend of sweat, hay, and horsehide was no match for her baby-powder-fresh deodorant. Where was a horse trough when she needed one?

"Lot number eighty-four! Last call!"

She flinched. Her heart skipped a beat then pounded painfully hard against her ribcage. Dreading the idea of mounting her horse in front of these roughneck cowboys, she swept the reins over Brandy's ears and grimaced. She could easily lead Brandy into the arena on foot, but this was the last chance to ride her. By golly, she wasn't about to let a few injured ribs take this away from her, too.

Earlier, she'd used an old grain bucket to climb onto Brandy's back, but she didn't think her pride could handle much more humiliation today. Now she truly understood what it meant to cowboy up.

"Look," she said, checking the cinch on her saddle, stalling mostly. "I don't mean to be rude, but I'm on deck. If you have any questions, we're listed in the auction catalogue."

"Fair enough," he agreed with a nod. "Good luck in there, and by the way," he added, leaning closer and catching her eye. "I'd have given you a ninety-five, easy." He propped her hat on her head, tapped it down, and then shot her a wink. His straight front teeth bit down on the end of his toothpick as his smile broadened, deepening a dimple in his cheek. The two-step between her heart and stomach suddenly turned into a full-blown jitterbug.

As he turned around, she could only watch as he sauntered down the wide aisles of the auction barn, his hips swaying in a slow, John Wayne kind of swagger as his large cowboy boots shuffled over the sawdust and straw-covered cement floor. He stopped at the exit door, standing nearly as tall and just about as wide. A stream of sunlight engulfed this huge cowboy and she wondered if he was some kind of an angel after all, sent by her father to escort her to the pearly gates.

She gave herself a mental shake. From the looks of things, J.D. was just another bullheaded rancher. Any gates *that* man would be escorting her to would be heavy and cumbersome and clear out on some pasture in the middle of God knows where. And if he was anything like her father, she'd be the one stuck opening and shutting those gates in all kinds of weather.

No, thank you. There'd have to be a hurricane in the Rockies before she'd step foot on a ranch again.

After the sale she was headed south to Colorado Springs. A new job awaited her at a company her father had co-founded over thirty years ago—before he'd given it all up to ranch.

Although it killed her to have to sell Brandy, Debra was

convinced that moving into the city was the best decision she'd ever made. Other than college, she'd never really experienced anything outside of ranching. It was time to broaden her horizons. Hang up her boot spurs and utilize her bachelor's degree to become a bona fide, eight-to-five career woman. Working behind a desk had to be a heck of a lot easier than busting her butt on a struggling horse ranch.

More importantly, this new job might be her only chance to earn back part of her father's legacy . . . as well as her pride.

Thankful the other cowboys left the vicinity, she wedged her scuffed cowboy boot into the leather stirrup and had to grit her teeth to keep the groan from escaping her throat. After a slight hesitation, she pulled herself up and swung her leg over Brandy's rump, landing hard in the saddle.

She closed her eyes and bit down on the inside of her cheek, curling over the saddle horn. Perspiration beaded her upper lip. Droplets of sweat rolled down her chest between her breasts. As the ache waned to a dull throb, she hauled in another gasp of air and managed to pull her shoulders back.

With new resolve, she urged Brandy the rest of the way down the aisle and halted in front of a dilapidated wooden door, the only thing that separated Debra from losing a piece of her heart.

Of all the new doors that had opened in her life, this was one door she wanted to bolt shut!

Hoping to get another glimpse of the tall cowgirl and her buckskin mare, Joshua "J.D." Garrison flicked his toothpick into a pile of straw in the parking lot, then stepped inside the rear area of the auction barn. His heart sped up a notch when he found the pair waiting up front near the arena door.

Everything about the lady was long: her muscular legs, her suntanned arms, and her hair. A silky ebony braid matching the color of the horse's mane swished the rounded curves of her tight faded jeans. The two of them together painted a picture he could gaze at over and over.

She turned and met his glance beneath the rim of her well-worn, black Resistol. His heart gave a swift kick against his chest, the same feeling he'd gotten the moment she'd looked into his eyes when she'd stood to her full height. Something about those big, round honey-speckled eyes made him wonder if he'd met this gal somewhere before.

She held his gaze for a split second before she faced the arena door, jutting her small chin forward. It was the same look of determination she'd given him earlier when she'd refused his help. He couldn't contain a grin. This was one strong-willed cowgirl.

He pulled the collar of his denim shirt to his nose and breathed deep. Even over the strong aromas of the barn, her earthy female scents and soft baby powder lingered on his clothes. Sexier than any perfume he'd ever smelled.

An involuntary shudder rolled down his back as he thought about how perfect she'd felt pressed full-length against him, nestled right below his chin. Her oversized men's work shirt barely concealed full rounded breasts under a tight-knit tank top. Her double-hearted western belt buckle wedged slightly below his own silver buckle, and he had to admit, she definitely wasn't a little gal.

At six-five, he usually had to bend over to hold a woman in his arms like that, and even then, most of the women he knew wouldn't get near him after he'd spent the day in a hot, smelly horse barn.

Catching another glimpse of this cowgirl's backside, he knew that she wasn't afraid of a little dirt on her jeans or sweat on her face. She had a good seat in the saddle and took that fall from her horse better than some cowboys he knew. She'd gritted her teeth and got right back on her horse without any assistance from him. She knew how to get things done, regardless of a little pain and discomfort.

Other than his two younger sisters, he'd never met a woman with such determination and grit, and as a pickup man for local rodeos, he'd met more than his share of those cute little buckle bunnies. They all liked the idea of being with a cowboy, flirting with him at the rodeos and trying to seduce him at the dances afterward. They just didn't particularly care for all the dirt and manure that came along with the image when the sun came up the next morning.

Ever since his father had died when Joshua was just thirteen, he'd dreamed of turning their ranch into one of the premier horse breeding and training operations in Colorado. His nights were short and his days were long and grueling. Not exactly a city girl's idea of living the high life, a fact he reminded himself of every time he thought about getting serious with a woman.

A red roan gelding stuck his head over a nearby stall, nuzzling Joshua's chest. He scratched the horse between the ears, then made another glance at the tall brunette. She didn't look like the kind of gal who was into one-night stands, and although the idea of pursuing this long-legged cowgirl appealed to his physical needs, he swore a long time ago he'd never open himself up to what would inevitably lead to heartbreak in the end.

He turned his attention to the pretty buckskin with the four white socks. Maybe the owner was off-limits, but he'd been searching for a good horse for his ten-year-old cousin to ride in the next Little Britches Rodeo. With her soft dark eyes and easy disposition, the horse would make a perfect mount for Dillan.

As he grabbed the auction catalogue from his back pocket, a wave of guilt tugged at his heartstrings. He remembered how he'd left Dillan that morning in the hospital. The ten-year-old's big blue eyes had shone with tears of disappointment after Joshua had told him he couldn't ride along with him today.

Born with a congenital heart defect, Dillan had undergone a heart transplant last summer, and the prognosis looked good. But Dillan had been running a fever earlier in the week, and lately, he was short of breath more often, taking longer naps in the afternoons. He hadn't been out to the ranch for a ropin' lesson in over two weeks. The doctors thought he might be rejecting his new heart and had hospitalized him yesterday morning to run some tests. As much as Joshua had wanted to bring him along today, it would have been too tiring for him. Getting Dillan his own horse might just be the ticket to help him feel better again.

Flipping through the catalogue, he stopped at lot number eighty-four and read through the vital statistics of the buckskin mare. *Lazy W Ranch?*

He caught another glimpse of the horse, then read through the information again. According to the catalogue, the mare was sired by Lazy W's Black-Eyed Bandit, the same stud that had sired his father's prized chestnut mare, Golden Sunset.

A bead of sweat rolled down Joshua's brow, stinging the corner of his eye. His gut tightened. His throat went dry. Like he'd done a million times since he was thirteen, he replayed the events of the last day he'd spoken to his father, wishing he could somehow turn back the clock and re-do that fateful morning when his dad and Golden Sunset were both still alive.

After all these years, had he been given a second chance to redeem himself?

The arena door rattled open. The buckskin reared slightly, prancing backwards. Joshua swept off his hat and swiped his face with the sleeve of his denim shirt.

He knew he had to have her . . . *the horse,* he reminded himself, as the pretty cowgirl ducked under a wooden beam and entered the center ring.

"Hey, J.D." His younger brother and veterinarian, stood near the exit door, giving an impatient glance at his watch. "I need help getting this new bay mare loaded. I gotta be back at the clinic by eight."

"Yeah, okay, I'm coming." Making one last glance over his shoulder, he crammed his hat over his head then hustled down the corridor toward the parking lot.

He had to make this quick.

A crowd full of potential buyers lined large cement bleachers rising from floor to ceiling. The smells of sawdust and horses now blended with a thick haze of cigarette smoke.

Debra's stomach churned. Her nostrils burned. She reined her horse to the counter and checked in with a gray-haired auctioneer, then sent up a silent prayer, her fervent hope that a loving family would take Brandy home today.

She'd had a private buyer lined up to buy Brandy last week, but when that deal fell through, she'd had no other choice but to take her chances here at auction.

"What do you say, folks?" the auctioneer called out. "Let's get the bidding started at eight hundred dollars."

Debra clicked her tongue and took Brandy into an easy canter emphasizing the mare's calm presence and honey-smooth stride in a show ring. Sawdust kicked up into the spectators standing near the tall corral. Gritting her teeth, Debra ignored the jolts of pain with every bounce and turn of her horse.

Numbers and bids rolled off the auctioneer's tongue in a nauseating resonating sound with an occasional jump in pitch. Two ring men watched for any movement from the crowd, indicating an increase in bid.

A loud, "Yeeeaaahhh!" rang out from one as he pointed to a bidder in the back.

The other yelled, "Yoooo!"

Her heart squeezed tighter with every hundred-dollar increment. This was happening way too fast.

She made one more turn around the ring when a sudden silence engulfed the arena. As if she'd been caught in some kind of a vacuum, the anticipation sucked the air right out of the building. The bidding had stopped.

Her knuckles whitened as she clenched the leather reins. With Brandy's bloodline and training, it was going to take a heck of a lot more than fifteen hundred bucks to get *this* horse.

Debra faced the auctioneer and spoke with firm conviction. "Not enough."

"This little lady doesn't look too happy, folks." He pulled out Brandy's documentation. "The horse is registered under the American Quarter Horse Association and has thrown some nice futurity babies. She's got the depth and balance you want in your mares and has an extensive open show record in Western Pleasure." Reading further, he added, "She's broke for trail and great with kids. Who'll give me one thousand six hundred dollars?"

Debra glared down at Mr. Boyle, the short stocky man with a barrel-shaped chest holding the last bid. Her father had barely been lowered in the ground when Mr. Boyle, the neighboring rancher, had bought their entire spread—the house, the livestock, even the tractors and equipment. Although grateful he'd paid fair market value, digging her out of a huge mountain of her father's gambling debts, she'd opted to take her chances here at auction rather than let Brandy wind up with Mr. Boyle.

She ran a protective hand over Brandy's neck, knowing firsthand how he treated his horses. He rarely called in a vet or a farrier. Battered fences surrounded his large spread, and with broken-down watering systems, she hated even to think what would happen to her father's ranch under Boyle's ownership.

"Fifteen hundred going once!" the auctioneer called out.

Oh, God. This was it. Maybe she could no-sale. Unfortunately, she was staying in a motel until she could find a place of her own. There was no way she could afford this horse short of stashing it in the backseat of her SUV.

"Fifteen hundred going twice!"

She tugged her hat down, bracing herself for the inevitable slam of the gavel. Her hopes of Brandy going home with a loving family faded faster than a pair of jeans washed in bleach.

"Yoooo!" a ring man's excited voice pierced the air.

Brandy shied and spun around. "Easy, girl." Debra gripped her legs tighter, calming her prancing horse.

"Looks like we've got some excitement, folks," the auctioneer chimed in. "We got us another bid. One thousand six hundred dollars. Let's have some fun!"

Debra whirled around as the crowd parted near the back of the arena, where a man at least a head taller than the others charged straight for the center ring. Her breath caught in her throat when she realized he was the same man with the goatee she knew only as J.D.

He wedged his booted foot on the bottom rung of the metal fence then vaulted over the top with ease, landing a few feet in front of her. He straightened, thumbed his hat back, and with his gaze riveted on hers, shuffled into the corner of the tall corral. A ticket with the number 121 stuck out of the pocket of his blue denim work shirt. The sleeves were rolled up to his elbows, exposing those same muscular forearms that had been wrapped around her just moments ago.

The ring man yelled, "Yeeeaaawh!" as Mr. Boyle upped the bid to seventeen hundred dollars.

She held her breath waiting to see if J.D. would continue the bidding race. With his eyes locked on hers, he countered the bid with the slightest nod of his head and flashed her an absolutely melt-in-your-boots kind of smile that made her toes curl. Her face flamed hotter than a firecracker and probably just as red.

Adrenaline surged through Debra's body—not as a result of the excitement in the arena, but because of the disconcerting stare from the cowboy in the corner. His gaze, fixed and unwavering, narrowed on hers—*not* on her horse, but *her,* Debra Walker, who'd never had a man look at her like that in her life.

Debra had spent most of her life at the ranch, and so most of the men she knew were either old and gray with hair growing out of their ears, or young and cocky with a mouth full of chew in their cheeks. From the few moments she'd spent in this man's arms, she could vouch that he was a virile young cowboy probably in his late twenties, and his teeth were pure white with no yellowing stains from tobacco. As to whether he was cocky? Jury was still out on that one.

The auctioneer's voice jumbled into a maze of numbers going higher and higher. There was no turning back. She trotted Brandy in a circle. Her fingers hurt from clenching the leather reins. Sweat droplets trickled down her chest into the valley between her breasts.

The auctioneer yelled, "Six thousand going once!"

Debra flinched, unaware of who even held the last bid.

"Six thousand going twice!"

The crack of the wooden gavel echoed in her ears.

"Sold for six thousand dollars to bidder number one twenty-one!"

Debra gasped, the impact of the sale hitting her with the force of a Rocky Mountain rockslide. Events of the past two months tumbled down around her, making her feel trapped. She'd buried her father, lost the ranch, and now Brandy was gone, too.

She thanked the auctioneer then urged her horse toward the exit. It was final. Now she had to summon the courage to hand the reins over to Brandy's ruggedly sexy new owner—if she didn't ride off into the sunset first!

CHAPTER TWO

Unfastening the braided cinch on her saddle, Debra peered over Brandy's back and locked gazes with that same cowboy as he approached her stall. Each long stride brought him that much closer to taking away the last remnant of her life as a rancher.

He swept off his hat and nodded. "Howdy," he drawled, twisting his hat in his hands. "Looks like we meet again."

She barely managed a nod before she tugged the saddle from her horse then dumped it on the cement behind her. Taking an extra moment to let the pain in her ribs subside, she squatted in front of the Billy Cook original, won at a Western Pleasure competition her senior year in high school. With an emotional lump blocking her airway, she trailed her fingers over the engraved initials and the intricate carvings in the leather. The day she'd won this was the first—and the only—time her father had ever told her he was proud of her.

He'd never actually told her he loved her, but being proud was the next best thing.

"Everything okay?" J.D. asked, his voice low and sounding genuinely concerned. His familiar, lizard-skin cowboy boots slid into view beside her.

She gave a forced laugh and stood, brushing her palms over her jeans. "Yeah. Guess I didn't know how hard this was going to be. My dad usually handled all the transactions after the sales." Hoping to keep from getting all tongue-tied in front of this man, she avoided his gaze and focused on a large, silver belt buckle with the initials J.D.G. emblazoned on the front.

Bad move. The buckle only drew her attention to his lean hips and snug-fitting Wranglers, reminding her just how close they'd been earlier. He was nothing but a solid wall of muscle, smelling like he'd been sent from heaven.

She had to force herself to extend her hand in greeting. "Um, I'm Debra Walker."

Wrapping his large, tanned hand around hers, he gave her hand a firm squeeze. "Joshua Garrison. My friends call me J.D."

Her grip tightened.

Garrison? Joshy Garrison? As he held on to her hand an extra moment, a small tremor raced up her arm and landed smack dab at the base of her heart. An image of a young, scrawny cowboy with shaggy, dusty brown hair flashed through her memory. He'd had the deepest brown eyes and a smile that had made the most adorable dimple in his cheek.

She slowly lifted her gaze up his broad chest until she landed on those delicious dark brown eyes, the color of Hershey's Syrup. With that same dimple almost winking at her, Joshua settled his hat on his head then arched his brows, zeroing his gaze on their hands. Only then did she realize it was *she* who hadn't relinquished the handshake.

Tugging her hand from his grip, she stepped back and tucked her trembling fingers into her back pockets, praying he didn't recognize her. Remembering how she'd carried on around him when she was eight made her stomach flop. "So, do you have any questions or concerns before I hand her over to you?" She grabbed a grooming brush from the gear bag then brushed the horse's hide where a sweaty imprint from the saddle remained.

"Actually, now that you mention it, I do have kind of a strange question."

Strange? She puffed a wisp of hair from her eyes and warily returned his gaze. "What did you want to know?"

"Well," he drawled, resting his hands on his hips and cocking a leg off to the side in a wide masculine stance. He tilted his head to the side, scanning her from the tip of her hat down to the scuffmarks on her cowboy boots, making no qualms about staring. He raised his gaze and slipped her a lopsided grin. "You don't remember having a big old paint when you were a kid, do you? Looked at you kind of crossed-eyed?"

She felt her mouth gape open. "Big John?"

"That's the one," he said through a chuckle. "I don't know if you remember me, but I used to visit the Lazy W Ranch with my dad when I was twelve. There was this freckle-faced, skinny little gal with black, braided pigtails hanging down to her waist. Every time we showed up at the Lazy W, she'd come charging out of the house and bombard me with a huge hug and a batch of her mama's homemade cookies." He bumped his hat back and shook his head. "I remember she always wore cowboy boots two sizes too big and galloped around the ranch yard on a pretend horse, using a stick as a whip." He stepped closer and tipped her hat back, his lips quirking into an ornery grin. "Was that you?"

Hearing him describe her to a T, she pressed her palms over her eyes and groaned. "That would be me."

"Don't that just beat all," he said through another chuckle, moving her fingers apart so he could see her face. "I knew you looked familiar. I believe I gave you one of my old riding crops. When my father started looking at that big paint, lickety-split, you hopped on him bareback and rode off into the pasture so's your daddy wouldn't sell him."

With a racing heartbeat, she reached around the corner of the stall, grabbing an old crop from a hook. "Does this look familiar?"

He took the crop and ran a finger along the white and black braided shaft. "I'll be doggone. You kept it all this time?"

She gave a small shrug. "I figured it was good luck. Dad never did sell Big John. We kept him around till he died last fall at the ripe old age of thirty-three."

Joshua shook his head and smiled. "We must have come out to your place, what, every couple of weeks that summer?"

"Every other Thursday, if memory serves me right." She had to contain a grin, remembering exactly how often he used to visit. As an only child, she'd always wanted a big brother to look up to. She'd marked off the calendar days till he'd shown up at their ranch, even washing her hair and taking a bath the night before. For a girl who wouldn't go near the tub except on Sundays before church, that was a pretty big deal.

Lordy, had he grown up.

Although her hygiene had drastically improved, she suddenly felt like that same awkward little girl with freckles and pigtails. She unfastened Brandy's bridle, hoping to conceal the rush of excitement of being near this man again. "We must have polished off a few dozen cookies that summer."

"I remember. You always wanted me to push you on that old tire swing in your barn. Never stopped jabbering either. Talked about horses, different methods of training, and well . . ." He rubbed his whiskery jaw with a grin. "Horses."

"And you always listened," she said through a smile. "You even taught me how to halter-break a foal. Don't laugh, but it got so lonely at our place, there were times I pretended you were my big brother."

"A brother, huh?" He pulled a piece of straw off her shoulder and for the briefest of moments, his gaze flicked to her lips. She thought maybe her heart had actually stopped beating before he stepped back a pace. "You do kind of remind me of one of my sisters. Heather would get so attached to her horses she'd have lived in the barn if my mom had let her."

"Sounds like me. My mom finally fixed me up a bunk in the tack room so I could stay whenever a mare foaled." She let out a wistful sigh. "I always loved hearing about your family. You have two sisters and a brother, right?"

"Yep. Heather, Jared, and Megan. You've got a good memory."

"You were a great storyteller. Gosh, there were times I would have given anything to have a brother or a sister."

He patted Brandy on the neck and gave a throaty chuckle. "There were times when I probably would have given anything to let you have them." Gesturing his head toward Brandy, he asked, "So, what's the story? Why are you selling her?"

"Well," she said, stroking her hand over Brandy's back. "To make a long story short, my father died a couple of months back and left everything to me." *Along with a half-million dollars in gambling debt.*

Not wanting to get into details about her father, she added, "There was no way I could handle a place that size on my own, so I sold everything to a neighboring rancher. But Brandy deserves better, someone who'll ride her and groom her, and won't set her out in some rundown pasture and neglect her. It's a huge relief to know she's going home with you."

"What about your mom? Didn't she want to keep the ranch?"

She gave a short cynical laugh. "She and Dad divorced about a year ago. She grew up in the city and never did adjust to ranch life. She lives in a condo in Denver now. She's happier than she's been in a long time."

He scratched the back of his head, bumping his hat down on his forehead. "Dang, losing your dad and your ranch at the same time must be rough. I'm sorry. I lost my dad when I was thirteen. In fact, it was the fall after we visited your ranch."

"Oh, Joshua. My father never told me. I always wondered why you never came back to visit." Remembering the awful end to her own father's life, she wondered if Joshua's father had been caught up in some sort of a ranching accident. She was almost afraid to ask. "Mind if I ask what happened to your dad?"

"Killed in a small plane crash." He blew out a loud gust of air, a hint of mint whisking into her senses. He gave what looked like a frustrated shake of his head as he looked down and flicked a clump of hay away with the toe of his boot. "The carburetor supposedly froze up on him in the mountains, didn't have anywhere to set it down. But that was a long time ago," he added, resting his hands on his waist. "Sorry I never made it back out your way. Things got kind of crazy for a while. My mom wanted to sell our place, too, but I convinced her to stay. I've been trying to keep it going ever since."

"I remember your father. Dad had nothing but good things to say about him. He definitely knew his horses, that's for sure."

"Oh, yeah. Dad knew it all," he quipped, sounding a bit cynical. Handing her the crop, he added, "Better hang on to this."

With a little regret, she shook her head. "Please, keep it. Good thing I didn't have it in the ring. You don't know how close I came to riding off with Brandy like I did Big John." She tried to joke, but a hitch in her voice probably gave her away.

"Have you checked into boarding Brandy somewhere? I know lots of reputable stables. I wouldn't even hold you to the sale."

"Believe me, Joshua. I've checked into all the options, but unfortunately, I was left with quite a bit of debt. And besides, I'm starting a new job tomorrow and will be moving away from the area anyway. I wouldn't be able to afford the fees even if I found a place." Knowing there was nothing else she could do, she said, "Brandy's a hundred percent sound and I'll guarantee that for thirty days. My mother's number is on the documents. She'll know how to get a hold of me if you have any problems."

"I already have the release papers. Everything looks in order."

He surprised her when he took her hand, his eyes peering into hers. "I still think you should keep this, Debra." He curled her fingers around the shaft of the crop and gave her hand a gentle squeeze. "Who knows? Maybe you'll need it again someday."

She stared at the crop, but mostly at Joshua's large, slightly callused hand covering hers, feeling the warmth and the strength, wishing she could somehow infuse some of that into her own body as she headed down a new path in life. She raised her lashes and met his gaze, melting into that incredibly sweet smile she'd missed all these years.

Where was he two years ago when she took over the ranch and needed a big brother to rely on? Someone who was bigger and stronger, and far more knowledgeable than she when it came to making sound ranching decisions.

"You said you're starting a new job tomorrow. Mind if I ask where you're headed?"

Hoping to keep her mind focused on her future, she tugged her hand from Joshua's grip, tossing the crop in with the rest of her gear. "Colorado Springs. I'll be the new contracts administrator for Walson Technology. They provide computer network support for some of the largest customers in the United States. They've got divisions in Boston as well as California."

"Yeah," he said, rubbing his chin. "I'm familiar with Walson. I've got a good friend who works there. Her husband and I used to play football together in high school and college. Her name is Jasmine King. Look her up. She's one of the sweetest ladies I know. I'm sure she'll be glad to show you around."

He tugged out his billfold and handed her his business card. "You and your father never made it down, but our place is located north of Colorado Springs a ways. That's my number and cell phone. I can be reached anytime day or night. If you need any help getting settled, or have any problems at Walson, you be sure and give me a call."

"Problems?" she repeated. "What kind of problems?"

He shook his head and returned his billfold to his back pocket. "Nothing. Forget I said anything. Can I help you out with your gear?"

"Thanks, but other than my duffel bag, I've just got my saddle and bridle. I put the saddle in the tack auction this morning, but I was only offered eight hundred bucks, so I decided to no-sale." She hesitated, chewing on her bottom lip before she asked, "Unless you'd be interested? It's a personalized Billy Cook Western Show saddle," she quickly added. "I won it at the Denver Livestock Show and Rodeo in a Junior Western Pleasure competition. With the leather bridle and reins, it's worth at least two thousand bucks."

He narrowed his eyes. "You're selling your saddle?"

"Like I said. I was left with quite a bit of debt, but I'd be willing to cut you a deal and let it all go for fifteen hundred."

Arching his brows, he glanced down at the saddle and shook his head. "I can't buy your saddle." His voice turned curt and abrupt. "And you and I both know a saddle like that's worth at least four grand."

At his quick retort, she wondered if he could even afford such an expensive saddle. He wasn't exactly dressed like a man with money, and he did say that he was still trying to make his father's ranch a go. She wondered if he could really afford her horse in the first place.

Embarrassed for even asking about the saddle, she gave a heavy swallow and patted Brandy on the neck. "You're right. I shouldn't have mentioned it. I'm sure a place like yours has plenty of saddles," she added, not wanting him to realize she knew he couldn't afford it. "Besides, I can probably get more out of it on eBay."

He let out a loud gust of air. "It's not that I don't want your saddle, Debra, I just think you're being a bit hasty about selling it." He stepped closer and cupped a large warm hand over her shoulder, forcing her to turn around and look up at him. "Are things that bad, honey? What happened to your dad?"

Her stomach fluttered when he called her honey, but by the pitying look in his eyes, she knew he was just feeling sorry for her. She never should have told him about her dad or the ranch. Hoping to avoid the subject of her father, she simply said, "Heart attack, but everything's fine, Joshua, really. It's no big deal."

"No big deal, huh?" He lifted his thumb and gently rubbed a tear away from the corner of her eye. "And I suppose these tears are just allergies?"

Angered at her vulnerability, she stepped away from his touch and swiped her eyes with the sleeve of her denim shirt. Knowing she didn't want to have the saddle around, reminding her of a past she was trying to forget, she shoved her hands on her hips and narrowed her gaze. "Do you want the damn saddle or not? Either way, I'm selling it."

His jaw muscles twitched. His eyes narrowed and he gave a slight shake of his head, obviously still disapproving of her decision to sell. He yanked out his checkbook and started writing a check. "I want you to consider this a loan. I'll store your saddle at my place."

"But—"

"This is not a negotiation," he said, tearing out the check and handing it to her. "I want you to know you're always welcome to come ride Brandy any time."

She took the check and almost choked. It was made out for the full four thousand dollars. "Oh, Joshua. I can't—"

"You can and you will," he insisted, scooping her saddle off the floor. "And if things don't work out at Walson, I've been looking for a good hired hand. I could sure use a dedicated horsewoman with your expertise and knowledge." His expression softened into a grin. "The pay might be lousy, but the company's good."

Grateful for the money, she folded the check and stuffed it into her back pocket. "I appreciate your generosity, Joshua, but the day I set foot on a ranch again I'll eat my chaps. I'm focusing on my career now. After being stuck out on my father's ranch all these years, I'm actually looking forward to living in the big city. Maybe I'll check out some of the tourist sites, take in some of the nightlife."

"Nightlife, huh?" He looped the bridle and reins over the saddle horn and smiled. "Take it from me, honey, there's not a nightclub in town that'll beat lying on a blanket under the star-studded Colorado skies. Especially if you've got the right company." He winked, then gave her a heart-stopping smile.

Feeling an annoying warmth cover her face, she turned and wrapped her arms around Brandy's neck, giving her one last hug. "Hey, sweetheart. You be a good girl for Mr. Garrison."

She looked up at Joshua, her voice sounding choked when she spoke again. "Be careful when you're loading her, she gets kind of nervous when she's being trailered. And she hates storms," she added quickly. "Her mama was killed by lightning when she was just a baby."

"I'll be sure and keep that in mind," he said with a contemplative nod. "Anything else?"

"Well," she said, gingerly slinging her duffel bag over her shoulder. "She likes baby carrots and little green apples, and watch out when it comes to oats. She's kind of a pig. Puts on weight easy if she hasn't been exercised."

"Sounds like a few girls I know," he said, giving her an ornery half-grin.

She gave a sad laugh that sounded more like a pathetic sob. She took in several aching breaths, knowing there was no way she could stand here and watch Brandy being led away. "If you'll excuse me, I need to settle a few things with the sales office. It was good seeing you again, Joshua. Take good care of Brandy."

As Debra flipped her silky ebony braid over her shoulder, Joshua could only watch as her long slender legs carried her down the corridor in that familiar, determined cowgirl stride. He stroked Brandy's neck and stared into the mare's soft, dark, almond-shaped eyes.

Somewhere deep in the recesses of his heart, he knew he'd found more than a good brood mare and a horse for Dillan. Debra's fiery independence and her obvious love of horses almost matched his own. Hearing how she'd lost her father and the ranch all in one fell swoop damn near broke his heart.

As he led Brandy out to his truck and trailer, a dull ache filled his chest. The last time he'd come anywhere close to feeling this way about a woman was ten years ago, when his fiancée had dumped him the day before they were to be wed. Flew off to the east coast with another guy.

Frustrated at where his thoughts had led, Joshua stored Debra's saddle in the tack section of his trailer, then gave another glance over his shoulder as she emerged from the sales office. She met his gaze from across the lot and gave a small wave before she headed over to her silver SUV. As she threw her gear into the backseat, he gave a disbelieving shake of his head, remembering all that crap about her wanting to become a career woman and moving into the city.

Unlike his ex-fiancée, who'd been a rich, pampered socialite, raised in the elite social circles of Colorado Springs, Debra was a homegrown country girl down to the soles of those well-worn cowboy boots. Whether she'd admit to it or not, that lady had horse in her blood. She was fooling herself if she thought she could just walk away from it all.

As he tied Brandy into the fourth angled trailer stall, the thought of never seeing Debra again made his chest tighten. He took in several slow, deep breaths, trying to convince himself that the reason he felt this way was because Debra reminded him so much of his sister. Knowing Debra all those years ago, he felt an obligation, if only to her father, to keep an eye on her. Act as a big brother of sorts now that she was on her own in a strange new city.

But more to the point, to keep her away from Robbie Nelson, the new president of Walson Technology.

Joshua slammed the trailer door shut, blowing out a heavy gust of frustration at the thought of Debra going to work with that low-life scum.

Like the rankest bull being let out of a rodeo chute, ten years of pent-up anger shot from his soul. If Debra encountered any problems at her new job, he'd personally ride that bull into the ground.

Exhausted after finishing a long shift at the Outlook Steakhouse, Jasmine King rushed up a plywood ramp leading to the front porch of her white, two-story house. The toe of her shoe caught the edge of a raised floorboard, and she made a mental note to give J.D. Garrison a call to come fix the platform.

With a thankful smile, she tapped the piece of wood into place with her shoe, remembering how J.D. had wrangled several of her husband's old high school buddies into constructing the wheelchair-accessible ramp.

Milten, J.D., and the star quarterback, Glen Frost, had been known as the Three Musketeers in their high school years. The three of them together were unstoppable and had led the Academy Falcons to the state championships two years in a row.

Glen Frost had gone on into the Air Force Academy, eventually becoming an F14 fighter pilot. J.D. and Milten had each won a full-ride football scholarship at Colorado State University. J.D. graduated with an degree in equine science, then moved back home to ranch fulltime.

But Milten loved the game of football and hadn't been able to get enough of it. His senior year of college, he'd been drafted into the pros, signing a three-year contract with the Kansas City Chiefs. He was invincible—right up until his car accident nearly a year ago. Now Jasmine would give anything to watch him walk across the living room floor.

With a heavy sigh, she entered the foyer and reached into her purse for a dark plum lipstick. Using the entryway mirror, she applied the gloss to her full lips then pinched her light brown complexion, hoping to look halfway awake. Managing the weekend shift at the Outlook Steakhouse as well as putting in overtime at Walson Technology during the week was beginning to wear her down.

For the past three months, her boss, Robert Nelson, had been in negotiations with the Air Force for the acquisition of a multimillion-dollar computer maintenance contract. If Walson won, they would begin monitoring and maintaining computers at various bases throughout the United States. But competition with larger computer companies was steep. Rumors had started circulating that if Walson didn't win this contract, the Colorado Springs division was in jeopardy of being shut down—just like the two divisions in Texas.

She closed her eyes, praying it wouldn't come to that. Where would she turn? Her job at the restaurant barely covered the nursing expenses for Milt. With their savings nearly depleted, she didn't know where she'd go if Walson shut their doors.

She opened her eyes and waggled her finger at her reflection. "Don't even go there, Jasmine King. Be thankful you have this job in the first place."

Shortly after Milten's accident, she'd run into Robert Nelson at the hospital. He'd been escorting his father, Stan Nelson, to a therapy appointment. Stan had suffered a stroke a few months before, and had handed the Rocky Mountain division of Walson Technology over to Robert to run. Having graduated from the same high school as Milten, Robert had offered her a job almost on the spot.

After all she and Milten had been through in the past year, she had to keep a positive attitude. Negative thoughts would only discourage her husband.

She pulled a hair pick from her purse and smoothed a few curly tendrils away from her face. Born with thick, African-American curly brown hair, she wore it straightened, sleeked down to her shoulders—the way she'd worn it when she and Milten had first met back in college. He used to say it brought out her high cheekbones and accentuated the jade green in her eyes.

Putting on her best smile, she plopped the lipstick in her purse, kicked off her pumps, then padded down the hallway to the master bedroom. Her heart always gave an extra beat whenever she saw Milten. Today, he was wearing a green and blue Hawaiian shirt, gray sweats and navy blue slippers. He was sitting in a recliner, staring out the bedroom window. A football lay in his lap.

Across the street, two neighbor girls, no more than ten, splashed in a large aboveground swimming pool. Although he normally had a much darker brown complexion than hers, he looked pale and drawn after months of being confined in a hospital.

He'd suffered a major head trauma and massive swelling of the spinal cord. Doctors hadn't given her much hope. But after months of bed rest and physical therapy, the swelling had significantly reduced. Since being released from the rehabilitation center a month ago, he'd regained almost full use of his arms and upper body and was eating solid foods. His vocal cords had sustained severe injury, so he used hand movements and a clipboard to communicate.

But it was his memory that worried her the most. He'd been in a coma for a month after the accident, and when he came out of it, he didn't recognize her and had no recollection of his life prior to that night. But now, almost a year later and with extensive therapy and repetition, he'd regained almost all of his basic skills. She'd repeatedly told him who she was, but the doctors said between the trauma of the accident and all the medications he'd been under, he might never fully remember everything.

As if sensing her presence, Milten turned and gave her a wide smile. All her anxieties whisked right out the window. Whether he was running for a touchdown or just gazing into her eyes like he was doing right now, it didn't matter what he remembered as long as they were together.

She crossed the room, slouched on the side of the recliner, gently taking hold of his hand. "Hey, baby. Sorry I was gone so long." She looked over at a short, plump woman with silver-blue hair. Her boss had recommended Mrs. White, and she'd been his nurse since Milten had come home from the rehabilitation center. "Thank you so much for coming over on a Sunday afternoon. The nurse I hired for the weekends should be back from vacation next Friday."

"It was no trouble, Mrs. King." She looked over at Milten. "We've got some good news. Say hello, Milt."

He opened his mouth and made a choking sound. He swallowed then made the same noise again. This time she heard, "Jazzy."

She cupped her hands over her mouth. "Oh, Milten. You remembered." She wasn't sure if her elation was because he'd actually spoken, or because he'd called her by the pet name he'd had for her since their first date, their freshmen year in college. She'd been a cheerleader and he was the starting linebacker for Colorado State University.

For several moments, his gaze bore deeply into hers, reigniting that old attraction she'd felt for this man in college. "Does it hurt to talk?"

He wrapped his arms around her waist. "Scratchy."

"This is wonderful. What else do you remember? Do you remember when we met?"

He gave her a squeeze and simply choked out, "No . . . spare." His lips curled into that sweet grin he'd given her the night he'd helped her with a flat tire in the parking lot after a football game. He'd had to drive her clear back to her dorm, where they'd talked for hours in the parking lot. She lowered and brushed her lips against his, feeling the warmth and the tenderness she'd missed for almost a year.

Mrs. White cleared her throat. "I was reading this article to Milt this afternoon. He's been as cranky as a grizzly bear on a cold winter's morning ever since."

Jasmine took the Sunday paper from Mrs. White. It was the front page of the sports section, featuring a local high school football team at a summer training camp. She read the caption underneath the picture. "Washington Trojans gear up for another bid at the state championship."

She hadn't met Milten till college, but she knew that he'd played for the Academy Falcons in high school. "Do you remember playing against the Trojans, sweetie?"

He pursed his lips. "Fuzzy," he ground out.

Mrs. White filled in more of the details. "Everyone around these parts knows that there's been a school rivalry between the Falcons and the Trojans for nearly thirty years. The picture must have sparked some memory of his high school days."

Milten looked down at his legs, his fingers curling into a fist. Jasmine's heart ached. As frustrated as she felt right now, she couldn't begin to imagine the discouragement Milten must be experiencing. At the time of his accident, he was one of the nation's top leading defensive lineman and had just become a free agent in negotiations with the Denver Broncos for a multimillion-dollar, four-year contract. To go from a viable, strong adult supporting his family to a paraplegic totally dependent on everyone else had to be excruciating.

Hoping to lighten his mood, she folded the newspaper and set it aside. "Hey, now, we should be celebrating. I'll give J.D. a call. He'll be glad to hear the news. Do you remember J.D. Garrison?"

Milten gave a crooked grin. "Saved . . . my ass . . . more than . . . once."

She laughed. "What about Glen Frost? Do you remember him?"

"Iceman?"

As she blew out a huge breath of relief, tears stung the backs of her eyes. "I'll have to give them a call and see if they can stop by for a visit." Hoping to finally get an answer about his accident, she asked, "Do you remember what happened the night of your accident? The police said you might have dodged a deer, but they're not sure."

He closed his eyes, his knuckles whitening as he clenched the ball in his lap. His Adam's apple bobbed heavily as he swallowed several times. He pursed his lips and gave a slow shake of his head. "Can't . . . remember."

"Be patient, Milten," Mrs. White said, giving him a motherly pat on his arm. "You've been on a lot of medications for several months. Give it time." She headed toward the door. "I think I'll leave you two to get reacquainted. I'll see you first thing in the morning, Milt."

Jasmine smiled. "Good-bye, and thanks again for helping us out."

After Mrs. White scurried out the door, Jasmine leaned over at the waist and stayed just a whisper's length away from his lips. She breathed deep, taking in all that was her husband. His hand slid up her back and curled around her neck, pressing her gently against his mouth. It was a slow, sensual kiss that brought back so many wonderful memories. An unexpected sob escaped her throat.

She wrapped her arms around Milten's shoulders and squeezed. "I'm sorry, baby," she said next to his ear. "This is so overwhelming. I've missed you so much."

He dragged his hand along her ribcage and tugged her closer. "Sweet . . . Jazzy," he murmured huskily. "Thanks . . . for not giving . . . up on me."

"Never. We're a team. I'll always be here for you." An overwhelming weight lifted from her shoulders. If she had to dig out his old scrapbooks and photo albums, she'd help him get all of his memory back.

And, with any luck, figure out what actually happened the night he plunged off the side of Pikes Peak Highway.

CHAPTER THREE

Joshua jabbed a pitchfork into a pile of musty straw and horse manure, heaping it into a wheelbarrow. He vigorously shoveled another load, then dumped it on top.

He'd been out cleaning horse stalls since dawn this Monday morning, worries about his cousin Dillan making for a long and sleepless night. Their worst fears had started to come true. Dillan was rejecting his new heart.

Grabbing the handles of the wheelbarrow, Joshua pushed it out to the back of the barn, emptying the load into a mound the size of a small hill. The stench of manure stung his nostrils as it tumbled out of the cart. He usually used a skid loader to do this job, but he needed to vent some of his frustrations. Mucking out stalls the old-fashioned way seemed the perfect outlet.

He stepped back and filled his lungs with the warm July air to clear his senses. Sweeping off his hat, he wiped his gloved hand over his beaded brow, staring up into the early morning skies. Only a few jet streams zigzagged across the canvas of pale blue. A hawk circled above, cawing and screeching, as if sending some kind of ominous warning.

After he'd left the auction last night, he'd stopped by the hospital to see Dillan. Now he couldn't get the image out of his head. It seemed in a matter of hours after he'd left him yesterday morning, Dillan's condition had deteriorated. Tubes, monitors, wires, all poked and prodded his lifeless little body.

As soon as Joshua had touched his frail, tiny hand, Dillan had opened his eyes . . . then he'd smiled. He actually smiled.

Dear God. What a courageous little trooper.

Joshua's chest tightened, and he had to swallow a lump the size of a football that seemed to have lodged in his throat ever since he'd visited Dillan. He sent up a silent prayer, something he'd been doing more and more lately, not sure it did any good, but not sure what else he could do.

The low rumble of a car engine drew his attention to the top of the hill. His sister's blue minivan pulled into the graveled driveway, parking in front of his folks' three-bedroom ranch home. He'd grown up in that little yellow house till he'd moved away to college. After he'd acquired his degree, he'd moved back and held down a full-time job in the city, saving up enough money to buy several of his own acreages surrounding his mother's spread.

Now he lived in an old renovated cabin located on the outskirts of his property near Elk Ridge Ravine. Not exactly South Fork, but it was secluded, far away from the city. Quiet. No hassles. Alone. He wouldn't want it any other way.

Two vivacious kids dressed in their Sunday best jumped out of the sliding door. His six-year-old nephew, Kyle, and his four-year-old niece, Katie, spotted him and darted across the grass-seeded lawn.

"Guys!" Heather yelled as she came around the van. "Stay away from the horses in your good clothes!" She gave Joshua a big smile and waved before sliding the van door shut.

Heather wore a pretty pink, short-sleeved blouse tucked into a long denim skirt that hung down to the tops of a pair of brown dress cowboy boots. Her brunette hair was styled neatly in a long French braid that hung down to her waist. His thoughts immediately turned to Debra, remembering how her ebony braid barely brushed the curves of her slender hips.

As Heather trotted down the hill, he found himself comparing the two women. Besides their long hair, they both had those same expressive brown eyes and exuberant smiles. Debra was a good few inches taller than Heather, and definitely fuller through the bust line, he couldn't help but note. Even though she'd tried to conceal it with an oversized work shirt, Debra had a figure any guy would drool over.

But without a doubt, it was her eyes that had captured his heart—from the moment she'd stared up at him, when he'd held her in his arms after she about passed out. If truth be told, he didn't know if his restlessness was because of Dillan's illness or the fact that he couldn't get Debra's big brown eyes out of his head.

He'd tried to call her at Walson Technology twice this morning, wanting to make sure she'd made it in okay last night. But she'd been in a meeting both times and hadn't been reachable.

All morning, he'd tried to convince himself that the feelings he had for her were more like that of a big brother toward a sister. But as Heather trotted toward him with a loving smile on her face, he knew the difference. The heated desires that swirled through his body at the mere thought of seeing Debra again were anything but brotherly.

Maybe he shouldn't try to see her. Pursuing her would only lead to another heartache in the end. He should just leave things the way they were. Uncomplicated. A date with a beautiful woman now and then. No commitments. No hassles.

Secluded . . . alone.

A bead of sweat broke out above his brow. Maybe he'd swing by Debra's office this noon and surprise her for lunch. Nothing romantic. Just two old friends getting reacquainted. He owed it to her dad, after all.

He just hoped he didn't run into the new president of Walson Technology while he was there. His knuckles whitened as he gripped the handles of the wheelbarrow, dreading a confrontation with that man. Before Robert Nelson had moved back to the area a year ago, there'd been rumors of his divorce. That in itself was a little retribution for the hell he'd put Joshua through ten years ago.

He shoved the wheelbarrow off to the side and breathed deeply through his nose. Maybe running into good ol' Robbie boy wouldn't be so bad. If a few . . . words . . . were exchanged, lunch would be that much sweeter.

"Uncle Josh! Uncle Josh!" Katie squealed with delight.

Joshua hunkered down and intercepted Heather's two charges before any damage was done to their clothes. "Hey, you two. Slow down."

"Where's the new horsies?" Katie asked, practically jumping to peer over his shoulder.

"They're eating on a bale of hay over there. See that pretty buckskin with the four white socks?"

"The one with the white blaze running down her face?"

"Yep. That's Brandy. That red dun over there is Cinnamon." He tugged off his leatherwork gloves and held the tips of Katie's tiny fingers. "You sure look pretty. Did you get a new dress?"

"Yes, she did," Heather answered breathlessly after her jaunt down the hill. "I told them they could *look* at the new horses, but not to go anywhere near them in their good clothes." She gave Katie a reprimanding glare and waggled her finger. "Is that understood, young lady?"

Katie kicked a rock with her patent leather, shiny black shoes. "Yes, ma'am."

"So why are they all dressed up?" Joshua asked, standing and resting his hands on his waist.

"The homeschool group I'm involved with is singing at Mrs. Kendrick's nursing home." Bud Kendrick's ranch bordered Joshua's property on the other side of Elk Ridge Ravine. Since

Mrs. Kendrick's diagnosis with Alzheimer's last year, she'd been staying at an area nursing home. Heather looked up toward the main house. "Mom wanted me to swing out and pick her up, then we're meeting Brad at his office for lunch."

"Yeah," Katie piped up. "Gramma Kara and Grampa Brad are taking us all to the Pizza Palace. Wanna come?"

Hoping to catch Debra for lunch, he rubbed the back of his neck and shook his head. "I'd sure like to, punkin, but I've got a lot of work to do around here." He reached down and ruffled Kyle's hair. "Howdy, pardner. You look pretty spiffy, too."

Kyle whirled around and buried his face into Heather's long, denim skirt, cupping his hands over his ears. Making a small moaning sound, he bounced his forehead against her stomach, autistic traits he'd displayed since he was a toddler.

Katie climbed on the bottom rung of the fence. "C'mere horsie, horsie," she called, then blew through her lips. Her attempted whistle sounded more like a gust of air.

Heather shoved her hands on her slender hips. "Katie, climb down from that fence and march yourself right up to the house. Kyle?" she said, tugging his hands from his ears. "Why don't you go see if Grandma Kara has any pancakes?"

Joshua couldn't help but smile as he watched the two rambunctious kids race up the yard. Even though Kyle rarely spoke, he understood everything. And give the kid a piece of rope, he could tie any knot known to man. The camp he attended once a month taught the children outdoor skills, which came in handy here at his ranch.

He glanced over at Heather. "Do they know about Dillan?"

"I told them he was very sick and can't play for a while. But I don't think they understand how serious his condition is."

"I don't think *any* of us understands," he grumbled, frustrated at the whole situation. Joshua would give him his own damned heart if he thought it would save Dillan. "Mom said he made it through the night without any complications. After I'm done here I'm headed in to visit him at the hospital."

He strode to the corral and looked over at the new buckskin horse he'd bought for Dillan. Debra had raised a feisty little mare. Brandy had no problem establishing herself at the top of the pecking order right from the start.

Joshua's black gelding quarter horse loped over to the fence. "Remember the first time Dillan sat on Evening Star?" he asked, stroking a hand over the horse's neck.

Heather draped her wrists over the fence and smiled. "Yeah, he called him Eating Tar."

"I'll never forget the time he and Jared and I all rode out to Buffalo Ridge. Dillan wanted to camp like *real* cowboys. Didn't even want to sleep in a tent. We sat up till midnight gazing at the stars." He grabbed an old lariat that dangled from the corner fence post. "I've been teaching him how to lasso. He's been so weak this last month, I was afraid to do much more than trail ride." He slowly coiled the rope into loops, then draped the lasso over the post.

"How long have you been out here?" Heather asked.

"Since six. Couldn't sleep anyway." He made a quick glance at his watch. Almost ten-thirty. He still needed to shower and stop by Milten King's house on the way to the hospital.

At least there was good news. Milt's wife had called late last night, excited that Milt's memory had started to return. He'd even asked Joshua to stop over this morning. Maybe this meant he'd remembered more about what had happened the night of his accident.

Police thought he'd dodged a deer and lost control. The only thing that bothered Joshua about that theory was all the skid marks up and down Pikes Peak Highway going around the curves. Unless there was a whole herd of deer, why the hell had there been so many marks?

"Have you placed an ad in the paper yet?" Heather asked, her voice holding a slight edge.

Knowing where this was headed, he darted Heather a sideways glance. "Nope. Haven't had the time."

"Gee. Maybe if you hired someone, you'd have more time." She crossed her arms over her chest. "Honestly, J.D. Now that Jared has his own clinic and Brad is in the middle of the Blue Ridge Condo Development, you can't possibly expect to run a ranch this size all by yourself. Between the training, all these auctions, and helping out at the neighbors, if you don't at least get some part-time help, you're going to work yourself right into the grave."

Not in the mood for one of his sister's lectures, he jammed the pitchfork into the ground and headed toward his cabin. "Do me a favor then. I'm a registered donor. Be sure and give Dillan my heart if I do."

After meeting with the director of marketing, the vice president of sales, and the manager of human resources, Debra's cheeks ached from the smile she'd had pasted on her face since she'd arrived at Walson Technology early this morning.

Now, at a few minutes after twelve, she found herself in the executive office of the president, a plush corner office with an extraordinary panoramic view of Pikes Peak. Cheyenne Mountain glistened from a set of windows that spanned the length of two entire walls. She could even see a glimpse of the giant red sandstone monuments of Garden of the Gods National Park.

Seeing Colorado in all its splendor made her ache to be out there and feel the warm sunshine on her face. She took in a relaxing breath, wishing she could smell the pine trees, but instead was engulfed by a mixture of burnt coffee and leather upholstery from the elegant couch ensemble positioned in the corner.

Fortunately, the view across from her on the other side of a mahogany executive's desk wasn't all bad either. Her new boss, Robert Nelson, was finishing a phone call he'd been tied up with since she'd arrived in his office promptly at noon.

Sitting in a maroon leather wing-backed chair, Debra pressed a palm to her stomach, hoping to stifle a low growl. The granola bar she'd eaten at six had worn off around nine-thirty during her tour through Field Engineering, where the core of Walson Technology operated. A staff of computer specialists rotated around the clock, doing phone support for various customers throughout the United States. The administrative staff was just down the hall on the fifth floor, nearly deserted except for a few cubicles arranged in the middle.

Her office, or more accurately, her cubby, was an eight-foot-square cubicle with six-foot dividers covered in gray tweed cloth. A computer workstation was positioned in the middle of a gray Formica countertop with a maroon swivel office chair pushed underneath. Not exactly the plush atmosphere Debra had envisioned in her new career, but at this point, anything beat manure-filled horse stalls.

She caught Robert's gaze and returned his smile with a smaller one of her own. As he finished scribbling something on a yellow legal pad, she crossed her legs, arranging her three-tier broomstick skirt around her calves. A short, fitted, southwest tapestry jacket complemented a burgundy rayon blouse underneath.

Her mother wouldn't recognize her. Other than the simple black dress she'd worn to her father's funeral, faded jeans and cowboy boots made up the greater part of Debra's wardrobe. Relieved to be off her feet, she rotated her ankles, her no-nonsense black pumps from Payless not as forgiving as her worn leather cowboy boots.

"I'll be waiting for his call, Lieutenant. My assistant and I look forward to meeting you later this week." Robert gave her a brief wink before pulling out a small Palm Pilot. "What day works best for you?"

As he set up an appointment with whom she assumed was from the Air Force, Debra still couldn't believe this was her new boss. Probably only in his late twenties, he had thick, jet-black hair stylishly combed into smooth waves behind his ears. A tailored crisp blue dress shirt stretched across a set of lean shoulders, the sleeves tapering down to his wrists. Gold cufflinks secured the cuffs, which were monogrammed with his initials. She couldn't help but notice his long tanned fingers and buffed square fingernails. She'd bet there were no calluses on those hands, or dirt under his nails. He was, to be quite honest, the cleanest-cut, most striking man she'd ever seen.

She brought two fingers to her lips, suppressing a yawn, her sleepless night catching up with her. After she'd left the auction barn last night, she'd arrived in Colorado Springs, checking into a motel on South Nevada. She'd found the place on the Internet, drawn by the affordable rates and the fact that it was located only two blocks from Walson. Unfortunately, it didn't look anything like the picture on the website. She hadn't been able to sleep a wink the entire night. Between loud bass music bellowing through an adjoining wall, and police sirens going off every five minutes, she'd lain there awake for hours.

More than once during the night, she'd found herself wishing there was a six-foot-five-inch, two-hundred-and-twenty-pound big brother standing guard outside her door, or better yet, inside her room sharing a batch of double chocolate chunk cookies and a glass of milk. Her stomach gave a nervous flutter as she envisioned Joshua filling her doorway with that same adorable smile she'd remembered him having the summer he'd visited their ranch.

Her father had met Joshua's father at an auction in April of that year, and they'd made several trips to the Lazy W throughout the summer. The last time Joshua visited their ranch was a late October day. She'd just stepped off the school bus, only to watch the taillights of the Garrisons' horse trailer rumble out of the long, graveled country lane. Without warning, her father had sold them his most prized chestnut mare, Golden Sunset.

At the age of four, Debra had witnessed the birth of the filly and had named it after the spectacular golden hues of the Colorado sunset. Her father had let her raise that filly like it was her own. Even though she was only eight, to have Goldie sold right out from under her had been earth-shattering.

She'd waited for weeks for the Garrisons' big blue Dodge pickup truck to pull into their drive so she could at least hear about Golden Sunset. But neither Joshua nor his father had ever shown up at their ranch again. Why hadn't her father told her about Mr. Garrison's plane accident?

She gave an exasperated sigh, knowing exactly why. She was his little girl. He kept a lot of things from her and would have done anything to keep her from getting hurt . . . including sacrificing his own life for hers.

An icy chill swept down her spine. With the temperatures kept in a climate-controlled atmosphere at seventy-two, she knew the prickling on her skin wasn't because she was cold. Haunting images of her father's lifeless body lying in the middle of a cattle pen plagued her day and night.

Knowing the real reason she hadn't slept in over two months, Debra wished she'd never run into Joshua last night. As much as she'd like to call him, catch up on old times, she couldn't risk letting her heart care for another rancher.

She couldn't bear to watch another man throw his life away

on a bunch of horses only to end up in disappointment . . . or worse.

A small tap at Robert's door sounded from behind. Robert glanced up and nodded. "Come in, Jasmine," he said, setting the phone in the cradle. "I'd like you to meet the newest member of our team."

A pretty young woman of African-American heritage whisked into the room. She had lovely light brown skin and honey-brown hair that was straightened, sleeked stylishly to her shoulders. Her sea-green eyes sparkled when she approached with a smile.

"Hi, I'm Jasmine King. You must be Debra Walker. I've heard so much about you."

Debra stood and took her outstretched hand, wondering if this was the woman Joshua had told her about last night at the auction. "Nice to meet you, Ms. King."

"Please, call me Jasmine. We're going to get pretty chummy with all the work we have to do." She turned and set a document on Robert's desk. "This is the paperwork from personnel you requested. It's too bad about Carolyn. She'll be hard to replace."

Still sitting behind his desk, Robert steepled his fingers and looked up at Debra, his dark gray eyes narrowing on hers. "I think with the right training and guidance, Miss Walker should have no problems taking over where Carolyn left off."

Wondering who this Carolyn person was and why she left, Debra gave a wary smile. "I assure you, I'll give Walson a hundred and ten percent."

"Is there anything else you need before your meeting this afternoon?" Jasmine asked. "I'd like to run home and see Milten for lunch."

"Do you have those financial reports ready for the Air Force?"

"They're coming off the printer now."

"Good. I should be all set then. How's Milt doing these days?"

Her face perked into a warm smile. "Much better. They've backed off on all his medications and he's sitting up and eating on his own. He's even getting back some of his memory."

Robert sat forward and started stacking several documents together. "Maybe I'll swing by the house sometime. I haven't seen him since he came home from the rehab center."

"I'm sure he'd love it. He gets a little stir-crazy with just the nurse and Oprah Winfrey to keep him company." She looked over at Debra. "I'll see you later. I should be back by one. If you have any questions, don't hesitate to ask."

"Thank you. I will. I look forward to working with you."

As Jasmine hurried out of the room, Robert rose from behind his desk. "I can't tell you how nice it is to finally meet Little Debbie Walker." His lips twitched into a crooked grin. "The way my father talks about you, you'd think you were his own daughter."

Being called Debbie was about as irritating as hanging onto coarse rope with blistered palms. She stepped closer to his desk and lowered her shoulders. "I haven't been called that since I was still in pigtails and stood as tall as a hitching post. Please, it's Debra now."

He gave an easy chuckle and picked up his tailored, pin-striped jacket hanging over the back of his chair. He spoke as he slipped his arms through the sleeves. "As far back as our fathers go, I'm surprised we haven't met before today."

"I'm afraid my father didn't take me a lot of places after we moved out to the ranch. In fact, I've only been down to Colorado Springs a few times with my mom." Hoping to avoid the topic of her parents altogether, she asked, "So how is your dad doing? He looked remarkably well at the funeral. I could hardly tell he'd had a stroke."

"I know. His recovery is amazing. He also struggles with arthritis and occasionally the pain gets him down, but," he added, adjusting the cufflinks at his wrists, "early retirement has done wonders for his morale. He hasn't had much to do with the business in months. He and my mom are vacationing in Hawaii as we speak."

As Robert came to a stop in front of her, she realized she was actually looking down at him. Standing two inches taller with her pumps on, she found herself slouching, a habit she'd formed in middle school when she was a good foot taller than most of the boys. She motioned her head to a picture of a little girl, sitting on the edge of his desk. "She's beautiful. Is she your daughter?"

He reached behind him and picked up the photo. "You wouldn't know it by looking at her. She's a spitting image of her mother. This is Shelly Lynn."

Debra smiled and stepped closer to get a better look. "How old is she?"

"She'll be ten this fall."

"She is absolutely adorable. Her mother must have lots of blond curly hair."

"And lots of everything else, I'm afraid," he said with furrowed brows, arranging the picture on his desk. "She and I divorced a while back, and now Shelly Lynn lives with her in Boston. Since I moved back to manage this division, I've only seen my daughter over the holidays."

"I'm so sorry. It must be hard to be away from her."

"Excruciating, if you want to know the truth. She's growing up so fast."

Debra's heart went out to Robert. It was obvious how much he loved his daughter.

He turned and slid his hands into the pockets of his trousers. "From what my father tells me, you've experienced some tough times yourself. I'm sorry to hear about your dad. Sounds like he had a string of bad luck these last few years. Are you getting everything settled with his estate?"

She lowered her gaze to her fingers, hoping to avoid the subject of her father. "It'll be a few weeks before everything's finalized, but I'm afraid it's going to take a lot longer than that to get used to the fact that everything's gone."

He gently gripped both of her shoulders and lowered his voice. "I'm sorry, Debbie. Did I upset you?"

She became engulfed with his cologne. Her nose tickled, feeling like a sneeze was about to erupt. She'd sneezed once since she'd injured her ribs, enough to know she didn't want to go through that torment again. "No. I'm fine," she assured, stepping back and casually dabbing at the tip of her nose. "It's exciting to know our fathers started this whole company from the basement of their homes. Walson has come a long way since then."

"You've come a long way yourself," he said, giving her another once-over from head to toe. "And to be quite honest, when Dad told me he'd hired you, I was more than a little hesitant. A country bumpkin coming straight off the farm into corporate America is a big jump."

Country bumpkin? Debra stiffened at his demeaning remark. It was obvious she still had to prove herself to Robert. She tried to give him a confident smile. "I assure you, Mr. Nelson. I won't let you down." As she'd let her father down.

"Please don't take offense," he said quickly. "I wouldn't have let Carolyn go if I hadn't had the utmost confidence in your abilities. I'm afraid my dad never really trusted Carolyn from the start, personally and business-wise. She tended to talk about things that were classified. We were worried about the security of our contracts."

Still unsure about her new position, she said, "Speaking of contracts, I was hoping to get a copy of your current agreements between Walson and your customers. I'd like to get a handle on them before working on the Air Force proposal."

He gave a low chuckle. "Don't you worry your pretty little head about the contracts, Debbie. Jasmine and the manager of accounting are the only ones with a secret clearance to work on contracts. As for the Air Force proposal, I'll be handling all the negotiations myself."

Ignoring his patronizing attitude, she tugged at the lapels of her jacket, looking down at him. "I don't understand. I thought I was hired as the contracts administrator. How long will it take for me to obtain my secret clearance?"

His brows arched, almost making him appear confused. "Maybe my father didn't explain your position very well. Jasmine was promoted to contracts administrator to replace Carolyn. You were hired to *assist* Jasmine. You won't be needing a clearance yet."

"Oh." She swallowed, suddenly feeling about two inches tall. "I guess I misunderstood."

"If there's a problem—"

"Oh, no," she interrupted, sounding almost desperate. "Believe me. I'm grateful for the opportunity to work here. The job market is tough right now. It seems everyone is laying off instead of hiring."

"Signs of the times, I'm afraid," he said without qualm, sweeping a tendril of ebony hair over her shoulder. "You shouldn't have to worry about that, though. Just stick close to me and learn the game, and I guarantee you'll be into management in no time. I'm afraid that's something Carolyn never quite grasped."

Learn the game? Now she had to wonder exactly why this Carolyn person was fired in the first place.

Before she could question him further, he motioned toward the door. "I cleared my schedule and thought we'd grab some lunch. Do you like Italian?"

"Italian's fine. I just need to go back to my desk and grab my purse."

As they left his office and headed toward her cubicle, he asked, "Are you all settled into Colorado Springs?"

"I'm staying in a motel until I can find an apartment. Maybe you could recommend a few places."

"As a matter of fact, I'm staying in a complex up in Woodland Park that has a few empty units. Hot tub, indoor pool, lots of security."

After the night she'd spent in her motel, finding a safe, secure location was of top priority. Unfortunately, her budget would barely be able to afford a hot shower, much less a hot tub. She stepped slightly ahead of Robert, a little uncomfortable with his closeness. "Sounds perfect, but expensive."

"Not really. I'm close friends with the owner. He could probably swing you a good deal on a lease."

Unsure about moving into the same complex as her new boss, she nodded and stepped inside her cubicle. "I'd like to get familiar with the area before signing anything. I'll let you know."

She grabbed her purse from the bottom drawer of the filing cabinet and bumped it shut with her foot. As she stepped in front of Robert, he gripped her shoulders from behind, stopping her abruptly in her tracks.

"Garrison? What the hell are you doing here?"

Debra jerked her head up, her heart jumping to her throat. *Joshua?*

Like yesterday at the auction barn, her gaze settled on that big cowboy as he strode down the central corridor straight toward her and Robert. Instead of tight, faded Wranglers, Joshua wore pleated tan trousers with a crisp, western cut dress shirt of the same color. A dark russet-colored silk tie and shiny dark brown leather cowboy boots finished off his ensemble. He looked more like a business executive than a rancher.

But it was his expression that made her stomach twist into a knot. Unlike yesterday, his chiseled jaw was clenched shut and he had absolutely no hint of a smile. His gaze met hers briefly before diverting to the man grasping her shoulders from behind.

"Look what the buzzards dragged in from Boston," Joshua ground out as he stopped in front of them. "Debra?" he asked, lowering his voice, glancing at Robert's hands, practically digging into her flesh. "Everything okay here?"

Robert tugged her back against him, almost as if he were using her like a protective shield. "What do you want, Garrison? How'd you get past security?"

Joshua gave a mocking laugh and looked down at Robert over her shoulder. "If Hank Zitler is your company's idea of security, then you've got more problems than I thought. That man hasn't been right since high school."

"You don't belong here, Garrison. Don't you have a cow to milk or something?" Robert pressed down on Debra's shoulders, sending a stabbing pain through her ribcage.

"Robert, please!" she gasped, jerking away and backing into the filing cabinet.

Joshua mumbled a curse and quickly stepped closer, touching her elbow. "Debra, are you all right?"

"Yes, of course. I'm fine." She took in a quivery breath, then gave the lapels of her jacket a swift tug to compose herself. "For goodness sakes. What's gotten into you two?"

"How do you know Debbie?" Robert growled, directing his question toward Joshua.

Joshua's eyes narrowed on Robert, but he didn't answer.

She tucked a strand of hair behind her ear and interjected, "Joshua and I are old friends, Robert. Our fathers used to do ranch business together." She made a nervous glance toward Joshua. "How do you two know each other?"

"It doesn't matter," Joshua answered, lowering his voice.

"Did you forget, honey? We made arrangements to go to lunch today. I'm sorry I'm late."

"Lunch?" she repeated, not sure she'd heard him right. She'd been so upset about losing Brandy yesterday, she couldn't remember if they'd agreed to lunch. Did he just call her honey?

The way he'd spoken to her so affectionately at the auction barn, she'd assumed his endearment had been because she'd been so upset about losing Brandy. He'd simply felt sorry for her, kind of like a big brother taking care of a little sister. But standing here now, he didn't show any kind of pity in his eyes. In fact, there was something else she couldn't quite put a finger on behind his warm, dreamy brown expression.

She nervously switched her weight between legs, now feeling as wobbly as a newborn foal.

Robert puffed out his chest, his eyes only coming up to Joshua's chin. "A classy lady like this is way out of your league, plow boy. Try across the street at the Waffle House."

Joshua made no comment, nor did he bat an eye as he held Robert's gaze in check. Tension loomed thicker than a midsummer dust storm in the prairie. What was the history between these two men and how was she going to get out of this mess?

CHAPTER FOUR

The shrill ring of Robert's cell phone made Debra flinch.

Robert gave a muffled curse, reached inside his jacket pocket and read the caller ID. "I have to take this call, Debbie. I've been waiting for it all morning." He turned to Joshua, his voice lowering as he spoke through gritted teeth. "Have her back in one hour. She and I will be tied up in a meeting the rest of the afternoon." Stepping in front of her, he took hold of both her hands, blocking Joshua's view. "We'll have to plan on dinner tonight. I'll pick you up at your motel at eight then we can take that tour of my complex. With my connections, we'll have you moved in by next weekend."

Before she could get a syllable out of her mouth, he turned on his Italian-loafered heels and strode down the long corridor toward his office. She flinched when Robert's door slammed shut. With her heart still beating erratically, she turned and faced Joshua, lowering her voice. "What was that all about? How do you know Robert?"

Joshua cleared his throat, looking more than a little guilty as he made another glance toward Robert's office. "It doesn't matter. Let's just say we go way back."

An awkward silence fell between them and she found herself switching her weight back and forth between legs. She tried to hide her trembly fingers by smoothing the front of her skirt. "Um, did I miss something yesterday? I don't remember setting a lunch date with you, but then again," she quickly added with a short laugh, "my mind wasn't exactly focused."

He raked his fingers through his hair and shook his head. "Actually, no. I just said that to rile ol' Robbie boy. Sorry for barging in on you like that. I tried calling this morning, but they said you were in a meeting. I hope I didn't intrude."

"No, actually, I'm kind of relieved. I've had so much thrown at me this morning I kind of needed a break from it all."

"Good. I don't feel so bad now. Tell you what," he said, loosening the knot in his tie. "Why don't I start all over?" He flashed her that toe-curling smile and gave a slight bow. "Miss Walker, I'd be honored if you would join me for lunch."

Flattered that he'd even thought about her today, she tilted her head and gave him a wry grin. "Is Mexican still your favorite food?"

His smile broadened, his dimple giving her that little wink that made her heart pitter-pat inside her chest. "Do you want mild-hot or clear-your-sinuses hot?"

"Now that you mention it," she said, breathing deeply, his masculine scent a wonderful contrast to Robert's irritating cologne. "My nose is feeling stuffy today."

"I've got the perfect place. I was hoping Jasmine was still here, too. Is she around?" he asked, peering over the cubicles.

"No, she just left to meet her husband for lunch. Is she the friend you were talking about last night at the auction?"

"Yeah. I just came from their house. I must have passed her on the way down." He motioned his head toward her desk. "Is this your office?" he asked, stepping inside her cubicle, cutting the already small area in half.

Still a little disheartened with her new career beginnings, she lifted her shoulders with a shrug. "Yep. This is it."

"How'd it go this morning? Any problems?" He picked up a file and started flipping through it.

She quickly took the file. "No, everything's fine."

He began flipping through her Rolodex. "Have you talked to any of your customers?"

Peering over the cubicle wall toward Robert's office, she lowered her voice. "You're going to get me fired on my first day if you keep this up."

"Believe me, that wouldn't be a bad thing." He kept flipping through her card file.

"Joshua, please," she huffed, covering the cards with her hand. "What's wrong with you? He just wanted to take me to lunch. No big deal."

"Look, I didn't want to say anything yesterday, but he's got quite a reputation. And I'm not just talking with the ladies. He's already shut down two divisions in Texas. I've heard rumors that some of your customers haven't been too happy since Robert took over this division. I wouldn't put it past him to close this one down as well."

She knew all about the offices in Texas. There were two other divisions in the United States, one in San Jose and one in Boston. Since the upheaval in the Middle East, both divisions, as well as the Rocky Mountain office, had shown a remarkable amount of growth over the last two years. Judging by the reaction between Robert and Joshua, she couldn't help but wonder if there was more to Joshua's concern than the economic outlook of Walson Technology.

He propped an elbow on the wall partition, giving her a speculative glance. "What's this about you moving into his complex?"

Somewhat embarrassed, she shook her head and held her hand over her heart. "Oh, no. That was just a misunderstanding."

"I'll just bet," he murmured with a hint of cynicism. "The way he was touching you, I thought maybe he was bothering you or something. Was he? Because if he's giving you any kind of trouble . . ." He trailed off, obviously thinking the worst of an innocent situation.

She shook her head. "If you're concerned about . . . well, you know, Robert coming on to me or anything, you don't need to worry. I can handle myself."

"Maybe so, but I know Robbie better than anyone else does. He doesn't have a decent bone in his body. I trust him about as far as a rooster can spit."

She couldn't help but laugh. "Roosters can't spit."

"Exactly. He uses women for his own personal gain, then drops them when he's got what he wants. He likes his liquor strong and his women fast and beautiful."

"See there?" she said through a laugh, hoping to lighten the mood. "I don't have anything to worry about."

"Don't sell yourself short. You're as pretty as they come in these parts. In any parts, for that matter," he added. "I just don't want him hassling you."

Feeling a warm flush on her cheeks at his compliment, she shook her head. "Trust me, Joshua, I learned a long time ago how to handle guys." She looked down and pulled her lapels over her blouse, self-consciously covering the huge swells of her breasts. "When I was sixteen, a ranch hand from the neighboring farm attacked me out in the barn. Believe me, after I introduced him to my knee, he was singing soprano for the next month at church."

Joshua stared at her for a brief moment, and she wished she'd have left that last bit of information out.

"I'm sorry, Debra. Were you . . . hurt or anything?"

"Just bruised up a bit," she answered, knowing full well that if her father hadn't shown up, she might have been raped. She slouched her shoulders and studied her fingers. "After that, Dad was pretty protective. He never let a guy come within ten feet of me. Made me wear bulky work shirts over a T-shirt so I wouldn't be so, um . . . distracting. Don't get me wrong," she nervously added, turning toward her desk and straightening files. "I wasn't a target of a lot of men's affections anyway. I think my height intimidated the guys in high school, and the few I hung out with in college had all been friends. Folks say I'm a spitting image of my father. Great if you're a guy," she joked, stapling two documents together.

He stepped up beside her and touched her arm, forcing her to face him. "It seems the lady has a little self-esteem problem." When she looked up and met his smile, he bent his legs slightly, leveling his gaze with hers. "Hasn't anyone ever told you how pretty you are?"

She looked down at her feet, her size twelves not exactly her idea of pretty. "My father used to tell me I was the prettiest little filly east of the Rockies, but aren't fathers supposed to say that to their little girls?"

"Since I'm not a dad, I wouldn't know." He touched her chin, forcing her to return his gaze. "But I *am* a red-blooded American male, and I completely agree with your father on this one."

Without batting an eye, he swept several wayward tendrils from her shoulder. "I don't think I've ever seen you with your hair down when it's not in a braid or pigtails. It looks nice. In fact," he said, stepping back and openly gazing at her from her head to her toe, "you look great. All of you," he assured her with a boyish grin.

She smoothed her palms over her skirt, feeling a warm blush work its way up her chest. For some reason, when Robert had been this close and looked at her like that, she'd felt uneasy, kind of icky actually. But with Joshua, it felt right. It felt nice. "Thanks," she said with a genuine smile. "Thought I'd shuck the tomboy appearance. I'm a career woman now. Better look the part. Although," she added, rotating her ankles, "my feet aren't exactly thrilled with the transition."

"Well, you looked good as a tomboy, but if a career woman is what you're after, it definitely suits you. But do me a favor." He gently pressed his hands on her arms, lifting her up slightly. "Don't slouch. My sister used to do the same thing when she was in high school. I'm going to tell you what I told her. You're a beautiful young woman with a good head on your shoulders. Stand tall and be proud of what the good Lord gave you." With his dreamy brown gaze bearing into hers, he gave her a warm smile that made her want to do more than slouch. Her knees felt about as strong as wet straw.

"Okay, okay." She straightened her posture, bringing her eyes level with his mouth. "Is that better?"

His gaze darted to her lips then back to her eyes. "Absolutely perfect."

For a moment, he held her gaze hostage, and she hoped she wasn't actually drooling. He was so startlingly handsome and sexy, and God, he smelled good. The hay and manure from yesterday had been replaced with something spicy and fresh and woodsy. She stepped back and openly scanned him from his thick wavy brown hair down to his shiny brown cowboy boots. "You clean up pretty nice yourself." She flicked the end of his tie. "Your ranch must have a rigid dress code."

He chuckled and ran a finger under his collar. "Actually, I have a meeting this afternoon with my banker and I just came from the hospital. My ten-year-old cousin's pretty sick. He had a heart transplant last summer. Looks like his body is rejecting it."

"Oh, Joshua. I'm sorry. What do the doctors say?"

"It's still too soon to tell. They've changed around a bunch of his medications. I guess all we can do now is wait."

"And pray," she said softly, reaching out and gently touching his arm.

"Believe me, I've put in more than a few requests over the years. Sometimes I wonder if He even hears me." He glanced at his watch. "Maybe we should get going. We only have fifty-two minutes left. I wouldn't want you late for your meeting with ol' Robbie boy."

Wondering what the history was between those two, she slung her purse over her shoulder and headed toward the elevator.

"Listen," he said, matching his strides to hers. "I'm really sorry for barging in on you like this. I had my cell phone turned off at the hospital and thought maybe you'd tried to call. I kind of hoped to take you and Jasmine to lunch. Guess I missed Jasmine."

They approached the end of the corridor and she punched the down button for the elevator. "I didn't get a chance to talk with her. What's wrong with her husband? Is he sick?"

"He was involved in a freak car accident about a year ago. Paralyzed him from the waist down. It's a shame. He was in the pros playing for the Kansas City Chiefs and had just become a free agent."

She pursed her lips. "Hmmm. You're talking about football, right?"

He rubbed his bearded chin, his mouth twitching as if he were trying to contain a grin. "Don't watch much sports, huh?"

A little embarrassed, she shook her head. "I caught the Super Bowl on TV this year, but only because Toby Keith was singing," she admitted with a wry grin.

He chuckled. "Milt helped take the Chiefs to the Super Bowl two years in a row. He could've pretty much picked where he wanted to play. He knew the risks when he stepped out alone without signing with anyone, but it was between seasons. The accident ended his career."

"Oh, my gosh. That's awful."

"I stopped by his place before going to the hospital this morning and he seemed kind of upset about something. I think he's worried about Jasmine working so hard. She also holds down a job at a local restaurant just to make ends meet."

"I had no idea. She seems like a nice lady. Be assured, she won't have to work so hard now that I'm here to help."

The elevator doors slid open and they stepped into the empty car. As they descended to the first floor, she was acutely aware of how close he stood, the back of her jacket barely brushing his shirtsleeve. A few people entered at the second floor, forcing her to nudge closer. The heat from his body, the scent of his aftershave, and the aura of pure man surrounded her with a heady feeling. When they hit the lobby, she quickly strode ahead of him, the air conditioning in the lobby a cool relief to her heated skin.

A security guard came around the corner, his walk more of a limp as he favored his right leg. She'd met him briefly that morning when she'd obtained a temporary badge; his demeanor had been gruff and not at all friendly.

"Ms. Walker," he hollered, not sounding as if he was in a better mood. "We didn't get your security paperwork filled out this morning. I'll be needin' you to fill out all the forms after lunch so we can overnight it to our headquarters in Boston by three."

"Yes, sir. I'll do that as soon as I get back. I promise."

He and Joshua exchanged a curt nod of acknowledgment, but no words were spoken. She entered an extra-wide glass revolving door and when Joshua stepped in close behind, she leaned close and whispered, "Somebody sure takes his job seriously. Is he always so gruff?"

Joshua gave a quick glance through the glass over his shoulder. "Don't let Hank intimidate you. He took a pretty bad hit playing football in high school. Suffered a severe concussion and really hasn't been the same since. He screwed up his knee pretty bad, too. Underwent several surgeries and is lucky to be walking without a cane. He's got a wife and four kids to support now. Probably has a lot on his mind."

As they stepped outside onto the pavement, the afternoon Colorado sunshine made her already warm face feel like an inferno. He gestured toward a solid black, long-bed four-by-four pickup truck with a four-door crew cab parked in the front visitor spot.

Oh, Lordy. She'd always been a sucker for a pickup man.

Joshua cranked the air conditioning to high, his temperature still climbing as he chastised himself for the way he'd handled things at Walson with Robbie Nelson. But something had snapped when he'd seen Robbie touching Debra, or more aptly, groping her. It'd taken all Joshua's strength not to plow his fist right into the weasel's perfect face right then and there. His gut still churned now that he knew some rednecked ranch hand had tried to have his way with Debra when she was so young and innocent.

With his anger reduced to a low simmer, Joshua pulled his truck into the parking lot of a rustic Tex-Mex restaurant. The hostess escorted them to a cozy corner booth, where they sat across from one another and munched on nachos and drank iced teas. The sounds of silverware and glasses clinking around the restaurant were mixed with low conversations of people in the neighboring booths.

Fluorescent lights shone through the stained-glass fixtures above their heads, casting a soft glow on Debra's hair. Shades of iridescent purple glimmered throughout the ebony tendrils cascading into loose waves down her front. She was undoubtedly the most beautiful woman he'd ever clapped eyes on, although to be honest, he preferred her in tight jeans and cowboy boots.

But she was a career woman now, he reminded himself. How

did she put it yesterday? She'd eat her chaps before stepping foot on a ranch again? Well, he'd see about that. They made edible panties. Why not chaps?

Debra peered over the rim of her glass and caught him staring. She gave him a pretty smile, her face turning a soft shade of pink. "So how come you never went on to play football in the pros with Milten? Looks like you could have had a pretty good shot at it."

He shook his head, feeling a warm sensation cover his own face. "Nah, I never really dreamed about it like Milten. My heart was always on ranching. Even after working in the city for several years, I couldn't wait to get home every night to be around my horses."

"You worked in the city?"

"Sure did. I had to build up enough capital before I could expand. Guess I don't have to tell you how hard it is to keep a ranch going these days."

She gave a forced laugh. "Believe me, I learned firsthand how tough it was."

"I'm sorry, Debra. I didn't mean—"

"It's okay," she said waving off his remark. "Ranching is a tough business. Why do you think I'm sitting behind a desk shuffling paperwork? At least now I can depend on a steady paycheck every week and get my bills paid."

Wishing he'd never mentioned his previous job, he asked, "So how is the city life treating you? Are you enjoying the nightlife?"

She smiled and poked a chip in and out of the hot sauce. "Not yet, but I can tell it's definitely going to be quite a switch from the country. Before Dad died, he and I were the only ones living at the ranch. The city isn't nearly as quiet." She brought the chip to her mouth and gave a loud chomp as she bit into the tortilla. "My friends all lived and worked in the city, and with everything that needed to be done around the ranch, I rarely got to see any of them. I think that's why I always hated being an only child. I got stuck doing all the grunt work Dad didn't like to do."

She gave a wistful smile. "I was always so jealous when you told me about the fun things you did with your family. That's why I want to have a huge family of my own someday."

After seeing Dillan struggle with his new heart, Joshua didn't think he could bring even one child into this world, only to be poked and prodded and put through every painful medical test they could make up. He cringed just thinking about it. "So, tell me . . ." He paused, wondering how set she was on having kids. "Just how *huge* are we talking?"

"Four to start," she said matter-of-factly. "Two boys, two girls. I want to live in a huge two-story colonial house with a wide wraparound porch. Oh, and a dog. My mom was allergic and we could never have one. Kids definitely need a dog."

What fantasyland did she live in? He had to chuckle. "I think your mother read you too many fairy tales as a child. Life isn't that easy."

"Sounds like you're speaking from experience. You said you're not a dad, but what about a wife? Are you married?"

Knowing how close he'd come to being a husband, he shook his head and ran the tip of his finger around the edge of his tea glass. "I'm definitely not married. To be honest, I don't think I'll ever go that route. Things get way too complicated."

"Now, Joshua," she admonished with a waggle of her finger. "If you've never been in love, how can you say you'll never get married?"

Remembering how Michelle had ripped his heart out nearly ten years ago, he blew out a loud gust of air. "I didn't say I've never been in love."

"Oh," she said, looking down at her napkin. "Mind if I ask

what happened?"

Sorry he'd even brought up Michelle, he picked up his tea, giving his shoulders a slight shrug. "She ran off with another guy the day before our wedding. How's that for an ego booster?"

"Ouch. Guess I'd be a little altar shy, too. I'm sorry."

Hoping to steer the conversation away from him, he leaned forward and smiled. "You sure remind me of Heather. She always wanted marriage and kids."

"Did she get them?"

"Yep. A boy and a girl. Unfortunately, Kyle was diagnosed with autism just after his third birthday. She's tutoring him at home now, but it's tough. Her husband left her last month, and I get the impression he's not coming back this time."

"This time?"

"Let's just say he's a jerk and leave it at that. My brother and I fill in as much as we can. I remember how hard it was growing up without a father. Kids shouldn't be alone." His expression softened into a smile. "I've been giving Kyle riding lessons this summer. I'm telling you what, the minute that kid gets in the saddle, it's like he becomes one with the animal. He's doing great."

"I've heard of horse therapy for autistic kids. Sounds like it's working."

"Yeah. I think Kyle likes being treated like a normal kid. Makes him feel grown up."

The waitress arrived with their meals and set a steaming plate of chicken fajitas and green peppers in front of Debra. Sizzling beef fajitas with rice and beans smothered with white cheese sauce was set in front of J.D. He forked a mound of seasoned beef strips onto a tortilla, hoping to hear more about her father. "Do you feel like talking about your dad? Yesterday, you said he had a heart attack. Had he been having heart problems?"

"Well, um," she stammered, bringing a napkin to her lips. "The doctors said he'd had a few minor instances before that, but nothing that warranted a hospital stay." She took a drink of tea, but wouldn't look him in the eye.

Not sure if she was telling the whole truth, he said, "I remember the Lazy W had a thriving business. What happened to the ranch?" The sparkle in her eyes seemed to have been replaced with a sudden sadness, and he hoped he wasn't upsetting her. "Hey, if you don't want to talk about it, just say so. I completely understand."

"It's all right," she said through an exhausted sigh, leaning back against the seat. "To be honest, I haven't really talked about it with anyone other than my mom. And she's not exactly sympathetic. She never wanted to move to the ranch in the first place."

"Can you tell me what happened? My sisters tell me I'm a great listener."

She smiled and met his gaze. "Your sisters are lucky to have you."

She sat forward, straightening the salt and pepper shakers. "I guess it all started about six years ago. Dad decided to convert to exotic animals. He'd found an investor and started a herd of buffalo. We installed special reinforced fences and bought new trailers and equipment. Unfortunately, the market was tough and he didn't have a big enough herd to make any major profit. When the buffalo didn't pan out, he'd tried raising a herd of bull elk while still raising cattle and breeding horses. For the first time in years, our ranch turned a profit."

"So what happened?"

"A couple of years ago, right after I graduated college, in fact, Dad injured his back. Laid him up for the entire summer and into the fall. I think that's when things all started going downhill. Meat prices dropped, and the threat of chronic wasting disease kept restaurants from putting venison on their menus. To make a long story short, the ranch took a nosedive in profits, and my father resorted to gambling."

Joshua stiffened, remembering how his own father had visited the casinos at the Indian reservations. Dang near left his mom and them without a dime in the end. The only reason she'd been able to keep their place was because of an inheritance from her father. Debra obviously hadn't been so fortunate.

She sat forward and grabbed a tortilla chip. "I tried my hand at running the place by myself. But in retrospect . . ." She paused, scooping sauce onto her chip. "He would have been better off hiring an experienced foreman. Maybe things would have turned out different."

"How different?"

"Come on, Joshua," she said through a noisy crunch. "I can lift a bale of hay with the best of them, but there were some things I just couldn't handle. I never admitted it to my father, but there were several times when I had to ask our neighbor for help starting a tractor, fixing a fence, or getting a water trough unfrozen during the winter. And when it came to training? I could never do it like Dad. He said I wasn't firm enough and that I got too emotionally attached to the horses."

"That's not a bad trait to have. Just means you're compassionate."

"That's not the only thing," she said, rolling her eyes. "Last summer, Dad was gone for the weekend and one of his prized mares went into early labor. The foal was breech and the vet couldn't get out to the ranch in time." She closed her eyes and shook her head. "God, Joshua. It was horrible. I couldn't pull it out. The mare and the foal both died."

Joshua's chest swelled with empathy. He'd never lost a foal or a mare in labor, but after watching Golden Sunset die, he knew firsthand the kind of guilt she must be enduring. He reached across the table and touched her chin, forcing her to look up at him. "That wasn't your fault, honey. Even I've had trouble pulling foals, and I'm twice your size."

Moving away from his touch, she leaned against the booth. "I don't want to talk about the ranch. I'm starting down a new path now. I get the weekends off and I'll finally have a place where there will be people to interact with who can actually carry on a two-sided conversation. Horses are great listeners, but they sure don't have a lot of opinions."

"I don't know," he said, rubbing his chin. "Horses don't tend to worry about things like benefits and overtime."

"True," she agreed with a laugh.

Eyeing her carefully, he sat back and draped his arm over the back of the bench, crossing his ankle over his knee. "You don't give yourself much credit, do you?"

"Credit?" she repeated. "What do you mean?"

"Sounds to me like you were running the whole show, taking care of your dad, running the operations of the ranch. And from the little I've been around Brandy, your training methods are right on the mark. You should cut yourself a little slack."

"You weren't around, Joshua. You don't know what it was like."

"I've got a pretty good idea. Not a lot of people know this, but my dad used to hit the tables. If it weren't for my grandfather's inheritance, I'd probably be a city slicker, too."

Her eyes widened. "Your father gambled? I never would have guessed."

"Most people didn't know that side of him. He was one of Colorado Springs' golden boys. Everyone loved him."

"I wish I could say that about my dad. He didn't have a lot of friends in the end."

The waitress refilled their glasses and left the check. When Debra pulled out several ones from her billfold, he reached across the table and covered her hand. "My treat."

"Are you sure? It's really not—"

"Put your money away, darlin'. I've got you covered." He gave her hand a squeeze, and for a moment they just sat there, gazing into one another's eyes. He rubbed the pad of his thumb over her knuckles, trying unsuccessfully not to notice how right her hand felt in his. He wondered if all of her was this soft underneath those stuffy business clothes.

She tugged her hand away and tucked her money inside her purse. He gave a quick glance at his watch. "I'd better get you back. Wouldn't want you late for your big meeting." He stood and pulled out his billfold, flipping a twenty on the table.

She shuffled to the edge of the booth then wrapped her arm around her midsection. When she braced a hand on the table, she grimaced as she pushed her way to standing.

Quickly moving in front of her, he gently touched her side. "Debra? I've seen enough fallen cowboys to know the telltale signs of injured ribs. Be honest with me. Did you hurt yourself yesterday at the auction barn?"

"No, no. I'm fine," she answered without looking him in the eye. "Just ate too much." Her voice sounded breathy when she spoke again. "How's Brandy doing? I miss our little talks. You're not one of those horse whisperers who can read their minds, are you?"

"Why?" he asked, taking hold of both her hands. "Is she keeping deep dark secrets that you don't want me to know about?"

Tilting her head in a shy gesture, she answered, "No. Just my innermost thoughts. Come to think of it, you'd probably be bored to tears reading her mind."

"I doubt that," he assured with a smile, dropping his gaze to her lips. A speck of hot sauce at the corner of her mouth begged for his attention. Although a napkin would work, he had a much

Colorado Pickup Man

better remedy for this particular situation, but seeing as how they were in a public place, he opted for the less intrusive method. He gently swiped the tempting morsel with the pad of his thumb. "Hot sauce," he explained huskily, licking the sauce with his tongue. An involuntary shudder raced straight up his arm and landed smack dab at the base of his heart.

A brother, he reminded himself. She only thought of him as a brother. That's what he'd tried to drill into his head ever since he'd met her at the auction barn yesterday afternoon. But somewhere between his heart and his brain, signals kept getting crossed.

She lowered her lashes and quickly swiped her mouth with her fingers. "I've never been too graceful at the dinner table. Drove my mother crazy."

"Guess I have something in common with your mother then." He winked and tugged her toward the exit. "Come on. We'd better get you back to work. Wouldn't want you to miss your big meeting with ol' Robbie boy."

He drove to Walson and walked Debra to the front doors. "Tell Jasmine I stopped by. Maybe I'll catch her next time."

"Sounds like Milt's got a tough road ahead of him."

"Yeah. They're amazed at his recovery. Milt and I actually used to rodeo together."

"Really?"

"Yep. He was a heck of a heeler in the team roping event. I ordered him a handicapped-equipped saddle and hope to get him out to my ranch when he gets stronger. Maybe the horse will give him a sense of freedom from the confines of a wheelchair."

"Milt's lucky to have you as a friend. I hope I get a chance to know Jasmine better."

"I invited them to a rodeo Friday night. Why don't you come with them?"

81

Jacquie Greenfield

"A rodeo?" she repeated, sounding a little wary. "I haven't been to a rodeo since high school. I suppose there'll be bucking broncs and lots of manure."

"I suppose now that you're a sophisticated career woman you don't want to get your boots dirty," he teased.

"Oh, no, it's not that. It's just . . ." she paused, looking down at her clothes, smoothing her palms over her skirt.

Wishing she would open up and talk to him, he tipped her chin up. "It's just what, then?"

"I don't know. Guess I'm afraid being around all that stuff will bring back some memories—and not all of them good. I watched my dad fracture an arm and twist an ankle trying to break in a green horse. And as you witnessed yesterday, I've had my share of bruised backsides from being thrown." Her nose wrinkled into the cutest expression as she rubbed her hind end.

He gave a low chuckle and caressed his hand up and down her arm. "It's a rodeo, Debra. It's where the cowboys come out to play. You don't have to do a thing except buy a ticket and plant your pretty little fanny on a metal bleacher. I'll even provide a cushion for your abused derriere."

"Okay, okay," she said, pressing her hands against his chest. "I'll think about it."

Her hands still on his chest, her gaze settled on his lips. They stood so close he could smell the Starlight mint she'd eaten after their hot-hot Mexican meal. He gave a heavy swallow. The signals between his heart and brain were suddenly jumbling with the anatomy below his buckle.

Sliding his boots to the outside of her black pumps, he slouched slightly to catch her eye. "Debra?"

"Hmmm?" she answered dreamily, slowly lifting her gaze to meet his.

He tugged her closer, speaking right next to her mouth. "I suggest you quit looking at me like that, or getting fired will be

82

the least of your worries right now."

Her face flamed redder than the chili peppers in the hot sauce. She shook her head and backed away toward the front doors. "I'm sorry, I was just . . . Anyway," she said, pressing her palms to her cheeks, "maybe I'll see you Friday. Where should I meet you?"

"Don't worry," he said with a smile, her nervousness a nice change from the bold and flirtatious buckle bunnies that swarmed around him at the rodeos. "I'm never in one place for long. I'll find you."

CHAPTER FIVE

Friday morning, Jasmine awoke to the classical music on the radio. She rolled over and lazily draped her arm across her husband's chest, her fingers tracing circles in the tiny black tufts of hair. "You awake?" she asked softly.

When he didn't answer, she gazed up at him. His eyes were closed, but his lips were curled up just enough to know he was awake and listening.

She smiled and snuggled in closer, draping her leg over his thighs beneath the covers. The feel of his skin next to hers was pure heaven. She only wished Milten could experience the same wonderful sensations. Maybe in time . . .

"I wish I didn't have to go in to work today, but at least it's Friday." She placed a soft kiss on his chest. "The new girl seems to be working out. Her name is Debra Walker. She's a hard worker and a quick study. Turns out she's a friend of J.D.'s. I think she'll be at the rodeo tonight."

He gave a heavy swallow. "Tonight?"

"Yeah. Do you remember the last time we went to the rodeo?"

His brows furrowed. "I remember . . . doing an autograph signing."

"That's right. You helped J.D. raise money for his little cousin's medical bills. He had a heart transplant last summer."

"Dillan?" he asked, his voice sounding scratchy.

"That's right," she said with hopeful anticipation. "What else do you remember?"

He dragged his hand to his forehead. "Weren't you sick that night?"

She nodded. "I had the flu. You wanted to stay home, but I didn't want you to let Dillan down. Now, of course, I wish you'd have stayed with me."

"I'm sorry, Jazzy," he murmured, stroking her arm.

"Don't be. It wasn't your fault. I just wish you hadn't been in such a big hurry to get home. Glen said when you dropped him off at his mom's condo in Woodland Park that you were worried about me."

Milten tried to speak but was overtaken by a wave of gut-wrenching coughs. She quickly sat up and stuffed a pillow behind his back, elevating his head. Bracing most of her weight on her knees, she straddled his midsection so she could reach over to the nightstand for a glass of water. "Here, baby, drink some of this." She held a straw to his mouth.

He took a long drink, then slumped back on his pillow, exhausted.

Worried, she set the glass on the table. "Maybe you shouldn't be doing so much talking. The speech therapist is stopping by this morning. I'll ask her what she thinks." Not wanting to get ready for work yet, she grabbed an envelope from the nightstand. It was from Milten's high school class reunion committee. Still straddling his waist, she asked, "Did you get a chance to read the letter from Shelly Whipstock?"

He shook his head. "What's . . . ol' Shelly Belly . . . want now?"

Giving him a loving smack on the chest, she quickly skimmed through the letter, acutely aware of Milten's large warm hands now splayed over each thigh, sending a rush of warmth through her entire body. "They're having your ten-year reunion over the Labor Day weekend. Wow, that's only a month away. It says there's a baseball game and a family picnic Friday night, then a black-tie affair at the Antler's Adam's Mark Hotel Saturday."

He shook his head. "Not going."

"Oh, Milten. Everyone wants to see you. Look how much you've recovered. Tell you what. Since you remembered Shelly Whipstock, I'm going to dig out all your old yearbooks this weekend. Maybe it'll trigger more of your memory to return."

A muscle ticked at the base of his jaw, his eyes narrowing in anger. She'd seen this look enough to know when a subject was closed for discussion. Before he could make another objection, she pressed two fingers to his lips and whispered close to his mouth. "Shhhh, I don't want to fight with you right now."

His gaze intensified as something else flashed in the depths of his midnight blue eyes. His fingertips started tracing circles over the bare skin of her outer thigh near the rim of her panties. He used to do that whenever he wanted to make love to her, but he was still so weak she figured he probably wasn't even aware he was touching her.

She reached over and switched off the bedside lamp. Rays of early morning sunshine filtered through the blinds, illuminating their bedroom with a soft yellow glow. Her favorite concerto was playing on the radio, the same music that was played at their wedding.

When she went to lie down beside him, he wrapped his hands around her hips, stopping her so she stayed on top of him, her knees bracing most of her weight. Her tummy did a little flip when his gaze lowered to her lips, lowering further down to her neck then her chest. She suddenly felt self-conscious as he openly stared at her breasts, the tips shamelessly hardening under his intense scrutiny.

Having seen this expression many, many, many times before his accident, she met his heated gaze and gave a playful arch of her eyebrows. *This had always been his favorite nightie.* Craving the simple affection of stroking one another, she spoke as she traced the words *I love you* onto the bare skin of his chest. He closed his eyes and slid his palms around to her backside, gently cupping her bottom.

Not sure what his intentions were, she licked her lips, and spoke in a soft, sultry voice. "I'm going to try and get home early tonight to get you dressed for the rodeo. I can't wait to see you in cowboy boots and jeans."

Milt's eyes barely opened, his lips curling into a sleepy grin.

When his palms and fingers started massaging her derriere, goosebumps rose on her arms. Her skin turned hot. "I always loved you in tight faded jeans sitting on top of your horse. You've got to be the sexiest man I've ever known."

His Adam's apple bobbed heavily as he slid the index finger of each hand under the elastic rim of her panties, then slowly circled around toward the apex of her thighs. She held her breath and bit down on her lower lip as both his fingertips met in the middle, the sensations sending a spasm of heat shooting up to the roots of her hair, all the way down to her toes. Her legs weakened and she felt herself instinctively lowering on top of him.

Almost afraid she was dreaming, she whispered, "Milten?"

With his gaze boring into hers, he pressed her downward till she settled on a very hard mass, covered only by his thin cotton boxers.

"Jazzy," he growled. His hands wandered freely underneath her teddy.

The warmth of his hands splaying over her skin ignited a flame deep below her belly that hadn't flickered for almost a year. She leaned over and covered his mouth with hers and could feel the fast beat of his heart under her palms. Although she loved his wonderful touch, she didn't want him to overexert himself either. She took his hands and intertwined his fingers with hers, raised them above his head and placed them on either side of his pillow. "You just lie there and let me take it from here." When he didn't resist, she placed a soft kiss over his lips then kissed along his prominent square jaw back to his ear, nibbling at his earlobe. When his breathing deepened and his fingers tightened their grip on hers, she couldn't help but smile. "Remember me?"

He rubbed his cheek against hers and ground out, "Always."

As the sun streaked through the blinds and the radio played a soft serenade, she made love to her husband as if it were the very first time. Her Milten was definitely back.

Nearing the end of her first week at Walson, Debra made a mental calculation of how many years she had to go before retirement. She almost groaned out loud. Spending her next forty years inside an eight-foot partition didn't exactly set her blood to pumping. She was quickly coming to the conclusion that her aspirations of becoming a high-powered career woman might have been way off-track.

Kicking off her shoes under her desk, she rotated her ankles and let out an exhausted sigh. Looking through the opening in the cubicle's partition, she glanced into an exterior office where she could see out the windows and catch a glimpse of the late-afternoon sky. From the little she could see, the sky over Pikes Peak was turning a majestic purple as dark gray clouds slowly rolled in over the tip.

Still staying at the Peak View Motel, she hoped to do some apartment hunting this weekend. Maybe she'd find a place that wasn't so close to the city, maybe near some hiking trails. Robert's complex in Woodland Park came to mind.

After she'd cancelled on Robert Monday night, feigning a headache, he'd invited her to lunch on Tuesday and had taken her out to his condo development in Woodland Park. The manager toured her through several available units and had even agreed to a month-to-month lease. If Robert hadn't given her the impression that he wanted more than just a business relationship, she might have considered moving into his complex. Not sure what her feelings were yet, she didn't want to sign anything that she would later regret.

She really did like his father, Stan Nelson, but as much as she adored the man and appreciated everything he'd done for her, before Debra could become completely independent, she had to square away her father's last debt.

Several years ago, when Debra was still in high school, her father had approached Stan Nelson about investing in the conversion of the Walker ranch into buffalo farming. Friends for most of their lives, her father and Stan had made a gentleman's agreement with a simple handshake. Other than the word of her mother, a deposit slip of a hundred thousand dollars was the only form of proof that the loan actually existed. Her father had promised to pay back the loan with interest, along with a percentage of the profits in five years.

The five years had been up over a year ago.

Debra hadn't even known about it until the funeral, when her mother had mentioned the outstanding debt with the Nelsons. The sale of the ranch barely covered the debts owed to the bank, so when Stan had shown up at the funeral and offered her this job, she'd accepted it only on the terms that he allow her to pay back every last cent her father still owed the Nelsons, plus any interest. Of course, being the compassionate man Stan Nelson was, he absolved Debra of any responsibility of the loan, saying she'd been through enough with her father and losing the ranch.

But she wasn't raised that way. If it took her the next twenty years, she'd pay back every last cent and clear her father's name once and for all.

"You over there, Debra?" Jasmine hollered over the partition.

Debra stacked two files together and set them off to the side. "Yeah, just typing up the minutes from this morning's meeting. What's up?"

Jasmine walked up from behind and dropped a stack of files on her desk with a thud. "I'm officially leaving you in charge of getting these purchase orders filled out and signed by Robert. Most of them are for parts we need to maintain the Connelly Communications contract, but there's two or three for Saint Anthony's Hospital as well. I put a list in each file of what needs to be ordered, so they should be pretty straightforward."

Flipping open the top file, Debra inwardly cringed. The Rocky Mountain division stocked and maintained a multimillion-dollar computer parts inventory that was located on the first floor. She flexed her fingers. It looked like a good two to three more hours of work. Pushing paperwork wasn't exactly how she wanted to spend a Friday night, but she forced a smile anyway. "No problem. I'll get right on them."

"Oh, there's no rush. Next week's fine. These are just the orders we need to restock our inventory. Carolyn Strome used to do them, but she got way behind when she and Robert started working on the Air Force proposal. Don't tell anyone I said this, but if legal found out how far behind we are, I'd probably be fired right along with Carolyn."

Debra's stomach tightened. "Is she the woman you and Robert were talking about on Monday?"

"Yeah. It came as a surprise to all of us."

"Do you know what happened?"

"You mean you don't know?" Jasmine's eyes widened in an incredulous expression.

Debra placed a hand over her heart, which was suddenly beating faster. "Why would I know what happened?"

"I just assumed . . . well, you being so close to the Nelsons and all."

"What are you talking about? I've never even heard of Carolyn Strome before Monday."

"Oh, well, it's no secret, Debra. We all know who you are. Your father was one of the co-founders of Walson Technology. I'm just surprised they didn't put you right into management."

Trying to keep her voice steady, she asked, "Are you saying they fired Carolyn just to give me this job?" Her earlier speculations were right then. "But Stan . . . I mean Mr. Nelson," she quickly amended, "offered me this position over two months ago, shortly after my father died."

Jasmine gave a quick lift of her shoulders. "Maybe they just kept her on until you had everything settled with your father's estate." Glancing over the partition toward Robert's office, she lowered her voice. "All's I know is when she left here last Friday, she and Robert were attending some extravagant charity event with all the bigwigs of the company."

"Are you telling me Carolyn and Robert were dating?" This was sounding more and more like a soap opera.

"If you talked to Carolyn, they were practically engaged."

"So what do you think happened?"

Jasmine made another nervous glance toward the corner office. "It's not for me to say. You'll have to ask Robert." Checking her silver wristwatch, she said, "It's almost four. I was hoping to leave early tonight and get Milten ready for the rodeo."

The rodeo. Debra'd thought about the rodeo all week, coming up with a thousand reasons why she shouldn't go, but they were all outweighed by one reason she should—that gorgeous hunk of a cowboy who'd somehow lassoed her heart.

"I think Milten remembers when he used to rope with the guys." Jasmine's voice sounded enthusiastic. "J.D. even ordered a special saddle for Milt to try out at his ranch."

"J.D. mentioned he and Milt used to rope together."

"All through high school. The two of them won all kinds of

buckles. The night of Milten's accident, he and J.D. even did a celebrity exhibition to help raise money for J.D.'s little cousin, Dillan."

Remembering Joshua's concern for his cousin, Debra hoped the little boy was improving. "Joshua said Dillan's rejecting his new heart. Have you heard any news?"

"Milt talked to J.D. this morning. Said Dillan's home now and is adjusting to the new meds. J.D. even drove him out to the ranch to see his horses."

An emotional tug grabbed Debra's heart. She wasn't sure if it was because Dillan was feeling better, or because she missed Brandy so much. "That's great news. Sounds like Joshua takes good care of everyone."

"Next to Milten, he's the sweetest man I know. He'd make a great catch if he'd just allow himself to open up to someone again."

Joshua's comments about never getting married made her ask, "So he's never been serious with anyone since high school?"

"Not that I know about, and as close as he and Milten are, we've never even seen him date anyone more than a few times." Jasmine made another glance at her watch, obviously wanting to get home. "Are you sure you don't mind if I leave early? The new speech therapist was there this morning. I can't wait to find out Milten's progress."

"Of course. Go. Take care of that husband of yours. I'll get all these POs put in first thing next week and get our contracts back on track."

"Thanks, Debra. We'll see you tonight then?"

Debra smiled and nodded. "I'll look for you in the stands."

As Jasmine hurried down the corridor toward the elevator, Debra gave a wistful sigh, wondering if she'd ever feel that kind of love for a man—and preferably before she became an old maid.

With her thoughts on Joshua, she stacked all the files off to the side and shut down her terminal. It was after five before she grabbed her purse and headed out of her cubby.

Clinking keys drew her attention down the hall to where that same security guard, Hank Zitler, was locking all the exterior office doors. Trying to be friendly, she slung her purse over her shoulder and waved. "Good night, Hank. Have a good weekend."

"It's after five on a Friday. Not many people stay late on a weekend."

"Yeah, I had to finish up a few things. I'm meeting Jasmine King and her husband later on tonight, so I'd better get going." She reached in her purse and fished out her keys.

Hank limped up beside her as she headed toward the elevator. "Dang shame about Milt. Him doing so good in the pros and all."

"I understand he was in some kind of a car accident?"

"Yeah, he was thrown a good twenty feet from his Jeep. A grove of bushes broke his fall."

Debra cringed. "That must have been terrifying for Milt. But Jasmine sounds optimistic. She says he's getting his upper body strength back and is starting to remember everything."

"Is that so? He remember any more about his accident?"

"I don't know. You'll have to ask Jasmine."

Resting his hand on a two-way radio attached to his belt, he punched the down button of the elevator. "Do you need an escort out to your car?"

Glad to see Hank had a soft side, as well as appreciating the offer, she smiled. "Thanks, but it's still light out. I'll be fine."

"Okay, then," he said, stepping back. "You have a nice weekend."

"Thanks. I'll see you Monday."

As Hank limped down the corridor, checking doors to see if

they were locked, Debra made her own impatient glance at her watch, waiting for the elevator to open. Hearing about Joshua's ranch made her excited about getting to the rodeo.

As the door slid open, Robert called out as he was leaving his office. "Hold the door, Debbie."

She gave an exasperated roll of her eyes, wondering how to get him to quit calling her Debbie. She gave a tentative smile then entered the empty car, pushing the hold button.

With a briefcase in one hand, he stepped into the car beside her, his lips forming into an easy smile. His deep-set, dark gray eyes seemed to take her in with just a glance. "I didn't get much of a chance to see you today. How was your first week of work?"

As the doors slid shut, his cologne made her nasal passages tickle and she wondered if she was actually allergic. "Good," she said, dabbing at the end of her nose. Although her ribs didn't bother her as much as they used to, the idea of sneezing still didn't sound too appealing. "My fingers get the brunt of the deal, I'm afraid. I'm not used to doing so much computer entry. But I'm not complaining," she quickly reassured him.

"Any luck finding an apartment this week?"

"I'm going to try to hit a few places tomorrow."

Robert loosened his tie. "Big plans for tonight?"

"As a matter of fact, Joshua invited me to a rodeo."

"Is J.D. your boyfriend or something?" His dark brows arched in speculation. She sensed a sudden tension in his spine.

"Boyfriend?" she repeated, placing a hand over her heart. She felt a warm flush on her face. "Oh, no. Like I said, our fathers used to do business when I was little. We're just friends now."

"That's a relief. I'd hate to see you dragged down by the likes of him. Take it from me, sweetheart, he never was one to please the ladies. Always rushing off to tend to his horses and broken-down ranch. From what my father says, things were never the

94

same after his dad died."

Irritated at the egotistical remarks he'd made about Joshua, she stepped away from him. But something he'd said made her wonder if maybe they were actually true. Not about keeping the ladies happy, of course, but about his ranch going downhill. Monday at lunch, he'd said he had to meet with his banker. Maybe things were worse off than she first thought. Now she felt guilty for taking the check he'd given her for the saddle. She still hadn't cashed it. Maybe she'd just hang on to it for a while longer.

"What about tomorrow night?" Robert asked, his persistence definitely his strong suit. "A friend of mine is having a dinner party. I told them I'd bring a date. Ever since my divorce, his wife has this thing about fixing me up with all her friends."

Remembering what Jasmine had told her about Carolyn, she had to know if it was true. "I don't mean to get personal, but what about Carolyn Strome?"

He gripped his briefcase tighter. "What about her?"

"Well," she said, tucking a strand of hair behind her ear, "I heard you two were pretty serious at one point. Is that true?"

Turning and punching the lobby button again, he answered, "I'm afraid the rumor mill has exaggerated a bit. We knew each other in college and went out a few times. Nothing serious. Unfortunately, Carolyn was looking for a husband with deep pockets. Her definition of love had nothing to do with the heart and everything to do with money."

"I'm sorry, I didn't mean to pry."

"No big deal. Some women are like that, I'm afraid, but you . . ." He paused, stepping closer and sweeping a tendril of hair from her shoulder. "I knew even before I met you in person that you were different. My dad has never doted on anyone like he has you. Not even my ex-wife."

His breath smelled of stale coffee and something else she

couldn't quite put a finger on. Maybe he drank one of those flavored lattes. He leaned a shoulder against the wall and smiled. "You still haven't answered me about tomorrow night."

She took a tentative step back, pressing against the rear of the elevator, not sure it was a good idea dating the president. And that's what he was doing, asking her for a date, wasn't he? She didn't have a lot of experience in that arena, and in light of what had happened to Carolyn, she didn't want to do anything that might jeopardize her job.

Hoping to get off the hook, she said, "I'm flattered for the invitation, but I was going to visit my mother this weekend. It's her birthday and I don't want her to spend it alone." Debra wasn't going up till Sunday afternoon, but he didn't have to know the details. She breathed easier when the elevator doors slid open. "If you'll excuse me. I should be going."

She shuffled past him, his heated gaze on her back sending a little tremble of apprehension down her spine. She couldn't decide if she was intimidated by this man or flattered by his personal attentions.

"How about next Saturday, then?" he called after her. "My folks are getting back from Hawaii. They want me to bring you to the house for a little dinner party."

Debra whirled around and spoke as she walked backwards toward the parking garage. "Next Saturday?" she asked, wondering if it was a good idea to keep brushing off the president of the company. Since Stan and Martha Nelson were the hosts, how could she possibly turn it down after everything they'd done for her?

As if sensing her hesitation, he added, "If you're worried about your mom, bring her along. I'm sure my mom would love to visit with her. Come on. Everyone will be there."

"Everyone?"

"Yeah. Most of upper management for sure. It'd be a good

chance for you to mingle and get your name around."

"Is this a dress-up thing?" she asked, giving him a small smile.

"Semi-casual is fine, but you might want to do a little shopping." He gave her a thorough perusal and shook his head. "These long skirts and button-up blouses you've been wearing are a little, shall we say, old-fashioned. You're not a country bumpkin anymore, Debbie. Amanda from accounting is up on all the latest trends. Maybe she could give you a few pointers. Oh, and be sure and buy a bikini. Everyone usually ends up in the pool before the night's out."

A bikini? The closest thing she had to a bikini was a pair of cutoff shorts and a tank top. She looked down at her attire, straightening the lapels of her navy blue business jacket.

So the skirt hung down to her shins. So the ruffled blouse buttoned at her neck. Since she didn't have a lot of clothes and was on a limited budget, she'd bought most of her clothes from a Denver thrift shop and had borrowed a few items from her mother, this blouse being one of them. She shuddered. Maybe Robert was right. She could be the poster child for Country Bumpkin U.S.A.

"Have a good weekend, Debbie. I'll tell my mom you're coming."

Hoping to appear confident, she strode to her SUV with long, determined strides. She'd never had someone as distinguished as Robert Nelson give her a second glance. Wasn't that what she wanted? A born and bred city boy with money to boot? They could date, take in the nightlife, and if everything went well, they could carry the Walson legacy into the next generation. So why was she in such a big hurry to brush him off?

She knew exactly why. *Joshua.* She silently chastised herself as she adjusted the strap of her purse over her shoulder. He was a struggling rancher. He worked from morning till night, busting his hump for a bunch of horses—*just like her father.* Joshua resembled everything from her former life that she was trying to forget.

She gave a frustrated grunt, upset that she'd let her heart get so emotionally attached to Joshua. Sliding her key into her door, she made a quick glance over her shoulder, catching a glimpse of Robert unlocking the door to his silver Lexus. Maybe she should be more receptive to Robert's attentions. Going out with him would open her eyes to all kinds of things she'd missed out on over the years.

She slid behind the steering wheel and adjusted her rearview mirror to get another look at her boss. Her stomach tightened at the thought of actually going out with such a powerful man. But if she ever wanted to make it in the corporate world, she had to shed this country bumpkin image.

She'd already committed to meeting Joshua at the rodeo, but after tonight, she was through with that kind of life. A rancher was *not* who she was anymore.

Before she glanced away, Hank pushed through the glass doors to the garage calling out to Robert. "You can't do this, Nelson. You owe me!" he yelled, hobbling up to the driver's side window.

Robert revved up the engine.

Hank banged on the window. "Nelson, you son of a bitch, open up!"

Startled, Debra switched on the ignition to her SUV, then rolled down her window an inch, wondering what Hank was yelling about. She cast a glance over her shoulder toward the commotion. Robert had lowered his window halfway and Hank had leaned closer, ducking inside the car, making it impossible for her to hear what he was saying. Whatever it was, Robert didn't seem too receptive. His tires squealed on the smooth cement surface as he sped away from Hank, practically running him over.

Hank picked up a rock and hurled it at Robert's Lexus, using every expletive Debra had ever heard and some she hadn't. Raised around roughneck ranch hands most of her life, she thought she'd heard every combination of curse words.

What was going on between Hank and Robert?

Jasmine frantically raced up the ramp to her house, where an ambulance sat parked with its lights flashing in the driveway. "Mrs. White, what's wrong?" she screamed as she sprinted down the hall. She almost ran into Mrs. White coming out of the bedroom.

"Calm down, Mrs. King," she soothed, cupping her pudgy fingers over Jasmine's shoulders. "Milten spiked a fever this afternoon and his blood pressure is a little high. When he started having trouble breathing, I called his physician and he ordered Milten to be admitted right away."

"I want to talk to him," she cried, straining to look over the nurse's shoulder.

"The ambulance technicians are preparing him for transport. Why don't you pack a bag for him so you can follow him to Saint Anthony's Hospital?"

"What happened? He was fine when I left him this morning."

"I'm not sure. After lunch, he started getting stomach cramps. I monitored him for a while, but he seemed to be getting worse. That's when I called and made the arrangements. I tried you at work but you'd already left."

Jasmine scooted around Mrs. White and knelt beside the gurney carrying her husband. "Milten? Sweetheart? Can you hear me?" She grabbed his hand and squeezed.

His grip tightened as he mumbled something inaudible through his oxygen mask.

She couldn't help but wonder if making love to him this morning had been too much. She slid the mask up so she could give him a kiss. "I love you, baby. I'll get your bag packed and meet you at Saint Anthony's. Maybe some antibiotics is all you need."

"Ma'am?" The EMT flipped up the rails on the gurney. "We're ready for transport."

After a quick change into her favorite boot-cut jeans, Debra grabbed her black Resistol and drove up Pikes Peak Highway through Woodland Park. She passed Robert's condominium complex, his two-story duplex right out in front. A wrought-iron fence surrounded the facility with an access-coded security gate. The units had a clear view of the mountains off in the distance.

She nervously bit down on her bottom lip, wondering if she should take advantage of the month-to-month lease the manager had offered her earlier in the week when Robert had led her on a tour through the facility. Tomorrow was Saturday. If she didn't find anything more affordable, she'd call and find out if the offer was still good.

A couple of miles out of town, tall pole lights illuminated the rodeo grounds and outdoor grandstand. Dozens of riders on horseback loped outside the large arena. She parked behind the livestock barn, bought a ticket and suddenly felt like she'd just stepped back inside a world she used to love. Clapping and hollering by rowdy rodeo fans sent a wave of excitement clear to her bones. A country swing song played over the loudspeakers as she scanned the fairgrounds. Canvas tents lined the pathways, with vendors selling everything from food and beer to cowboy hats, t-shirts, saddles, and tack.

She walked through several tents, pricing saddles, taking in all the wonderful aromas of leather and horse. She kept her eyes open for Jasmine and her husband, but saw no signs of them. She did a double take when she spotted Hank Zitler sitting on the edge of a table filled with T-shirts. He was smoking a cigarette and drinking a beer.

Remembering the earlier confrontation between him and Robert, she was more than a little surprised to see him here. She gave a hesitant wave and strode over to where he sat. "Hey, Hank. I didn't know you were into rodeos."

He snorted as he blew out a stream of smoke. "Little lady, I'll have you know I was lassoing these calves before I could even walk. Won me several belt buckles in my younger days."

She remembered Joshua telling her how Hank had injured his knee in high school and wondered if he could still compete. "Will you be roping tonight?"

He straightened and looked over at a woman who was wearing a sling around her shoulder. She glanced up and shook her head. "I'm afraid Hank's competition days are over. Had a little mishap on the football field in high school."

"Mishap, hell," Hank grumbled through a slurred drawl.

"Now, hon, don't get into that again." She extended her good hand to Debra. "Hank's manners are a little lacking, I'm afraid. Hi. I'm his wife, Nadine."

"Nice to meet you, Nadine. I'm Debra. I work with Hank at Walson." Speaking to Hank, she said, "Joshua told me you'd injured your knee. I'm sorry."

"Don't need no one's pity, least of all J.D.'s." Hank stood and crumpled his plastic cup, swaying slightly. "I need another beer." He stumbled around Nadine, bumping into her arm, and staggered through a flap at the back of the tent.

"Uh-oh," Nadine said, giving a visible wince as her husband rammed into the hind end of a horse. He let out a low curse, then weaved around the mare. "Something's got him awful upset tonight. He hasn't drank like this in almost a year."

"When I left work tonight, he and Robert Nelson had an argument. I'm not sure what it was all about though."

"He's been putting in extra hours and his knee has been bothering him again."

Debra watched as Hank leaned a hand on a hitching post and started rubbing his bum knee. "Looks like he's in some pain. Is he taking anything?"

Nadine pursed her lips and shook her head. "He got hooked on painkillers a while back. Doc won't prescribe nothing too strong now. He needs to go to therapy, but insurance won't cover the sessions."

A little girl interrupted, asking Nadine to buy a T-shirt.

She gave an apologetic smile to Debra. "Sorry, hon. Selling these T-shirts helps keep bread on the table for our kids. Every little bit helps. Are you staying for the dance? Maybe we could talk more later in the pavilion."

"Dance? I really hadn't planned on it. I'm meeting Milten and Jasmine King. Depends on what they want to do, I guess."

"Well, it was nice meeting you. Have fun."

Debra wandered out of the tent and made a quick scan for Jasmine and Milten. Her ticket was for the opposite side of the grandstand. Hoping to find a shortcut, she hurried past the livestock barn behind the rodeo arena to get to the other side.

The bawling of calves made her slow her steps as she peeked inside the barn. Several pens were filled with young black Angus calves for the calf-roping event. Another large pen held at least twelve rank bulls for the bull-riding competition.

She stopped and leaned an elbow on the top rail of the fence, breathing in the pungent smells of fresh hay and manure. Maybe her fears about coming here tonight hadn't been justified. Like Joshua said, all she had to do was set her butt on a bleacher and watch the cowboys play.

A loud ruckus drew her attention to a pen holding several

large steers. Her eyes widened. Two cowboys were wrestling with one of the steers that had climbed halfway out of the chute. One of its foot-and-a-half-long curling ivory horns was wedged between two wooden slats.

She jumped up on a gate and clenched the top rung, her knuckles turning white. With her heart in her throat, she watched helplessly as the two men wrestled to free the beast. From their matching red, white, and blue, star-spangled western shirts and ankle-length black leather chaps fastened around their hips, she assumed they were in the steer-roping event.

The beast jerked free from the fence, ramming into the other steers in the pen. The man who had freed the steer fell backwards, landing flat on his back in the sawdust-covered aisle. His hat flew off. Debra's heart slammed against her chest.

Joshua?

As if she were replaying a horror movie, images of her father flashed through her mind. Bloody images. Long, curling ivory horns. Agonizing screams.

Determined not to freeze up this time, she jumped down and hightailed over to Joshua's side, dropping to her knees. "Joshua?" She cupped his face with her hands. "Are you okay? Do you need an ambulance?"

CHAPTER SIX

Staring into a pair of wide, honey-speckled eyes, Joshua blinked to make sure he wasn't imagining things. "Debra? What are you doing back here?"

"Are you all right? Can you breathe?" she asked, pressing her hands against his chest.

His senses were filled with the scent of fresh mint, spring wildflowers, and a hint of her soft baby powder scent he'd come to adore. Instead of a fancy business suit, she wore a blue denim vest with a sequined red star embroidered on the front. The low-scooped neckline of her white T-shirt underneath gave him a tantalizing peek at the generous swells of her breasts. Her cheeks were rosy pink. Her hair fell freely over her shoulders, piling onto his chest. He didn't think he'd ever seen her looking so pretty.

This was the Debra he'd missed all week.

"Joshua? Are you okay?"

"Well, now," he drawled. "I am having a little trouble catching my breath. But then again," he said, patting her hand, "there is a gorgeous woman pressed against my chest."

She gazed down at her hands, her fingers curled tightly into the poplin material of his western shirt. She let go and fell back onto her haunches, panting, trying to catch her breath, only making her that much more incredibly desirable. "I . . . I saw you wrestling with the steer. I thought you were hurt."

"Nah. The critter just got a little ornery, is all." He had to contain a grin, knowing Debra had come to his rescue. But he also noticed the fear in her eyes, her gasping for air. The steer must have really spooked her. He grabbed his hat off the ground, then stood, offering his hand to help her stand. "I see you found the rodeo grounds. Are Jasmine and Milt here?"

"I don't know." Her answer was short and abrupt. She ignored his hand and shoved herself to her feet. "You could have been killed, you know. You act as if you just gave a frisky dog a bath, for goodness sakes." She slapped her palms on her jeans then tucked a strand of hair behind her ear. "I'm sorry I interfered. I'd better go find Jasmine."

"Debra? Is something bothering you?"

She slung her purse over her shoulder then jammed the toe of her boot into the dirt floor of the barn. "When I saw you fly backwards, I thought . . ." She gave an irritated shake of her head. "Nothing, just forget it." She tried to move around him.

"Hold on, darlin'." He took a quick step in front of her. "Are you mad?"

"No, I'm not mad."

He scratched the back of his head, bumping his hat down. "You sound mad."

"It's not you, it's just . . ." She shoved her hands on her hips, obviously upset about something. "This was a bad idea. I never should have come here tonight." She headed for the door.

He angled in front of her, blocking her path. "Hold on there, honey. I didn't mean to scare you. Please, talk to me."

For a long moment they just stood there, staring into each other's eyes, both breathing heavily, but he knew the hard pounding of his heart had nothing to do with the steer.

She blew out a loud gust of air and stared up at the rafters, shaking her head. "I'm sorry if I sounded mad. I guess I just didn't want anything to happen to you, too."

She must have been thinking about her father, and again, he

wondered if his death was more than a heart attack. "As you can see, no harm done. But I gotta admit, I've never had a woman come to my rescue before. It was kind of nice."

His younger brother, Jared, gave him a hard clap on his shoulder. "My brother hasn't seen a steer he ain't tamed yet, ma'am. I don't believe I've had the pleasure, J.D."

With a little hesitation, Joshua moved aside. "Debra, this big lug is my younger brother, Jared. Jared, this is Debra Walker. She grew up on the Lazy W Ranch. She's the owner of the buckskin quarter horse I bought last weekend for Dillan."

Jared pulled off a leather glove and extended his hand. "Nice to meet you, Debra. She shore is a beauty." He cracked a grin and slipped her a wink. "The horse is pretty, too."

Glad to see Debra's expression soften into a tentative smile, Joshua asked, "Who does she remind you of, Jared?"

"Well, let's see," he said, rubbing his chin as he openly scanned her from her hat down to her boots. "With legs that stretch from here to Texas and a smile as wide as the Mississippi, I'd say she's a dead ringer for our sister, Heather. Although this little lady's hair's a lot prettier."

"You two are brothers, huh? I thought I noticed a resemblance, and I don't just mean your smooth talking and adorable matching outfits. You two could be twins."

Jared gave a husky chuckle. "We've been called worse."

The rodeo announcer called for the opening ceremonies to begin. Jared grabbed a partial bale of hay. "It was nice meeting you, Debra."

"You, too, Jared."

Joshua set his hand on her lower back and walked Debra outside the barn. "There's a dance in the pavilion afterwards. Promise you won't leave?"

"I don't know." She tugged at her pretty denim vest, looking hesitant. "I can't dance. My father showed me how to do the country two-step, but beyond that I'm afraid you're going to need steel-toed boots."

He chuckled at her expression, tapping her hat down. "I'll take that as a challenge. And by the way, you look great. I definitely prefer this look over the career girl any day."

"Thanks." Her blushing cheeks made her about as pretty as the sunset. Tilting her head, her smile turned a little ornery. "Did you bring my cushion?"

He tipped his head back and gave a loud bellowing laugh. "I could probably scrounge up an old saddle blanket."

She craned her neck around and smacked her cute little behind, reminding him of an upside-down heart. "I think these jeans are the only padding my fanny needs."

He couldn't agree with her more.

"How's your little cousin doing?" she asked. "Jasmine said he came home yesterday."

"Yeah, he's doing great so far. He got to see Brandy and is already talking about the Little Britches Rodeo."

"That's wonderful. I guarantee he'll do great with Brandy."

He froze when she leaned close and pressed her hands on his leather vest. Standing on the toes of her boots, she reached up and tipped his hat back and placed a tender kiss on his cheek. His heart shuddered at her unexpected gesture of affection. He closed his eyes briefly, her fresh wildflower scent overriding all the smells of the barn.

"Be careful out there tonight, cowboy," she murmured softly into his ear.

He slipped his arm around her waist. "You bet I will."

When she drew apart, she stayed just a few inches from his face, the brims of their cowboy hats barely touching.

"You sure you're all right, darlin'?" he asked, inching his fingers farther around her waist, tugging her closer.

She let out a deep breath and smiled. "I am now." She

reached up and tweaked his chin. "You sure have changed since you were twelve. The beard's a nice change. Makes you look rugged."

It took all his strength not to plant a kiss right on those luscious pink lips. He'd wanted to kiss her from the first moment she'd gazed into his eyes at the auction barn. But if he kissed her here in the middle of the livestock barn, he'd probably scare her off for sure.

She pulled from his arms, turned around, and trotted toward the grandstand.

Watching that sweet little fanny zigzag through the crowd, Joshua rubbed his bearded chin. "Rugged, huh?"

"Now there goes a nice lady, J.D." Jared stepped up beside him, coiling his lasso into loops. "Don't let her slip away."

J.D. veered away from Jared, loosening his chaps, suddenly tighter around his waist, a notch. "It's not like that, Jared. We're just friends."

"Friends, huh? It's not what it looked like to me. Is that what you want?"

"Hell, I don't know." Joshua's spurs jingled as he strode over to Evening Star, his black gelding quarter horse. "She's made it clear she doesn't want anything to do with ranching."

"That's ridiculous."

"To us, maybe. Now she's trying to become some damned career woman. Thinks it's all her fault her father's place went under. I get the feeling she thinks I'm doomed to suffer the same fate."

"You two have more in common than you think."

Afraid of where this was headed, Joshua asked anyway, "Why's that?"

"Ever since Dad died you've been hell-bent on turning your ranch into some kind of a showplace, buying up land till you don't know what to do with it, yet you won't even get part-time help to muck out the stalls. It's like you've got this gigantic chip on your shoulder, like you're trying to prove something to the world by doing it all by yourself. It wouldn't mean you're a failure if you hired a hand to help out now and then."

"It's kind of hard to afford a good hired hand these days."

"That's a load of crap, J.D." Jared whipped off his hat and banged it against his leg. "Shoot. You've got enough money stashed away to start three ranches if you wanted."

Joshua gave a swift tug to the cinch of his saddle, surprised that Jared knew so much about his financial situation. A few years ago he'd invested in a little company in Iowa that manufactured automatic waterers. Along with the five hundred acres he owned in prime Black Forest real estate, the last time he'd checked with his banker, he was worth well over seven figures. So why didn't he take everyone's advice and hire someone? He knew exactly why. His father. Dad had never hired anyone. He'd always done it on his own. Could he ever measure up to his father's success?

Joshua gritted his teeth and swung into the saddle.

"You're going to kill yourself if you don't at least get some part-time help, J.D. Hell, Dad had half the herd you've got and he had all of us working for him."

"I'm not Dad, so back off."

"What is it with you? I can't even talk about Dad without you biting off my head. You ever going to tell me what happened between you two that last day?"

Joshua crammed his hat low over his forehead. "It's none of your damned business. Now, if you don't want to end up in that pen of steers over there, you'd best drop the subject permanently." He gave Evening Star a gentle nudge with his spurs, urging him into a canter toward the rodeo arena. If he never thought about that day again, it'd be too soon.

★ ★ ★ ★ ★

Debra finagled her way through the stands and found her seat just as the announcer called for the parade of horses to filter into the rodeo arena for the opening ceremonies. Dozens of riders lined up for the traditional parade in front of the grandstand. Cowgirls in bright metallic western outfits carried several advertising banners. The El Paso County Rodeo Queen displayed the United States flag and rode in last.

After the national anthem, everyone thundered out of the arena. Debra glanced at her watch, then made another sweep through the crowd, concentrating on the handicapped-accessible seats located in various locations, but she didn't see any signs of Jasmine or her husband. They should have been here by now.

Debra still couldn't shake her anxiety from watching Joshua wrestle with the steer. She hadn't even bothered to ask him which event he'd entered. Obviously, steer wrestling, or was it the saddle broncs? Flashing a glance of dread toward the corral of bulls, she gulped. *Surely not?*

The announcer introduced the first event, the saddle broncs. As in bareback riding, the cowboy had to stay on his mount for eight seconds, spurring the hard-bucking horse, hoping to get a high score. If he fell off before the eight seconds, dropped the reins, or touched his equipment, he'd be disqualified.

The announcer came over and introduced J.D. and Jared Garrison as tonight's pickup men. She gave a heavy sigh of relief at knowing they weren't actually going to compete tonight. Even though they were right in the middle of all the action, assisting the cowboys during and after their rides and then herding the livestock into the corner pens, at least they weren't setting their butts on a bull.

She locked gazes with that rugged cowboy on horseback standing near the fence. Joshua tipped his hat and nodded, flashing her that same melt-in-your-boots kind of smile he'd given her at the auction barn. She found it hard to blink as he reined his horse around and faced the bucking chutes at the end of the arena.

She glanced at her watch, then scanned the crowd, but still saw no sign of Jasmine or Milten. Across the arena, she found Hank watching her. He took a swig of his beer and shoved away from the fence, staggering into one of the T-shirt tables. Nadine hurried to his side, but he only pushed her away and stumbled to the other side.

Even though he was obviously drunk, Debra's heart went out to Hank. She remembered how hard it had been on her father when he'd injured his back two years ago. Instead of alcohol though, her father had resorted to gambling. Knowing how that had turned their family upside down, she just prayed Hank wasn't taking his aggressions out on Nadine.

Bucking chute number four clanged opened, releasing a big paint named Overeasy. Debra quickly diverted her attention to the horse as it jumped and spun in circles in an effort to throw the young cowboy from its back. The rider held on with one hand while the other swung in rhythm with the spinning bronc. After what seemed an eternity, the buzzer sounded, signaling the end of the eight-second ride.

Debra expelled a huge gust of air, not even aware she'd been holding her breath the entire ride. Her eyes widened when Joshua and Jared sprinted from the sidelines, hazing the bucking bronc. The rider grabbed hold of Joshua's waist and swung to the ground. Returning to a full gallop, Joshua raced up beside the spinning bronc, reached over, and loosened the cinch. Still at a full gallop, he pulled out his lariat and expertly lassoed the horse's neck, slowing it to a trot. Together, he and Jared led the horse to the stock pens in the corner.

An exhilarating shiver raced down her spine. It was an amazing sight as the two pickup men worked side-by-side with one goal—protecting the cowboy. She didn't take her eyes off Joshua the rest of the evening as he gripped his horse with his powerful thighs, reining in to rescue another fallen cowboy. Joshua's broad shoulders and bulging arms took her breath away as he remained in control of all the action in the arena.

After the last bull ride, the crowd stood and filtered toward the exits. Debra's breathing turned rapid as Joshua galloped straight toward her. She stumbled down the metal bleachers till she landed on solid ground directly in front of him.

"What'd you think of our modest little rodeo?" he asked, coming to halt at the fence.

"It was great, but I could do without the bull riding."

"Where's Milt and Jasmine?" he asked, looking around at the milling crowd filtering out the exits.

"I don't think they came. I haven't seen them all night." She reached over the fence and patted his horse on the muzzle. Although the horse was breathing heavily, it stood perfectly still under Joshua's direction.

Joshua leaned over the fence and offered his arm. "Hop up here. You can help me unsaddle Evening Star before we head over to the pavilion."

Debra gulped and followed his large rugged arm clear up to his broad shoulders, past his muscular neck, finally landing on his eyes. Knowing her ribs would not like to hop anywhere right now, she backed slowly away. "How about I meet you there? I want to put away my purse."

"Sounds good."

"Hey, I met Hank's wife earlier. She seemed pretty nice. She said they'd be over there, too."

He glanced over his shoulder, toward the T-shirt tents, then back to Debra. "Was Hank drinking?"

"Actually, it looked like he'd been drinking all night."

"Damn." Joshua resituated in the saddle and shook his head.

"Hank can be a pretty mean drunk. I've had to break up more than one fight over the years. Nadine's a nice enough lady, but I really don't want you hanging around them."

Amused by his overprotectiveness, she perched her hands on her hips. "You sound like a big brother now."

"Sorry. Old habits die hard I guess. I'd better go. Jared's waiting. Promise me you'll save the first dance?"

She smiled and glanced at his boots. "I hope those have a brick in the end."

He let out a bout of hearty laughter, as if she were kidding. Reining his horse around on his back hooves, Joshua made a kissing noise, taking off at a full gallop across the arena. He halted on a skid near a huddle of cowboys by the bucking chutes.

Loud music from the pavilion reminded her of the dance. Debra's heart fluttered hard under her chest, doing a little jig with her stomach at the mere thought of dancing with that big cowboy.

A candy bar. She always got a little jittery when she hadn't eaten for several hours. She grabbed a Hershey bar from the concession stand and strode around to the back of the livestock barn, heading toward her SUV. She made a quick peek inside at the pen of steers waiting to be loaded into the semi. An unsettling shiver raced down her spine as a bloody image flashed through her mind. Loud, agonizing screams.

How many times had she gone over that fateful day in her head since her father had been killed? If it hadn't been for her stupid mistake, he never would have been hurt. He'd still be here today. She choked down the last bite of candy bar then closed her eyes, feeling a sting of moisture behind her lids. "Oh, Daddy," she whispered. "I'm so sorry."

"Okay, boys!" a young male voice called out. "Let him go!"

Debra jerked her head around and saw three good-sized boys, no more than twelve years old, standing over a pen of black Angus bull calves. Kids, usually between the ages of twelve and eighteen and wanting to try their hand at bull riding, rode these young bulls. But they weren't the small baby calves used in the calf-roping event. These animals were half-grown, rank bulls in training, and they probably weighed over a thousand pounds each.

No adults were supervising the trio as the blond-haired boy wearing chaps straddled one of the bigger bulls. It didn't have horns, but two one-inch nubs protruded from its head. Another smaller boy opened a gate swinging into an adjacent pen. The bull calf jumped out of the chute, bucking and twisting, trying to throw the young rider. The boy held on for at least five seconds before he was flipped up in the air, landing with a thud on the hard dirt floor of the barn.

Debra's heart raced. The boy screamed then rolled several times before coming to a stop. The bull bucked away toward the corner, trying to kick off the cinch. Swinging around in the corner, he pawed the ground, snorting, lowering his head toward the boy.

Debra vaulted over the fence. "Get out of here!" she yelled at the boy, frantically waving her arms. He tried to move but screamed and grabbed his leg. Without hesitation, she took several long strides toward the boy and dropped beside him. "Is it your leg?" she asked through heavy breaths.

The boy's face wrinkled in an expression of agony as he moaned and grabbed his knee. Taking a quick glance over her shoulder, she saw the bull take off on a dead run straight toward them.

She scooped the boy in her arms. "Hold on!"

"Mister! Mister!"

Halting Evening Star in front of his horse trailer, Joshua glanced over at Jared and motioned his head toward a redheaded kid running out of the livestock barn. "What do you think this is all about?" Joshua swung to the ground and hitched his horse to the trailer.

The kid ran up and grabbed his arm. "We need help!"

"Whoa. Slow down, pardner. What's wrong?"

"In the barn," he gasped. "My friend's hurt. There's a lady in the pen of bulls!"

"I'll get my bag!" Jared yelled, heading for the cab of his pickup. "I'll tell the EMTs to head that way. They should still be here."

Sprinting after the hysterical young cowboy, Joshua asked, "What happened?"

The kid yelled over his shoulder. "Travis tried to ride one of the bull calves. A lady jumped in to keep it from charging him!"

They rounded the corner of the livestock barn and Joshua's heart plummeted to his stomach. "Debra?"

She was crouched on the ground on her knees, holding her stomach with one arm. The half-grown bull was still loose, standing and snorting in the corner. It lowered its head, looking intent on taking a run at Debra.

Joshua let out an ear-piercing whistle and grabbed a lasso hanging on a post. He leaped over the fence, landing between Debra and the bull. Yelling and waving his arms, he diverted the bull's attention away from Debra.

Angling straight for the beast, Joshua hurled the lariat over its neck and yanked it taut. The bull twisted and bucked, almost whipping the rope out of his hands.

"Open the other gate!" he yelled.

One of the boys jumped down and opened a gate that led into the next pen. The bull ran inside, still kicking its back legs. As soon as the bull cleared the fence, the boy swung it shut, allowing Joshua to let go of the rope.

He turned around and lunged toward Debra, who was still

hunched over on her hands and knees. "Sweet Jesus." He blew out a heavy gust of air and gripped her shoulders. "Honey, are you all right?"

"I . . ." she gasped. "I . . . can't . . . breathe." She leaned in against him.

He wrapped his arms around her waist, holding her up for support. "Let me help you lie down. You might have hurt your back."

"No. I'm . . . okay," she panted through a muffled breath. "Just . . . pulled . . . a few muscles."

"Do you have any pain in your neck?"

"No. Just . . . need . . . to catch . . . my breath."

Dear Jesus, he'd never felt this helpless in all his life.

After several seconds and a few gulps of air, her breathing started to deepen. She slowly raised her head and spoke in a hoarse whisper. "I think . . . I'm okay now." She took in another quivery breath, deeper and sounding more relaxed.

He swept her hair from her neck and spoke near her face. "Why don't you lie down? My brother will be here any minute. He can take a look at you."

She took in another breath then craned her neck around, bringing her face within inches of his. For an instant, her gaze flicked to his mouth, then back to his eyes. He was surprised when the corner of her lips kicked into a crooked grin.

"I could probably . . . get more air . . ." She paused and licked her lips. "If there wasn't a big cowboy . . . squeezing me so hard."

It was only then he realized he'd completely circled her upper back and was holding her firmly against his chest. He blew out a heavy gust of air and pressed his lips against her temple. "Dang, lady. You scared the hair right off my chest."

She gave a short laugh then coughed before she looked up

with a smile. "The critter . . . just got . . . a little ornery, is all."

Not amused at her attempt at humor, he carefully eased her back against the fence.

"She all right?" Jared vaulted over the rail and dropped down beside them with his bag in his hand. Two EMTs hurried over to the injured boy.

Debra nodded and swiped a strand of hair from the side of her face. "I just pulled something when I picked up the boy. I've lived through worse."

Wondering what that meant, Joshua rubbed his hands over her arms, then helped her straighten her legs.

"Is the boy okay?" she asked, peering over his shoulder.

Jared opened his vet bag. "The technicians are looking him over now."

She shoved her hands on the ground and tried to stand. Joshua gently cupped her shoulders. "Don't get up yet, honey. I want Jared to take a look at you first."

"No," she adamantly shook her head. "Go help the boy."

Jared flashed a small light into her eyes, then sat back and whipped out his stethoscope. "Let me take a listen, Debra. Make sure everything's working okay."

Without waiting for her to answer, Jared pressed the end to her chest. "Take a nice slow breath," he said, moving along her sternum and around to her back. Tugging the ends from his ears, he began palpating her stomach.

When he poked her ribcage, she flinched and grabbed his hands. "Ouch!"

"Sorry about that, darlin'. I think you might have cracked a rib or two. You should probably get an x-ray, as well as a blood oxygen test to make sure you didn't puncture a lung or anything."

She shook her head. "No. I'm fine," she insisted in her usual defiant tone. "I don't need an x-ray. Go help the boy."

Jared gave him a worried glance. "She should see a doctor."

"I thought he was a doctor," she said, her expression wary.

Feeling a little guilty, Joshua tried to give her a reassuring grin. "He is, but of the four legged-variety."

"Well, thank you, but if it's all the same to you, I'd just as soon go home." Her voice was breathless and strained. She didn't sound fine. She stared up at Jared and motioned her head to the pen behind them. "Please. Go help the boy. He needs you more than I do."

"You're going to be pretty sore for a few weeks, and you probably shouldn't drive. If you need a prescription for pain—"

"No. I don't need anything. I've got a bottle of pills at home that made me sick. Believe me, with three cracked ribs, puking my guts out is the last thing I want to do right now."

Three cracked ribs? Joshua looked at Jared and gestured his head toward the injured boy. "Better go see to him. I'll make sure she's taken care of."

As Jared hurried over to the boys, Joshua massaged Debra's outstretched legs, frustrated at her bullheadedness. She was so damned determined to do everything on her own, she wouldn't let anyone near her. He breathed deeply, his own breathing just now starting to even out. He caught her familiar scent of wildflowers and baby powder mixed with a hint of milk chocolate. His frustration was replaced with a feeling he'd tried to deny all week.

Not convinced she was okay, he leaned close and tucked her hair behind her ear. "Honey? How did you hurt your ribs? Was it last week at the auction barn?"

She tipped her head back against the fence and closed her eyes. "No. I hurt them in a ranching accident two and a half months ago." She paused and gave a shrug of her shoulders. "Last week I just jarred 'em a little bit."

"Jarred 'em a little bit?" he repeated with incredulity.

"Really, Joshua, I just want to go home." Her big brown eyes shone with unshed tears. "I think God's trying to tell me something. I'd better get out of here before the barn collapses on me."

When she attempted to stand, he wrapped his arm around her waist and eased her to her feet. She swayed and grabbed his hand. He gently tugged her to his side and pressed his mouth against her hair. "Easy now. Don't want you passing out on me." He had to chuckle, glancing down at her face. "This is the second time this week you've about fainted on me. I didn't know I had this kind of effect on women."

She tried to laugh, but grimaced as she clutched her ribs and leaned back against the fence.

He slid his boots on the outside of hers, keeping a grip on her arms. "Come on, honey. I'll drive you home. Where are you staying?"

"At the Peak View Motel."

"On South Nevada?" he verified, feeling the hairs on his neck stand.

"Yeah, but I'm okay. You don't need to drive me."

"Do you know what kind of neighborhood that's in? Smack dab in the middle of the red light district. Hell, there's drive-by shootings at least once a month in that area."

"It's all . . . I can afford . . . right now." Her voice was weak and breathy. "It's really not . . . that bad. I'm on the second floor," she justified in her next quivery breath.

"Didn't Walson give you relocation expenses?"

"Yeah, but not much. I'm hoping . . . to be into an apartment . . . by next week."

Bracing his hands on the top rung of the fence, he leaned close to her face and boxed her in. For a brief moment, neither of them moved. His gut instinct told him to haul her pretty little ass off to the emergency room, then get her the hell out of the Peak View Motel.

"What happened?" he asked, trying to lower his voice.

"The boys were riding—"

"No. I mean before," he interrupted, carefully sliding his hand around her waist. "What kind of ranch accident? How'd you hurt your ribs?"

She shook her head and braced her palms on his shirt. "It was stupid. It shouldn't have happened." Her fingers curled into the poplin material of his western shirt, using him to hold herself upright. "This isn't the place . . . to go into all that." Mere inches from his face, her gaze flicked to his lips before diverting over his shoulder. "Shouldn't you see about the boy?"

He cleared his throat, trying to focus on her honey-speckled eyes, not on her shiny pouty lips, wondering if she tasted as sweet as the chocolate on her breath. "Don't worry about the boy, darlin'. Jared and the ambulance techs will take care of him. It's you I'm more concerned about right now. I'm parked just over there." He motioned his head toward his quad cab pickup and trailer. "Why don't you jump in with me? We'll come back tomorrow and get your SUV."

"Really, Joshua. I can drive. You don't need—"

He pressed a finger to her lips. "I'm not arguing with you this time. Now either you let me drive you or I'll carry you straight over to that ambulance and strap you into a gurney myself." Her lower lip trembled under his touch. Tears brimmed her lashes before she fluttered them down over her eyes.

He slid his fingers around the nape of her neck under her hair. "I never thought I'd meet anyone as stubborn as my sister. When Heather was twelve, she hobbled around for three days with a broken foot after a horse stomped on her. I finally had to hoist her over my shoulders to get her into the emergency room."

Her eyes almost bulged out of her dirt-smudged face. "You wouldn't!"

He couldn't help but chuckle. "From the sounds of it, your ribs probably don't want to be hoisted anywhere right now. I'd prefer if you'd go of your own accord."

"I'm not going to the hospital," she declared. "Now are you going to move or do I have to stay in this pen all night?"

He rubbed his whiskery jaw, contemplating the idea. Spending the night lying on a bed of straw with this beautiful lady didn't sound all bad.

"Joshua?"

"What?" He arched his brows.

"I was joking."

He smiled, reached down, and picked up her purse and her hat from the ground, then wrapped his arm around her waist. "Come on. I'll help you to my truck."

"I'm okay," she tried to reassure him through a jagged breath. "I don't need any help." She grimaced, then hunched over, giving a muffled curse. "I knew this was a bad idea. I don't belong here."

Guilt stabbed him in the heart. Now he regretted ever making fun of her abused derriere. "Come on, darlin'." He carefully lifted her into his arms.

"No!" she gasped, wriggling in his arms. "I'm too heavy!"

Holding firm, he tugged her closer, bringing his face right next to hers. "Honey, I've wrestled steers five times your size. Now be a good girl and let me help you."

A lone tear dripped from the corner of her eye as she spoke in a choked whisper. "I'm so embarrassed."

"Don't be," he reassured her. "You may have saved that boy's life. I'm just glad you didn't get hurt worse." He pressed a kiss to her forehead, the salt and warmth of her skin arousing every nerve ending on his body. The thought of this sweet lady being

121

injured jarred him to the core.

She wrapped her arms around his neck. "I thought it was the devil himself charging me."

"Easy, honey. Everything's okay now." He took slow, easy steps toward his truck. His heart shuddered as she relaxed and rested her head on his shoulder, snuggling her face against his neck.

"My father had to carry me." Her breath was warm as she spoke into the side of his neck. "It was all my fault."

"What was all your fault?" When she didn't answer, he looked down and found her eyes closed. He approached his truck, bent his knees, and gave a slight tug at the passenger side door handle. He carefully deposited her on the bench seat, then loosely strapped the seatbelt around her waist. He remained hunched in front of her, wanting desperately to kiss her, smooth away all her pain, both physical and emotional. What kind of hell had this lady lived through in the past few months? Maybe even years?

She opened her eyes and gazed at him through slitted lids. "Thank you," she said through a strained whisper. "I'd probably be a slab of hamburger if you hadn't shown up when you did."

He smiled and tapped the end of her nose. "All in a pickup man's line of duty, ma'am."

She started to laugh, but quickly grimaced, holding her stomach. "Shit," she whispered under her breath.

"Ah, your true colors are coming out," he commented with a grin.

She looked at him out of the corner of her eye. "I grew up on a ranch, remember? You haven't even begun to see my true colors."

Giving her leg a gentle squeeze, he said, "Rest. I'll just be a few minutes with the horses."

He shut her door, then hurried around and unsaddled Evening Star. Flashing lights of the ambulance drew his attention near the barn. Jared jumped in his truck and waved. "I'm meeting them at the hospital. Looks like a broken leg. Let me know if Debra has any problems."

As Jared sped out of the rodeo grounds, Joshua led his horse into the trailer and secured the black gelding next to Jared's sorrel mare. After locking the gate, Joshua rushed to the driver's side door and slid in under the steering wheel. Debra turned and gave him an exhausted smile.

"You okay?" He reached over and rubbed the backs of his knuckles over her cheek.

"Hmm-huh. Just tired."

"Sleep. I'll wake you when we get there." As he switched on the ignition, she rested her head back against the seat and closed her eyes.

Now the dilemma. Where should he take her?

She didn't want to go to the hospital, and there was no way he'd leave her alone at the Peak View Motel for the rest of the night. There was only one logical place.

Hopefully, she'd sleep the whole way and wouldn't know where they were headed.

CHAPTER SEVEN

Silence startled Debra awake. She blinked several times, then focused on the dark gray dash of a pickup truck. *Joshua's pickup.* Rubbing her arms, she cringed, remembering the events of the past couple of hours. The rodeo, the bull—the whites of his eyes were still ingrained into her memory.

She turned her wrist and checked the time. Almost eleven. With a grunt, she shoved herself upright from her scrunched position against the door. Her chest didn't hurt too badly. At least she could breathe now without gasping.

Through a grimace, she straightened and focused on a dilapidated two-story barn through the windshield. An apprehensive tightening of her throat told her she was at Joshua's ranch. Why hadn't he taken her to the motel?

A pole light cast a yellow glow over the peeling red paint of the barn, turning the building to a dingy orange. An old rusted grain elevator led up to an opened door into the loft. The Walker Ranch had used the same method for moving square bales of hay into the barn. She'd always hated that old thing. The rusted gears grinding and rattling made her ears ring. Half the time it didn't even work, and she'd ended up lugging the bales up to the raft and stacking them herself.

Wrapping her arm around her waist, she carefully pushed the truck door open, taking slow and easy movements as she climbed down to the running board. Stepping onto the ground, her senses were immediately bombarded by the smells of the farmyard. Horse manure, fresh-cut hay, diesel oil from the tractors and fuel barrels, all mixed with the distant smell of rain, warning her of an approaching storm from the west. She swallowed heavily at the thought of being caught in a storm this late at night.

Outdoor spotlights illuminated the overhang of a newer steel building with at least a dozen horse stalls cordoned off at one end in the corral. Several horses stood sleeping in a three-legged stance around a large round bale of hay, their tails switching the occasional fly. Several telephone poles stood around what looked like a lighted roping arena. Beautiful white vinyl fences seemed to glow in the dark as they stretched for acres out across the pasture and up and down the graveled lane. She'd seen pictures of ranches like this in magazines, but had never actually visited one. Not exactly the kind of place she'd envisioned Joshua owning.

Maybe Joshua had decided to unload his horses before he took her to the motel. Although grateful for his assistance, she didn't like the idea of getting back so late. She hated to admit it, but the characters lurking around the parking lot at the motel made her hair stand on end. Hopefully, tomorrow she could find an apartment and be moved in by the first of August, the following weekend.

She glanced toward the horse trailer. Joshua had already unloaded his horses. Seeing no sign of him, she shut the truck door, tucked her fingers into the front pockets of her jeans, and strode toward the corral. Her heart swelled when Brandy raised her head and whinnied, then started plodding toward her.

Debra looked around at the other horses, wondering if by the slightest chance Joshua still had the pretty chestnut mare, Golden Sunset, the horse the Garrisons had bought so many years ago. She saw no sign of the mare and held her hand up as Brandy sniffed her fingers. "Sorry, sweetie. No treats tonight.

Have you been a good girl for Joshua?"

As if Brandy understood, she tossed her head and whinnied. Debra pressed a kiss to the mare's face, wishing she could saddle her up and take her for a ride. She still hadn't gotten used to the idea that she might never ride her again. A yellow cat sauntered out of an opened barn door and rubbed against her leg, meowing softly.

She squatted down and picked up the cat. "Hi, kitty. Where's Joshua?"

"Did you get a good nap?" Those same lizard-skin cowboy boots slid into view directly in front of her. She licked her lips and slowly raised her gaze up a pair of jean-clad legs, dusty and extremely long. His large silver belt buckle with his initials emblazoned on the front drew her gaze to his midsection. It seemed an eternity before she made it clear up to his broad shoulders. Her earlier speculation that they were a yard wide didn't cover the expanse by half.

He hunkered down in front of her, bringing him to her eye level, thank goodness. She didn't think she had it in her to go up any farther on this man, but now that he was here directly in her line of vision, she seemed to be mesmerized by the deep dark chocolate of his eyes. The color reminded her of the creamy hot fudge she could only find at the Frosty Freeze back in her hometown of Prairie, Colorado. She licked her lips and imagined sharing a bowl of ice cream with Joshua on a hot summer's night.

She'd tried all week to think of him as a brother, but to be honest, the flutter in her heart, the feelings swirling through her body, and the sexual thoughts running rampant in her mind at this very moment would be considered downright immoral between a brother and a sister in her Christian upbringing.

As if he could read her mind, he smiled, his adorable dimple winking at her as he rubbed his chin, the growth from his beard only making him that much more incredibly sexy. "You must have been pretty tired the way you slept through all the racket I made unloading my horses. How're your ribs?"

"Not too bad. My muscles are probably just sore from lack of use. I'm sorry I fell asleep on you. I haven't exactly been sleeping well since Dad died." With the cat secured in her arms, she started to push up with her legs. Joshua quickly wrapped his arms around her waist, helping her stand. She gave a grateful "thanks," and brought the kitty to her chest.

With the warmth of his palm splayed across her lower back, he scratched the cat's head with his other hand. "I think you've got a friend. This old tom rarely lets anyone pick him up without clawing their eyes out."

She looked around the ranch yard. "You've got a quite a place here. How many brood mares do you have?" She stared over at the corral of horses.

"A dozen good ones, or thereabouts. Most of my mares are ones I've trained or have proven performance records, like Brandy's, before they're ever bred." He took two long strides and climbed over the fence, then gathered several black rubber feeding bowls from the pens. "Limiting the number of mares allows me to take excellent care of the babies. About half the year's foal crop are sold as yearlings, and the others are sold after I've started them under saddle. I also offer services of some of the trained stallions for stud fees."

She set the cat on the ground and strode up next to the corral. "My father had up to two dozen brood mares at one point. Looks like you're doing well." *So far,* she thought with a little cynicism. Her father's ranch had been thriving at one time, too.

She followed him into a feed and tack room just off the entrance of the old red barn, then leaned a shoulder against the door jam, taking in all the wonderful aromas of sweet oats and the leather conditioning oil from the saddles and tack. Her saddle was tucked neatly in the corner draped over a barrel. It took all her strength not to go over and touch it, run her fingers over the intricate carving in the leather.

Instead, she focused her thoughts on Joshua's ranch. "No other livestock?" she asked.

He spoke as he measured out a large cup of sweet oats, mixing them with a mixture of vitamin-fortified grain pellets. "Not right now. The neighboring rancher raises black Angus cattle. He lets me train some of the finished horses on them. We help him out during branding season, and my brother and I participate in team penning events."

She stepped inside and held the bag of corn while he measured out another bucket. "It seems like right after Dad got kicked by Whiskers, he began to lose interest in our place."

"Whiskers?"

"Yeah, he was a feisty palomino with long whiskers and a temper to match. Kicked him in the stomach, slamming him into the fence."

"Ouch. You mentioned he'd started gambling. Was that before or after the horse accident?"

"He'd dabbled in it ever since I can remember, but more so after his injury. Some nights he didn't get home till almost dawn."

Joshua picked up the bowls of oats and headed toward the pens, where several horses trotted up to the gate, snorting and pawing the ground, anticipating the treats. Debra shuffled across the dirt ground to the corral, offering her hand to a young chestnut who sniffed her fingers. A low rumble of thunder alerted her to the storm quickly approaching from the northwest.

She brushed her hands on her jeans and stared up at the house. "Do you live here alone?"

He set the last bucket down, then hopped over the fence,

landing beside her. "Nope. My mom and my stepfather, Brad, live up at the main house, but they both work downtown at his architectural firm. They flew off Wednesday to Seattle for an architect convention. They're scheduled to fly in sometime tomorrow."

"So where do you live?"

He motioned his head somewhere in the distance beyond the new steel barn. "In an old log cabin that's been on the property for at least a hundred years. It's basically one big room with a bedroom, kitchen, and a bathroom. Brad helped me update it and run plumbing. It's completely insulated and even has an old wood stove to fire up in the winter."

"Sounds like a cozy little love nest," she teased, then regretted it when his lips curled into an inviting grin.

"Maybe you'd like to come and have a look."

When his eyes twinkled with a hint of seduction, she gave a quick shake of her head. "No. Um, we should probably get the rest of your chores done before the rain starts." She gave another quick glance around at his ranch, hoping to change the subject. "Is this all your mom's land?"

Still smiling, he shook his head. "Just a few acres and the house. I've bought up several hundred acres surrounding their place and put up the new steel barn. Brad and Jared both own a few mares, so they help me out in the evenings and on the weekends. Jared lives in town over his vet clinic."

Another rumble of thunder reverberated all around them, getting louder as the storm approached. Her pulse quickened. She brushed her hands over her jeans and started up the ranch yard toward his truck. "Listen, I hate to be an imposition, but would you mind taking me back to the motel now?"

He hustled up beside her. "You're not staying at the motel, Debra. You're staying here with me."

"Excuse me?" She jerked around, the abrupt movement sending a jolt of pain through her ribs. "What do you mean?" she asked, clutching her waist. "I'm staying here?"

"It makes perfect sense. The way you're holding your middle you shouldn't be driving, and I don't want you staying alone."

"You want me to stay here at your ranch?" she clarified, looking in the direction of his cabin. Her stomach tightened, forcing acid up her throat. She didn't know if her anxiety was from the thought of staying alone with Joshua, or because of all the painful reminders this ranch brought to mind of her father's place.

He followed her gaze and almost laughed. "Don't worry, Debra. You can stay up at my folks' house in Heather's old bedroom. I'll stay down the hallway in my old room in case you need any help."

Thunder rumbled in the distance and a horse whinnied and ran into the paddock. The wind picked up, whisking leaves to the ground. Her breathing shortened and she headed toward his truck. "If it's all the same to you, I'd rather just stay in the motel."

He chuckled as he easily kept up with her long strides. "Hell no, it's not all the same." As she reached the door, he braced a hand on the roof of his truck, not allowing her to enter. Cupping her shoulders, he slowly turned her around to face him. "Look, honey, the way I see it, you got two choices. Either stay here with me and get a good night's sleep, or I take you to the hospital to get some x-rays, check out of your motel, then go find a decent hotel in a safe part of the city. It'll be early morning by the time you get to bed, but you make the call."

Knowing she wouldn't have health insurance until her probationary period was up at Walson, and also understanding that the doctors probably couldn't do anything for her anyway, she shoved her hands on her hips, meeting his intense gaze just a few inches from her face. "I'm not going to the hospital, Joshua."

"Fine. You're staying here with me then." Something in his narrowed gaze told her he wasn't backing down on this.

A raindrop splattered on her arm. Through an exasperated gust of air, she said, "Fine. I'll agree to stay, but first thing in the morning I'm getting my car back. I need to find an apartment. I don't want to be a burden on you."

"Debra, you're not a burden. In fact, you're more than welcome to stay out here as long as you want. Mom and Brad work all day and are always gone somewhere in the evenings. You'd practically have the whole house to yourself."

Not to mention living just across the yard from the most sexy man on earth. "I don't think that'd be such a good idea. I'm sure your mom wouldn't appreciate you offering her home to a total stranger."

"You're not a stranger, Debra." He trailed his fingertips down her arms till he captured both her hands with his. "There's something you should know about the Garrisons. We stick together and go out of our way to help our friends and loved ones. I'd like to think we're friends after all these years."

"Of course, but—"

"But what? My mom will kill me if she knows an old friend of the family was off in some motel room alone in a new city and with cracked ribs to boot."

She hauled in a shaky breath and tugged her hands from his grip, too tired to argue with him anymore. "You're just a real take-charge kind of a guy, aren't you? Are you always this way with your sisters?"

He looked down at the ground and shoved his fingers in the front pockets of his jeans. "They tell me I can be a little overbearing at times. Guess it kind of comes with the big brother territory."

Was he actually blushing? She tipped his hat back and gave him a crooked grin. "It's okay. I guess I'm not used to having someone watch over me like this, other than my dad. And he was more of a control freak, always telling me what to do. It didn't matter if I was doing it right or not. If it wasn't his way, it wasn't the right way."

He held up both palms and surrendered. "Okay, okay. I won't tell you what to do anymore."

Another raindrop splashed on her arm, followed by a sudden gust of wind that whisked leaves all around. The horses snorted, prancing nervously in the corral. One nickered, bucked its rear legs, then ran off into the pasture behind the barn.

Her mind flashed to the last day she'd seen her father alive. A rising tide of panic made her knees tremble. Lightning flashed and was followed immediately by an explosion of thunder. The rain turned into a downpour and, in the next instant, turned into pea-sized hail.

"The horses!" she gasped, heading toward the corral.

Joshua firmly grabbed her elbow diverting her toward his parents' house. "I'll take care of the horses. Go up to the house and wait for me there."

"No! I want to help!"

He shook his head. "You're hurt. I'm not going to let you make it worse."

"Ugh! What was that about you not telling me what to do?"

"This is different," he grumbled, tugging her through the side door of his parents' house, entering a good-sized mudroom. He gently pushed her down onto a wooden buckboard bench. Rain poured off their hats. Their clothes were drenched. Wind whistled through the window as hail pounded the glass windowpanes.

"The gate to the back pasture is closed, so the horses can't get out to the ravine. Both barns have large overhangs, so they have plenty of cover." He tossed his hat on a set of antlers on the wall. "There's a few new foals I need to get into the main barn, but they'll be huddled by their mamas so I shouldn't have any problems."

"I want to help, Joshua."

"I don't need any help." He hunkered down in front of her and cupped his hand under her knee, tugging off one cowboy boot, then the other. He gave her calf a gentle rub. "There's some aspirin in the bathroom cupboard if you need it for your ribs. Heather's still got some old clothes in her bedroom. You're about her size. Go change into something dry and I'll be right back."

He stood and glanced out the window. Hail pounded against the glass. Debra stood abruptly and grabbed his arms, suddenly fearful for Joshua. "If you're not back in twenty minutes, I'm coming out there. Will you check on Brandy?"

"Take it easy, darlin'. I'll take care of everything." His gaze flicked to her lips before he pressed a kiss to her forehead. "I won't be long, I promise." He grabbed a rain poncho from a hook then reached up to a shelf above her, yanking down a box. He found a flashlight and ran out the door.

With her heart racing, she followed him to the door and watched as the flashlight made a strobe-like affect as he ran toward the barn. She closed her eyes, telling herself she was being silly. It was just a rainstorm.

Convinced he was okay, she turned and strode into the kitchen just off the mudroom, flipping on the light. Fluorescent lighting above a ceramic-tiled island illuminated a spacious eating area. Oak cupboards lined the walls leading into a great room with a vaulted ceiling. She was surprised at how much bigger the ranch-style house looked on the inside. A set of large brown leather couches faced a stone fireplace set off in one corner with rows of bookshelves flanking the sides. It was one of the coziest homes she'd ever seen.

The wetness on her skin made goose bumps raise on her

arms and she wished she were snuggled down in front of a roaring fire with Joshua, sharing a mug of hot cocoa . . . or anything else that might warm them up. She couldn't help but smile. Maybe staying here alone with him wouldn't be all torture.

Heading down the hallway off the living room, she found the bathroom, grabbed a hand towel from the rack, and pressed her face into the soft terry cloth. After several calming breaths, she caught a glimpse of her drenched reflection and almost groaned. She looked like a tattered rag doll that had gone through the washing machine. She scrubbed her face and hands, noticing two other doors adjoining the bathroom.

Rehanging the towel on the rack, she peeked through one and switched on the light. She had to blink to make sure she wasn't imagining things. At least two hundred horse figurines were displayed on a shelf that wrapped clear around the room. A poster of wild mustangs, running across a creek with water splashing all around their legs, hung near a white painted desk. Dozens of ribbons and trophies won at various horse events lined a shelf above the counter. Debra couldn't help but relax into a smile. If she were twenty years younger, she'd swear she was in horsie heaven.

She looked at the other door and pushed it open a crack. Instead of horses, this one had shelves lined with football trophies and yet another filled with belt buckles won at various rodeos. A bulletin board covered in old newspaper cutouts hung over a desk in the corner. Her gaze focused on one picture in particular of three football players covered in mud. They were standing behind a three-foot-high trophy. Although his hair was long and straggly, she recognized Joshua immediately, standing in between two other men. The caption read, "Three Musketeers Lead Falcons to State Championship." She read further and realized the one on the right was Milten King. Was this Jasmine's husband?

Lightning flashed. The lights flickered before a sudden darkness overcame her. She blinked hard, then froze. *Relax, Debra. It's just a power outage.*

Flashlight. She needed a flashlight.

Walking mummy-like, with her hands outstretched, she felt her way through the bathroom, down the hallway, and into the kitchen. She made her way into the mudroom and over to the far wall where she remembered Joshua leaving the box with the flashlights. Lightning lit up the room, giving her enough time to get a glimpse of the box. She rummaged through the contents and found a few candles, a box of matches, and, thankfully, another flashlight.

She flipped it on and blew out a heavy gust of air, trying to calm her ragged breathing. A narrow beam of light filtered through the darkness from the flashlight, leading her into the living room. She bumped into the couch, slouched down on the cushion, giving an audible grunt of pain, of frustration, but mostly worry. Joshua had only been gone a few minutes, but it felt like hours. Her ribs ached, and now her head was starting to pound. She set the candles on the table and lit both. The flames flickered, dancing with streaks of lightning that flashed through the windows.

She thought she'd never have to feel this way again—worried about a storm, angry that she wasn't able to help . . . scared that she'd have to live the last day of her father's life all over again.

The mudroom door banged open, then shut again. The familiar sounds of boots being dropped on the floor made her release an anguished breath. She scooted to the edge of the couch and called out, "Joshua? Everything okay?"

"Yeah," he hollered through the door. "How 'bout you? Looks like we lost power."

"Yeah, I found some candles and a flashlight."

"Where are you?" he hollered from somewhere in the mud-room.

"In the living room, on the couch," she clarified.

The strobe of his flashlight crisscrossed the room as he emerged from the mudroom. The light beams danced with the flicker of the candle flames on the ceiling as he approached her in the dark.

"Horses okay?" she asked with a shaky voice, though she wasn't sure if she was nervous about the storm or because she suddenly realized she was all alone with this incredibly sweet and sexy cowboy . . . in the dark.

He hunkered down in front of her and pressed his hands on her knees, giving her a reassuring squeeze. "The horses are fine. Brandy's in the barn. There's nothing to worry about."

"I don't know what's wrong with me. As many storms as Colorado gets this time of year, you'd think I'd get used to them by now."

He slicked a few wisps of wet hair away from her face. "Don't like storms, huh?" His voice was warm and genuinely concerned.

"They never really bothered me till Brandy's mother was killed by lightning. I think that's why I try to get the horses into the barn whenever I see a storm coming."

He started caressing her arm. "Megan was always afraid of storms. She used to sneak under my covers when she was little."

Remembering all those years when she'd huddled under her covers, Debra tugged at a lock of wet hair hanging down her front, flicking the drenched ends with her thumb. "I didn't have a big brother to go to, and my dad never let me come into their bed. Didn't want me to turn into a scaredy cat afraid of my own shadow. Sometimes I'd bury myself under three pillows, clutching Brownie."

Warmth radiated from his large hands as he slipped them

around the sides of her back, nudging her closer. "Who's Brownie?"

"My stuffed horse. I got her when I was three for being potty-trained. Worked like a charm."

He chuckled. "Be assured, honey. The horses are all standing and accounted for."

She touched his cheek with the backs of her fingers and smiled. "My big brother the hero." Her resistance low, she leaned forward and wrapped her arms around his neck, pressing her cheek against his face. "Where were you about two and a half months ago?" she whispered into the side of his face.

"Hey, hey, hey," he soothed, stroking her back. "I'm here now. Everything's going to work out."

Warm breath feathered her temple, making her insides puddle around her feet. His hair was soaked. Water dripped down the side of his face. He smelled of rain and horse and mud, and *Oh God*, why couldn't her father have lived and been here now? She closed her eyes, envisioning her dad, giving another hard squeeze.

"Not that I mind, or anything, but you're making it incredibly difficult for me to breathe."

A little embarrassed by her display of affection, she drew away and lowered her hands to her lap. He remained kneeling on the floor in front of her, situated slightly between her knees, his hands rubbing the outside of her thighs. Lightning flashed, illuminating his prominent features, the broad silhouette giving her a sense of protection from the outside forces. Unfortunately, it was the inside forces she was worried about right now.

"Hey, are you hungry?" he asked. "Since the electricity is out, your choices are ham and cheese, or my personal favorite, peanut butter and applesauce." When she opened her mouth to speak, he pressed a finger over her lips. "Don't knock it till you try it. Beats jelly any day."

"I know." Her speech came out slow and breathy as she gazed into his eyes. "You used to share your sandwich with me whenever you visited our ranch that summer. Your mom always packed two. I've been a convert ever since."

Lightning flashed through the room just as his gaze lowered to her mouth. Her heart actually stopped beating. Although the thought of kissing this man had crossed her mind at least a thousand times this week, she didn't actually think a guy like Joshua Garrison would be interested in someone as plain as a girl just off the farm like Debra.

She looked down at her dirty, rain-soaked jeans and felt like that same awkward eight-year-old little girl with scraggily pigtails who thought Joshua hung the moon. Now, here he was, looking nothing like that twelve-year old boy, kneeling in front of her, so close she could feel his warm breath fan her face.

She gave a nervous laugh. "I feel like that annoying little girl who wouldn't stop pestering you when we were kids. Remember? I always pretended to be your little sister."

"Debra?" His gaze bore deeply into hers, reaching clear to her soul. Even as a little girl, he could do that: look at her and almost know what she was thinking.

"What?" she finally answered.

"I'm not your brother."

She swallowed heavily, trying to control her racing heartbeat. "I'm very aware of that fact, but it helps me to keep things in perspective."

He gave a low, throaty chuckle and wedged in even closer. "Then you need a new perspective. Would you mind if I kissed you?"

CHAPTER EIGHT

Every instinct urged Joshua to back away now before he crossed over that thin line separating friends from lovers. But as he knelt in front of Debra in the darkness, breathing in her tantalizing scents of wildflowers and rain, he found it hard even to move. Now he remembered why he'd found her so charming as an eight-year-old little girl. It was her exuberance for life and the sparkle in her eyes. Every time he looked into those big, round eyes he felt some kind of a bond with her. Maybe it was their love of horses, or maybe their connection to their fathers. Either way, he wanted to kiss her, taste the sweetest woman he'd ever met.

"Yes," she finally said, her whisper barely audible over the pummeling rain on the roof.

"Yes, you're hungry?" he asked, not sure what she was answering. "Or yes, I can kiss you?"

Her lashes fluttered over her eyes. "I . . . I'm not sure."

He gave a low chuckle, suddenly nervous about kissing this pretty lady. Braced on one knee, he scooted closer and brushed a whisper-soft kiss over her shiny, wet mouth. He felt a slight quiver in her response and had to close his eyes.

Dear God in heaven. Something shot right through him, as if *he'd* just been struck by lightning. When he started to pull away, she followed him and drew in a deep breath, sucking his breath right from his soul.

Sweet little Debbie, he groaned inwardly, pressing more firmly this time, lingering for an extra second as she exhaled deeply into his mouth. The kiss was an exploding, delirious experience. More than he'd ever imagined one kiss could bring. He ended the kiss with several short kisses, going back and forth between her top and bottom lip.

Regrettably, he drew away from her, but just enough that he could still feel her warm breath on his face, the tip of her nose barely brushing the end of his. Her eyes were closed and she looked about as dazed as he felt. One more second and he'd have her pinned down on the end of the couch, and he'd be kissing every square inch of her rain-soaked body.

Thunder echoed all around them in a barrage of tympani drums. They both flinched. She ducked her head onto his chest, and his arms instinctively shielded her from the storm as she cringed into his embrace.

"It's just thunder, darlin'," he murmured next to her ear.

She curled more tightly into his chest, so he held her for a few moments, stroking the palm of his hand over her curled spine. After the thunder dissipated, he gradually set her apart and sat back on his haunches, glimpsing a trail of wetness on her cheeks. He didn't think it was from the rain.

He remembered the ranch hand who had attacked her and wondered if he'd been clumsy with her. Reaching up, he brushed the pad of his thumb under her eyes. "I'm sorry. Was I too rough?"

"No. God no. It was perfect." She gave a small laugh and quickly swiped at her eyes. "Jeez, I think I've fantasized about my first real kiss since I was ten. I guess I didn't expect it to affect me like this."

He gave a disbelieving shake of his head. "What are you saying? You've never been kissed before?"

She fluttered her long lashes and flicked at her fingernails. "I told you. After the incident with the ranch hand, I stayed pretty much to myself. Even in college, I commuted back and forth most weekends, and during the week I never stuck around after class because I had to help Dad with the chores."

Joshua's chest swelled. He suddenly felt as if he'd just stolen a piece of her heart—charged right in and took it without even thinking about the consequences. Although it was only a kiss, were they ready to be more than just friends?

He knew what she wanted: a commitment, marriage . . . kids. He didn't know if he'd ever be ready for that kind of a relationship. Unfortunately, he knew from experience that having a casual affair would only end with someone getting hurt. He couldn't risk that either. Debra meant more to him than any other woman he'd ever known.

He bowed his head. *God, I'm an idiot. I never should have kissed her.*

"It's pathetic if you think about it," she added with a short laugh. "I'm a twenty-four-year-old college graduate, and I've never even had a relationship with a man. Do you know how embarrassing that is to admit?"

"Ahh, don't be embarrassed, sweetheart. You're an extremely attractive young woman with a strong head on your shoulders. If anything, it just means you're waiting for the right one. I'm sorry if I crossed over the line of friendship."

"No. I wanted you to kiss me. Please, don't be sorry." Her eyes widened. "Unless it was really bad. I probably didn't even do it right. Did I?" She gripped his forearm and practically pleaded, "As my oldest and dearest friend, Joshua, you have to be totally honest with me."

She was making this very hard on him in more ways than one. The swelling in his jeans and the tightening of his chest were pretty damned good indications that she'd done it more than right. Ignoring his gut instinct to back off, he cupped the soft, delicate features of her face between his work-roughened hands and smiled. "Debra, it was perfect. You're perfect. In fact, I'm going to kiss you again just to prove it." Leaning in, he covered her sweet, heart-shaped lips with his, only confirming his suspicions that he'd not only stolen a piece of her heart, but she'd taken a piece of his.

Her mouth parted slightly and a small moan escaped the back of her throat. Her fingers tightened their grip on his shirt as she practically melted against him. Deepening the kiss, he tilted his head and covered her mouth, pressing her to the back of the couch.

As he wedged further between her legs, her knees instinctively gripped his waist, as if she were holding on for dear life. It was hard to believe she'd never done this before. Regrettably, he placed a departing kiss on her lips, barely touching her, not even breathing. *Sweet little Debbie. Why did you come into my life after all these years?*

The house lit up as the electricity returned. The refrigerator kicked on, the humming noise blending with the noise of the ceiling fan.

She squinted, adjusting to the brightness. "Whew. I feel like I just woke up from a very strange dream. One minute I was being charged by a bull, the next you were kissing me to tears."

His parents' phone rang, jarring him back to his senses.

"Saved by the bell," she said through a nervous laugh, pressing her palms against his chest, giving him a slight push away from her.

"Saved from what?" he said with a grin, wedging in closer. "My folks have a machine."

"Joshua?" Debra's shiny mouth twitched with a crooked grin. "That look in your eyes has me a little nervous. If you don't mind, I think I'd like to go back to my old perspective." When the phone rang a second time, she swung her legs together and said, "Tell you what. You get the phone and let your *little sister* fix the sandwiches."

"A sister, huh?" he repeated with an incredulous laugh, tugging on her hand to help her stand. "I think it's a little too late for that, darlin'."

She reached up and pressed a palm to his cheek, her own cheeks shining with a pretty rosy glow. "Friends, then? I don't think I'm ready for anything more right now."

He covered her hand and pressed a kiss to her palm, knowing she was right, but not liking it just the same. "Friends it is, then. Lead the way."

She slowly backed away from him, her gaze never quite leaving his till she turned and headed toward the kitchen. As the phone rang, blood mercilessly continued to concentrate on his anatomy below his buckle. Hoping to conceal his bulging perspective of this woman, he made his way to a wooden bar stool on the other side of the kitchen island, catching a full view of Debra's cute rump as she bent over at the waist and rummaged through the refrigerator.

Maybe staying here alone with her wasn't such a good idea. Knowing she was just down the hall in Heather's old bedroom would be like setting a barrel full of oats in a corral of hungry horses. The temptation to taste all of Debra's sweetness might be too hard to resist.

When the phone rang for the fourth time, she craned her neck around and caught him gawking at her. "What? Do I have something on me?" She strained to look at her backside.

He chuckled. "Nope. Everything's absolutely perfect."

On the fifth ring, she stood and shoved her hands on her slender waist. "Are you going to answer that or sit there and ogle my fanny?" When he gave her a big smile, she held up her hand and laughed. "Don't answer that."

He drew his head back in mock surprise. "Oh, so, you want me to ogle your fanny?"

"No! I meant answer the phone!" She threw her hands in the air. "Ugh! That's it. I'm calling a cab right now."

He gave a deep belly laugh. "I'm just teasing. That's what big brothers are supposed to do, you know."

The answering machine picked up. "This is Jasmine King. I'm trying to find J.D. Jared said I might find him here."

Debra bumped the refrigerator door shut with her hip. "Wonder what Jasmine wants."

He picked up the phone and turned off the machine. "Hey, Jazz. We missed you at the rodeo."

"J.D.? I'm so glad I found you." Her voice quavered and he thought she might be crying.

"What's wrong?" he asked. "Where were you tonight?"

"At the hospital. Milten's had some kind of a setback. They're getting ready to move him into the ICU now."

"ICU? What happened?"

"I don't know. He was fine when I left him this morning. When I got home, the ambulance was taking him to the hospital."

"What did Mrs. White say?"

"She's not sure what happened. He started having stomach cramps and trouble breathing. They've got him on the ventilator now and he's stabilized."

Joshua glanced at his watch. "I can be down there in twenty minutes. Where will you be?"

"You don't need to come out in this storm. Milten's mom arrived a few minutes ago. I just thought you'd want to know."

He rubbed his brows. "I'm sorry you have to go through all this, Jazz. We'll be down first thing in the morning. Do you want us to bring you anything?"

"Us?" Jasmine repeated.

"Yeah, Debra's here with me. She decided to try her hand at bull fighting and injured herself."

"She what?"

"She's actually a hero. She jumped in and saved a kid from a loose bull. She may have saved him from being killed."

Debra rolled her eyes, obviously unaware of the danger she'd been in.

"Is she all right?" Jasmine asked.

"I think so, but I didn't want to leave her alone tonight. She's staying at the Peak View Motel, of all places. Doesn't your company give any better relocation packages?"

"Walson's pretty tight when it comes to budgeting those kinds of expenses. Has she found an apartment?"

He remembered Robbie's suggestion at her moving into his complex and he had to keep his voice level. "Not yet. Heather's staying in a nice complex. Maybe they have a few units available. With any luck, Debra will be moved in by next weekend."

"I don't know why I didn't think about this before, but she's more than welcome to stay in our upstairs. With Milten being confined to the main floor, we rarely use the spare rooms. She'd have her own bathroom, phone, and cable hookup. She's welcome to stay there as long as she wants."

Joshua glanced warily at Debra, knowing how hell-bent she was on doing things on her own now. "Are you sure?"

"Absolutely. I won't take no for an answer. The room's got a bed and a dresser. All she has to worry about is her own sheets and towels, that sort of thing. Otherwise, she's got free rein of the house. I'll probably be here at the hospital for the next several days anyway. It'll be good to know someone's at home in case I need anything."

"Sounds perfect. You can convince Debra when we stop by in the morning. You sure you don't want me to come down tonight?"

"Positive. You take care of that girl. She's a sweetie. I'm going to need her to help me at Walson if Milten doesn't show any improvement by Monday."

"I'm sure she won't let you down. Good night, Jazz. He'll get through this."

"What happened?" Debra asked before he'd even clicked off the phone.

"Milt had some kind of a setback. He's in the ICU." He set the phone back in the cradle.

"I don't need a babysitter, Joshua. If you want to go down there, I'll be fine here alone." Lightning flashed, followed by an immediate roll of thunder. Debra flinched and tried to hide her unease, but he could see the fright in her eyes. He'd never seen anyone so terrified of storms before.

He shook his head. "Jasmine said he's sedated and stable now. We'll stop by first thing in the morning. Good news, though. You won't have to go back to the motel, and you won't have to be stuck out here with me."

"What do you mean?" She walked around the island and set a sandwich and a glass of milk in front of him.

He flipped the bread up and gave a low chuckle when he saw peanut butter and applesauce. "Decided to go with the old stand-by?"

"Yeah, thought it'd be nice for old times' sake. So what's the good news?"

"She wants you to stay with her. They've got a big two story and since his accident, they don't even use the upstairs. She needs someone to help her out while Milt's in the hospital anyway, get the mail, keep an eye on the place, that sort of thing. I don't think she likes staying alone. You'd be doing her a big favor."

Debra pulled out a stool and slouched down beside him, staring at her sandwich. "I can't imagine what she's going through. This must be a total nightmare."

He draped his arm around her shoulder and squeezed. "Milt's

got a strong will and a determined spirit, honey. He's not going to be held down for long. Trust me, *sis,*" he gave her a small wink, getting her to smile. "He'll be home in no time."

Debra crammed a pillow over her head, hoping to muffle the loud thunderstorm raging outside the Garrison house. With every lightning flash, all she could see were images of her father's lifeless form lying in the middle of the cattle pen.

Her heart beat hard. Her legs felt like wet cement. Even her breathing was painful, almost a déjà vu of the night her father had died. Another loud rumble made her jump. She tossed the pillow to the floor and focused on the red neon numbers of the clock sitting on the bedside table. Three o'clock. Only twenty minutes later than the last time she'd checked. It seemed the night was crawling by slower than a turtle on depressants.

Food. Junk food in particular usually helped her sleep and calmed her frazzled nerves. She made her way down a dark hallway to the kitchen and opened the refrigerator, squinting from the bright light. She pursed her lips, making a quick scan of the contents. Not much to choose from since Joshua's folks were out of town. She checked the fruit drawer and found an over-ripened peach. Bumping the door shut, she took a large slurpy bite and savored the cool juice and soft peach as it slid down her throat.

A small desk lamp cast a soft yellow glow over the kitchen and living room. She took another bite and imagined Joshua with his sisters and brother growing up here, laughing, playing games. Two boys, two girls. That was the kind of family she'd always dreamed of having someday.

The shelves in the living room were filled with colorful clay projects each child had made over the years. Several portraits were displayed in a grouping on the wall next to the fireplace. The pictures looked like they ran from the previous Christmas, and included Heather and her husband with their two kids, clear back to when Joshua was a baby sitting on his mother's lap, the dimple in his cheek even more adorably cute than it was now.

The wind outside blew the rain in torrents against the windowpane. The glass shook. An eerie howling noise made her skin crawl. Did the Garrisons' house have a basement?

Maybe some aspirin would help calm her nerves and help alleviate some of the discomfort in her midsection. She retraced her steps down the hallway and stopped at the bathroom door. She switched on the light and clamped her eyes shut, then squinted till she adjusted to the brightness. The adjoining door to Joshua's bedroom was cracked open, a low snore reminding her she was definitely not alone. Her chest tightened, her stomach fluttered. It took all her strength not to peek into his room, get a glimpse of the man who'd kissed her to tears just hours before.

Aspirin. Fumbling through the medicine cabinet, she found a bottle of pain relievers then spotted a half-empty bottle of Stetson Cologne for Men. Glancing quickly over her shoulder, she unscrewed the cap and took in a short breath. Joshua's unmistakable scent aroused all her senses. Now she knew why he always smelled so good. She dabbed a few drops at the pulse point of her throat, then between her breasts. Maybe now when she closed her eyes to sleep, she could pretend he was there with her, holding her, protecting her from the storm. She screwed the lid on and set the bottle on the shelf.

The faucet to the sink creaked as she turned it on and tossed two aspirin to the back of her mouth. She cupped her hand under the cold stream, gulping several drinks of water. The lights flickered off then back on. She sputtered and almost choked as she fumbled for the knobs. Another wind gust whipped against the house. It sounded like the roof was being ripped off the rafters. She hurried to Joshua's door and peeked through the crack, knowing she should just go back to bed—or hide *under* her bed.

A pole light from the barn shone directly into Joshua's window. Even through the rain and hail, a yellow glow streaked across his room, illuminating a large figure sprawled on top of a quilt-covered twin bed. Her eyes widened. His broad shoulders practically stretched from one side to the other, his torso bare down to his jeans. Did he always go to bed half-dressed?

He looked so peaceful with his brows perfectly arched, his mouth slightly parted. And those lips. How was she ever going to be around this man and not think about his kiss? He stretched and turned his head, his bare feet dangling over the end of the bed frame. She had to cover her mouth, stifling a giggle. He looked like papa bear sleeping in baby bear's bed.

Another bolt of lightning flashed, immediately followed by an explosion of thunder. She jumped and backed against the door, the doorknob cracking against the wall.

Joshua jerked upright. "What's the matter?" He rubbed his face and shook his head like a dog.

"I-I'm sorry," she stammered, trying to come up with a good reason for being caught in his room. "I guess I got turned around in the dark. I thought this was Heather's room."

"Are you all right? Are your ribs bothering you?"

"A little. I found some aspirin in the bathroom." Needing to explain further, she quickly added, "The storm. The hail. I thought the window in Heather's room might break." She blew out a loud gust of air. "Guess I'm being silly." She jumped at the sound of another loud clap of thunder, then held her hand over her rapidly beating heart. "The storm must be right on top of us." Her voice quivered over the reverberating thunder. "Do your folks have a basement?"

"Yeah, but I really don't think we need to go down there."

He reached over and turned on a bedside clock radio and tuned it to a country station. "There. If there's any warnings, the radio will let us know."

She turned to leave. "I'm sorry I woke you. Good night."

"Debra, wait. You don't have to leave."

She halted in her tracks.

"Don't take it wrong or anything, but you're welcome to stay with me till the storm passes."

She shook her head and spoke with her back to him. "Oh, no. It's really not necess—" she gasped midsentence when lightning lit up the room. She whirled around and clutched her arms around her waist. "Where's Brownie when I need her?"

Still on top of the covers, he scooted to the other side of the bed and pulled down the blankets in front of him. "Come on. Crawl in here, *sis,*" he emphasized, patting the bed.

Even as he spoke, she took small hesitant steps toward him. "Oh, no, there's barely room for you as it is."

"There's plenty of room. I'll stay on top of the covers so it's no big deal."

She swallowed. "Do you always sleep on top of your covers with your jeans on? I mean, it doesn't look very comfortable. Don't you keep a set of pajamas up here that you could wear?"

"Darlin', I haven't worn pajamas since the sixth grade."

"Oh . . . ohhhh," she repeated, widening her eyes and wondering exactly what he did or didn't wear to bed. "I think I'd better go back to Heather's room now."

He laughed, fluffing his pillow. "Come on, honey. No monkey business. Just a big brother protecting his little sister. You trust me, don't you?"

When another loud bang sounded outside, Debra practically leapt into his bed, sliding under the blanket with her back to him. "Sounds like the roof is being ripped off."

"There's a loose hinge on the shutter door in the rafters on the old red barn. I keep hoping the whole thing will just blow away. Then I can justify building a new one."

"Do you think the horses are okay?"

"The horses are fine. There's plenty of shelter for them to get under. I already put Brandy in the barn with a few of the other foals and their mothers, so there's nothing to worry about." He slid his arm under her neck then tossed the covers over her shoulders. He reached around her and snugly tucked the edge of the blanket clear up to her chin. With only the blanket separating them, he wedged in from behind and tugged her closer. His brawny arms surrounded her as his knees fit perfectly into the concave of hers.

But she didn't feel nervous, or that his motives were sexual. Closing her eyes, she let out a loud sigh of exhaustion. Feeling his strength wrapped around her, it seemed all her energy drained right down through her toes, which at the moment were brushing against the tops of his bare feet, both sets hanging off the end of the bed.

Thunder exploded outside, making the house rumble. "I hate this," she whispered, barely audible over the noise. The radio gave no weather alerts as they played a slow Faith Hill song, appropriately titled "Breathe."

"It's just thunder. It's not going to hurt you in here."

"I know. I tell myself that every time there's a storm. But ever since . . ." She trailed off and bit back a sob. "I'm sorry, Joshua. I'm just so tired. The moment I close my eyes, I see him lying there. Helpless. It was all my fault."

She curled the blanket in her fist and pressed it against her mouth, knowing it was too late now. She'd gone over the what ifs in her mind a thousand times wishing she'd done things differently. But she had to live with her mistakes and hope she didn't make the same ones again.

CHAPTER NINE

Joshua stared down at this sweet angel in his arms and almost shuddered. He wanted to pull her close and caress all of her pain away. When he'd found her standing at his door, wearing only a long T-shirt of Heather's, he'd sworn Debra was some kind of a beautiful apparition sent to him in his dreams. Taller than Heather by a few inches, Debra's curvy physique filled out the T-shirt, which hit just barely at the lower rim of her panties. The skin of her long legs practically shimmered from the glow of the pole light.

Glad he'd worn his jeans to bed, he hoped the extra padding of blanket between them disguised the heated desires she'd ignited deep below his belly. He didn't mean for this to be sexual. He just wanted to offer her support, get her to open up about her father, and help her through a difficult time in her life. She needed a friend right now.

But God, she smelled like she'd been sent from heaven. Wildflowers and fresh peaches wafted into his senses. He caught a whiff of something else, something familiar. He lowered closer to the side of her neck and took in a subtle breath. He couldn't keep the grin off his face. She obviously found more than just aspirin in the bathroom cupboard. It took all his strength not to place a kiss behind her earlobe, find out if she tasted as sweet as she smelled.

She really was an angel. An angel with broken wings. Was there anything he could do to help her fly again? Or, in her case, get her back in the saddle?

He smoothed her hair down with the palm of his hand, admiring her long ebony tendrils cascading over his pillow. The ends tickled his bare chest and arms. Hoping to get her to relax, he swept a few strands from her face, then traced his fingertips along her jaw down to her chin. She let out a small contented moan as she tipped her head back, allowing him to stroke from one side of her face to the other. Her skin was as soft as silk, smooth as satin.

Looking down from the top of her head, he caught a pretty view of her closed eyes, her long black lashes skimming her cheekbones. Her small pointy nose was set in perfect harmony above her heart-shaped lips. Lips he didn't think he could ever get enough of even if he did have his way with her, which, of course, was strictly off limits—at least tonight.

He lowered himself, speaking softly near her ear. "Do you want to talk about your father?"

She clenched her eyelids together, her long lashes pressing against her cheeks.

"I know it's hard, but are you the one who found him?"

She sniffed and quickly swiped her eyes with the blanket, trying to keep from crying.

He pulled her tighter against his chest, hoping to get her to open up to him. "It's okay to cry around me, honey." He rubbed his hand up and down her arm through the blanket. "Heather and Megan have been crying on my pillow for years. I have lots of experience."

"This is silly. It's just a storm. I don't know why I'm crying."

"I don't think it's just about the storm, darlin'. You've been through hell these past couple of months—years, the way it sounds—and you haven't had anyone to lean on. Who took care of all the funeral arrangements?"

She rubbed her nose with the sheets. "Why are you asking that?"

"Just answer the question." He reached over her and grabbed a box of tissues from the nightstand.

She pulled one out and dabbed at her nose. "Even though Mom and Dad had been divorced a year, my mom was still pretty upset. I took care of most everything."

Joshua set the box on the table, remembering how his mother had fallen into a severe depression, leaving him to practically raise the other three. Even after she'd met Brad, the others still came to him for most of their problems. But at least his mother had two sisters who'd helped with all the funeral arrangements. He smoothed her hair from her face, staring down at her perfect profile, illuminated only by the soft glow of the barnyard pole light shining through the pouring rain. "Do you have any other family?"

"My father was an only child. It was his Uncle Charles who died and left the ranch to my dad."

"So, dealing with the hospital, the funeral home, calling your friends, it was all dropped in your lap?"

"It's not as bad as it sounds. Word travels fast. The worst part was picking out the casket. We found a pretty copper-trimmed casket with a picture of a quarter horse embroidered on the satin lining. It was beautiful—as caskets go, I mean."

With her back still curled against his stomach, he braced his weight on his elbow and tucked a strand of hair behind her ear. "What about settling his estate, selling the ranch?"

"Remember, Mom moved out a year ago, and before that, she never did like to deal with the banks and left the books up to Dad. That's probably why we didn't know about all the loans and debts he'd driven up. It'll be a few months before everything's finalized."

"In other words, you're handling all the financial transactions, too."

"It hasn't been that bad. Stan Nelson has helped with the banks and getting the place sold."

He stiffened at the mention of the Nelsons. Just how well did she know them?

"We were lucky to get fair market value out of the land from Mr. Boyle, which, given the size of his corporation, didn't make much of a dent in his pocketbook."

Joshua had heard of the Boyles. A prominent stock contractor for local and regional rodeos. "He's got quite a monopoly in eastern Colorado. No wonder your father had so much trouble getting ahead."

"Don't remind me. Mr. Boyle was a mean old cuss who never got married and had different ranch hands rotating through his place every year. Since we'd taken over my great uncle's ranch, Mr. Boyle had acquired thousands of acres. It was getting harder and harder for us to compete."

"You said your father had a heart attack. Didn't he smoke?"

"I guess so."

"You guess so? From what I remember, the man had a Winston in his mouth even when he ate."

"Okay, so he smoked."

"You don't think that had a little to do with his heart attack?"

"I know what you're doing." She flipped on her back and pulled the blanket up to her face, blotting her eyes.

"It wasn't your fault, Debra. You couldn't have prevented his heart attack."

"You don't know the whole story, Joshua." She stared up at him with big shiny brown eyes, her cheeks wet and her nose an adorable shade of pink. "There's so much you don't understand."

"So tell me so I can understand." He laid his hand on her stomach, making a gentle caress through the blanket. "Please, honey. You can't keep this bottled up inside you."

She looked up at the ceiling and shook her head. "God, it just makes me sick every time I think about it. It happened so fast. One day everything was fine, then poof, everything was gone." A flash of light streaked across the room followed by a roll of thunder. She cringed, turning her face into his chest with her arms curled between them.

Trying to keep his mind off the searing warmth of her body, he cupped her chin between his thumb and forefinger, forcing her to look up at him. "From what I've heard, things weren't fine for several months before he died."

"More like two years. I know exactly how bad it got."

"Tell me then. I want to help you, Debra. Sometimes just talking about it makes you feel better."

She hauled in a shaky breath, then spoke as she exhaled slowly. "It seemed like it all started after Dad hurt his back. We were vaccinating our horses for the West Nile virus. I hated giving our horses shots and made my father do them." She wrinkled her nose.

"I know what you mean. I get a little queasy around needles, too. Jared does all that stuff for me."

"What I should have done was given the shot myself," she huffed.

"Just tell me what happened," he insisted, hoping to keep her on track.

"Okay, okay. We were in the stall giving Whiskers the vaccination. I was holding onto her halter and she reared back, jerking away from me. She bucked and kicked Dad right into the fence. He fractured his lower back and was laid up for the rest of the summer. He never really got back to his old self. He practically lived on painkillers."

"Was he able to walk?"

"Yeah, but he was still in a lot of pain. It seemed like he completely lost interest in the ranch. I had no choice. I had to take over. He started going into Denver, telling us he was hitting a sale or going to a farm auction. But then the credit card bills started showing up."

"From the casinos?" he guessed.

She nodded. "At first it was just a few hundred dollars. He and Mom would go 'round and 'round, arguing about them, then he'd storm away mad. Before we knew it, the credit cards were maxed out. Soon bank statements started showing up. He'd taken out a farm loan, but had missed several payments, so we were in danger of foreclosure. He even cashed in all his stocks, retirement plans, life insurance policies, everything he could get his hands on and could liquidate."

"All for gambling?" he asked, shocked that it had all come down to the tables.

"That's when Mom left." She looked up at him almost pleading. "He turned into a different man, Joshua. He started selling all the high-dollar horses until all we had left were just a few brood mares. He even sold Black-Eyed Bandit. That stallion alone brought in twenty-thousand dollars."

He arched his brows. "You still had that ol' boy around?"

Her lips tipped into a tentative smile. "You remember him?"

"Yeah. He sired a chestnut mare my dad bought that summer we visited you."

Her smile brightened. "I know exactly what horse you're talking about. Her name was Golden Sunset. I used to call her Goldie. I was devastated when Dad told me he'd sold her. But when he told me you guys bought her, I felt better. I looked for her tonight in the corral, but I'm sure you got rid of her a long time ago."

Inwardly, he cringed. How could he tell her what really happened to Golden Sunset? Hoping to steer clear of the topic for now, he said, "Hey, we're getting off the subject. Why don't you skip ahead to the day your father died? Was there a storm?"

She nodded. "There were watches and warnings posted all day for high winds and hail. We were culling out the small heifers, getting ready to take the last twenty head of steer to a sale in Boulder on Sunday."

Remembering how dangerous it was to get cattle loaded into a trailer, he was almost afraid to ask. "Who all was there helping you besides your father?"

She pushed away from him and sat up, folding her long legs beneath her Indian style. "You have to understand. We didn't have the money to pay for hired hands."

"What about the neighbors? Mr. Boyle?"

Avoiding his gaze, she situated the blanket over her lap and shook her head.

He gave a frustrated sigh and raked his fingers through his hair. "Okay, so it was just you and your dad. Then what happened?"

"Well . . ." She swallowed, folding and unfolding the edge of the blanket, although the way her eyes were glazed over, he knew she wasn't even aware she was doing it. "If you remember our place, we had two holding pens that opened into a larger sorting pen. On the south end, a squeeze gate opened into a narrow aisle that herded them down to the chute, which led them into our old stock trailer. It took us most of the afternoon before we culled the heifers and got them into the holding pens. By then, the rain had started to come down in bucketfuls and the corral turned into a sludge-podge of mud and manure. I had my old yellow rain slicker on and with the hood over my head, it was hard to see, much less move around very quickly." Her fingers curled around the blanket, her knuckles whitening. "We got most of the steers down the squeeze chute without too much trouble, but then—" Lightning lit up the room. She gasped and stared out the window.

He covered her hand and squeezed. "Then what, honey?"

"The hail started. Ping-pong-ball-sized hail," she emphasized, still staring out the window, as if going back in time.

"Where were you standing?"

"My father was up at the loading ramp, prodding them into the trailer. I was inside the squeeze chute behind the last steer, goading him forward. I remember being slammed into the gate." She absently rubbed her ribcage, her voice choking as she spoke through choppy breaths. "I couldn't breathe. I thought a lung had collapsed. Turns out it was just a few cracked ribs. There was a small puncture in my right lung, but nothing serious."

Nothing serious? "What happened next?"

"All I can remember is Daddy scooping me into his arms, yelling my name. He carried me all the way up to the house and laid me on the couch in the living room." She shook her head. "He never should have carried me, Joshua. Since his accident, he'd lost all kinds of weight. I was too heavy. And with his lower back, he had troubles lifting a fifty-pound bag of feed, much less a six-foot grown woman. He was coughing and clutching his chest. He could barely catch his breath."

"Do you think he was having a heart attack?"

"I don't know. Maybe. He went back outside in the storm alone. After about a half-hour, I went out to the porch to see if he needed help. Not that I could've done much. It hurt so bad I could barely call out his name, and with the storm, there was no way he could've heard me. I couldn't see him anywhere. He must've opened the gate because the steers were bawling and huddled in the middle of the pen."

"So where was he?"

She closed her eyes then started rocking her upper body back and forth. "At first I didn't see him, but then . . ." she paused, giving a heavy swallow, her whole body trembled. "One of the steers shoved him out of the middle of the herd, pushing him clear across the corral. He rammed Daddy into the fence, not just once, but over and over."

He barely heard her next sentence. "He was still alive, Joshua. He was screaming in pain. He felt the whole thing." Tears now streamed down her soft pink cheeks in a river of emotion.

He sat up beside her and pulled her into the crook of his shoulder. "It's okay, honey. You don't have to go on."

"When the steer was through with him," she went on as if she didn't even hear him, "the monster flung him aside like an old rag. I crawled through the fence. The mud was so thick. My ribs. I couldn't breathe. God, Joshua. All I can remember is the blood. There was so much blood."

"That's enough, Debra."

"I finally got to him," she added. "But he wasn't moving. Blood streamed into the muddy water. I tried to do CPR, but with my ribs, and the mud and . . . oh, God. I kept praying that his eyes would open, or that his lips would quirk into that silly grin he always used to give me."

"Sweet Jesus," he said, pressing his lips to her temple. "Don't do this. I'm sorry you had to go through it all by yourself."

She stopped shaking and stared straight ahead, looking at a spot on the wall. "I wanted to die." Her voice was low and even. "I wanted the steer to kill me, too."

The look of desperation in her eyes stabbed him in the heart. He slid his palms over her cheeks, tipping her face up to his, trying to get her to focus on him. "Don't say that, honey. Don't ever say that. It was an accident. It wasn't your fault."

She blinked, as if bringing herself back to his room, out of the corral, away from her father. She took in a deep breath and blew it out, shaking her head. "It *was* my fault. If I hadn't screwed up and let the steer get turned around, I wouldn't have been hurt. Dad would still be here today."

"Honey, if a thousand-pound steer wants to get out of a chute, there's not a whole hell of lot you can do but get out of the way. And from the sounds of it, you were squished into the gate, making that near impossible. Please, you have to let this go. It wasn't your fault. None of it was."

She pressed her fists against his chest. "He shouldn't have carried me. His heart—"

"He was protecting you, Debra, just like you protected that boy tonight. You didn't think twice about your ribs when you jumped in and carried him to safety. It was the same for your father."

"But if I'd been bigger, the steer wouldn't have—"

"Size doesn't matter. I weigh twice again as much as you and look how that steer tossed me right out of the pen tonight. You have to let this go, darlin'. You can't go through the rest of your life blaming yourself for something that was out of your control."

When she started to object again, he couldn't help himself. He lowered his head and covered her lips, wanting to kiss all her pain away, make her forget every gory detail of that night. She sank into him, her shoulders dropping back before she let out a heart-wrenching sob right into his mouth.

He dragged his lips back to her ears and gently tugged her closer, murmuring into her ear. "It's okay, baby. Just let it all out."

A low, guttural moan sounded next to his ear. "I miss him so much," she cried, tears of pain coursing down her cheeks onto his neck.

"I know you do," he murmured in a gravelly voice. With every gut-wrenching sob she let go, a part of his heart went right along with it. Hearing how much she missed her father made him realize just how much he missed his own father. Joshua closed his eyes and gave her a careful squeeze, the warmth of her breath consoling a part of his own grief.

After several minutes, her shoulders stopped shaking and her sobs became soft hiccups. He eased her down into a reclining position with his head propped against the headboard. He couldn't help but notice how she willingly turned toward him and melted into his embrace. He pressed a kiss to the top of her head and murmured, "Just close your eyes, honey. It's all over now."

"I'm so tired," she whispered, giving a long yawn.

"Shhh, don't talk anymore. It's time to sleep and make new dreams. Think about all the good times you had with your dad. Don't let what happened to him erase all the fun times you shared. Those will always be in your heart."

With her eyes closed, she said, "There's something else I forgot to tell you." She rubbed the tip of her nose and gave a small sniff.

"What is it?"

"Well? It's weird. It's probably just my imagination." She spoke through another long yawn. "Or maybe the storm just confused me."

He smoothed her hair away from her face, trying to get a better look at her expression. Her eyes were closed, her lashes curling up from her lids. She looked like she was almost asleep. "What is it Debra? What's weird?"

She snuggled in closer to his side. "The last thing I remember . . ." She paused then finished barely over a whisper, ". . . is a set of taillights leaving our driveway."

"Taillights?" he repeated. "What taillights? I thought you said you were alone."

When she didn't answer, he looked down and found her completely asleep. Her muscles were twitching, like she was already into a dream. It seemed she'd fallen asleep before he'd even stopped speaking.

But he was wide-awake. His mind started going over everything she'd told him about the night her father was killed. The steer kicking her, the storm, her father being rammed into the fence. And through it all, she was alone.

Or was she? Had someone been at their ranch the night her father was killed?

She said he'd been gambling, and Joshua wondered if his death was the result of more than being gored by a steer? Maybe he could get in touch with the Prairie Police Department and get more information about her father's accident. In all likelihood, it probably was lightning as she said, but it wouldn't hurt to at least check it out.

Feeling his protective nature take over his emotions, Joshua tugged her closer, wrapping his arms around her, sorry he hadn't been there for her over the years.

She looked so peaceful with her fingers curled under her chin as she rested against his chest. He started caressing her arm, stroking her softness with his fingertips. He knew she was totally unaware of the fact that she was no longer covered by the blanket. Her T-shirt rode clear up to her waist, exposing a pair of frilly pink panties edged in lace. Funny, he hadn't pictured her as the pink and frilly type, but then again, he hadn't seen her as the high-powered career type, either.

He couldn't keep his gaze from dropping down to the generous mounds of her breasts pressed fully into his side, barely concealed under her thin cotton T-shirt. He was tempted to kiss all her pain away, starting at her eyes, then her cheeks, landing on that delicious full mouth, slightly parted and reminding him of a fresh, ripe strawberry. He took in a steadying breath and blew it out slowly, trying to keep his desires in check. It'd been a long time since he'd enjoyed the breath of a woman on his skin.

Way too long. And even then, he'd never felt this strong need to nurture and protect her, not only from the elements, but from her own self-condemnation as she fully carried all the blame for everything that had ever gone wrong at the ranch. He only regretted not being around for her when she was alone, juggling the ranch duties on her own.

Trying to keep his mind focused on Debra, and away from his libido, he swept the blanket up over her legs, loosely tucking it in around her waist. He pressed a kiss to her temple near the corner of her eye, tasting salt from her tears. Low, rolling thunder reverberated throughout the room. She didn't even move. With her in his arms, he scrunched down onto his pillow, allowing her face to rest just under his chin. Looking down at the top of her head, he pressed a kiss to her hair, his fingers grazing the skin of her arm. She felt good nestled beside him, like this spot was made only for her.

The rain and wind lessened and they lay there in the yellow-gray darkness of his childhood room. Funny, this was the first time he'd ever had a girl back here. Truth be told, he'd never even had a woman overnight in his rustic, cozy cabin back by Elk Ridge Ravine. He'd never wanted to share either with anyone before . . . before he met Debra.

Joshua's trusty rooster, Rusty, startled him awake, serenading him with an off-key cock-a-doodle-do. Soft breath fanned his skin. A long slender arm draped across his chest. He looked down and smiled, finding Debra snuggled by his side, her long leg casually draped over his.

He glanced over at the bedside clock. Almost eight. He hadn't slept this late in years.

She stirred and gave a little moan. Then her body stiffened.

He guessed that right about now she realized where she was.

"Please tell me I'm dreaming," she said without opening her eyes.

He chuckled. "Okay, you're dreaming," he said, giving her shoulder a gentle squeeze. "Anybody in it you know?"

She groaned and covered her mouth. "Is it really morning?"

" 'Fraid so."

She looked up with widened eyes. "I fell asleep on you?"

"Right again."

"Oh, Joshua. I'm so embarrassed."

He smoothed her hair from her face. "Don't be. You were exhausted. When's the last time you had a good night's sleep?"

She gave a loud yawn into her hand. "I can't even remember that far back." Letting out a contented moan, she unabashedly draped her arm across his bare torso, comfortably settling her hand on his chest.

He had to force himself to keep his breathing steady. He stared up at the ceiling, counting from one hundred backwards. At number eighty-two, he looked down and found her with her eyes closed again, her lips pressed together in a small smile of contentment. When her fingertips started doing soft slow circles in his chest hair, he had to grit his teeth. He knew she had no idea the affect her innocent gesture was having on him. He also didn't know how much more he could take before he yanked off this quilt and found himself on top of her, tasting every square inch of her soft peaches-and-cream skin.

Looking up at him, she interlaced her fingers on his chest and perched her chin on the backs of her hands. Her lips curled into an incredibly sexy, sleepy grin.

"What's that smile about?" he asked, tucking a strand of hair behind her ear.

"I don't know. Guess I didn't realize how nice it was."

"How nice what was?"

"Snuggling with someone in a thunderstorm. Maybe you could teach me how to like storms after all." She arched her brows with a hint of playful seduction.

He chuckled and wrapped his arms around her waist, gently hauling her up so her mouth was just inches from his.

"Darlin', you keep that up and I'll teach you more than just weather appreciation." He laughed at her somewhat startled expression and tugged her back into the crook of his shoulder. "Sorry. As hard as I tried to think of you as a sister, I'm afraid my perspective got a little clouded. I didn't mean to make you uncomfortable."

She sat up and propped her head against the headboard, dragging the quilt up to her chin. "This is so humiliating."

He laughed and turned on his side. "I was just razzing you. I'm glad you trusted me enough to confide in me last night. I would never do anything to jeopardize our friendship. I hope you know that."

"Oh, no. I'm not talking about us having . . . well . . . you know." She fluttered her lashes down, avoiding his gaze.

He had to force himself to keep from laughing. She was so innocent and pure, only making her that much more adorably sexy.

"I'm embarrassed that I unloaded on you last night, bawling like a newborn calf. I don't think I've ever cried like that before in my life. My father made sure I wasn't some sissy girl who cried at the scrape of a knee. Even when I broke my arm, I didn't cry."

He leaned on an elbow, resting his head in his hand. "How'd you break your arm?"

"I was thirteen and I got between a calf and her momma." She held her arm out in front of him and flexed her fingers. "Believe me, I never did that again."

"You've sure had your share of run-ins with farm animals."

"It's not just the livestock I couldn't handle. See this?" She pointed to her forearm.

The yellow glow from the sunrise made her skin look silky

smooth except for a jagged line running from the crook of her elbow clear up to her wrist. He traced his finger over what he assumed was a scar. "Is this from your broken arm?"

"Nope. Got that from barbed wire when I was ten. Thirty-two stitches." Flipping the covers off, she kicked up her right leg and pointed to a scar on her shin. "Got twenty-five stitches there when I was eleven. Guess what that was from?"

"I'm afraid to ask." He reached up and traced his finger the length of her shin, trying not to notice how incredibly smooth and sexy she was lying next to him . . . in his bed . . . wearing only a thin cotton T-shirt. Trying to keep his perspective, he scooted away from her, hoping she didn't notice his growing arousal.

"You know that little wheel that's supposed to hold up the tongue of a trailer?"

He arched his brows. "It didn't hold?"

"Scraped right down the front of my leg. Cut my jeans and all. I was lucky it didn't land on my foot."

"Dang, lady. Even big tough cowboys don't get banged up as much as you have."

"Which only proves my point." She blew out a loud gust of exasperation, swinging her legs over the side of his bed. "I don't belong on a ranch."

As she huffed out of his room, Joshua swung his legs over the side of his bed. "Way to go, Garrison." He dragged his fingers through his hair. What could he say? It was killing him, the way she blamed herself for all her father's problems. Only now did he fully understand why she was so determined to get away from ranching.

He headed down the hall and heard the faucet running in the bathroom. He found her hunched over the sink, splashing water on her face. He leaned his shoulder against the doorframe, jamming his hands into the front pockets of his jeans. "I'm sorry,

Debra. I hope you don't think I was making fun of you. What can I say to make you feel better?"

"Nothing," she said, shutting off the faucet.

He stepped up beside her and handed her a towel.

She spoke as she blotted her face. "You were just stating the obvious." She turned around and leaned on the edge of the counter between the two sinks, picking at a string on the towel. She rubbed her bare feet together and wouldn't look at him. "I'm so grateful you came along when you did last weekend. Knowing Brandy is with you gives me such peace. It allows me to get on with my life, to get my feet planted on the right path."

"And you think the right path is behind a desk at Walson shuffling paperwork?"

"Yes . . . no . . . ugh, I don't know." She blew out a loud sigh, obviously frustrated with her situation. "What do you want me to say? That I miss the ranch? That I miss seeing the horses every night? Okay. I miss them. I miss them so much it hurts. It's killing me not being able to see Brandy and take her out for a ride. But guess what?" Her voice choked as she flung her hands in the air. "The ranch is gone, Daddy's gone, everything's gone. That part of my life is over."

He gently grabbed her shoulders just as she looked up into his eyes. Her face was red and tear-stained, and God, she was beautiful. "Don't do this, Debra."

Her voice was a whisper when she spoke again. "I shouldn't have come here, Joshua. Everything about this place reminds me of what I left behind.

He swallowed a lump forming at the base of his throat, wanting to hold her, wishing he could tell her he was here for her now. But she was right. He was everything she was trying to get away from. He never should have brought her here.

"Tell you what," he said, taking hold of her hands and rubbing his thumb over her fingernails. "Why don't you get cleaned up and we'll go visit Milt and Jasmine at the hospital? Get you as far away from my ranch as possible." He tried to joke, but deep down his heart ached. Would she ever want to come back? "After that, we'll get your vehicle and settle you in at Jasmine's. I'll feel a lot better knowing you're in a safe neighborhood."

"Always the big brother, I see." She gave him a loving jab in the stomach then looked down at her bare feet, tugging her shirt down over her thighs. He knew this was her polite way of getting him to back off.

He regretfully stepped away and gestured toward the cupboard. "There's towels in there and there should be plenty of shampoo and stuff in the shower. Mom usually keeps some extra toothbrushes around. Rummage around and make yourself at home."

"A shower does sound good."

"Are you a coffee drinker?"

"This morning? Yes. Strong and black, and by the way," she added, her lips quirking into a crooked grin, "just so you know, I don't normally crawl into bed with guys when there's a little thunder. I think that incident with the bull and thinking you'd been killed made me a little anxious."

He had to chuckle. If she'd never been kissed, she'd never even had a man hold her in his arms either, much less been in bed with one. He touched her chin, forcing her to look up at him. "And just so you know, I've never had a woman crawl into my twin bed before, either. Mom never allowed girls back here. You're my first." He gave her a quick wink before he asked, "Does this mean I shouldn't expect you out scooping horse stalls this morning?"

"Ha. I think I'll let you have all the fun."

He gave a forced laugh, inwardly feeling like his chest had been poked by an electric cattle prod. His ex-fiancée, Michelle had never wanted to be a rancher's wife. She'd wanted a job, a career, a house in the suburbs with a white picket fence and a ten-foot-square lawn. After all these years, had he let himself fall for another woman who wanted nothing to do with his dreams?

Chapter Ten

The smells of disinfectant and ammonia always made Joshua's stomach curdle. Other than visiting Heather in the hospital when she'd had her two kids, he didn't have anything but bad memories from Saint Anthony's, first of his father's death, then Milt's accident, and more recently, Dillan's illness. He just hoped Milt's setback was only temporary and he could go home with his wife where he belonged.

"You dreading this as much as I am?" Debra asked, nudging his shoulder as they rode up the elevator.

He looked down at her from the corner of his eye. "Not too thrilled with hospitals either?"

"Not especially." She slid her fingers into the crook of his elbow and let out a deep breath. "I never got to say good-bye to my dad."

He patted her hand, knowing exactly how she felt. By the time he'd arrived at the emergency room after his father's plane crash, his dad was already dead. He never should have gotten into the cockpit in the first place. They'd only just got the plane back from the mechanics, and because of Joshua, his dad didn't do a pre-flight inspection.

Maybe if his father hadn't been so angry and upset . . .

He rubbed his eyes, not wanting to dredge up that old story. The events of the previous night still had him worried. Debra's story had haunted him all night long. Knowing she'd witnessed the brutal death of her father made his gut churn. But it was

171

the taillights she'd seen that had him concerned. After more than two months, would there be a way to know for sure if anyone else had been there?

He'd like to get hold of the Prairie Police Department, but the thunderstorm had left quite a mess at his ranch. Unbelievably, the old red barn still stood intact, including the rafter in the loft. As soon as he could get Debra settled at Jasmine's, he had a full day of clearing debris and downed tree limbs. Maybe he'd give the newspaper a call and place an ad. A hired hand didn't sound all bad right about now.

They strode off the elevator and followed a wide corridor, passing several doors till they finally arrived at the Medical ICU waiting room. Several families camped out in the small room. Pillows and blankets had been strewn into corners and draped over chairs, signifying a long night they'd spent worrying about their loved ones.

"J.D.?" A warm, familiar voice sounded from the far side of the room.

"Mrs. King." He stepped around two kids putting a puzzle together on the floor. "How's Milt this morning?"

"Not as good as they'd hoped. Jasmine is in with the doctors now. She'll be out in just a few minutes. It's so nice to see you again."

He looked up and found Debra leaning against the door, her normally tan complexion as pale as the eggshell paint on the wall. Maybe this was too much for her to handle so soon after her father's death. He caught her gaze and waved her over, then set his hand on her lower back. "Debra, this is Milt's mom, Mrs. King. Mrs. King, this is Debra Walker. She and I have been friends since we were kids. She works with Jasmine over at Walson now."

Mrs. King touched Debra's hand. "Good to meet you, dear."

Color started to return to Debra's cheeks as she gave Mrs.

King a warm smile. "I'm sorry to hear about your son. I've never met him, but the way Jasmine dotes on him all day, he sounds like a fighter. My prayers are with all of you."

"Debra? J.D.?" Jasmine's voice sounded from behind.

Joshua turned and met her weary smile, then held out his arms. "Hey, Jazz. How's the big guy doing?"

"Oh, J.D. He's so sick again." She immediately fell into his embrace. She was so petite, only coming up to his chest. "I don't know what could have happened."

"Did the doctors have anything else to say this morning?"

"No. They said it could be just about anything. An allergic reaction to his medicine, stress, you name it. In all honesty, they may never know. Sometimes things just happen with no apparent cause."

"Is he awake? Can he have visitors?"

"He's still sedated, but they hope to take him off the ventilator this morning and move him to a private room this week. Maybe you can see him then." She rubbed the pads of her fingers under her eyes and gave Debra a teary smile. "Thanks for coming down. I hope one week was enough training. I'm afraid you'll be on your own for a few days."

"Don't worry about Walson. You just make sure Milten comes home soon."

"Did J.D. ask you about moving into my place? I'd love for you to stay with us."

"Are you sure you're prepared for a houseguest? I really hate to impose, especially at a time like this."

"Your timing couldn't be more perfect. I hate coming and going to an empty house. It makes me realize how much I'd miss Milt if he ever . . ." She trailed off, her eyes turning misty.

"Hey," Joshua said. "Milt's not going to let a little flu bug get him down."

"You're right. It's just been a long exhausting night." Jasmine

173

grabbed her purse and pulled out a set of keys. "This long gold key is to the house, and the two short silver keys are to my administrative filing cabinets at work. Get in and find what you need."

"Don't worry. I'll take care of everything," Debra assured her.

"I'd better go. I want to be there when they take him off the ventilator."

Joshua and Debra walked Jasmine down the hall toward the ICU visitors' entrance. They each gave Jasmine a hug before she disappeared behind the double metal doors into the ICU.

Debra pressed her fingers to her lips. "Oh, Joshua. Why did this have to happen?"

He quickly folded her into his arms and pressed a kiss to her temple. "Like you said, Milt's a fighter, honey. He's going to pull through this and be home in no time." When he gave her a squeeze, she grimaced.

He cringed and stepped back. "Sorry about that. I forgot about your ribs."

"It's okay. Your hug was the medicine I needed anyway."

"Maybe you should go down to the emerg—"

"No, Joshua," she interrupted. "I'm fine. Let's go get my stuff from the motel before I get charged for another day."

They checked out of the motel, had an early lunch, then spent the rest of the afternoon getting a few essentials for Debra's stay at Jasmine's. It was after six before Joshua pulled up in front of the Kings' house. They still needed to pick up her vehicle from the rodeo grounds.

He carried in her luggage, which only consisted of two old suitcases with broken straps. He spotted an old faded stuffed horse with only one eye and chuckled. Stuffing Brownie under his arm, he carried it upstairs where Debra was hanging a few blouses in the closet of the spare bedroom. "Guess you'll have to rely on Brownie the next time there's a storm." He plopped it on the bed.

"Yeah, she's about the only one I can count on these days."

That comment struck a nerve. He wished there was some way he could convince her that he was here for her now.

She started to yawn, then grimaced and slumped down onto edge of the bed. "Whew. I'm more tired than I thought."

"Tell you what, why don't we get your SUV tomorrow?"

"Actually, that would be great. I think I'll just take a long hot soak in the tub and go to bed early."

"Sounds like a good idea." He shot her a teasing wink that made her smile. He hunkered down in front of her and placed his hands on her knees. "Will you be okay here by yourself tonight? You could probably twist my arm into camping out in the living room, you know, in case you get scared again."

She laughed. "I think I can manage. You can take off your big brother hat now. I'll be fine. Thanks for running me around and taking care of me last night and today."

"What time do you want me to pick you up tomorrow?"

"I don't know. Since it's Sunday, I was hoping to find a church nearby. My faith is about the only thing that keeps me going these days." She tried to make light of her feelings, but the sadness in her eyes gave her away.

"To be honest, I haven't been to church in years, but the Garrisons have always gone to the Rockrimmon Church of Christ. It's just up the hill about two blocks. Heather's on the welcoming committee. If you want, I'll let her know you're coming."

"That'd be great. If I can roll out of bed tomorrow, I think I'll check it out. Maybe you could meet me here around noon."

When she started to stand, he shook his head and swept her legs off the ground and settled them onto the bed. Pressing her shoulders gently down onto the pillow, he said, "Rest. You don't need to walk me out." He found himself lost in her gaze. Her pretty ebony hair cascaded over the crème pillow shams beneath her head, the soft comforter forming to the perfect curves of her breasts and her hips. She was undeniably the most beautiful woman he'd ever known. Would he ever be able to hold her in his arms again? Feel her softness, be as close to her as he was last night?

"Joshua?"

"What?"

She arched her brows and gave him a teasing kick in the leg. "Friends?"

He smiled, bent over her, and braced his hands on either side of her at the waist. "Absolutely." Unable to resist, he pressed a kiss to her soft, satiny cheek, lingering for an extra moment, breathing in her fragrance of wildflowers and baby powder, wishing he could do more. "Sweet dreams, darlin'."

She wrapped her arms around his neck. "Thanks for everything. You really are an angel."

Regretfully, he strode to the door and shut off the light, then headed downstairs, passing Milt and Jasmine's master bedroom on the main floor. The bed was in disarray and the lunch tray and glasses still cluttered the nightstand and table. Wanting to help any way he could, he picked up the dishes and almost tripped over a clipboard lying on the floor. It was the notebook Milt used to communicate. He picked it up, noting the top page was blank except for traces of blue ink that had soaked through from the magic marker.

He narrowed his eyes, turned it front and back then held it up to the light. He thought it said, "Don't hurt Jazzy." Adrenaline surged through his body. Whom did Milt write this to and why would they want to hurt Jasmine?

He ripped out the page from the notebook and rifled through magazines and various pieces of mail looking for anything else out of the ordinary. He glanced in the trashcan and found several sheets of paper crumpled in a ball. He flipped through all of them, but most were just brief messages indicating food that Milt wanted or requests to change a channel on the television. He shoved the note into his pocket and carried the dirty dishes into the kitchen. He'd bullied his way into Dillan's room last week. He just hoped he could get in to see Milt tonight.

Rising early Sunday morning for church, Debra dressed in a dark denim jean skirt and a short-sleeved yellow blouse with a V-neck collar. She drew the sides of her hair back, binding it with a gold clip, leaving several ebony wisps framing her face. Her cheekbones were a rosy pink after applying a little rouge, although the way her thoughts kept drifting to the intimate night she'd spent with Joshua, she didn't think her cheeks needed the extra coloring. She'd dreamt of him most of the night, wishing she were still in his arms, snuggled cozily in his twin bed. His penetrating gaze, his sumptuous, gentle kisses, and the velvety touch of his strong hands ignited something deep in her soul she'd never felt before.

But she couldn't allow herself to think beyond friendship. She'd never forgive herself if she caused Joshua's ranch to go under like her father's. With a heavy heart, she tidied the bedroom and bathroom, then went downstairs and began straightening the living room. Several photo albums and a high school yearbook were sitting open on the coffee table. She picked up the yearbook, dating back ten years. That would have been the year Joshua graduated.

She sat down on the couch and immediately turned to the senior pictures at the back of the book. She smiled. Joshua's hair was longer and thicker, combed into waves behind his ears, but his eyes were a dreamy coffee brown that seemed to be focused on her. His face was thinner and his lips were curled into a delectable grin, his dimple still adorable.

She let out a wistful sigh and stroked her thumb over his image. *Total hunk.*

Flipping to the front of the book, she thumbed through several pages till she came to the football photos, and there they were, the Three Musketeers, all lined up across the back row, practically towering over the rest of the team. What she'd give to go back in time and watch those three in action.

Going to the next page, there were several candid shots of the football games, some of them played in the rain; one was of Joshua alone as he held up the ball after a touchdown. She came to a picture from the homecoming game and her breath caught in her throat.

Joshua stood with his arm around a short blond cheerleader. They'd been crowned king and queen. The caption read, "Sweethearts Forever." *Michelle Davis?* Was this the girl who left him heartbroken at the altar?

Debra fanned through several pages and found Joshua and Michelle together in at least a half-dozen pictures. They'd even been crowned prom king and queen, though Michelle seemed chubbier at the end of the year, and neither of them seemed to have that smile they'd had back at homecoming.

She flipped through to a picture of what looked like a very young Robert Nelson. It was a drama photo of the winter play, *Grease.* He'd played Danny, of course. Her eyes widened when she saw the blond who'd played Sandy. Michelle Davis. They made the perfect pair. Robert, with his hair slicked back in shiny ebony waves, and Michelle wearing skin-tight, black leather pants.

Then it hit her.

Joshua said Michelle had run off with another guy. Was it Robert Nelson? That would definitely explain the animosity between the two men.

The phone rang. She set the book on the coffee table and answered, "Hello, King residence."

"Debra?"

She smiled and relaxed into the couch. "Morning, Jasmine. How's Milten?"

"The doctors said he'll probably be in the ICU several more days, maybe longer."

"He'll pull through this, Jasmine. Just give him time. How are you doing? Did you get any sleep?"

"I got a few hours this morning in the lounge. How about you? How'd your first night go?"

"Great. I really appreciate you letting me stay here. I have to admit, it was pretty creepy at the motel." Catching a glimpse of Milten and Joshua in the yearbook, she said, "I found Milten's high school year books. If he looks anything like he did back then, you've got yourself quite a catch."

Jasmine gave a little giggle. "Did you see their football photo? You can see why they carried the team to the state championship."

"They sure were cute back then. I mean, they're gorgeous now," she clarified with a smile. "But, oh man, they were a bunch of studmuffins, weren't they?"

"You don't think I married Milten for his money, do you?" It was good to hear Jasmine laugh. "Their ten-year reunion is over Labor Day weekend," she went on to say. "I dug those yearbooks out of the basement, hoping to help Milt get some of his memory back. Some things he remembers, but others are still a blur."

Debra flipped through several more pages, stopping at the pictures of homecoming. "Who was this Michelle Davis that Joshua's with in about every picture? Was she his high school sweetheart?"

"I never met her, but Milten said they were practically joined at the hip. Rich debutante type. Drove a fancy car, captain of the cheerleaders, very popular. Maybe you know the type?"

"Only too well," Debra said with a little envy.

"He'd asked her to marry him and had even set a date."

"Wow. Right out of high school? That seems kind of young."

"I probably shouldn't tell you, but Milten said J.D. had gotten her pregnant."

Debra gasped and held her hand over her mouth. "He *had* to marry her?"

"It wasn't a shotgun wedding, if that's what you mean. I guess they were planning to get married, but this just bumped things up a bit. Unfortunately, she miscarried in the third trimester."

"Oh, no. That's awful."

"According to Milten, being the gallant gentleman he was, Joshua still wanted to go through with the wedding, but she up and left him for another guy."

Looking down at Michelle with Robert, Debra was almost afraid to ask. "Do you know who she ran off with?"

"J.D. doesn't like to talk about it and I've never asked. I didn't meet Milten until college. The three of them have kind of an unwritten pact. They stick together and keep each other's secrets."

"Do you think she's why he's never married? I mean, do you think he's still in love with her?"

"Could be. As long as I've known him, he's never even been serious with anyone. Many have tried," she added. "But I think it's going to take someone pretty special to get inside his heart. Know anyone, Debra?" Her voice was laced with honey.

"What do you mean? Why would I know someone?"

"Come on, girl. I saw you two yesterday. You make the perfect couple."

"We're just friends, Jasmine. We've known each other since we were kids. If anything, he sees me like a sister."

Incredulous laughter sounded in her ear. "You believe what you want, but I know my J.D. well enough to know that he's been bitten by the love bug. Now you just have to figure out how to cure what ails him."

An unsettling wave of nausea made Debra's stomach pitch. She swallowed and closed her eyes, knowing it was her own ailments that were a bigger hurdle to clear. "It would never work," she heard herself say.

"Girl, love has a way of making things work. You just listen to your heart and the rest will fall together. Hey, I have to go. The doctors are here. I just thought I'd touch base this morning. I talked to Robert and apprised him of the situation. You'll be on your own for several days. If you have any problems, ask him or give me a call."

Debra hung up, and for a moment, she just sat there on the couch, staring at Joshua's picture, wondering . . . fantasizing. *Listen to her heart,* Jasmine had said, but how could she when her head butted in and reminded her of the kind of life Joshua led. Up at dawn doing chores, working fourteen-hour days and sometimes till the early morning hours, only to get up and do it all over again, day in and day out. In short, Joshua was working himself into the ground . . . *just like Daddy.*

As she went to close the yearbook, several newspaper clippings flitted to the floor. She scooped them together and started shuffling them back in order. They were mostly candid shots of Milten playing football in high school, in college, and then for the Kansas City Chiefs. A headline from his high school days drew her attention as she smoothed out another clipping. *Tragedy Dampens State Football Playoffs.*

Milten's team, the Academy Falcons, were playing the Washington Trojans in the championship game. Debra went on to read how one of the Trojans had been injured in the final play of the game, knocking him unconscious. No names were mentioned, but it said the boy had suffered a severe concussion and a broken leg. He even had to be life-flighted off the field.

She remembered what Joshua had told her about Hank Zitler and her heart skipped a beat. Was Hank the boy in this article? She read further, hoping to find out more, but no names were listed. Maybe Joshua could fill her in.

Hoping to clear her head—and her heart—she set the books aside, grabbed her purse, and headed outside into the fresh Colorado morning. Puffy white clouds drifted over the top of Pikes Peak across a sea of endless blue sky. Squirrels scurried up and down telephone poles, precariously skittering across the high wire to another pole. Birds were singing in a synchronized melody as they flitted from one evergreen tree to another.

She breathed deeply, trying to stay positive about her new lease on life. So the landscape was filled with tract houses, occasionally alternating paint schemes to break up the monotony. So the yards were only twenty feet by twenty feet with one lone tree planted in the middle of grass that had to be watered twice a day just to stay green. And so the dogs had to be on a leash or remain in a kennel because of city ordinances. She could get used to the suburban life. Millions of people lived that way every day. Why not her?

She strolled up the hill and approached the massive double doors of the Rockrimmon Church of Christ. As she entered the lobby, beautiful angled designs and stained-glassed windows filled her with a spiritual warmth. She was immediately filled with a sense of welcoming peace. Several greeters stood in the doorway of the sanctuary. She studied each one and spotted a tall brunette with a French braid hanging down to her waist. Debra knew in a heartbeat that this was Joshua's sister. Other than the fact that the other woman didn't have black hair, Debra felt like she was looking into a mirror. The woman stood with two small children tugging on her long, blue denim skirt. Debra smiled. She definitely liked Heather's taste in clothes.

"Good morning, I'm Heather Thomas." She held out her hand in greeting.

"Hi, I'm Debra Walker."

Her eyes lit up. "Ah, you're the one J.D. told me about."

Debra nervously smoothed her palms over her skirt. "I hate it when people say that."

"Don't worry. I've never heard him talk about anyone like he does you, and I can see why. You're very pretty. He tells me you've recently lost your father?"

Debra twisted her purse in her hands. "Yes. About two and a half months ago."

"I'm sorry. I know you're new to the area, so if you ever need a friend—" Her little girl grabbed onto her arm and Heather spoke with a laugh. "Or if you'd just like to babysit, give me a call. This little monkey is Katie."

"Hi, Katie." Debra smiled and saw the little boy hiding behind Heather's skirt. "And this must be Kyle. Joshua told me a little about him." She squatted down to his eye level. "Hi, I'm Debra. I'm a friend of your uncle Joshua."

Kyle buried his face into his mother's skirt, cupping his hands over his ears. Debra stood and gave an apologetic smile. "I'm sorry. Did I scare him?"

"No, he's just wary around strangers. After he gets to know you, he'll open up more."

"Well, I'd better find a seat. Does it matter where I sit?"

"Not at all. I'd love to chat more after the service if you have time."

"I'd like that. I'll look for you then." Debra sat toward the back on the end of a pew and immediately bowed her head, lifting up a prayer for Milten and Jasmine. She also sent one up for Joshua's little cousin and, lastly, one to her father, apologizing over and over for letting him down.

The congregation stood and she pulled out a hymnal. Her heart wasn't into singing this morning so she found herself just listening to everyone else around her.

A man nudged in beside her and whispered, "Is this seat taken?" A familiar, sexy baritone drifted into her ears. The same intoxicating cologne she'd dabbed on her neck Friday night surrounded her in a cloud of heavenly bliss.

Her feet seemed velcroed to the carpet and she couldn't even move. She slowly lifted her gaze up his black western-cut trousers, which narrowed at his firm, trim waistline. Her gaze skimmed over a maroon chambray shirt and a black leather vest before she finally met his dreamy Hershey-brown gaze.

His muscular arm wrapped around her lower back, his sides pressing full length against hers. Pressing his lips next to her ear, he spoke in a husky murmur. "Are you going to move over or do I have to go clear down front and sit in front of the preacher?"

With his soft whiskers tickling her neck and his warm breath fanning her face, she covered her mouth, stifling a giggle, and scooted over. "Sorry about that. Is that better?"

He moved inside the pew, slid his arm around her waist and tugged her back by his side. "Now it is." He slipped her a little wink then pulled her hymnbook between them.

She couldn't speak, much less squeak out a note, as his low baritone drifted melodiously into her ear. *Oh, boy.* Keeping her distance from this man was going to be like keeping a baby calf from its mama.

She leaned close and asked, "Why aren't you in the choir?"

He just smiled and kept singing. After they sat down, their shoulders and legs brushed against each other. She wiped her trembly hands on her jean skirt, hoping she made it through this service without fainting. She'd fainted once in church when she'd made her First Communion. Knocked a candle over and about set her hair on fire.

The pastor asked for special prayer requests, and someone stood, asking that everyone pray for Milten and Jasmine King. She and Joshua exchanged a sad smile, each putting in a silent prayer for both of the Kings. Heather stood and added Dillan McNeil's name to the list. She asked that everyone pray for a quick recovery and that his heart would adjust to the new medication.

Joshua bowed his head and closed his eyes, his compassion for his little cousin evident in his strained emotions. Without hesitation, she slid her hand under his elbow, interlacing her fingers with his. Keeping his eyes closed, he squeezed her hand, slowly letting out what sounded like an agonizing breath.

He didn't let go of her hand the rest of the service.

She just hoped nobody quizzed her on today's sermon.

CHAPTER ELEVEN

Never had Joshua been so inspired during a church service before. But since he couldn't even remember the sermon, he wondered if his spiritual inspiration had more to do with this gorgeous angel sitting beside him than the holy setting.

Debra was breathtakingly beautiful with her thick, ebony hair glistening down her back. She had it pulled back with a gold clip, wisps of hair framing her perfect oval face. Unlike her first day of work, she only wore a touch of mascara on her long curling lashes. Her tanned complexion and rosy cheeks were the only color she needed to bring out her natural beauty.

When the congregation started singing the closing hymn, he found himself lowering his voice as she harmonized with the melody. He could never figure out how to do that, but she took his breath away. If the choir director ever got wind of her, she'd be asked to sing at every wedding and special event.

It'd been a long time since Joshua had been to church. He only attended this morning because he'd known Debra was going to be here. After his father was killed, he'd felt unworthy, undeserving of any kind of love and forgiveness. It was only once he'd started dating Michelle several years later that he'd allowed anyone to get inside his heart. And even then, he'd never talked to her about his father. But now, surrounded by his friends and family, all praying for Dillan and Milt, he suddenly realized he wasn't alone. The weight on his shoulders somehow seemed lighter.

After the song ended, he escorted Debra to the nave of the church, where Heather and her two little cohorts were huddled together with his mom and stepfather. As he looked at Heather's long brunette hair hanging down her back and listened to her easy laughter drifting across the church lobby, he couldn't get over how much alike she and Debra were, not just their looks, but their passion for horses and dreams of family and children.

"I met your sister," Debra whispered. "She's very nice. I told her I'd talk with her, maybe get registered."

"Sounds good." Hoping to spend more time with her, he asked, "What have you got planned the rest of the day?"

"I told my mom I'd come home for a visit. It's her birthday tomorrow."

"She's in Denver, right?" He rubbed his jaw, still worried about Debra driving. "I'm headed up to Camp Forester this afternoon. They're located about twenty miles east of Castle Rock. We could stop by there for about an hour, then swing up to Denver and pick up your mom. If you wouldn't mind Kyle tagging along, we could take her out for a nice birthday dinner."

"Sounds great. My mom loves kids, but what's Camp Forester?"

"It's a special camp for kids who have some kind of disability or a terminal illness. I usually take Dillan and Kyle up twice a month to give their parents a break and do a little volunteering. Dillan's been going since he was a toddler. He's still too weak for that kind of trip today, so I'm just taking Kyle. He loves it, but Heather can't get up there very often. So what do you think? Want to ride along?"

"Sure. I'd love to. It'll be a nice surprise for my mom. I talked to her this week and told her that you bought Brandy. She asked if chocolate chip was still your favorite cookie."

He gave an easy chuckle and squeezed her hand, happy to

see her smile brighten. "My folks are here. Want to meet them?"

"Sure, that'd be nice. I'd like to thank them for letting me stay in their home Friday night."

He led her across the marble floor of the lobby and directed his attention to his parents. "Mom, Brad? I'd like you to meet Debra Walker. Debra, this is my mom, Kara, and my stepfather, Brad Dalton."

Debra held out her hand. "Nice to meet you, Mr. and Mrs. Dalton."

"Please, call me Kara. As far back as our families go, I feel like we're old friends. Joshua told us about your father. Do you know I still remember how Dave used to talk about the Lazy W Ranch? He sure thought a lot of your dad."

"My dad liked doing business with him, too. I always looked forward to the Garrisons' visits. They'd usually surprise me with a new horse pick or an old set of spurs."

"Have you found a place to stay?" Brad asked. "I've got several contacts in town if you need help."

"Thank you, but I'm already settled in with Jasmine King. Joshua's been more than kind in helping me out. He's the epitome of big brothers." The way she kept referring to him as a brother made Joshua wonder if that's all she felt for him.

His mother touched his arm. "Shelly Whipstock called last night. She said she hasn't received your RSVP for the reunion. I told her you'll let her know this week."

He'd received two notices in the mail and hadn't even opened them. He shook his head. "Tell her I'm not going."

"Not going? You were the president of the class, for goodness' sake. Shelly said they were even having a silent auction for the Kings. You have to go."

"I'm already scheduled to go up to Boulder for a sale."

"Maybe Jared can do the sale," his mother suggested.

"I said I'm not going, so you can tell Shelly Belly to quit

bugging you."

Mom gave her typical disapproving shake of her head. "Now that's the Joshua I know." Touching Debra's arm, she added, "It was nice meeting you. We'd love to have you out for supper some night."

"Sure. That'd be great," she answered, but her eyes betrayed her smile. He knew she had absolutely no intention of going back out to his ranch any time soon. Would she ever be ready?

With his mood suddenly spiraling downward, he motioned to a few people standing near the door. "Come here. I'd like you to meet an old friend of mine."

Still irritated that his mother had even brought up the reunion, Joshua guided Debra over to an old high school buddy, Glen Frost, now a captain in the U.S. Air Force. He and Glen had spent many a long night together all through high school and college, either on double dates or just hanging out at the Pizza Palace. Besides Milt, Glen had always been the one friend he could trust.

Two young women stood beside him, their giggles echoing in the church lobby. His military haircut and Air Force blues only increased Glen's inherent ability to lure women. With a friendly slap on the shoulder, Joshua grinned. "Hey, Iceman. Trying to impress the ladies with that getup?"

"Hey, J.D." He gripped Joshua's hand in greeting. "It's been a long time, buddy." The two girls giggled and tiptoed out the front door of the church.

"So, what brings you back to the Springs?" Joshua asked. "I thought you were stationed out east somewhere?"

"I got transferred to Peterson Air Force Base. How about you? Still breaking your back out at that ranch of yours?"

Debra's spine straightened under his touch. Hoping to steer clear of any discussion about his ranch, he diverted the conversation. "Glen, I'd like you to meet a friend of mine. This is Debra Walker. Debra this is Glen Frost. He's a pilot for the Air Force."

Debra's eyes widened, and she was clearly impressed, as were most women who met Glen. She took his outstretched hand. "I've never met a real pilot before. I can't tell you how much I appreciate all you guys do for our country."

Glen leaned close to Debra and turned on his charm. "So how'd a sweet thing like you get hooked up with this ugly mug?"

She spoke with a shy laugh. "Believe it or not I knew him when all he had was a little peach fuzz on his upper lip. He was all skin and bones and had hair down to his shoulders."

Glen gave a friendly punch to Joshua's gut. "And you've kept this pretty lady a secret all these years?"

"We lost touch after my dad died. I met up with her last weekend at a sale. Bought her horse," he added with a grin.

"Maybe I oughta check out some of these auctions. You wouldn't mind boarding a horse for me if I found me a good, uh . . . brood mare, now would you?"

"Glen, you wouldn't know a good brood mare if it bit you in the . . . hind end."

"No, but I can spot me a good owner a mile away. It's all in the eyes."

Joshua gazed directly into Debra's eyes. "You got that right, brother." A pink glow colored her cheeks, making her outshine the stained-glass windows. When she gave a shy smile, her straight white teeth almost sparkled in the morning sunlight. Remembering how perfect her lips felt against his, he could only imagine running the tip of his tongue over those ivory surfaces, showing her just how much more perfect a kiss could be.

"I got a notice about the reunion," Glen commented. Another topic Joshua had hoped to avoid. "You going this year?"

"Nope. Got a sale that weekend. Already got four colts listed in the catalogue."

"Get Jared to do the sale. The whole team's coming back."

Along with Michelle, Joshua wanted to add. "Sorry, Glen," he said through gritted teeth. "Not this year."

"How's it going to look when the class president doesn't even show up for the reunions, especially when he lives in the same hometown? Not cool. We could rent out a limo and double date like old times. What do you say?" He turned on his charismatic smile and wrapped his arm around Debra's shoulder. "Think you could twist J.D.'s arm into treating you to a real Cinderella evening?"

Debra clutched her cross necklace and warily looked up at Joshua.

He tugged her closer to his side. "I didn't come over to discuss reunions. Did you hear Milt's back in the hospital?"

Glen's expression immediately turned to one of concern. "No. What happened?"

"Not sure. Doctors are still running tests. The good news is he's starting to get back some of his memory. He recognizes me now and even asked about you."

"That's great. Maybe I'll stop over there this afternoon."

"He's in the Medical ICU and only family members are allowed to see him. Jasmine would probably love the company though." He slid his hands into the pocket of his trousers, the paper he'd found at Milt's crinkling under his fingertips.

Heather walked up behind them. "Hey, Glen. You're looking good as ever. It's been a while since I've seen you."

"How's it going, Heather? Kyle sure is getting big."

"Don't I know it. I think he's taking after his uncles." Looking at Debra, she said, "When you get a minute, would you like to fill out a registration card?"

"Sure. I can do it right now if you want," Debra said, then turned toward Glen. "It was nice meeting you. I haven't met

Milten yet, but I'm starting to understand why you three were known as the Three Musketeers."

As the ladies hurried off, Glen motioned his head toward Heather. "I hear your sister's having trouble. Her husband still gone?"

"Afraid so. She's had it pretty rough."

"Think she'd ever consider dating again?"

Joshua rubbed his brows, watching his sister talk to Debra. "She's vulnerable right now, Glen. Don't go messing with her heart unless you're serious."

"I've known her all my life, J.D. She's practically my little sister."

Knowing Glen's feelings for Heather were anything but brotherly, Joshua cringed. A jolt in his own heart made him realize his feelings for Debra ran deeper than he'd allowed himself to believe.

Glen shook his head. "You know I would never intentionally hurt her. I just thought maybe she'd like to see a movie with me or go out to dinner sometime."

Joshua gave his good friend a smile. "I'm sure she'd love it, but you mess with her heart, or anything else for that matter, and you mess with me. Understand?"

"Loud and clear."

Turning his back on the ladies, Joshua fiddled with the note in his pocket. "I wanted to talk to you more about Milt, but I didn't want Debra to hear."

"What's up? Sounds serious."

Joshua lowered his voice. "I stopped over to see him this week before he got sick. He was worried about Jasmine and wants her to quit Walson." He showed Glen the paper he'd found on Milt's clipboard.

"Looks like it says 'don't hurt Jazzy.' What's this all about?"

"No clue. I got in to see Milt last night but he was on the

ventilator and was pretty doped up. He tried to tell me something but the nurse caught me and kicked me out. I guess we'll just have to wait till he gets stronger before we get any answers. You ever thought anymore about the night of his accident?"

"Every time I visit my mom."

"What do you mean?"

"Remember? I had Milt drop me off at my mom's because I'd had too much to drink. Maybe if I'd stayed with him, he never would have encountered the deer. You know what they say, timing is everything."

Joshua shook his head. "Guess I'm not the only one with the case of the guilts."

"What have you got to feel guilty about?"

"I'm the one who asked him to do the appearance at the rodeo that night."

Glen clapped Joshua on the shoulder. "Come on, J.D. Neither of us had any control over what happened that night. The deer population is out of control. Hundreds of people every day have some kind of a mishap with a deer or some other kind of animal on the roadway. Milt just didn't have any room to swerve. As far as that note goes, it could be nothing. Why don't you wait until Milt is feeling better and ask him about it." Motioning his head toward Debra, he added, "She's a nice lady. Not like any of the women I've seen you date before. Bring her to the reunion. You can't let what happened between you and Michelle ruin the rest of your life. It's time to move on."

"My not going to the reunion has nothing to do with Michelle. I told you, I've got a sale."

"You're talking to the Iceman, remember? You can't snow me. Don't blow it and lose this one, too."

"It's not like that, Glen. Debra and I are just friends."

"Friends, huh? It's not what it looked like to me." Glen

headed toward the door and spoke over his shoulder. "If I didn't know any better, I'd say you were whipped. See you later, buddy."

Joshua stared over at Debra and smoothed his hair behind his ear. *Whipped?* No way. He had everything under control.

He strode up behind her. Katie was on her lap, touching her suntanned face, stroking her hair behind her ears. Kyle hid behind Heather, peeking through his fingers. Debra giggled, trying to get Kyle to laugh. Joshua's heart swelled bigger than his chest. He could see how much she loved children, and they obviously adored her. Without a doubt, she'd make a good mother someday.

He squatted next to Debra and tweaked Katie's cheek. "Hi, puddin'. Did you meet my friend?"

"Oh, yes, Uncle Josh. She's so pretty."

He chuckled and slid his hand over Debra's knee, squeezing gently. "She sure is." He loved how Debra's face reddened whenever she received a compliment. He ruffled Kyle's hair. "What's the matter, pardner? Aren't you going to say hi to Debra?" He growled playfully, edging toward him. Kyle giggled and ran toward the doors. Joshua easily caught him, swinging him in the air and tickling him. Kyle screamed in a fit of laughter.

Katie jumped off Debra's lap and ran over to him. "Do that to me, Uncle Josh!"

He deposited a dizzy little boy on the marble floor and swung Katie in the air, tossing her high then catching her. Her high-pitched squeals were mixed with Heather's nervous cry. "J.D.! Not so high!"

He laughed and tickled Katie before setting her down. He met Debra's wide smile and sparkling brown eyes. "Are you next?" he asked, stalking toward her.

She backed up, grabbing Heather. "He wouldn't, would he?"

"I wouldn't put it past him. He threw me in the creek behind our house on my sixteenth birthday. All my friends were there. I've never been so embarrassed in my life."

Debra gave him a wry grin. "You wouldn't want me to divulge a little secret to Heather, now would you, Joshua? Remember the time when you and I went out to the creek behind our barn?"

Joshua narrowed his eyes, not sure what she was talking about. The only thing he remembered was the one time they'd gone fishing and he'd slipped down the bank right into a muddy thicket of thorn bushes.

His face reddened and he started to laugh.

Heather shoved a hand on her waist. "What secret?"

Joshua held up his palms in retreat. He'd had to strip clear down to his skivvies because he'd gotten stuck in the mud and the thorns tangled in his jeans. Remembering the look in his father's eyes, when he'd run up to the truck, still made him shrink in his boots. "Okay, truce," he said with a laugh. He bent over and grabbed Kyle's hand. "Come on, pardner. Let's go visit Camp Forester."

Debra felt like she was floating on a cloud the rest of the day. They drove up to Camp Forester, where Joshua filled in as a tour guide and helped lead the children on a trail ride. Her heart overflowed with joy whenever she saw Joshua with the children, telling them jokes, teaching them how to hold a lasso, or just letting them sit on his lap while they told him about some of their problems at home or at school. They even shared their peanut butter and jelly sandwich picnic afterward.

The counselors had asked her to lead an art project where they'd constructed animal habitats out of shoeboxes. It was the most wonderful experience, seeing their eyes light up with excitement as they rode horses and participated in the arts and crafts. Some of the kids were autistic like Kyle, some had Downs syndrome, and others were undergoing treatment for various forms of cancer.

Before they left, they were both hugged by everyone. Joshua even got a thank-you card from one of his younger female admirers. His eyes misted over and he admitted later that every time he visited, he wished there was more he could do for them.

They'd picked up her mom and had all gone out to a steak-house for her birthday. They spent the evening reminiscing about old times, reminding Debra that her memories of their ranch hadn't been all bad. In fact, things had been fairly happy, up until her father had injured his back . . . the day she took over the ranch operations.

It was after ten before they'd dropped a sleepy six-year-old Kyle off at Heather's. They still had to drive clear up to Woodland Park and get Debra's SUV that she'd left parked at the rodeo grounds Friday night.

As they headed up Pikes Peak Highway, a soft country ballad played on the radio. Leaning against the headrest, she lolled her head to the side, staring dreamily at Joshua's chiseled profile. "I really enjoyed meeting your parents and your sister today. Kyle and Katie are crazy about you, and the way all those children clung to you all afternoon, I can't believe you haven't married and started your own family."

He shook his head and gave a little grunt, then stared out the window, but he didn't say anything.

She sat up and cocked her head to the side. "What was that little sound?"

"Nothing. You wouldn't understand."

She arched her brows. "Understand what? You look upset. What's wrong?"

Even in the darkened cab, she could see the muscles at the base of his neck twitch. She wondered if she should just keep quiet, but something was obviously bothering him. With the fold-down center console separating them on the bench seat, she reached across and touched his forearm. "Joshua? What is it?"

He blew out a loud gust of air, still staring out the window. "I don't know. It's the whole marriage and family thing."

She shook her head, confused. "You're right. I don't understand. Can you elaborate?"

"I wish I could, but it's hard to explain. It's hard for *me* to understand sometimes." He turned and met her gaze. "To be honest, I don't think I'll ever be able to venture down the marriage path, Debra. There are too many risks."

"Risks?" she repeated. "Is this about the woman you almost married? Are you afraid you'll get hurt again?"

He whipped off his hat and tossed it on the dash of his truck, then raked his fingers through his hair where a crease from his hat remained. "I guess a part of me is afraid that could happen."

She gave a heavy swallow. "Do you still love her?"

He didn't answer right away, his eyes narrowing as if taking her question to heart.

"I'll always love what we had together," he finally admitted. "She was there for me during a difficult time in my life. Looking back though, we were never ready for marriage. We were too young and wanted different things in life."

"So, you're waiting till the right one comes along who shares your hopes and dreams. Isn't that what everybody wants?"

"I don't know. It's more than just marrying the right woman, though."

"What is it then? I don't want to pressure you, but can you help me understand?"

He adjusted an air vent, allowing the cool air to blow directly onto his face. "Take Heather, for instance. Do you know how hard it is on her, raising two kids alone, and one of them is autistic? I mean, Jared and I help out whenever we can, but she's pretty much the sole caregiver for Kyle and Katie."

"Heather's a strong woman. She's doing a remarkable job with her kids and she seems pretty happy."

"Yeah, it's amazing isn't it? Her husband treats her like crap and she still figures out a way to find a smile."

"I guess I'm not following. What does your not marrying have to do with Heather? You'd never leave your wife and kids."

"You got that right," he grumbled. "I guess I just get kind of frustrated after visiting all those kids every month."

"You sure looked like you had a good time to me."

"Don't get me wrong," he said, looking in his rearview mirror then over at her. "I'm not frustrated at having to visit those kids. I love going up there and spending time with them. It's just that whenever I see what some of them have to live through, it tears my gut up. Then I think about Dillan and all the crap he has to go through on a daily basis. I don't ever want my child to go through what those kids are experiencing."

He stared out the window, his voice filling with frustration. "And then I see what's happened to Milt and how his and Jasmine's lives will never be the same. I don't ever want to be that kind of a burden on anyone." He turned and looked her square in the eyes. "Especially my wife."

As he held her gaze, she swallowed heavily, not sure how she should respond to that. When he looked back toward the road, she had to give herself a mental shake to remember what they were even discussing. "Jasmine doesn't see her husband as a burden, Joshua. If anything, this tragedy has brought them closer together. That's the beauty of a good relationship. When one is hurting and sick, the other is there to console and make him feel better. You can't be afraid of what might or might not happen a year or fifteen years down the road."

"But that's what I have to think about. I lost my dad when I was only thirteen. In fifteen years, I could have a teenage son. Do you know how hard it was growing up without a father?" He looked through the front windshield, his jaw muscles twitching as he swerved around a car to pass. "We were lucky. My mom eventually ended up marrying a great guy. Unfortunately, Brad hadn't been so lucky."

"Did something happen to Brad?"

"He lost his father before he was born. His mom remarried a guy who turned out to be a drunk. Used him and his brother as punching bags. It got so bad, his brother turned to drugs and did some pretty mean shit, almost landing in prison. Brad got caught up in the middle of it all and was sent to some kind of a work farm that taught him about horses, life skills, and more importantly, respect. It probably saved his life."

"I had no idea."

His fingers clenched the steering wheel, his knuckles whitening. "And what about Kyle's autism and Dillan's congenital heart defect? What if I have some kind of a genetic disorder that I could pass on to my kids?"

"I understand your concerns about children. My great uncle had Parkinson's before he died. But I can't *not* have kids because of what they *might* inherit. If you're worried about passing on some kind of a genetic defect, have your DNA tested. Science has come a long way in the past ten years."

He shook his head. "It's more than genetics. Can science guarantee *I* won't be killed, leaving a widow and kids for her to raise alone? Or worse, to marry someone who'll beat the crap out of them?" He looked her straight in the eye. "I'll answer that for you. No, it can't."

She pulled her head back and crossed her arms over her chest. "Sheesh. You have got to be the most pessimistic man I've ever met. Is this how you're going to live the rest of your life? Worrying about what *might* happen in the next ten minutes? Tomorrow? Next year? Lord, talk about a miserable existence. How do you walk out your front door in the morning?"

He groaned and rubbed his eyes. "How did we get on this subject anyway?"

"I'm sorry if I'm broaching a sensitive topic, but no one is guaranteed a perfect life. You're not alone and neither is Heather. You've got each other. You're both surrounded by family and people who care about you . . . and love you." A jolt in her own heart made her realize she'd already fallen into that last category. Not wanting him to know the depths of her feelings, she faced the front, straightening her jean skirt over her legs. "Other than my parents, I was usually alone. I didn't have any brothers or sisters to turn to. That's why it's so important that I have my own family someday."

She was surprised when he reached across the console and took hold of her hand. "I'm sorry, honey. I wish I could have been there for you."

"I know you do," she whispered, covering his work-roughened hand with hers. "That's what makes you so sweet. The way you reach out to people and help them, I can't imagine you living the rest of your days all by yourself. Half the joy of having a place like yours is to see it develop over the next several generations. Don't become an old codger and end up hoarding your land with no one to share it with."

He cocked his head to the side giving her a wry grin. "Like Mr. Boyle?"

"Exactly. From the little I've seen of your ranch, you've got a beautiful place. Don't let your fears of marrying and bringing children into this world paralyze your dreams."

"Wow." He gave a low chuckle, giving her hand a gentle squeeze. "As much as I've heard you run yourself into the ground about your father and your ranch, it's too bad you can't focus some of this positive energy on your own life."

"Believe it or not, I am staying positive. I've put my past behind me and am trying to move on. I failed miserably as a rancher, but I'm not going to let that keep me from reaching other dreams. And I don't think you should live your life by what might or what might not happen in fifteen years. Find someone who shares your love of ranching and can work alongside you and help you achieve your goals. That's the one thing my dad had going against him, Mom never really supported him, and it finally tore them apart."

He leaned his elbow on the center console and brought their hands up so they were between them. "So you think I'm wrong about marriage, huh?" He glanced quickly at the road, then looked her square in the eye. "I don't suppose you know anyone who wants to get married and who loves ranching as much as I do? You know, someone who doesn't mind a little dirt on her jeans or the long hours and hard work."

Her mouth gaped open, but she couldn't make a sound come out now if her life depended on it. She knew he had feelings for her, but was he seriously talking to her about marriage? She gulped, not sure what to say. Besides, as successful as he already was, she'd hate to be the cause of any bad luck that might keep him from reaching all of his dreams.

As if sensing her hesitation, he let go of her hand, then touched her chin, closing her mouth. "Don't worry, Debra. I was just kidding. Can't blame a guy for asking, though."

She gasped when he whipped his truck across the other side of the highway and slid to a stop on the graveled shoulder, facing oncoming traffic. She grabbed the dash and pushed up, looking out the window just as he lifted the gearshift into park. Although not in any danger of hitting a car, it was still unnerving to be sitting so close to the side of the cliff. "What's wrong?" she asked. "Why are we stopping?"

"This is where the police found Milt the night of his accident. Over there on those rocks." The truck's headlights illuminated a rocky crevice several yards down an embankment, descending into a steep ravine. Wanting to get a better view, Debra unfastened her seatbelt, flipped up the middle console, then scooted across the bench seat.

Gripping the steering wheel with one hand, she braced her hand on Joshua's shoulder with the other, and peered down the side of the cliff where a flat rock jutted from the base. "Oh, my gosh. And he survived?"

"Amazing, isn't it? He doesn't remember a thing."

"Hank said they found him in a grove of bushes." She looked farther up the side of the slope, several yards from where the police had found him. "Probably that grove of shrubbery up there."

Joshua's dark brows furrowed. "News to me. I came upon the accident an hour after it happened. He was lying out in the open on that flat rock. Where did Hank get the idea that he landed in some bushes? There weren't any eyewitnesses. The police got an anonymous call that said there was a Jeep in the ditch." He looked back at her and narrowed his gaze. "What else did Hank have to say?"

She looked down at the rocks Joshua had pointed out, trying to remember. "That's pretty much it. Said Milt was thrown from his Jeep and landed among some bushes. What were you all doing up here in the first place?"

"There was rodeo that night. Milt and Jasmine had flown in from Kansas City to do a celebrity appearance and autograph signing to raise money for Dillan. He even competed in the team roping event. We all stayed for the dance afterwards, but he'd gone home early to be with Jasmine. She had the flu."

He scratched his jaw, looking down the side of the cliff. "Hank had been drinking that night. Even got into a fight. I know because Milt, Glen, and I were the ones who broke it up. I made sure Nadine had the keys, but now I'm wondering . . ."

A shudder raced down her spine. Hair lifted on her arms. "You're giving me the willies," she said, rubbing her hands over her skin. "Do you think Hank ran Milt off the road?"

Joshua scratched the back of his head. "I don't know. A few years back he had his license suspended because of a DUI. Maybe I'm trying to make something out of nothing. With this latest setback, I've been thinking a lot about his accident. I'm hoping now that his memory is starting to return, and he'll be able to tell us more about that night."

Still a little uneasy, Debra gave Joshua's shoulder a reassuring squeeze. "I guess all that matters now is that Milt's alive. Let's just pray he gets better and comes home soon."

Joshua turned and met Debra's gaze, the muscles in his shoulders bunching under her touch. They sat so close she could smell the chocolate mint he'd eaten after dinner, feel the warmth of his breath fan her face. Incredible. No matter how hard she tried to convince herself they could never be together, she had absolutely no control over the hormones and sensual feelings that this man stirred deep inside her body. Right now, it was her breasts that had become annoyingly hardened at the tips.

His gaze lowered to her lips and for a moment she thought he was going to lean over and kiss her. "I suppose we'd better get you home," he said, his voice sounding low and husky as he brought his gaze back up to her eyes.

She licked her lips, giving a slow nod. "Yeah, it's getting late. I'm pretty tired." She resituated, staying in the middle of the bench seat, acutely aware of the heat radiating between them as their legs brushed against each other.

His lips twitched, as if trying to keep from smiling as he re-entered the highway. Reaching over her legs, he turned up the radio that was playing one of her favorite Toby Keith songs,

"You Shouldn't Kiss Me Like That." Still reeling from Joshua's kisses this weekend, she wondered if he knew just how much those words hit home.

She knew she should move back to the passenger side, but for the life of her, she couldn't seem to make herself move away. She'd always envied the girls snuggling up to their boyfriends in their cars. It was nice, she decided with a smile.

Gazing out at the magnificent chiseled rock jutting perpendicular to the highway, Debra let out a wistful sigh. This had always been one of her favorite scenic drives as a little girl. The way the road was carved through the middle of the mountain made for an amazing sight, as pines and aspens grew straight out of the rock.

They pulled into the rodeo grounds, and she couldn't help but shiver when she glanced toward the livestock barn. "Just drop me off so I can get the heck out of here. There's probably a bull or a steer lurking behind some door ready to charge me."

He shoved out his door and turned to offer his hand. Hooking the strap of her purse over her shoulder, she let him pull her across the seat till her feet swung down to the running board. When she stood, he wrapped his hands around her waist, slowly letting her slide down his front. Her feet finally touched the ground . . . maybe. The way her head was floating, she thought she'd landed on the moon.

"Easy now. Don't want you hurting yourself again."

She braced her hands on his shoulders and blinked, trying not to let her gaze slip to his lips. *Too late.* There they were, full and shiny with just a whisper's length of his soft mustache curling over his top lip. With his hands still wrapped around her middle, he gently tugged her closer till the sensitive tips of her breasts pressed snugly against his chest. His breathing turned heavier as his gaze lowered to her lips.

Oh, no, she couldn't let him kiss her. Just one more kiss would send her heart clear over the brink for sure. And now that she knew his feelings about marriage and family, there was no way they could have a future together. She fluttered her lashes down and lowered her head just as his lips landed smack in the middle of her forehead.

But he didn't back away, instead his lips remained sealed to her forehead, his warm breath fanning the top of her head. The wetness of his mouth on her skin seeped clear to her soul. It took all her power not to raise up on her toes and let those luscious lips caress hers the way he'd done during the storm Friday night.

Why not? she asked herself. Why not be like all his other girlfriends and be promiscuous, tossing her morals and everything her mother had taught her out the window? Her heart nearly jumped out of her chest when she thought about making love to this man. If the mere act of kissing him sent her into oblivion, they'd probably have to call in the paramedics if they ever did have sex.

Sex. Who was she kidding? Even *thinking* the word made her blush from her head down to her toes. She looked over her shoulder as if someone were near who could hear her thoughts. And there was someone there, maybe not in person, but in her conscience. The loud resounding voice that reminded her that she could never give herself to Joshua, or to any man, unless she knew he was prepared to marry her. And from listening to Joshua this afternoon, that didn't sound too promising.

With wobbly knees, she stepped back and looked down at her purse, avoiding his gaze. "Guess I'd better get going."

"Are you sure you're okay to drive?"

"Positive. You've done your big brother part. It's time I got back on my own two feet. Thanks for everything this weekend."

He opened the door to her SUV and took her elbow, helping her ease down into the driver's seat. As she fastened the seat-

---

belt, he shut the door. Wondering when she'd see him again, she switched on the ignition and pressed the power window button, lowering the glass. "With Jasmine gone, I'll probably be working late most of the week."

"I'll be pretty busy myself. I've got several buyers stopping out over the next few days and I've got a sale on Friday. There's another rodeo Saturday if you're interested."

She looked down at her lap, avoiding his soulful brown eyes. "Probably not a good idea right now." Remembering Robert's invitation, she was almost relieved for the excuse. "Besides, I've got a thing I have to go to."

"A thing, huh?" he repeated, obviously not believing her.

She looked up and met his doubtful expression. "Really. Robert said his folks are getting back from Hawaii this week."

"You're going out on a date with Robbie?"

She shook her head. "Oh, no, it's not a date . . . exactly."

"Exactly what is it then?" His voice had turned abrupt.

"His folks are just throwing a little dinner party," she said, on the defensive. "They wanted me to come. I'm even taking my mom. I'd hardly call that a date."

He looked around, still shaking his head. "I'll be honest, Debra. I'm not thrilled with the idea that you work for the guy, but I sure as hell don't want you going out with him."

Alarmed at his sudden irritation, she narrowed her eyes. "Are you ever going to tell me what happened between you two?"

"There's not much to tell," he said, bracing a hand on the roof of her SUV, staring down at her. "He's the jerk who stole my fiancée. Anything else you want to know?"

With her suspicions confirmed, she suddenly understood the whole situation. He still held a grudge against Robert and had obviously never stopped loving Michelle. She looked up and narrowed her eyes. "I guess that explains why you get all fired up at the mere mention of Robert's name."

"What the hell does that mean?"

"This is exactly what I mean. Listen to yourself. You're ready to spit nails right now. But I'm telling you, Joshua, the Nelsons have been wonderful to me and my mother, helping us settle my father's estate and getting me this job. They've been nothing but gracious since my father's death."

"Oh, this is rich. Now they're heroes? Don't tell me Robert's snowed you, too."

She jutted her chin toward him and crossed her arms over her chest. "No one is snowing anyone. Robert has gone out of his way to show me around and get me started at Walson. I don't have a lot of corporate experience, and he's giving me a chance to prove myself. But the fact remains, Robert is my boss. If I do decide to go to this *thing* next weekend, it's only out of respect for his parents. After all they've done, the least I can do is to show up and say thanks. Now if you don't mind, I'm tired and I'm not in the mood for your big brother act right now."

A throbbing pain worked its way behind her eyes. She pressed her fingers to her temples and lowered her voice. "I'm sorry, Joshua. I don't want to argue with you. A lot of things have happened in the last three months and I feel like I need some time to get settled into a routine. Get my mind focused on where I'm going, and quit thinking about the past."

"And anything that reminds you of your past," he added with cynicism.

She quickly looked up. "It's not that I don't appreciate everything you've done for me, but maybe it would be best if you just backed off for a while and gave me some space."

"Space, huh?" It was his turn to blow out a loud gust of air. "Sure, you got it. I've got a lot of *things* going on in the next few weeks anyway." His voice took on a sudden chill, his eyes narrowing. "Will you be okay getting back to Jasmine's?"

"Yeah. My ribs feel pretty good tonight."

He nodded and shoved away from her door. "Okay, then. Be sure and lock your doors when you get home. You're in the city now. Can't be too careful."

"Joshua?" Why did her voice suddenly sound choked? "Take care of yourself."

"You too. Maybe I'll see you around."

Without another word he turned on his boot heel and strode back to the driver's side of his truck. He climbed behind the wheel and revved the engine, giving it extra gas. With a curt flick of his hand, he motioned for her to go first.

As she drove down Pikes Peak Highway, he stayed a car's length behind her. She took her exit off the highway and gave Joshua a wave, but he only gave her a brief nod before speeding past, the engine of his V10 Dodge roaring with power. As the taillights flickered out of sight, she was reminded of the day she'd seen him and his father leave their ranch with Golden Sunset.

She blinked back the sting of moisture, wondering how long before she'd see him or Branded Sunset again.

CHAPTER TWELVE

"Thanks for the help, Jared." Joshua swung down from his tractor and yanked off his leather work gloves. He and Jared had just picked up three hundred small square bales from one of his pastures. He'd spent a little extra money on an aboveground watering system, allowing him to grow the higher-quality alfalfa, instead of shipping it in by the semi-load like a lot of his neighbors. Temperatures soared into the upper eighties this Friday afternoon, the dry heat typical for late August in eastern Colorado.

It'd been almost three weeks since he'd dropped Debra off at the rodeo grounds, and his mood had slowly gone from bad to worse. His only release had been to work his ranch. He grabbed the water jug out of the cab of his truck and nodded at the acreage behind the steel barn. "Next week I'm cutting the back pasture near the ravine. I'll put that up with the large round baler so I won't need any help. That cutting combined with this load should last me through the winter."

"I'd stay and help you stack what we got today into the barn, but the Kendricks have a sick cow I gotta doctor." The Kendricks were the only neighbors bordering Joshua's land who were still ranching. Everyone else had either gone bankrupt or developed their land into a rural subdivided neighborhood. Jared had always had his eye on the Kendrick place, hoping to open his own equine clinic someday. Joshua thought that maybe down the road a ways, he and Jared could form some kind of a partnership, using each other's expertise.

Jared checked his watch. "It's three now. I might be able to come back after five."

Joshua leaned against the wagon, using the sleeve of his shirt to wipe his brow. "Don't worry about it. I'll get most of it done by then anyway." He took a long gulp of water, cold droplets trailing down his sweaty, grimy neck.

"What's the status on Milt?" Jared took the jug and held the spigot over his mouth.

"The doctors think he should be able to come home as early as next week, hopefully before Labor Day weekend. They don't want to rush it though, and risk another setback."

"They ever figure out what happened?"

"Said it was some kind of a virus." Although Joshua's gut instinct told him it was more than a virus. How much more, he didn't know. He'd asked Milt about the note he'd found at Jasmine's, but Milt said not to worry and that he'd gotten everything worked out. So what, exactly, did he work out and with whom?

Jared slapped his straw cowboy hat against his leg, banging off the dust. "Mom wanted me to ask if you'd changed your mind about going to your ten-year reunion next weekend."

"Nope." Joshua dropped the water jug on the tailgate of his truck. "I told her, I've got a sale."

"Listen, I'd be glad to do the sale for you—"

"What's the big friggin' deal about this reunion?" Joshua flipped on the switch to the old corn elevator, the loud rumbling noise cutting off anything else Jared had to say. Grabbing a bale of hay by the twine, Joshua slung it on the rickety old contraption. Rusted gears and chains worked together to roll bale after bale up to the rafters.

"Is this about Michelle?" Jared asked, yelling over the grinding mechanisms.

"My not going to the reunion has nothin' to do with Michelle," Joshua shouted, more out of anger than because of the noise. Why did everyone think he still had a thing for Michelle? Truth be told, he hadn't thought about that woman in years.

So why didn't he want to go to the reunion? How about disappointment for one? Disappointment in himself. His senior year of high school, he'd been voted most likely to succeed by the whole student body. Now here he was, ten years later, and he was exactly what Michelle had said he'd be. A lowly farm boy struggling to make his ranch a success. No wonder guys like Glen and Robert attracted women like mineral ore to a magnet. They were rich and successful. Even Jared owned his own vet clinic.

What did Joshua have? A few lousy horses and some dirt.

"You seen Debra lately?" Jared grabbed a bale of hay and slung it onto the elevator.

"Nope."

"Glen said he saw her with Robert three weeks back. Some big party at the Nelsons'."

Joshua gritted his teeth, remembering the picture he'd seen in the society pages of the *Colorado Springs Gazette*. It showed Debra with Robert, and they were both wearing swimsuits, sitting next to his pool. She was obviously smitten with the whole Nelson clan. The more he thought about Debra going out with Robert, the more aggressive he became as he hoisted bale after bale onto the rusty chains. Once again, it would seem the rich and glamorous life of the Nelsons was too much to resist.

Jared shoved away from the wagon and jammed his hand on his waist. "You just gonna let him waltz in and take her away from you, too?"

"She was never mine to take! I told you, she doesn't want anything to do with me or my ranch."

"That's bullshit and you know it! Dammit, J.D. Get your

211

head out of your ass and talk to her."

"What are you? A fucking shrink now?" His fists clenched tightly in his gloves.

Jared reached over and flipped off the switch, silencing the noisy contraption. He took a deep breath and lowered his voice, his chest heaving as he spoke. "Look, I know you've had a lot of shit dumped on you over the years, taking over this place and practically raising all of us, then losing Michelle and the baby. It's like you've completely shut everyone else out of your life ever since. The only time I've seen you enjoy this place is when you're out here with Dillan or Heather's kids. But you can't live that way, J.D. You need your own kids, your own family to share this with. That night at the rodeo, I watched you with Debra. You became the brother I used to admire. Don't run from this one. She's what you've been missing around here."

"You're one to talk. I don't see a ring on your finger."

"Only because the right one hasn't come along. I'd love to settle down and have a family. But it takes a lot of commitment, and right now, I'm just getting my vet clinic off the ground. Maybe someday I'll find that one special lady. You know, the one that when you look into her eyes, you can envision your own children. That's when I'll know I've found the right one." He gripped Joshua's shoulder. "Debra's just lost everything she's ever known. She's scared as hell it's going to happen again and she's running. But she's heading in the wrong direction. Make her trust you, J.D. Don't wait till she's gone."

Having heard enough, Joshua flipped the switch back on, creating the same loud ruckus. After throwing several more bales onto the elevator, he looked up just as Jared sped down the driveway, kicking up a cloud of dust as he spun onto the graveled road. Joshua flipped off the switch and leaned against the wagon, his chest heaving for air, but his heavy breathing had nothing to do with lifting the bales of hay.

He'd been going out of his mind these past weeks thinking about Debra. He'd worked from sunup to sundown, hoping to be so busy he wouldn't have time to think about her. But during everything he did, whether it was working with the horses or just cleaning out the stalls, he'd dreamed of what it would be like to have her working beside him day in and day out . . . sharing a bed with him every night.

He studied the corral of milling horses and found a particular buckskin mare with four white socks. How the hell was he supposed to get Debra to trust him, when he didn't even know how to believe in himself?

As it neared five o'clock on a Friday afternoon, Debra rubbed her brows, feeling like she'd been working for Walson Technology four years instead of just four weeks. Walson was in the last phase of negotiating the multimillion-dollar agreement with the Air Force, and they were supposed to decide next week before Labor Day who would be awarded the new contract.

She'd filled out all the purchase requisitions that would update their inventory to comply with their contract requirements, but with Robert so busy in negotiations, he hadn't given them back yet.

Three weeks had gone by since Milten's setback. Jasmine had been coming into the office during the afternoons, spending the mornings and evenings at the hospital. Most nights she didn't come home till after eleven, then she was out of the house by six the next morning. That was *if* she came home at all. The doctors had wanted to keep Milten in the hospital till they were sure the virus had worked its way through his system, preventing any further setbacks. If he continued to improve, he could be home as early as Monday.

Although thankful he was headed for a full recovery, Debra knew it was time for her to find another place. The Kings didn't need a stranger intruding on their lives. Tomorrow was Saturday. With luck, she'd find an apartment and be moved in by next week.

Exhausted, Debra leaned back in her chair and stared at a picture of herself and Brandy taken the previous spring. She pulled it off the wall and wistfully rubbed her thumb over Brandy's image, wondering how she was, if Joshua was taking good care of her. Of course, she knew without a doubt Brandy was being well cared for, which made her miss that big guy even more. She hadn't seen or heard anything out of him since he'd dropped her off at the rodeo grounds three weeks ago.

Against her druthers, she'd gone to the Nelsons' party with Robert, but had also taken her mother along. Mom and Martha Nelson had spent the entire evening together, reminiscing about their old college days. Debra hadn't seen her mother that happy in years.

Mom had had a prestigious upbringing, living the life of a rich debutante in an elite crowd in Denver. She'd married Clyde Walker and they'd made a name for themselves in their prominent social set. Debra was six when her great uncle Charles died from Parkinson's and left the ranch to her father. He'd sold his half of Walson and had moved them away from the city, away from everything her mother had ever known. It was good to see her laughing and mixing with her old social set again.

Debra, on the other hand, felt about as out of place as a saddle bronc at an English Pleasure competition. Taking Robert's advice, she'd gone shopping with Amanda Truman, the lady from accounting, and had even bought a new swimsuit, although Debra had drawn the line at buying a two-piece. As it was, the one-piece maillot dipped dangerously low between her breasts and was cut high up on her hips. When everyone had slipped into their suits, Debra had refused to remove the wrap sarong the rest of the evening.

Not that Robert hadn't tried. He'd gotten disgustingly drunk and constantly had his hands on her every chance he could get, steering her from conversation to conversation like she was some kind of a trophy he was trying to flaunt. He'd even tried to kiss her at one point. If sticking his tongue down her throat could be called a kiss. Not wanting to upset him at his own party, she'd tactfully told him she had no intention of having a personal relationship with him. Thank goodness Mother had been along to chaperone them on the way home, or who knows how that night would have ended. Debra had avoided Robert ever since.

Amanda from accounting stuck her head in her cubicle. She was a short, petite woman, fresh from college with all the vigor of the Energizer Bunny. She'd jump through hoops of fire to help anyone.

Dropping a pile of requisitions in her in box, Amanda smiled. "Hi, Debra. Will Jasmine be back next week?"

"Let's keep our fingers crossed. They hope to have Milten stabilized enough to go home as soon as Monday. Why are you here so late?"

"With Jasmine gone, I got backed up on the billing. I was supposed to meet my husband at six, but looks like I'm going to have to cancel."

"I minored in accounting in college. Maybe I could take a look and help you catch up a little."

"Would you? That'd be great. I'd hoped to get off early tonight. It's our anniversary."

Debra smiled. "That's wonderful. How long have you two been married?"

"Three years. We got married in college." A flicker of mischief sparkled in her eyes. "Can you keep a secret?"

"Depends on what it is," Debra answered with a coy smile.

215

Amanda held her hand over her stomach, her face turning the color of a blushing rose. An instant tearing blurred Debra's vision. "Pregnant?" she mouthed?

Amanda nodded. "I haven't told anyone at Walson yet. I wanted to wait and make sure everything was okay, but I just can't stand it. I'm about to burst."

"I'm so happy for you." Debra stood and flung her arms around Amanda.

"I've never been so scared and so excited in my life!" Amanda almost squealed. "This is all Craig and I have ever talked about. We even put in an offer on a new home. There's a huge yard and the owners are leaving a swing set."

"A new house and a new baby?" Debra's voice cracked. Using the pads of her fingers, she carefully wiped under her eyes. "I don't know why I'm so emotional. You'd think I was the one who was pregnant." *Wishful thinking maybe.*

"Listen, if you can dig me out of this jam, I'll treat you to lunch every day next week."

Anything to avoid Robert, she thought. "I'm going to hold you to that. I'll start working on your files tonight."

"You'll need my password. They're pretty strict around here, but with Jasmine gone, I'm sure it'll be okay."

For the next thirty minutes, Amanda helped her get access to the accounting database. She mostly just had back billing for the month of July. "It looks like the two contracts are about to expire the end of August. Are they renewing?" Debra asked.

Amanda shook her head. "Robert hasn't said anything about them, but if we win the Air Force contract, we won't need them anyway."

"I don't suppose you have a copy of the Air Force proposal. I'd love to scan through it, see how something like that gets put together."

"To be honest, I haven't read through it myself. Carolyn was the one who was helping Robert. I just worked up the costs of each of the work stations that we'll be supporting throughout the United States, as well as the forecasted labor involved."

She typed in a command and was prompted for another password. "Use AF1 to get into the document. It's protected, so you can't make any edits from here. Only Robert and the legal department can make any adjustments."

"Great. That's all I needed anyway."

Amanda glanced at her watch. "Are you sure it's okay if I leave?"

"Of course. I was just going to curl up with a movie and a quart of ice cream anyway."

Amanda touched her shoulder, her smile suddenly looking a little sympathetic. "Craig and I were going to hit a movie. You're more than welcome to join us."

Debra laughed. "And horn in on your anniversary weekend? I don't think so. Now go," she said, shooing Amanda out of her cubicle. "I'll get these last few statements done and we'll start off Monday fresh and new. And hopefully, we'll hear good news about the Air Force contract."

"Thanks, Debra. You're a godsend. I can see why Robert speaks so highly of you. With Jasmine gone, you've virtually run this entire department singlehandedly. I have a feeling you'll be into management in no time." Amanda turned and practically skipped to the elevators.

Debra's heart overflowed with happiness for Amanda, yet at the same time, she couldn't help but feel a little envy. Here Amanda was younger than she and married, and now she was pregnant and about to move into a beautiful new house. She and her husband wanted the same things in life, shared the same dreams.

Would she ever feel that way? Excited and scared at the same time, knowing that soon there'd be a beautiful little baby to love and to hold?

Frustrated that nothing seemed to be going the way she'd hoped, she typed in Amanda's password, bringing up several worksheets. It only took her thirty minutes to get those finished and put into the queue for Monday morning's mailing.

Curious, she scanned through the second-quarter financial statement and was amazed at how much it cost to run a corporation this size. Between salaries, building costs, and insurance premiums, not to mention all the incidentals like travel expenses and business supplies, their profit margin barely made it into the black every month. Hopefully, if Walson was awarded the Air Force contract, that margin would increase dramatically.

She brought up the Air Force proposal and almost groaned. It was a ninety-page document. She'd be here till midnight if she wanted to read the entire thing. Looking over the cubicle at a nearly deserted floor, she had an idea.

Queuing up the document, she hit print. If she could get a copy printed while she finished up the billing statements, she could take the proposal home and read it over the weekend.

Hoping to compare contracts, she dug out the agreements between Walson and their other customers from Jasmine's filing cabinets and shoved them into her tote bag. Not exactly a romance book, but it beat watching reruns on television any day.

That night, Debra sat hunched over Jasmine's kitchen table, pouring over each individual contract between Walson and their customers. They were all in the last three months of their terms with no indications of renewing.

Debra had a sinking feeling in the pit of her gut. Was Robert putting all his eggs into one basket with the Air Force proposal? What if Walson didn't win?

Frustrated, she scooped out a bite of pralines and cream ice cream from a small quart-sized bucket in her hand. Shoveling the bite of sweet confection into her mouth, she savored a few moments of the only sheer pleasure she'd had all week. With Jasmine gone, it seemed she'd been swamped with work.

Digging her spoon into the container, she picked out a big fat praline and sucked off all the caramel and brown sugar. Finally reaching the nut, she scooped another bite of ice cream out and chomped down on all of it at the same time.

Reading through the Air Force proposal, she skimmed through all the legal jargon. The only thing that bothered her was the mention of the Boston division, listed several times throughout the document. By the time she got to the last page, she came to an unavoidable conclusion. This proposal was not for the Rocky Mountain division as she'd assumed.

If the Air Force accepted all the terms and conditions, support of the Air Force communications offices throughout the United States would begin in mid-October—from Boston.

Was Joshua right? Did Robert intend to shut down this division after all?

Hoping she'd missed something, she flipped back to the beginning of the proposal and scooped out another spoonful of ice cream. A light tap sounded at the front door. Startled, she inadvertently crammed the whole bite into her mouth, giving her an excruciating ice cream headache. She glanced at the clock on the wall. Who would be knocking on her door at ten-thirty on a Friday night?

"Debra, are you up?" Joshua's familiar low baritone called through the door.

She gave a relieved sigh, yet her stomach somersaulted with anxiety. Even with the separation these past three weeks, she'd found it harder and harder not to think about him, or dream about being with him . . . in his cozy little twin bed.

"Debra? You there?"

Pressing her tongue to the roof of her mouth to alleviate her headache, she padded barefoot through the living room and called out, "Yeah, I'm coming." She switched on the porch light and peeked through the sheer curtain covering the window next to the door. Blood from her head rushed quickly south. Why did she react like this every time she saw this man?

He was startlingly handsome in a pair of dark blue Wrangler jeans and a white golf shirt with Wrangler stitched over the breast pocket. A dark shadow of whiskers on his cheeks blended into the goatee covering his chin. She couldn't help but remember how soft his whiskers had felt against her lips when he'd kissed her at his ranch. If she let him in now, she didn't know if she'd be able to say no if he pursued her again.

Hoping to keep this unexpected visit short, she stuck her spoon in the ice cream, unlocked the dead bolt then opened the door two inches. "Joshua? What are you doing here so late?"

"Drove by and saw your kitchen light on. Thought I'd stop and say hi." He tucked his fingers into the front pockets of his jeans then leaned a shoulder against the door jam. "Hi."

"Just drove by, huh?" She nudged the door open a few more inches. "So, how's Brandy? She giving you any troubles?"

"I think she misses you. I haven't had much of a chance to exercise her and she seems to be putting on a little weight, but don't worry," he quickly added with a reassuring smile. "I hope to take her out this weekend. Maybe you know someone who'd like to help me out?" He arched his brows in invitation.

She looked down at the ice cream container and poked the spoon in and out, wishing she could join him. She hadn't thought about her father's ranch in a couple of weeks. She'd fallen into a pleasant routine, taking long walks every night through Garden of the Gods nature trails. She used to jog in college, but until her ribs were stronger, she'd limited herself to brisk walks. It wasn't the same as riding Brandy, but it still felt good to get out into the great outdoors. Did she want to ride Brandy and stir up all kinds of emotions she'd tried to store away?

"So, how've you been?" he asked, not waiting for her to answer. "Are you getting along okay here by yourself?"

"A little lonely if you want to know the truth. This big old house gets kind of quiet at night. With Jasmine gone, I haven't made too many new friends."

"Sounds like Milt might be coming home next week."

"I know. I'm hoping to find an apartment this weekend."

"Why? Jasmine said you could stay as long as you like."

"They're a married couple, Joshua. They need their privacy. I don't want to impose."

"Well, if you need some help, I'd be glad to show you around. Heather said there's a few empty units in her complex. I could take you by there and see if it's something you'd be interested in. And no, it wouldn't be an imposition. I know this town better than anyone. I'd feel a whole lot better knowing you were in a good, safe neighborhood."

"How can I say no to that? I'll let you know." Feeling her insides melt like the container of ice cream, she tugged her orange and blue football jersey down over her thighs, suddenly aware of him standing so close. A dog barked across the street as a car drove by out front.

Joshua shoved his hand on his waist and toed his boot into the door jam. "Well, guess I'd better let you get back to your ice cream." His voice was low, sounding disappointed. "Good night, then." He shoved off the door and turned around.

"Wait. Joshua?" She pulled the door wide. It might not be the wisest move in the world, but she didn't think she could take another three weeks without seeing this man. "Do you want to come in, get something to drink?"

He craned his neck around, warily looking at her over his

shoulder. "You sure?"

She smiled and gestured to the living room. "Absolutely. It's good to see you. I've kind of missed our little talks. I thought maybe you were trying to avoid me."

"Just giving you your space," he quipped, mocking what she'd said the last time they'd spoken.

"Thanks, but with Jasmine gone, I've had more than enough space. Please, take as much as you want."

He stepped inside and combed his fingers through his dusky brown hair, his muscles bunching the ribbed sleeves of his white golf shirt. Her heart fluctuated between a rapid beat and then not beating at all. Maybe this wasn't such a good idea after all. Her space seemed to have just shrunk by half.

Too late. He was already inside perusing Jasmine's country décor of teddy bears and hand-painted wooden knick-knacks. There was a framed print of three young children playing near a beach, another was of a little boy and a frog, and her favorite, a little girl with pigtails riding on a Shetland pony that Debra had added as a thank-you gift to Jasmine.

"You've really kept up the place. I don't think Jasmine was much of a housekeeper."

"I guess something had to take a backseat. Working two jobs and caring for Milt nights and weekends had to be exhausting." She set the ice cream on the coffee table.

He picked up a picture of her and Brandy at a competition she'd won several years ago. "You two sure made quite a pair."

She walked up behind him, peering around his shoulder. "Yeah, she's from a good bloodline. Black-Eyed Bandit was one of the most gorgeous stallions we'd ever owned. I knew it was too much to hope that you still had Golden Sunset. Gosh, she'd be around twenty years old by now."

"Debra? I need to tell you something." He set the picture down then started pacing the living room, rubbing the back of his neck. His brows were drawn together, his expression grim.

"What is it, Joshua? You look serious."

With his back to her, he braced his hands on his waist and stared up toward the ceiling. "I killed Golden Sunset."

Her heart slammed against her chest. "What do you mean? You killed Golden Sunset?"

"I've been trying to figure out a way to tell you, but I never knew where to start. I guess that morning would be as good a place as any."

"Joshua, are you sure you want to go through this?" She didn't know if she did.

"I really think you should know."

She only nodded, twisting her fingers together.

"It happened three weeks after we'd brought Golden Sunset home. Dad had been gone all weekend and didn't get back till late Sunday night. Early Monday morning, he told me to move the horses over to an adjoining paddock. It butts against the road leading up to our place and has its own entrance gate." He paused and stared toward the picture of her and Brandy. "Somehow, the gate was left open and all the horses got out onto the road. I rounded them all up . . . all but one," he clarified. "Dad was clear back by the ravine, so he didn't know what was going on till he heard the tires screeching."

"Oh, my gosh," she said, covering her mouth with her fingers. "What happened?"

He turned and met her startled gaze. "A delivery truck hit her broadside."

She pressed her hand tighter to mute the gasp from her throat.

Joshua pinched the bridge of his nose then slumped to the edge of the couch, his breathing turning heavy. "When Dad showed up she was writhing in pain. Her chest had been split open and her back legs were crushed."

Debra slowly lowered beside him on the couch and closed

her eyes, not wanting to hear any more. "You don't need to go on, Joshua. I understand."

He dropped his face into his hands, his voice sounding like a strangled murmur. "God. How could I have been so *stupid?*" His voice turned curt and filled with anger. "Dad told me to get the gun and put her down, but I couldn't. I froze. So he charged into the barn, brought out a thirty-thirty rifle and shoved it into my hands."

She had to swallow her own emotion building in her airway. "Please, Joshua. I don't want to hear any more."

"I couldn't do it," he continued anyway, staring down at the carpeted floor between his boots. "I ran off crying to the house and heard the gunshot from my room. It was the most horrifying sound I'd ever heard."

Sickened, Debra slouched against the back of the couch and didn't say any more. She *couldn't* say any more.

"That's not even the worst part."

Oh God, there's more?

"Shortly after that Dad headed out to his plane."

"I know you said your father was killed in a plane crash, but I didn't know he was a pilot?"

"Yeah. He flew a Cessna one seventy-two. We had a grass runway behind our house. It's all pasture now." He blew out a heavy gust of air. "Anyway, it was fall and the wind was coming in strong from the northwest and with the death of his prized mare, he had no business being in a plane. He didn't even take the time to do a pre-flight inspection. He never flew without doing that first. I tried to block him from getting into the cockpit. I screamed at him, but he shoved me out of the way. We argued for several minutes and I pushed him, yelling some pretty rotten things."

He rubbed his eyes in frustration. "I'll never forget it. For the longest time, Dad just stared at me. I don't know if it was hate or disappointment I saw in his eyes. But then he got right in my face and said I'd never be nothing but a wussy city boy, and that I'd never make it as a rancher."

"What did you do?"

"I told him I hated him and that he was a lousy father. Said I hoped he never come back." Joshua slouched to the back of the couch, his shoulder nudging against hers. "He never came back, Debra. I never saw him or spoke to him again."

They both sat there, staring up at the ceiling, not saying a word. The ache she'd felt for the loss of Golden Sunset was replaced with an even graver pain at the extraordinary loss of Joshua's father and the kind of guilt Joshua had carried around all these years.

"I couldn't figure out what I was doing wrong," he added, pinching the bridge of his nose. "I tried so hard to do things his way. Truth is, I thought I had the best dad in the world. He was my idol. I wanted to be just like him when I grew up." He swallowed heavily and shook his head. "Do you know that he never once told me he was proud of me, or that he loved me?"

She leaned her head on his shoulder, then slid her fingers over his large tanned hand and squeezed. "He loved you, Joshua. He might not have said it in so many words, but he did. My father never said those words to me either. And even though it got pretty bad in the last couple of years and some angry words were exchanged on more than one occasion, I know in my heart that he loved me."

"I was a big disappointment."

"You weren't a disappointment. When your father spoke to you like that, he was angry about what had happened to his horse. He had to vent on someone. It was a freak accident. He said those things because he wanted to make you tough as nails, drive out your compassion. Kind of like my dad making sure I never cried. They were both raised in the old school that made them feel they were less than a man if they showed any emotion."

"I don't think I ever told him."

She drew her brows together, perplexed. "Told him what?"

He looked down at her, his eyes filled with pain. "That I loved him."

"Oh, Joshua," she whispered. She reached up and stroked her hand over his whiskery cheek. "Your father knew in his heart that you loved him. All teenagers say mean things to their parents now and then."

"I feel like I let him down." His voice choked and he closed his eyes.

She stroked the skin of his forearm, where soft dark hairs blended in with the tanned complexion of his skin. "Don't you see? You've already proven your father wrong. You've got a successful herd with more land than you know what to do with. Your family is so close. I truly believe it's because you single-handedly stepped in and took care of everything after your father died—your mom, your brother and sisters, the ranch. You even went on to college and got your degree. He'd be so proud of how you've handled things all these years."

He gave her hand a squeeze. "Are you mad at me?"

"Mad?" Debra repeated, not sure what he meant.

"About Golden Sunset."

She shook her head. "I'm saddened, but not mad, and I certainly don't hold you responsible, or think you're any less of a man. It was just a freak accident." She couldn't help but remember how Joshua had said the same thing about her father's death. Was his death just a freak accident?

He stared toward the ceiling again and blew out a heavy gust of air. "I've never told that story to another living soul. I feel like I just lost a twelve-hundred-pound weight that had been sitting on my heart all these years."

"I'm glad you told me. It means a lot that you trusted me enough to confide in me."

With the pad of his thumb brushing the back of her hand, he lazily rolled his head to the side and gazed deeply into her eyes. "As my oldest and dearest friend, I just didn't want any secrets between us."

"Thank you, Joshua. You'll never know how much that means to me." Without another thought, she wrapped her arms around his brawny neck and squeezed.

He held her tight, stroking the back of her hair, his lips pressing against the side of her neck. Right now, she didn't care if he was a rancher, a doctor, or a ditch digger. Being in his arms was all she needed. He tugged her onto his lap and pressed his face into her hair, breathing deeply, the same way he'd done the night he'd held her in his twin bed.

"You always smell so good." His voice was heavy. His hands roamed up and down the bare skin of her leg, caressing her shin from her ankle to her knee, then higher up to the edge of her jersey. It took all her power not to haul this guy upstairs and try out her own double bed. Thinking of Goldilocks, she wondered if it would be *just right*.

Knowing her fantasies were getting the best of her, she released her hold and grabbed his hand, stopping it as it crept closer to the rim of her panties. For a minute, they both froze in each other's heated gaze. The moment his gaze lowered to her lips, she shook her head and pushed against his chest, scooting off his lap. Sitting forward, her bare legs brushed against his jeans as she tried to keep her jersey from sliding up to her hips.

With trembling fingers, she picked up the container of ice cream off the coffee table. "Wanna bite?" Her voice sounded shaky, unsettled. She swirled her spoon through the soupy mixture, hoping the coldness of the container would quench some of the fire burning through her body at this very moment.

He cleared his throat and braced an arm behind her on the couch, putting her snugly into the crook of his shoulder. He swept a strand of hair from her face with the other so he could see her clearly. "Depends on what you're offering."

She wedged the container between them. "Ice cream." She gave a nervous laugh. "Well, it used to be ice cream. Now it's more like caramel syrup and pecans. It still tastes good, though." She brought the container under his chin and offered him a spoonful.

He smiled and wrapped his fingers around her wrist, his eyes bearing into hers as he slowly slid the spoon into his mouth. "Mmmm," he sighed, seductively pulling the spoon from between his lips. His other hand had moved to her lower back, pressing her closer. "I've only had one other thing that tastes as sweet." He flicked his gaze to her lips, then met her eyes again. He still hadn't let go of her wrist.

With his warm caramel breath fanning her face, she licked her lips, her heart deciding to go on a full-blown marathon. If he kissed her now, there was no way she would be able to stop at just one kiss. As it was, she was ready to rip off her jersey and pour the whole container of caramel syrup all over her body and let him lick it off.

"Tea?" she asked, barely hearing herself over the blood rushing through her head.

His lips twitched into a smile, his dimple winking at her as if he could read her mind. "Tea would be good," he said, letting go of her wrist.

"Whew," she said standing. "It's hot in here. I, um . . ." she stammered and pointed to the kitchen. "I'll just be a second."

CHAPTER THIRTEEN

Feeling the heat himself, Joshua could only smile as he watched Debra sprint into the kitchen, unsuccessfully covering a lacy pair of light blue underwear beneath her football jersey. What had he been thinking, stopping by here so late?

Scratch that. He knew exactly what he'd been thinking. Now how to stop thinking it was going to be the difficult part, maybe even impossible.

He rubbed his eyes, exhausted, yet he'd never felt better. Telling her about his father and Golden Sunset made him feel whole again. He hated having any secrets between them. And he had to admit, she was right about one thing. His ranch was already a success, and he knew his father would be proud.

Glasses and ice clinking drew his attention to the kitchen. He stood and strode over to the entrance then leaned a shoulder against the wall. All his tension seemed to drain right out of his body every time he came near this woman. Debra looked so natural without makeup, her hair hanging in a tousled mass of loose, wavy black curls, the tips brushing the curves of her narrow hips. From behind, her long silky legs seemed to go on forever underneath her jersey.

He'd never forget how she felt lying next to him in his twin bed, the way her feet rubbed the tops of his toes. And her scent. Her wildflower scent seemed ingrained into his memory, not to mention the smell of his cologne she'd dabbed on her neck. The sweet memory made him want to go up to her from behind and trail his fingertips from her pretty pink toenails all the way up the inside of her thighs and under that far too sexy football jersey.

He suddenly realized that *whipped* didn't even begin to describe his feelings for this woman. She was right in a way; he had been avoiding her these past three weeks, but it wasn't because he hadn't wanted to see her. In fact, he'd found himself daydreaming about her, picturing what their life would be like together. It always ended up with him thinking about what their children would look like: tall, dark hair, big brown eyes, and wide exuberant smiles. Remembering what Jared had said that afternoon, he knew without a doubt: he wanted kids in his life, but only with this woman.

Although the thought of marriage and kids still scared the hell out of him, the idea of growing into an old codger hoarding his land and having no one to share it with didn't sound like a picnic either. He wanted to work beside Debra, day in and day out, raising and training horses full time.

Therein lay the problem.

She was so convinced she was responsible for her father's ranch going under, that she thought she'd eventually cause Joshua's ranch to fail and that he'd follow her father's footsteps into financial ruin . . . or worse.

Was there anything he could say or do to convince her that that wouldn't happen? And, more to the point, could he convince himself?

"Sugar?" she asked, handing him a tall glass of tea.

"Dip your finger in it and taste it."

She furrowed her thin dark brows, dunked her fingertip into the tea, then sucked off the drip. He took the glass and smiled. "Perfect. That's all the sugar I needed." Her cheeks turned that delectable shade of pink that always made his heart beat faster.

"Joshua? Why are you here? That look in your eyes has me a

little worried."

He placed his hand over his heart and feigned innocence. "What? Can't a friend stop by and chat without having ulterior motives?"

"Friends. Right. So long as we have that clear." She quickly brushed passed him, her hair trailing over his arm as she turned the corner.

He took a long drink of tea, hoping to quench this insatiable fire that seemed to be getting hotter the longer he stood in her kitchen.

Stepping around the corner, he found her shuffling papers into neat piles on the table. The word *Classified* jumped out at him. He reached around her and picked up the top document. "What's this?"

"Nothing," she said, extracting the paper from his hand. "Just some work I brought home."

Sensing she was hiding something, he picked up another page. "Is this the contract between Walson and Connelly Communications?"

"Yes, and I could get fired if anyone knew I brought this home." She tried to grab the document from his hands.

"I won't tell anyone," he said, holding it in the air to keep her from reaching it. He turned his back toward her, blocking her with one arm while scanning through the first few paragraphs.

"Joshua, you're acting like a kid. There's nothing to see."

"You won't care if I read it, then." He quickly flipped through the first few pages, then turned to face her. "Looks to me like this contract is about to end. Are they renewing?"

"It's really none of your concern, Joshua. Please, just give me the contract."

He complied, but as she scooped the Connelly agreement together, he picked up the Air Force proposal. She gave a frustrated sigh and shoved a hand to her waist, holding out the other, waiting for him to give it back. Instead, he walked into the living room and started scanning through the document.

"Fine," she said to his back. "But if you get me fired, you've got to find me a new job."

He almost chuckled at that. With his connections, he could guarantee her a job just about anywhere in these parts. Pacing back to the dining room, he leaned a shoulder against the wall and flipped to the last several pages, coming to an overwhelming conclusion. "Did you know this contract is for the Boston division of Walson Technology?"

When she didn't answer, he tossed the papers onto the table. "I was right, wasn't I? He's shutting down the Rocky Mountain division as well."

"We don't know that for sure," she said, not sounding very convincing. "Maybe they entered the wrong address, or maybe Boston's just handling the procurement of the contract. I read through all their financial statements this afternoon. Ever since Robert took control of the company, their profits are up and their costs are down. Streamlining the divisions into one centrally located office where there's a high volume of technical and avionic advances, Walson has become one of the top engineering firms in the industry. You should cut him some slack."

"When are you going to stop defending the Nelsons? Don't you see? They're only in it for themselves. They don't care how many people lose their jobs. All they care about is the bottom line. While they're out living high on the hog, people like Jasmine and Hank will lose their livelihoods. No wonder he's kept this so confidential."

"We don't know for sure that's what they're going to do. We've got a huge parts inventory in our warehouse. Maybe we'll be maintaining that for this new contract as well."

Realizing this was a dead-end discussion, he had to lean back against the doorframe as she hurried past him again, setting a glass and a bowl in the sink. Frustrated, he followed her to the kitchen. He hadn't come here to argue, and he especially didn't want to talk about the Nelsons. Though he couldn't help but wonder: if the Rocky Mountain division of Walson was shut down, would she move away?

More specifically, would she go to Boston with Robbie?

Trying to hold on to his anger, he watched as she turned on the water and poured dishwashing soap in the sink. Hoping to smooth the edges between them, he stepped up behind her, barely brushing against her backside. He noticed she didn't flinch away. He breathed deeply, taking in all that was uniquely Debra, flowers and caramel and sugar, nothing but sweet morsels to tempt his senses.

When she started washing the dishes, he set his glass on the counter beside her and spoke next to her ear. "Need any help?" He swept her shiny ebony hair away from one side of her neck, his fingertips brushing the delicate skin of her nape as he draped the long tendrils over the other shoulder.

She gave a slight shiver. Her hands stilled in the sink of soapy water. For an instant, he thought she'd even stopped breathing.

As if she suddenly realized what she'd done, she cleared her throat and moved aside, grabbing a towel from a drawer. "Thanks, but I think I can handle a few dishes."

His heart gave a disappointed thud inside his chest. Taking her tactful rejection as a hint, he strode over to her refrigerator, hoping to quench another kind of appetite. He gave its contents a quick scan then reached in the fruit drawer, pulling out an apple. "Care if I have this?" he asked, biting into the tart red skin. "I haven't eaten anything since lunch."

She set the glass in the cupboard and leaned her hands on the counter behind her. "What if I said no?" she asked, her crooked grin flickering a challenge.

He kicked the door shut and took one step toward her, boxing her in the corner of the cupboards. "I'd share it with you. You know, from one friend to another, of course. Wanna bite?" He held it up to her mouth and smiled.

She gave a loud sigh of contemplation, her gaze switching from the apple to his eyes. "Okay, but then you gotta go. It's late and I need to get to bed."

"Couldn't agree with you more." He moved his boots beside her bare feet and watched as she bit into the apple next to his bite. She gave a noisy slurp as the juice dribbled down her chin. She laughed and tried to wipe it with her hand.

He caught her wrist midair, slid up to her palms, and interlaced their fingers together, bending slightly to level his gaze with hers. "Mind if I get that?"

She stopped chewing and gave a heavy swallow, leaving her mouth gaped open.

Without waiting for a possible rejection, he lowered to her chin. Using the tip of his tongue, he started below her jaw and followed the trail of juice to the corner of her lips. She still hadn't closed her mouth, nor had she breathed that he could tell. Her eyes were closed and he wondered if he should pursue this any further.

Tasting the apple on her skin, being so close to her luscious lips, he didn't know if he had it in him to pull away right now. He slid his lips along her jaw back to her ear. She pressed her cheek against his and gave a little moan into his ear, her warm breath fanning his heated skin.

That little sound made his whole body turn to fire. He dragged his mouth under her chin, avoiding the one place he wanted to kiss the most. Their fingers still intertwined, he drew their hands down to his waist, wrapping her arms around his back.

"How are your ribs feeling this week?" he asked, slipping

from her grasp and following the same path at her waist till his arms were wrapped around her back, his hands stroking the silky material of her jersey.

She spoke into his ear in a sensual whisper. "Better. I hardly noticed them at all."

When she kissed his earlobe, he groaned and drew away, but just enough to glance at her lips. "Guess I should let you get to bed."

"Uh-huh," she agreed with a slow nod. Her mouth remained open a whisper's length from his. Her sweet apple-pectin breath and shiny wet lips were a reminder of their sensual exchange of the forbidden fruit. His breath caught in his throat when her fingers brushed his waist, slipping through the belt loops of his trousers, tugging him closer.

Dear God in heaven, if he stood here another second he'd have those little blue panties of hers down around her ankles and be sampling all of her fresh produce. Sweet ripened cherries came to mind. He wanted to delve his tongue into her warm essence until she was begging for more.

When she ran the tip of her tongue from one corner of her mouth to the other, that was all it took.

"Hell's bells, woman."

The next thing he knew he'd covered her mouth with his own and had her pressed up against the counter. Whatever it was he felt for this woman couldn't be contained another second. It seemed like time stood still while he massaged her lips, warm as sunshine and sweet as honey. Her heart was beating hard, her chest rising and falling in shallow gasps as she breathed into his mouth. It felt like their souls were making a connection they'd both yearned for all these years.

He sucked in a quick breath when her tongue shyly slipped into his mouth, then quickly retreated. He smiled through his kiss and traced his tongue along her lower lip then the top. "It's okay," he whispered. "You're doing it right."

Responding to his invitation, she opened her mouth fully, allowing him to swirl their tongues together in a sweet dance of ecstasy. After what felt like hours of pure heaven, she murmured into his mouth. "I've never felt this way before. I feel like I'm on fire."

"I know darlin', it's the same for me."

As her hips writhed against him, he slid his boot between her feet, pressing his muscular thigh into the apex of her legs. She moaned and hesitantly parted her legs further, allowing him to wedge in harder. He wanted to be the one to take her to that peak of ecstasy for the first time. There were so many things he wanted to do with her for the first time.

He found her mouth again as she melted into his kiss . . . right into his soul. He slid his palms down her sides and slowly tugged the silky material of her jersey up over her hips, the heated skin of her thighs searing clear through his jeans. Wanting to feel every square inch of her, he caressed around to her back, his thumb brushing the lower swells of her breasts. It was only then he realized she wore no bra.

"Oh, Joshua, I don't know what you're doing to me, but you feel so good." When she flung her arms around his shoulders and dug her nails into the back of his neck, he couldn't help himself. He cupped a breast, marveling at how perfectly it fit into the palm of his hand, the size of a firm, newly ripened peach. Her whole body was just a cornucopia of fruit.

Her tongue delved deeper, her hips pressing against his, the hardened bulge behind his zipper giving her a good idea of what happened to him whenever she got near him.

She gave a startled gasp and pulled her hips back slightly. It was then he was reminded just how pure this woman was. Except for the ranch hand who'd tried to attack her in the barn, she'd probably never felt the arousal of a man in a heated state of passion before.

He slid his hands around to her lower back, linking his fingers together then drew away to see her expression. Her cheeks were flame red, her eyes big brown disks that couldn't hide her shock. He had to laugh. "Sorry about that, but now you know what happens every time I get near you."

"Every time?"

"And even when you're not," he confessed.

She rested her forehead against his chin. "Oh, Joshua. I don't know if I'm ready for someone like you. I mean, what if you're too . . ." she paused and looked up at him. "I've never . . ."

He gave a low, throaty chuckle. "It's okay, darlin'. Nothing's going to happen tonight. But be assured, when the time is right, I guarantee we'll be perfect together."

The ringing of the telephone broke into their moment. He ignored the intrusion and lowered to her mouth, pressing her against his zipper.

The phone rang again. She dug her fingers into the back of his hair, speaking through his kisses. "I'd better get that."

"Do you have a machine?" he asked ducking his head to her chest, kissing along the V of her jersey.

"Yes," she answered through a moan. "But I think I should get it. Maybe it's Jasmine." She met his mouth one more time before pushing hesitantly out of his embrace. With her dreamy brown gaze locked on his, she smiled, took in a deep breath, and blew it out as she slowly backed into the living room.

She turned and answered the phone on the third ring. "Hello?" her voice was breathy, alluringly sexy.

He walked up behind her and started sliding up her jersey, exposing her frilly blue bikini underwear. She pulled away and handed him the phone. "It's Heather. She sounds frantic."

"My sister?" Joshua took the phone. "Heather? What's up?"

"Thank God I finally found you. Jared said you might be at the Kings."

"What is it? What's wrong?" he asked, keeping his eyes on Debra. Her lips were slightly swollen, her face tinged with a rosy blush.

"Mom called. She said a pack of neighbor dogs got into the pen with the new foal."

"Son of a bitch," he swore, turning his back. "How's the foal?"

"Jared said it wasn't too bad. He's with her now."

"Did they get rid of the dogs?"

"They ran off before Brad and Jared could catch them. Mom called the police, but they didn't sound too concerned."

"When did it happen?"

"About an hour ago. We called your cell phone but couldn't get through." Giving a dramatic huff, she scolded, "Where have you been all day?"

Suddenly feeling on the defensive, he said, "I was at a sale in Denver."

"You've got to get some help. As big as your ranch has grown, you can't be two places at the same time."

"I don't need a lecture right now. I'll be out in twenty minutes." He slammed the phone down.

"What is it?" Debra pleaded. "What happened?"

"We've had some trouble out at my ranch."

"What kind of trouble? Do you need any help?"

"Some of the neighbor dogs got into the pen with one of the new foals."

Debra gasped and covered her mouth. "Is it all right?"

"I think so. Jared's out there now." He let out a curse. "I've seen a few stray dogs hanging around the past few days, but I didn't think they'd actually attack anything."

"We lost ten chickens the same way. Dogs can be the tamest

animals in the world, but when they travel in packs, I think their hunting instinct takes over."

"I'm sorry, I gotta go."

"Hold on," Debra said, hurrying toward the stairs. "I'm coming with you. I just need to throw on some jeans."

"Oh, no you're not." He took off after her and caught her arm. As much as he wanted to get her back out to his ranch, he didn't want it to be when there was an emergency. It would just confirm her fears that only bad things happened on a ranch. "I could be out there all night. I'll call you as soon as I know anything."

"But Joshua—"

"No buts, Debra," he said, wrapping his arms around her waist. He pressed another devouring kiss over those pouty pink lips, preventing her from arguing with him.

Knowing Jared was at the ranch tending to his foal and that there was probably nothing he could do tonight anyway, Joshua was tempted to start back up where they'd left off before the phone rang. When he pulled away, he could only smile. Her eyes were still shut and her head had drifted back so that her neck was arched. "You're making it very difficult for me to leave."

She flung her arms around his shoulders. "I don't want you to leave."

He groaned into the side of her neck. "That's not the wisest thing to say to a man in my current condition."

"Will you at least call me? Let me know what's going on with the foal?"

"I'll call you as soon as I get a chance." He looked down at her, still feeling the effect of their sensual interlude. Remembering how he'd lost his fiancé, he touched her chin, rubbing the pad of his thumb along the curl of her lower lip. "Will you go?"

"Go?" She gave a quick shake of her head. "Go where?"

"To Boston. Will you move out to Boston with Robbie if he asks you?"

She held a hand over her heart. "I hadn't even thought about it. I can't imagine being so far away from my mom." Shaking her head, she said, "Let's not even think that far ahead. We might be jumping to conclusions. I'll talk to Robert first thing Monday, and hopefully, we'll get this all straightened out."

"You just be careful around Robbie, Debra. There's more to that man than you'll ever know."

"You don't have to worry about me. I can handle myself."

"I do worry about you," he said, getting right in her face. "This isn't your father's horse ranch or a few little gambling debts we're dealing with anymore. Believe me, if the Nelsons find out you've been snooping around in the contracts, they could be far more dangerous than a pack of wild dogs."

Watching Joshua's taillights go down the road, Debra felt like she was ten years old again, when her daddy wouldn't let her go out to the barn when a mare was foaling. Said the horse was having a difficult delivery and he didn't want her to get in the way.

Was that why Joshua didn't want her to her go along? Because she'd get in the way?

After a restless night, the phone rang around seven o'clock Saturday morning. She reached over and grabbed the receiver and dragged it to her ear. "Hello?"

"Thought you'd like to know how the foal is doing." Joshua's soft, low baritone sent butterflies to her stomach.

"Oh, Joshua," she gushed, sitting straight up in bed. "I've been worried sick all night. How is she?"

"The foal is fine for the most part."

"For the most part?" she repeated, almost holding her breath.

"Jared had to put a few stitches in her hind leg, and other

than a sore tendon, she's as flighty as a June bug, prancing around in the back of her stall. She won't let anyone come near her. It's going to take a lot of time and patience to get her to trust me again."

"Well, if anyone can do it, you can," she said, slumping into her pillow.

A loud breathy sigh sounded in her ear. "Does that go for people, too?"

Debra closed her eyes. "What do you mean?"

"I don't know. You kind of remind me of that scared little filly. She used to love running out in the pasture, getting her nose into everything. Now she's huddled in the back of the stall hiding from the world."

"You think I'm hiding from the world?"

"Maybe not hiding, but definitely avoiding something that you once had a passion for, and it's pretty obvious you don't trust me."

"Oh, Joshua, it's not that I don't trust you. How can I make you understand that it's me I don't trust? You're already more successful than my father ever was, and I don't want to drag you down. I'm sorry if I've hurt you in any way."

The line became quiet. She rolled over on her side and clutched her pillow. "Are you mad?"

He gave a low throaty chuckle. "Did I act mad last night?"

She gave a wistful smile and squeezed her pillow. "Now that you mention it, you were very . . . attentive, for lack of a better word. But Joshua," she said, knowing she had to draw the line. "About what happened."

"Friends, right?"

She blew out a deep breath. "Yeah, friends. It was good seeing you, though. Did you get any sleep? You sound exhausted."

"I got a couple hours this morning. I've got a few things to do around here, then I'm heading up to Castle Rock and delivering a sorrel mare to Camp Forrester around one. Dillan's feeling stronger and his mom said he could ride along with me today. I even told him he could bring his dog. You know, 'cause kids need their dogs," he added with a hint of playfulness.

She laughed. "Yes, they do. Sounds like it'll be fun. Will you be gone all day then?"

"I should be back around four. I told my neighbor I'd be over and help him with his hay later this afternoon, then I've got some buyers coming out tonight to look at one of my trail horses."

"Guess I'd better let you go, then. You've got a full day planned." She wondered how long it would be before she would see him again. She didn't think she could survive another three weeks.

Neither of them said anything for several long seconds, each listening to the other breathe. Clenching the receiver, she finally asked, "Will you be stopping by the hospital to see Milt? Maybe I could meet you sometime."

"I'm not sure. I hope to stop by either today or tomorrow, but things are pretty hectic right now. I've got a sale to get ready for next weekend."

She glanced at a wall calendar above her dresser. "I can't believe it's almost Labor Day. Isn't that when your reunion is supposed to be?"

"I don't know. I guess so."

"So you're still not going?"

"Nope. I told you, I got a sale." His voice suddenly turned harsh. "I'd better let you go."

"Wait, Joshua?" She clenched the receiver and asked straight out, "When will I see you again?"

"I don't know, Debra. I guess that's up to you. I've got a ranch to run. You know where to find me." Without another word, he hung up.

Debra stared at the receiver, then held it to her heart. She didn't think she could go another minute without seeing him again.

She hung up and started to make a mental list of things she could do today. She wanted to go to the hospital and visit Jasmine and Milt. And with Milt's expected release next week, she needed to go apartment hunting. She'd passed a cute little complex not far from Walson. It wasn't nearly as extravagant as the facility Robert had shown her in Woodland Park, but at least it had a security gate.

Food. She needed to go grocery shopping. Joshua had eaten the last apple. Remembering their sensual interlude sent small spasms to the region between her legs.

"Laundry," she said, draping her legs over the side of the bed. She needed to throw a few things into the washing machine. With Milt coming home, she needed to get the place extra clean, run the vacuum, and dust the furniture.

Maybe this afternoon, she could take in some of the sights of Colorado Springs. Visit some of the national monuments. That would take a whole day in itself.

She headed downstairs and into the kitchen. Jerking open the refrigerator, she pulled out a half-eaten piece of strawberry cheesecake from yesterday's lunch. She grabbed a spoon and kicked the door shut with her foot. After three bites, she realized her anxiety had only worsened.

When she'd felt like this at the Walker Ranch, she'd always gone for a trail ride with Brandy. Right now, she'd give anything to be able to saddle her up and ride her into the early morning dawn. She wanted to hear the birds sing, smell the fresh mountain air, get away from the city for a while.

She wanted to quit hiding.

Taking in a deep breath, she tested her ribs for strength. It'd been almost three months since her ranching accident, and other than small twinges now and then, she felt relatively strong.

Dumping the empty platter into the sink, she took the stairs by twos and found her favorite pair of Rocky jeans and a T-shirt. After throwing on an oversized men's denim work shirt, she laced up her old worn cowboy boots and shoved her black Resistol over her head. Glancing at her reflection in the bathroom mirror, she couldn't keep the grin from spreading across her face.

"You make a darn good country bumpkin, Debra Walker." She tugged her hat low over her forehead, determined not to let Robert or anyone else make her feel like that was a bad thing or that she was any less worthy.

She glanced at her watch. Almost eight. The sun was creeping up higher over the horizon, turning the sky a dark, majestic blue. The birds were singing and the flowers were just opening up to the warm summer heat. With renewed strength, she headed outside, staring into the pink and apricot sunrise. Maybe she should call Joshua, make sure it was okay if she came out to ride Brandy today.

Nope, she decided, climbing behind the wheel of her SUV. She didn't want him altering any of his plans, and if she changed her mind on the way, no one would be the wiser. She just hoped she didn't get lost trying to find his ranch.

After a twenty-minute drive north toward the Black Forest, Debra pulled into a graveled lane and followed a grove of trees. She emerged near Joshua's folks' secluded yellow ranch house. No cars were parked in the drive and she didn't notice Joshua's quad cab pickup either. Not that she came here to see him or anything, but now she kind of felt like an intruder.

Maybe this was a bad idea. She should have called first.

Just as she lowered the gearshift into reverse, a tap sounded at her window.

CHAPTER FOURTEEN

She looked up and gave a relieved smile when she found Joshua standing there. He opened her door and leaned his hand on the roof of her SUV, looking altogether too appealing this early in the morning. A black leather vest spread open, revealing a blue and green plaid western shirt. His belt buckle sparkled in the big orange sun and her face warmed just being near him.

"Good morning, Sunshine. What brings you out here—and so early, I might add?"

She perused his acreage and gave a slight shrug of her shoulders. "I was in the neighborhood and thought I'd drop by to say hi. Hi," she said, mocking his excuse last night when he'd stopped by and visited her. "How's the foal? She okay?"

"She's real skittish and won't come out of the barn." He offered her his hand. "There's someone who misses you."

She took his hand and let him pull her to his length. He didn't step back, and he didn't let go of her hand either. With a sudden attack of nerves, she gave his hand a tight squeeze, not sure she could go through with this now that she was here.

As if sensing her unease, he leaned close and spoke in a low, comforting tone. "It's okay, darlin'. Nothing's going to happen. I promise. Just go for a walk with me. I'll show you around."

"Are you sure? I know you're busy with Dillan today. I'm sorry I showed up without calling, but I was afraid—"

"It's fine, Debra. I don't have to pick up Dillan till noon. To be honest, I'd hoped you'd take the first step and come out here on your own."

She glanced down at the corral where several horses grazed on a bale of hay. She spotted Brandy immediately. Her heart raced. He followed her gaze and gestured toward the corral. "What are you waiting for?"

She gave a little squeal and took off at a dead run. She didn't stop till she jumped high atop the fence rail and called Brandy's name. The mare perked her ears, then raised her head. Debra put her fingers between her teeth and whistled. Brandy immediately loped over to the gate, head bobbing.

Leaning way over the top rung, Debra wrapped her arms around her horse and squeezed. "Hey, girl. I've missed you so much." She dug into her pocket and pulled out a raspberry candy disk, offering the treat to Brandy. Jingling and a loud thud behind her brought her attention around.

Joshua dumped her saddle and the rest of her gear in a heap. "Looks like you're over your jitters. Think you can ride? I could show you around my property, tell you what my plans are."

She was so pumped, she jumped down from the fence and wrapped her arms clear around him, about knocking his hat off his head. "I'm so glad you're here, Joshua. Thank you. I would love to take a tour of your place."

He feigned a gasp and laughed. "Okay, okay. You're welcome, already." He set her away, but kept his hands loosely around her waist, his gaze darting between her eyes and her lips. The warm sunshine bathed his tanned face with a rosy glow. Debra held her breath, knowing in the next split second her entire body would turn to mush, like a cookie that was left in milk too long.

She wanted to feel his mouth on hers, taste the passion on his tongue. But if she allowed him to give her one more kiss, she didn't know if she'd be able to stop at just one kiss. And if they went that next step beyond friendship, where would that lead? A casual affair that would inevitably end up with one of them hating the other?

He started to lower to her mouth, but before he met her lips, she pushed away and tugged her hat down. "So, where's the foal?" Her voice had a slight quaver.

He let out a heavy breath through his nose. The muscles in his neck tensed as he rubbed his brows and nodded toward the old red barn. "First stall on the left." His voice was low, almost abrupt.

He gave an ear-piercing whistle, and she cringed. His black gelding quarter horse galloped up to the gate, snorting and pawing the ground. "I'll go saddle the horses and meet you out back of the barn."

"Thanks. I won't be long," she said, stepping back a few paces. She spun around and trotted inside the barn, trying to ignore the low grumblings coming from the brawny cowboy behind her as he strode toward the tack barn. How much longer could she stave him off? And did she want to?

She passed several stalls in the old dilapidated red barn. The moment she laid eyes on the foal, Debra wanted to cry. The little filly was huddled near the back corner and her legs were shaking like leaves. "Hey, sweetie," she cooed and held her hand over the stall.

The foal tossed her head a few times, pawing at the ground and backing into the wall behind her. Her short black tail swished back and forth, swatting away pesky flies. Slowly, Debra climbed over the fence and held her hand out to let her know she was a friend.

"Hiding from the world?" she asked softly, remembering Joshua's comments. "I know it seems easier in here, but look what you're missing out there. Green grass, warm sunshine. Come on, baby, you're a strong little girl. Don't let those mean old dogs control your life."

In a matter of minutes, the little filly nosed her way toward

Debra, sniffing her fingers. "That's a good girl. Want to come with me? Let's get some sunshine on that pretty face of yours." Debra led her out of the stall. The foal's knees were wobbly and still trembled, but she didn't pull away either. When they emerged from the barn in the sunlight, Joshua looked up from the hitching post, his lips spreading into a wide grin as he bumped his hat back on his forehead.

As they approached, he hunched over at the waist, offering his hand to the foal. "Looks like you made a friend," he said to the filly. "Maybe I oughta let Debra take care of you from now on." He glanced up at her from the corner of his eye. "She wouldn't even let Heather get this close. What'd you do?"

She gave a shrug. "I guess we're both tired of hiding from what we love."

He stood and rested his hand on his waist. "Any regrets about coming?"

"Yes." She stroked her palm over the filly's face. "Now I'm afraid I'll never want to leave."

He tipped her hat back, forcing her to look up at him. "That's nothing to be afraid of, honey. You're welcome here any time you want. Come on. I'll tour you around my property, point out the trails. If you want to come ride in the future by yourself, you'll know where you're going."

"Are you sure it's okay if I come here by myself? I mean, I could pay you. Maybe rent out Brandy from time to time."

He chuckled and leaned close to her face. "Yes, I'm sure. And no, you don't have to pay me to ride your horse."

Glad to see his mood had lightened, she smiled and let the foal run to her mama. Thrilled to see Brandy again, she stroked the mare on the neck. "Hey, girl. You ready to work off some of this weight?"

Joshua took hold of her elbow and held out the leather stirrup. "Let me help you up. I don't want you re-injuring yourself."

As soon as she swung into the saddle, she felt a huge smile spread across her face.

"Feel okay?" he asked, tenderly rubbing her lower leg.

Even through her jeans and boots, her whole body reacted to his simple gesture. "I feel absolutely terrific." She leaned over and hugged Brandy's neck. "I missed you so much, girl."

"You sure are a pretty thing sitting up there. You ready for a ride?"

"If you think you can keep up with me," she joked.

"Sounds like a challenge to me." He mounted Evening Star and nudged in beside her, their legs rubbing against each other. Their horses stayed side-by-side trotting through the paddock. They halted in front of a gate, and Debra waited while Joshua swung it open, allowing them to ride out into the pasture.

Over the course of the next two hours Debra soaked in the early morning sunshine, enjoying the fresh earthy scents of dew and wet grass. The birds were singing and chirping. Off in the distance was a spectacular view of Pikes Peak. An occasional low-flying jet streamed across the sky, coming from the Air Force Academy and leaving in its wake a low rumble of noise.

He led her along the property lines clear back to a creek near a thick grove of trees. Small waterfalls trickled over several boulders into the deeper part of the ravine. She stopped near the top of the ridge and took in a deep breath of the warm Colorado morning. "This is so beautiful out here. I've only been in the city a month and already I hate the smell and all the noise. I appreciate Jasmine letting me stay with her, but I'd love to find a condo or some place a little farther out of the city."

She was filled with exuberance when she saw the view from the creek. "Look at this view, Joshua. It's incredible. Have you ever considered building a house out here? My goodness, it's like we're the only ones on the planet. Do you think this is how Adam and Eve felt?"

He chuckled and rested his hand on his thigh. "I don't know about Eve, but I can vouch for Adam. If she looked anything like you, he probably thought he was in paradise no matter where they lived."

"Well, now," she drawled in her best southern accent. "That's about the sweetest thing anyone's ever said to me, Joshua Garrison." She tilted her head and gave him a shy smile. "Corny, but sweet."

Feeling uncharacteristically romantic, he leaned over his saddle horn toward her, hoping to give her a kiss.

Instead of returning his affections, she tugged her hat down, tightened the reins in her hands and yelled, "Yeeeaaahh!"

Dust and dirt clods churned the dried russet soil, almost clobbering Joshua in the face.

Holy shit.

He kicked Evening Star in the flanks and easily caught up with her. Rocks and spruce trees seemed to fly by as they raced toward the ranch yard. Sweat darkened both horses' hides as flecks of foam flew from their mouths.

Joshua's blood surged through his body. He'd never ridden with anyone who had such pure determination. Brandy's muscular legs were a blur of motion, her black tail almost brushing the forehead of Evening Star. Low, rumbling whickers sounded through the horses' heavy breaths. Twigs cracked, birds scolded as he and Debra sprinted headlong through their habitat.

If he'd found her irresistible before, there was no denying his heated desire for this woman now. Her muscular legs gripped her horse, her boots spurring it faster. When he saw her eyes, the way they glittered with excitement, he wanted to grab the reins and pull her down into the middle of the hay field. Feel her long legs wrapped around him, her lips on his. It'd been a long time since he'd wanted a woman like this.

Had he *ever* wanted a woman like this? Even with Michelle, he'd never burned just to hold her, to feel her hand snuggled tightly in his, to know her dreams and her fears. It had all been about sex with Michelle. He'd fended her off for two years, afraid something would happen.

Then it did. He'd been drinking. His judgment was clouded. Michelle's hands were too fast. The one time he'd succumbed to her temptation, he'd gotten her pregnant. They'd taken all the precautions, but still it had happened. Although he was certain she wasn't a virgin when he'd made love to her, she'd sworn he was the first. When she'd lost the baby in the third trimester and left him a week later, his whole world had fallen apart.

In retrospect, he was thankful they'd never married—especially now that he knew what he suspected was true love staring him square in the face. But he knew what Debra wanted, a commitment, marriage . . . kids.

Was he ready for that?

Was *she* ready for that?

Every time he'd get close, she pulled away. Was there any way he could get her to trust him long enough to convince her to return to ranch life?

Reaching the stable yard, Debra reined in her mount. The horses snorted, breathing heavily. "That was great!" She laughed, pulling back on the reins of her prancing horse. "I've missed that so much. You have no idea how good that made me feel!"

He laughed and reined in beside her. "You're an awesome rider. You gave me a run for my money. How do your ribs feel?"

She gave a slight shrug of her shoulders. "Not too bad, but the way I feel now, it was definitely worth it."

After they walked their horses around the ranch yard to cool down, he dismounted and wrapped the leather straps around the hitching post, then went to help Debra. He stepped beside her just as she swung down, her hands grabbing his shoulders as she slid to the ground.

She wavered and braced her hands on his chest, the heat from her fingertips searing right through his leather vest. "Sorry about that, cowboy. I didn't mean to jump on you."

He gripped her shoulders, bringing her closer. The warmth of their bodies touched full length. "That's okay." He smiled and tipped her hat back. "I'm a pickup man. I'm used to having people grab onto me." He moved closer, boxing her against her horse and breathed deep, sucking in an intoxicating scent of wildflowers, leather, and horse. He quickly lowered to her mouth.

His nose bumped into her hat. He cringed as she ducked under his arm.

"Um, I'll just go and get a grooming brush."

As she jogged off toward the tack barn, he gripped Brandy's saddle and bowed his head between his shoulders. Maybe it was his breath.

Or maybe she just didn't feel the same way as he did— although the sparkle in her eyes, the smile on her lips told him otherwise. Was it because of his ranch? Did she still think he was destined to fail like her father?

With a clenched jaw, he gathered air into his lungs, then headed toward the hitching post where Evening Star stood next to Branded Sunset. When Debra didn't return, he unsaddled Brandy and lugged the saddle into the tack barn, swinging it over an empty barrel. Unsaddling Evening Star, he draped his saddle on a barrel next to Debra's. After he hung the sweaty blankets side by side on a railing to air out, he looped both bridles together and hung them on the same hook.

He glanced down at the saddles, then up at the bridles, their reins intertwined. Trailing a finger along Debra's saddle, still warm from her body, he shuddered, feeling the bond to this pretty lady strengthen its hold on his heart.

Wondering where she'd disappeared to, he stepped inside the barn and heard her sweet voice as she talked softly to a horse in the back stall. Debra was sitting on the ground with the head of his new sorrel mare resting in her lap. "Looks like she's got colic, Joshua."

He nodded and draped his wrists over the top rail. "Yeah, I think she'll be fine, though. I bought her last weekend at a sale. With the change in diet, she started showing signs of colic earlier in the week. Jared came out and treated her for mild spasmodic shock. She was standing up earlier this morning when I checked on her. It'll probably be a few more days before she's up and at 'em."

"What's her name?"

He propped his booted foot on the bottom rung of the fence. "The papers call her Doc's Dandy, but it doesn't really suit her. Maybe you could come up with a good nickname."

Without looking up, she tilted her head to the side in contemplation. "John Wayne always had a sorrel quarter horse in his movies. You could go with Duke, or Duchess, since it's a mare. Or maybe O'Hara, for Maureen O'Hara. She starred in a lot of his movies."

"Big John Wayne fan, huh?"

"Yeah. Daddy and I had the whole collection. We'd stay up all night pigging out on popcorn and ice cream sundaes."

Joshua unhooked the gate and stepped inside. "My all-time favorite was *The Cowboys*," he said, hunkering down and giving the horse's neck a pat.

"Mine, too. I bet I've seen it a thousand times and I still cry whenever John Wayne dies."

"My dad's favorite was *McClintock*. We used to watch that

with him as kids." Joshua swept off his hat and set it on a post behind him, then raked his fingers through his hair.

"So, why does everyone call you J.D.?" she asked. "What does the D stand for?"

"I was named after my dad, David. Sometime in high school everyone started calling me J.D."

"Except me, you mean."

He smiled and tapped her nose. "And my mom."

Her lips turned into that pretty smile that always made his heart thump hard. The horse kicked and snorted. Debra turned and rubbed her palm over the mare's belly.

"You're good with them," he said. "Are you sure you're not the horse whisperer?"

She gave a short, cynical laugh and scooted away from the horse as if she didn't believe him. She stood, then rubbed her hands over her arms as she surveyed the barn, taking a moment to stare out a window above the stall. The midday sun shone brightly, sending fingers of sunrays into the ranch yard. Several horses stood motionless except for the switching of their tails.

"It's so peaceful out here, and the view is spectacular. I hate to admit it, but being stuck in a cubicle all day isn't exactly how I'd envisioned my new life. Don't get me wrong," she quickly defended herself. "It's nice receiving a steady paycheck, getting off at five, and going to bed by nine without every muscle in my body aching. I guess I'm still adjusting to the change. But you know what they say. You can take the girl out of the country—"

"But you can't take the country out of the girl," he quickly finished, standing behind her. Resisting the urge to touch her, he bent and spoke softly next to her ear. "You don't have to give up either, Debra. Lots of women work and live in the country."

She shook her head and moved away from him. "No way. As much as I love being here, I know from experience how fast things can go wrong."

"I know what I'm doing, Debra. You don't have to worry about me."

Staring up toward the hayloft, she blew out a gust of air. "I wish I didn't worry about you, Joshua, but I see you working so hard, busting your hump out here at your ranch all by yourself. I couldn't bear to see you end up like Daddy someday."

"Ahh, so now we're getting to the real issue." He turned away, raking his fingers through his hair in frustration. "You think I'm doomed to the same fate as your father."

"Okay, yes. I guess a part of me is afraid something is going to happen to you."

He gave a cynical shake of his head. "You and my father both. Gee, thanks for the vote of confidence."

"No, Joshua. You don't understand. You've got it all backwards. I'm afraid that I'll drag you down, that I'll be the one to keep you from reaching your dreams."

If he heard her run herself into the ground one more time, he was going to throw something. He tipped his head back and had to take a deep, calming breath to keep his voice level. "You know what?" he said, bending closer, getting right into her face. "From the moment we met at the auction barn, all I've heard is how *you've* failed, and how *you've* let your father down. That's a load of horseshit, Debra. Pardon my language, but I'm sick of hearing you run yourself down. You've got more brains and horse sense than half the ranchers around these parts. And you know what else? I'm tired of you comparing me to your father. I'm not your dad. I was born and raised on this ranch and learned from the best."

He stepped in front her when she wouldn't meet his gaze. "What was it you said the other night? We can't worry about what might or might not happen in fifteen years? It goes the same for you. Remember a few years ago when the rash of forest fires destroyed thousands of acres throughout Colorado and bordering states? It was tough, but we got through it and rebuilt. If I thought I needed more help, I'd hire someone in a heartbeat. Truth is, I love doing it by myself. Jared's around whenever I need him, and Brad helps me out quite a bit. And as far as my finances go, I've made some good investments over the years. I've got enough money in the bank to start three ranches if I wanted."

For the first time in his life, he felt proud. Proud of all he'd accomplished over the years. He didn't need a fancy title or a military uniform or a huge salary to prove his worth.

He gave a frustrated shake of his head. "What do I have to do to make you understand that I'm not your father? Man, I don't know whether to grab hold of your shoulders and shake some sense into you, or drag you down to the ground and kiss the living daylights out of you. Maybe that would convince you I'm not your dad."

She swung her head back, her jaw gaping open. "Ha, I'd like to see you try."

"Oh, really?" Joshua took two long steps toward her as she backed into the fence.

"Joshua?" she said, climbing the first rung of the fence backwards. "Don't you dare touch me or I'll—"

"Or you'll what?" he challenged, bracing his hands on either side of her, bringing his mouth right next to hers.

She pressed her lips together and closed her eyes, then turned her head away from him. A small tremor visibly shook her body and it was then he realized he'd scared her. She probably thought he was going to force himself on her like that ranch hand.

I'll be a son of a bitch. Standing alone in a barn with no one else around, of course he'd scared her. He chastised himself for threatening her, even in jest. He pushed away from her a few inches and tried to sound as gentle as he knew how. "It's okay, darlin'. I'm not going to touch you. I was only joking."

She didn't move. Her eyes remained clenched shut. Her chest rose and fell in shallow breaths. His gut tightened. "Damn, I didn't mean to scare you. Are you all right? Talk to me, honey."

She gave a heavy swallow but didn't answer. He stepped back and held up his hands. "Look, I'm not going to touch you. I'm sorry if I frightened you."

"No, you don't understand," she finally said in a shaky voice. She stepped down from the fence, her lashes slowly fluttering open. A shiny gloss from unshed tears shimmered in her eyes under the yellow glow of the sunshine streaming through the window. "You didn't scare me, at least not the way you think."

He warily stroked the back of his fingers down her arm until he touched her fingers, still quivering under his grip. "What is it then? You look like you're on the verge of tears."

"Do you want to know the real reason why I don't want you to kiss me?"

He lowered his shoulders and tilted his head to the side, trying to contain a smile. "I thought maybe it was my breath."

She gave a short laugh. "Your breath is fine, in fact it's part of the problem. You always smell so good."

He inched closer. "So, why don't you want me to kiss you?"

"Because of this," she said, reaching up and stroking her fingertips over his cheek, down his jaw to the whiskers covering his chin.

"I thought you liked my beard," he teased. "Said it made me look rugged."

"No." She laughed, making a tear drip down her cheek. She swiped her face then gave a little sniff. "I'm afraid . . ." she paused, then gazed into his eyes. "I'm afraid that if you kiss me even just one more time, I'm going to lose what little I have left of my heart." Her voice choked and he thought he'd never heard anything so sweet in his life.

He smiled and cupped her perfect face between his hands. "Where's the rest of it?" he asked, knowing full well that it was probably in the same place as his.

She curled her fingers into his shirt. "I don't think you fully understand, Joshua. After what happened between us last night at Jasmine's, I'm afraid if I let you kiss me, even just one more time, I won't be able to stop at just one kiss."

He pursed his lips and arched his brows, contemplating what she meant. Lowering his gaze to her shiny pink lips, he was reminded of sweet cotton candy. He let his gaze drop to her perfectly rounded breasts, the size of large fresh ripened peaches, then he scanned clear down to her boots, envisioning those delectable little toes that had rubbed against his bare feet the night of the storm. The night he held her in his arms in his cozy twin bed.

Nope, she was right. He definitely wouldn't be able to stop with just one kiss, either.

"You're doing it again." She stepped back a pace, wedging into the fence.

"Doing what?" he asked with a knowing laugh.

She crossed her arms over her chest. "What am I supposed to do when you look at me like that?"

"Like what?" he teased.

"Like you're going to devour every part of my body with your mouth?"

"I don't know," he answered through another laugh, pressing up against her. "Let me?"

She smacked him on the chest and huffed. "This isn't funny, Joshua. I'm not like all the other women you've dated. I can't just give myself to you and pretend it doesn't mean anything."

"Hold on," he said, backing up and giving her more space. "I've only had maybe two or three girlfriends over the years, and like I said, I've never brought them out to my ranch."

"Joshua?" she barely whispered. "I need to know what you want."

He dipped his head to the side of her neck and nibbled on the pulse point, beating as fast as his. "Isn't that obvious?" he answered, swaying into her while his hands roamed freely over her back.

"You're making it very difficult for me to keep my perspective." She cupped her palms over his cheeks and gently held him away from her face. "I told you my dreams. I want a husband, a home with lots of kids. Are you ready for that?"

Remembering Jared's lecture, he wasn't sure what he wanted. He flipped her hair behind her shoulder, trying to think of the right words to say. "What do *I* want?" he repeated, his voice lowering to a husky murmur. "I know what I *don't* want. I don't want to hurt you." He brushed the backs of his fingers over her sun-kissed cheeks. "I don't want you to have to work at a boring desk job that makes you miserable for the rest of your life, and I don't want to see you deny yourself the one thing that makes you happy." He motioned his head toward the horses out in the paddock.

"You're referring to horses?" Her voice sounded breathy and disappointed. "That's not exactly what I wanted to hear."

He stroked his thumb over her cheekbone. "I'm sorry, honey. It's the best I can do right now. I can't deny I have feelings for you, strong feelings, but I don't know if I'm ready for all that other stuff. You want a commitment, a ring, and if I know you as well as I think I do, you want a huge wedding with bridesmaids and a reception, and I'm sure there'd be horses riding off into the sunset by the end of the day."

She gave a sad laugh and closed her eyes. "You make me sound so juvenile."

"No, honey," he whispered and kissed the end of her nose.

"You should have all those things. I just don't know if I'm the one who can give them to you. It scares the hell out of me to think about being responsible for a wife and a family."

"Oh, Joshua, it is scary. That's why we need to back off before things get out of hand. If you're not ready for a commitment and I'm not ready to live on a ranch again, where do we go from here? I don't want to risk losing our friendship."

Wishing he knew the answer, he closed his eyes, circling his arms around her and bringing her full length against him. "You tell me, Debra, because this is killing me, not being able to touch you and hold you." Pressing his mouth into her ear, he added, "Make love to you."

"Okay," she murmured into his shirt.

"Okay, what?"

"I want you to make love to me, right here, right now. Forget everything I ever said about marriage. I don't care about anything else but being with you today."

He closed his eyes and almost cringed. "And tomorrow?"

"I . . . I don't want to think about tomorrow," she said, unsnapping the third snap of his shirt.

When she pressed her lips against his chest, he groaned, tunneling his fingers through her hair, knowing she was right in the first place. As much as he wanted to make love to her, to devour every part of her body with his mouth, he knew they weren't ready for that . . . at least not today. Maybe in time he would be ready to make a commitment and she'd be ready to return to ranching. But right now, he couldn't risk losing her because of a quick romp in the hay. She'd come to mean more to him than he'd ever imagined.

Dare he say he loved her?

He leaned his forehead against hers, his mouth almost touching hers as he spoke in an anguished voice. "I can't believe I'm about to say this, but we have to think about tomorrow, Debra.

As sure as Rusty will crow at dawn, tomorrow will come and then what? You say it won't matter, but it will. You've come to mean more to me than any other woman in my life. I don't want to risk hurting you."

The horse snorted and kicked her legs, struggling to stand. He tugged Debra toward the fence. "Watch out. Looks like O'Hara is feeling better."

Debra whirled around in his arms and leaned back against his chest. Their breathing was heavy with desire . . . with frustration. He wrapped his arms around her stomach, pressing into the lower swells of her breasts, wanting to feel them in his hands, watch her as he took her over the brink for the first time. He lowered and slid his cheek next to hers as O'Hara stood and shook the hay off her back.

Debra reached out and stroked her hand over the mare's face. "Easy, girl. You're going to be all right." Blowing out an exhausted sigh, she rested her head on his shoulder and closed her eyes, nuzzling her cheek against his. "So where do we go from here?" she asked, her voice a breathy whisper, as if she might cry again.

"Hell, I don't know. Maybe we could try dating for a while. See how things go."

"Dating is not the problem. It's the going home afterwards that's the problem."

He gave a low, throaty chuckle, totally in agreement. "Tell you what." He turned her around in his arms. "Next week is my class reunion. How about you be my date? I think Glen is going to ask Heather, and hopefully by then, Milt will be better. We could all go together in a limo. Do it in style."

"Sounds wonderful, but I thought you didn't want to go?"

He shrugged. "I'll admit a part of me didn't want to."

"Is it because of Michelle?"

He closed his eyes and groaned. "Am I that pathetic?"

"No, of course not. It's perfectly understandable you not wanting to see her again. Have you seen her since she left you?"

"Nope," he said and pulled from her arms. "Guess I didn't want her to think I've been pining over her all these years."

"Have you been?"

"No," he answered with a little irritation, then headed for the gate. "Do you want to go with me or not?"

"Yes, of course I want to go."

He took her fingers and tugged her out of the stall. "Come on then. Let's go get Dillan and head up to Camp Forester. I think O'Hara will be okay for a while. I'll leave a note for Brad to come out and check on her in a few hours."

"Have you ever thought about opening your own camp?"

He gave her a sideways glance and latched the chain. "What do you mean?"

"Like Camp Forester. I mean, you've got a great start. You could give riding lessons and reach out to kids just like Dillan and Kyle."

Her enthusiasm almost sucked him into the idea. Almost. He'd already let his father down once; if he tried something of that magnitude and failed, he'd never be able to live with himself. What if something happened to one of the kids?

He shook his head. "I wouldn't know where to begin, to start something like that. I think I'll just stick to breeding and training."

With their fingers intertwined, they strode through the barn and out into the sunlight. The crickets and the frogs were singing in harmony, fluctuating from loud to soft. Several doves took flight and landed on the roof of the red dilapidated barn. He wrapped his arm around her, keeping her as close to his side as possible.

Why did he suddenly get the feeling she could never be close enough?

CHAPTER FIFTEEN

Monday morning, Debra had just stepped off the elevator, determined to go directly to Robert's office and question him about the Air Force contract. She was afraid if she waited, she'd lose the nerve, afraid she might be fired for snooping into the top-secret files in the first place. She dropped her purse at her cubicle, then strode down the long corridor to the large corner office.

As she approached his office, it dawned on her why her father had sold out in the first place so many years ago. Surrounded by corporate greed and politics—no wonder he gave it all up to ranch. He might have had a horrible death in the end, but at least he'd spent the last days of his life doing what he loved the most. Ranching.

Now the question was, how was she going to spend the rest of *her* life?

Robert's door stood slightly ajar and she could hear him talking on the phone. Glancing around, she decided to wait right there till he was done with his call. She clutched the files to her chest and swept a loose tendril of hair into the bun that she had secured at the nape of her neck, hoping the hairstyle made her appear more professional.

"I've had it with you, Carolyn! Don't call me again."

Debra flinched, bringing her fingers to her mouth to prevent a gasp from escaping. Was he talking to Carolyn Strome? Looking around, she scooted closer to the door.

"Your threats aren't worth spit," he added with contempt in his voice. "You have no proof. It's your word against mine. Do you honestly think anyone is going to believe a gold digger like you? Get a grip, sweetheart. You're not getting another dime out of me. A month from now, I'll be clear across the country. Now I suggest you keep that pretty mouth of yours shut, or finding another job will be the least of your worries."

He slammed the phone down. Debra jerked away from the door and started hurrying down the hall toward her cubicle.

"Debra?" Robert's low voice called her from behind.

She froze in her tracks. "Yes?" she answered without turning around.

"I need to see you in my office."

She slowly turned around and gulped. "Right now?"

He straightened his tie. "If it's not too inconvenient," he said, smoothing a palm over the sides of his hair. "There's something I've been meaning to ask you."

Clutching the contracts to her chest, she retraced her steps to his office and pasted on a forced smile. "Actually, I was hoping to speak with you for a few minutes myself. Can I get you a cup of coffee or anything?" she asked, hoping to buy some time to get her heart back to a normal rhythm.

He shook his head. "Thanks, but I've had three cups since I arrived at seven this morning. I'm already agitated enough. Please, come in. How's your mother? Mom said she had a fabulous time at our party."

Still unnerved at overhearing his telephone conversation, Debra forced a smile, stepping across the threshold. "Mom had a wonderful time. They sure had a lot to catch up on. I think my mom has talked to your mom every night since." The door clicked shut behind her. Did he just turn the lock?

Inwardly, Debra cringed. Being alone with this man was the last thing she'd intended to happen. Hoping to keep this meeting as brief as possible, she headed for his desk.

"I thought we'd sit over here this morning," Robert said, gesturing his hand toward the maroon leather couch ensemble in the corner. His gaze did a swift scan of her attire from head to toe, her buttoned-up blouse and long blue business skirt, no doubt too prim for his tastes.

Waiting for her to sit first, he eased himself down beside her. "What's on your mind, Debbie?"

She squared her shoulders and set the files on the coffee table in front of him. "I've had a chance to read through some of our contracts as well as the new Air Force proposal and I had a few questions."

His brows arched as he slowly reached down to gather up the documents, but he didn't say anything. Feeling a need to explain, she said, "Jasmine and Amanda asked me to help them out with some of the accounting. I took the liberty of reading through them to get acquainted with the legal descriptions. I hope it's not a problem."

"Not at all," he said, totally taking her off-guard. "I'm glad you've taken the initiative to tackle something so complex. I'm sure you've got a lot of questions."

"First of all, the current contracts are due to be renewed in a month, and I wanted to make you aware of some of the discrepancies I've found before we write up the new terms."

He looked down at the stack of files and took in a deep breath, then tossed the documents on the table. "Actually, that's part of why I wanted to see you this morning. I'm afraid we aren't renegotiating any of our existing contracts. I'd planned to have you write up a letter and inform our customers next week."

"So, am I to assume you're hedging all bets on us winning the Air Force contract? Isn't that a little presumptuous on your part? What if—"

"From my sources," he said, interrupting her, "we'll be

awarded the contract sometime this week."

"Oh," she said, sounding surprised. "I have only one other question then. Throughout the document, you reference the East Coast facility in Boston with no mention of the Rocky Mountain division at all."

He nodded. "That's right."

She gave a confused shake of her head, her heart slowly sinking to her stomach. "I don't understand. What's going to happen to this division?"

He reached over and took her hand. "I'd hoped to keep this under wraps until we got the official word from the Air Force. But it looks like we'll begin computer support in October."

"In Boston?" she clarified.

"Yes, in Boston," he verified, placing his other hand on her thigh. "You have to understand, Debbie. Sometimes we have to make sacrifices for the better good of the whole company. Merging into two strategically located areas of the country makes the most sense right now. As fierce as competition in the technical market has become, consolidating the Rocky Mountain division with Boston and San Jose will make the best possible use of our technical capabilities and resources."

Pulling away from his touch, she stood and glared down at him. "When were you planning to tell us? October is only one month away. That doesn't give the employees much time to relocate."

He stood, shoving his hands into his trouser pockets, looking nonplussed at the situation. "That's why this has been kept under wraps for so long. Dad gave me the impression you were open for just about anything right now. With the expansion in Boston, there will be a managerial role opening that you could fill immediately."

"A management position?"

He cupped her shoulders and stepped closer, uncomfortably

close for her tastes. She had to force herself to remain grounded. "You've impressed me, Debbie. Since Jasmine has been so tied up with her husband, I'll be quite honest and tell you that I think your business skills are exceptional. And with your father and your ranch gone, I thought you'd jump at the opportunity to go to Boston with me. In fact," his eyes lowered to her lips, "I was hoping we'd take it a step further."

"A step further?" she barely repeated.

He massaged her arms, lowering his voice. "Think about it. You and me running this company just like our fathers did thirty years ago. We'd make a great team."

She just stood there with her jaw gaped open. This had all happened so suddenly, she didn't know what to think. On the one hand, this was the answer to her prayers. She could get back part of her father's legacy, just as she'd set out to do from the beginning. But it was her other hand that kept waggling a finger at her to follow her heart, and no way did it lead to Boston with Robert Nelson.

"What about my mom? I can't just leave her here by herself."

"She's not alone. She's got my mom and all her old friends. She's been on her own for over a year now since the divorce. That's the beauty of us going together. We can fly back anytime and see our folks."

"What about Jasmine? And Hank? And then there's Amanda and all the computer technicians on staff. Will they be relocating, too?"

"I know you've grown close to Jasmine, but with her husband being so sick, I doubt she's even in a position to move right now. As far as the others, we've put together a nice relocation package for a select few."

"A select few," she repeated, suddenly getting the bigger picture. "In other words, you're laying off everyone except management."

"Please understand this isn't personal, Debbie. Dad and I have gone over all the numbers. This is the best solution for Walson Technology."

"Isn't personal? Isn't your daughter conveniently living in Boston?"

"As a matter of fact, she is. And I'd love for you to meet her." He looked at her mouth again. "Go with me, Debbie. Let's turn this company into one of the top Fortune One Hundred companies."

Before she had a chance to react, he abruptly pressed his lips over hers, instantly jutting his tongue between her teeth. His breath tasted and smelled of stale coffee and something else she couldn't quite put a finger on, alcohol maybe? It was the same smell she'd noticed on his breath at his party whenever he got too close. Was Robert drinking on the job?

When his tongue reached to the back of her throat, she actually made a gagging sound. He obviously thought it was a moan of desire because he wrapped his arms clear around her waist and pressed his hips firmly against hers, the hardened bulge in his trousers letting her know exactly what he wanted.

At that moment, her nose tingled. She jerked from his hold just as a sneeze erupted. Then another. The third sneeze made her double over as she wrapped a hand around her midsection, each fit ripping through her ribcage.

"Hey, take it easy." Robert stepped back and pulled out a handkerchief from his back pocket. "Sounds like you're catching a cold. I hope it's not contagious. I can't afford to be sick right now." He wiped his mouth and blew his own nose. "Maybe you caught something while staying at Jasmine's. With Milten so sick, you should probably see a doctor."

"I'm not sick," she said, and almost laughed, realizing she *was* sick, but it had nothing to do with a cold. The idea of working for this man another day, much less gallivanting all the way to Boston to spend the rest of her life with him, made her want to do more than sneeze. Her stomach did a major roll.

Straightening, she pulled her shoulders back and looked him square in the eyes. "I'm not going to Boston with you, *Robbie*," she said with emphasis. "There's not enough money in the world that would justify spending another minute with you. Joshua was right. You're only out for yourself. If you'll excuse me, I have to stop by personnel and lodge a sexual harassment complaint, then I'm tendering my resignation."

"Big mistake," he warned, bracing his hands on the window behind her head, backing her against the ledge. "I've known most of these managers since I was old enough to walk. It would be your word against mine. And if you ever want to be more than a data entry girl, I'd suggest you reconsider my offer. I've got a lot of connections in Colorado."

She crossed her arms over her chest, hoping to appear confident and in control, while her insides hit eight point oh on the Richter scale. "What about Carolyn Strome?"

His eyes narrowed. "What about her?"

"I couldn't help but overhear what you'd said to her earlier. Maybe I'll give her a call. Find out exactly why she was fired."

She let out a gasp when he grabbed her hair at the back of her head. "Let me give you a piece of advice, sweetheart. You go anywhere near Carolyn and you'll regret the day you set foot in this building." Craning her neck farther back, he ground his lips hard against hers again.

Bile rose in her throat. She pushed him away, shoving him backwards onto the couch. "The only thing I regret is thinking I could actually work with a low-life scum like you. You're even worse than a pack of wild dogs." She turned and ran toward the door, swiping her lips with her hand.

As she struggled to unlock the office door, he came up behind her and twisted her arm behind her back. "I never should have listened to my father."

"Wh-what are you talking about?" She grimaced, straining to get away from his hold.

"The only reason I hired you in the first place was to keep an eye on you till you paid back every last cent you owe my family. I actually started to have feelings for you. I thought if we were married, I'd have instant access to every last dime that you've got coming to me." His grip tightened. "I guess it's onto plan B."

Plan B?

"I'm tired of waiting. Where's the money?"

With the side of her face pressed against the door, she could barely get the words out of her mouth. "Money? What money?"

"Don't play stupid with me. The money from your father's life insurance. It's been three months. Surely you've received a check by now."

She tried to shake her head. "There is no life insurance. I have no money. Please, let go. You're hurting me!"

"Liar!" He whirled her around and pinned her against the door, covering her mouth with his hand. She grimaced, but refused to let him know how much it hurt.

"My father may be a sap-hearted old man, but when it comes to business, I'm in control now. He gave your father my inheritance money from my grandfather, convincing me it was a sure thing. But your father failed, Debra, and it's way past time you paid it back. Either cough up the hundred grand with interest, or you're going to suffer a fate worse than your father's."

She stiffened, not sure what he meant by that. Jerking her face away from his hand, she said, "I told you. He didn't have any life insurance. He cashed out his policy before he died. I have no money. Your father said—"

"Forget my father. I'm in control now, and I'm tired of waiting."

Sheer terror was the only thing that fueled the rage building inside her now. Without another thought, she lifted her knee, nailing Robert directly in the groin. As he doubled over with a loud curse, she yanked the door open and fled to the elevators, punching the down button several times.

When the doors wouldn't open, she sprinted down the stairwell, taking the steps by twos all the way to the lobby. She didn't stop running till she was in her SUV with the doors locked.

Dropping the gearshift into drive, she squealed out of the parking lot, out into the warm Colorado sunshine. Robert wasn't going to get away with attempted rape. Somehow, she'd find this Carolyn Strome, and maybe together they could stop his abuse of power.

But right now, she wanted to get away from it all. She didn't know where she would go from here; she only knew she had to get away from Robert and all the greed of the corporate world.

She had to find herself.

A trail of dust kicked up behind Joshua's truck as he drove into the graveled lane leading to his ranch. Bud Kendrick had called him over this morning to help him load some cattle. Not that Joshua minded helping out the old man, but he had his own ranch to run.

He still had a whole field of cut alfalfa lying on the ground waiting to be baled. More rain was forecasted, and he might lose another cutting if it rotted and turned moldy. If that happened, he'd have to resort to buying his hay and having it shipped in by the semi-load like most of the other area ranchers.

Halting his truck in front of his parents' yellow ranch home, he spotted a silver SUV parked near the edge. His mood suddenly brightened. He stepped out of his truck and hollered,

"Debra?" He shut the door, looking around the deserted ranch yard, but saw no sign of her.

He strode toward the barn and searched the paddock for a buckskin mare with four white socks. He spotted Brandy immediately and couldn't contain a grin. There was a definite sweat mark made by a saddle on the mare's backside, a good indication that she'd recently been ridden.

The little filly that had been attacked by the dogs whickered and pawed at a palomino colt, playing in the corral. "I'll be doggoned," he marveled, enjoyingt the pretty sight, thumbing his hat back on his head.

Wondering what Debra was doing at his ranch on a Monday morning, he headed inside the steel barn and heard pawing and horses nickering from several stalls.

A few of the skittish two-year-old colts had been separated into adjoining pens. All the stalls had been mucked out and fresh bedding had been thrown down. He hadn't cleaned the stalls in three days, and the last time Brad or Jared had pitched in to clean stalls, Joshua had been down with the flu—and that was over five years ago.

He never did get around to putting an ad in the paper for a hired hand. There was a list of chores that needed to done and he was supposed to deliver a trail horse to a buyer up in Boulder tomorrow. Ironically, in his quest to better his father, he was doing more harm to his ranch by trying to do it all alone.

Admitting he needed help, he sure as hell didn't want some stranger on his property. He needed someone who was dedicated and wasn't afraid of a little hard work. Someone who did more than just fix fences and clean out stalls. He needed someone with a sixth sense where horses were concerned, a quality that couldn't be taught. It was an instinct bred in hearts from years of experience.

He needed Debra.

Thinking of going through the rest of his life as a lonely old rancher without anyone to share his life with made him realize that he wanted a wife. He wanted a family. He wanted kids, a whole dozen if possible. He wanted to fill this place with children . . . but only with Debra.

He knew he loved her more than life itself. But was she ready to move out here and become a rancher's wife? Not that he had a problem with her pursuing her dream of becoming a business-woman, if that's what she really wanted. A lot of women had both.

But he couldn't deny his own dreams of her working beside him every minute of the day, working and training the horses together. Crawling into bed every night, cuddling under their covers in thunderstorms. Making love all hours of the night until Rusty alerted them to another new day.

The grinding gears and the moan of the diesel engine of his old John Deere drew him around the barn to the back pasture. He had to blink to make sure he wasn't imagining things. Debra was driving the tractor with the big round baler on behind. Except for one last row, the whole field was almost all put up in large round bales.

A bead of sweat rolled down the back of his neck, reminding him how hot it had gotten this afternoon. The weather people had forecasted late afternoon storms all day, as a cool front was due to move in overnight. He glanced off toward the west. As predicted, a line of dark gray clouds was building in strength.

Hoping to help her finish before the storm hit, he jogged over to his cabin and made up a pitcher of ice water. He jumped in his truck and drove through the pasture, following the baler to the end of the row, where she was about a hundred feet from Elk Ridge Ravine. She turned the tractor and started heading back down the last row.

He sped up in front of her, caught her attention and signaled for her to stop. When she slowed the big rig to a halt, he whipped his truck into park, grabbed the jug of water, and jogged over to the tractor.

She remained in the cab with the diesel engine idling, pushing the door open with her booted foot. "Hi," she said, using the rim of her low-scooped T-shirt to wipe the perspiration beading her upper lip. He made another note to get the air conditioning fixed on the tractor cab.

Hoisting himself up onto the bottom step, he asked, "What are you doing out here?"

"I saw the storm coming and I thought you could use some help."

He held the cooler of water in front of her. "Thirsty?"

Without answering or looking up at him, she held her mouth under the spigot and took a long chug of water. Drips rolled down her chin, making streaks through the dust on her neck and in the valley between her breasts. Perspiration darkened the area in front, her T-shirt molding to her generous curves. Her shoulders were bare, her skin tanning in the afternoon sun.

Standing here so close in the enclosed cab he got a good whiff of her fresh wildflower scent. Combined with hay and perspiration and diesel fuel, they all mixed together to send his senses into a whirl. She was covered in dirt and straw, and God, he'd never seen her looking more beautiful. He'd better bail out now if he wanted to get the hay done before it rained.

"Why aren't you at Walson?" he asked.

She swiped her mouth with the back of her hand. "I quit."

The diesel engine of the tractor rumbled loudly all around them, the vibrations shaking their bodies in unison. Maybe he'd heard her wrong. He raised his voice and ducked his head inside the cab. "Come again?"

She switched off the ignition, leaned forward and positioned her face mere inches from his. But instead of raising her voice, she whispered, "I quit."

Although he wanted to give a whoop and a holler at her declaration, he said, "I don't understand. Why?"

She sat back and slouched against the torn vinyl tractor seat, expelling a huge gust of air. "Turns out you were right. Ol' Robbie boy is shutting down the Rocky Mountain division. He'll most likely be announcing layoffs by the end of the week."

"That son of a bitch hired you, then laid you off?"

She shook her head. "Oh, no, he offered me a full relocation package, even promoting me into management if I wanted. Said we could run the company together like our fathers had so many years ago."

"So why didn't you take it? Isn't that what you wanted?"

"Unfortunately . . ." She hesitated, picking at her fingernails. "He wanted more than just a business relationship."

His stomach muscles tightened. "What do you mean?"

She rolled her eyes. "It means he made a pass at me."

His fingers curled into a fist. "I'll kill the bastard."

Tipping her head back, she laughed, as if he were kidding. "Don't you dare. I'm going to handle this legally. I've already put in a call to human resources and lodged a formal complaint. I called the lady who was fired before me. Her name was Carolyn Strome. I thought maybe if she had the same problems, we could make a stronger case against him."

"What did she say?"

"I don't know, it's weird. She practically warned me to steer clear of Robert and made me promise never to call her again. If I didn't know any better, I'd say she was scared."

"Maybe he's threatening her."

Debra rubbed her arms and gave a noticeable shudder.

"Debra? What's wrong? Did he threaten you?"

"I guess you could say that, but it's not what he might do to me, but more of what he said that bugs me more than anything.

He said the only reason I was hired was to make sure I paid back all the money my father owed his family."

"What are you talking about? What money? I thought you had all your debts paid."

"All but one," she clarified. "Remember me telling you Daddy got an investor to give him some money to convert our ranch?"

He nodded, not liking where this was headed.

"Stan Nelson loaned him the money and my father promised to pay it back in five years with interest. That was over one year ago. Robert said the only reason he agreed to hire me was to make sure I paid back the loan, which I'd planned on doing anyway," she quickly added. "Apparently, Robbie's not as patient as his father."

"So what happened?"

"Robbie wants his money now. He thinks I received some kind of a settlement from Dad's life insurance."

"I thought you said he didn't have any insurance."

"He didn't, but Robbie doesn't believe me. That's when he forced himself on me and I introduced him to my knee."

If Joshua weren't so angry, he'd laugh. "I'd like to have seen that."

"I came straight out here from Walson. I didn't know where else to turn."

That told Joshua more than she knew. "Robert's not going to get away with this, honey. We'll get this Carolyn Strome and with your testimony, maybe we can even get him arrested for attempted rape."

She blew out a gust of air, rubbing her eyes. "I sure bring out the best in guys, don't I?"

"As a matter of fact," he said, giving her a smile, "you do."

She looked down at her T-shirt and laughed, but her voice quivered, betraying her emotions. "I borrowed some of Heather's old clothes. I hope she doesn't mind."

"Hey," he said, sensing she was on the verge of tears. "Are you okay?"

She closed her eyes and breathed deeply, then looked up at him and smiled. "I am now. I'm glad you're home."

"Home, huh?" He set the water jug on the floor of the cab, hunkering down in front of her. "I like the sound of that." He rubbed his hands over her jean-covered thighs.

"I called my mom," she said, reaching over and picking a piece of hay off his shoulder. She smoothed her hand over his arm, the gesture purely innocent, but the sensations of her fingertips rubbing his muscles made him want to tug her into a sensual embrace.

"I'm moving in with her till I can find a place of my own."

He had to do a double shake of his head. "Say what? Why? You know you can stay with Jasmine as long as you need to."

"We've been through this before, Joshua. They need their privacy. Now that I'm out of a job, I need to check out a few employment agencies in Denver, see what's out there. And besides, Robbie may be a low-life scum, but I still want to find a way to pay back Stan the money he loaned my father."

She gave a frustrated sigh and draped her wrists over the steering wheel. "If I can't find anything right away, I'll probably temp for a while."

Although it galled him that she had to pay them a dime, he admired her need to clear her father's name. He tilted his head to the side, looking up at her from the corner of his eye. "There's a job opening here," he heard himself say. "You could work for me." By the incredulous look in her eyes, he sensed an emphatic "no" about to roll off her tongue.

She looked him square in the eye and asked, "How much are you paying?"

There was no smirk, no indication that she was kidding. She seriously wanted to know what he would pay her to come work for him. *For openers, how about just a warm body to crawl into bed with every night and a pretty smile to start my day off every morning?*

"Well?" she reiterated, her brows arched in impatience, waiting for him to answer. "You made me an offer. Are you willing to put your wallet where your mouth is?"

He leaned his elbow on her thigh and rubbed his jaw, forcing his gaze to her eyes, not on her shiny wet lips. "Well, let's see," he said clearing his throat, trying to take her seriously. "How much you making now?"

She gave an amused laugh. "Not nearly enough. And I'll need benefits."

He chuckled and stood, leaning his shoulder against the cab of the tractor, having absolutely no intention of hiring this woman to do anything. If she wanted to work out here, day in and day out, it was going to be as his wife and nothing less. He just prayed she was serious about returning to ranch life. As she very well knew, ranching was a hard life with long, grueling hours. Was she willing to give up her dreams of being a career woman?

He hooked his thumb in a belt loop and propped his booted foot on the back tire of the tractor. "If I didn't know any better, I'd say you were serious. Why the change of heart? Thought you wanted the city life."

She gave a long, wistful glance over his acreage before she lifted her shoulders in a shrug. "I guess I came to the conclusion that no matter where I am, there are always going to be problems. Like you said, life isn't a fairy tale, and if I had to choose between being confined in a cubicle pushing paperwork all day long or working in the great outdoors with some of the world's most magnificent creatures, then guess what I'd choose, hands down?"

She looked up at him, passion flickering in the depths of her big brown eyes. "All the money in the world couldn't replace the feeling of satisfaction I get after a hard day's work on a ranch, Joshua. You could offer me minimum wage and I'd probably take it in a heartbeat."

"Done," he said, tugging the brim of his hat down. "I'll even credit you for a whole day's labor for cleaning out the stalls." When she looked up at him with eyes popping, he tapped her straw cowboy hat down over her forehead and had to force himself to keep from grinning. "Better hurry up and finish this last row before that storm hits." He motioned his head behind her to the dark green wall cloud quickly forming in the west.

When she turned around, her face drained of all color, her normally tanned complexion turning off-white. Her fingers trembled when she clenched her knuckles around the gearshift.

Remembering how deathly afraid she was of storms, he gripped her shoulders and spoke close to her face. "Hey, I just remembered. We need to herd the horses up to the barn before this storm hits. I don't want any of them running out into the creek. The water rises pretty fast. Why don't I take over the tractor and baler and you go close the gate to the back pasture."

He tweaked her chin between his thumb and forefinger. "Besides, I was only kidding about you working for me. I wouldn't feel right having you doing all my grunt work."

She flinched away from him. "Ha! I knew it! You weren't serious about hiring me at all. You say I had nothing to do with my father's ranch going under, but when it comes down to it, you don't trust me to work your ranch any more than my father trusted me to work his!"

She tried to push past him, but he braced an arm in her way. With her face mere inches from his, she narrowed her gaze. "Admit it, Joshua. You don't think I have the gonads to do a man's job!"

He had to bite his cheek to keep from laughing. This woman

could turn emotions on and off faster than an outdoor water spigot. He gripped her shoulders and firmly set her back down onto the tractor seat. "You may not have the gonads, lady, but you sure as hell have the spunk. You got a temper worse than any steer I've ever tangled with. Anyone ever tell you that?"

"Yes, as a matter of fact. Something else I inherited from my father, so if you'll excuse me, I need to go close the *gate*. It's been a few months, but I'm pretty sure I know how to latch a chain." She tugged her cowboy hat down, grabbed the water cooler, and scooted around him, about shoving him off the tractor.

She jumped down and charged toward his truck, huffing and puffing like she was about to blow her stack. He reached in the cab, shut all the vents, then hopped down, not knowing what would be worse, staying out here with Debra or being caught in the storm that was quickly approaching.

She slapped her palms on her dusty jeans and swung the back door to his truck open. "By the way," she said, flinging the water jug onto the floor of the backseat. "The PTO gets stuck on the tractor if you go around the end too fast, and I think one of the gears is about to bust off the baler."

"I know," he said bracing a hand on the door and looking down at her. "With you helping out around here, I'd hoped to have more time to fix things up. After you get that gate closed, I need you to start cleaning out the old red barn. I'm tearing it down and putting up a new steel building to match the other one. When all the kids show up next summer, I want this place to be one of the premier camps for kids in America. You can start in the loft then—"

"Wait. Back up," she said, giving him a double take. "You're opening an outreach camp for kids?" Her voice took a drastic turn, sounding almost excited.

"Depends." He moved closer and lowered his gaze to her lips

then back to her eyes.

"On what?"

"I need an office manager and someone to run all the business aspects of getting this thing off the ground. With Walson shutting down the Rocky Mountain division, Jasmine will be out of a job as well. I thought maybe the two of you could work together and acquire permits, apply for grants, get insurance, set up the marketing, you name it. Are you willing to put your college degree to good use and sit your butt in a chair and push paperwork?"

Her mouth gaped open as she blinked several times, probably trying to digest it all. "I don't know what to say," she finally said. "Are you sure? I mean this is a huge undertaking."

He cupped her shoulders and squeezed. "Do you trust me, Debra? Do you truly believe in me? You say I don't believe in you, but what about you? Do you believe I can make this outreach camp for kids a reality? Or do you think I shouldn't even try? That I'll never succeed?"

"No." She emphatically shook her head then wrapped her arms around his neck. "I mean yes. I trust you and I know you'll be a huge success." She drew back, shaking her head. "But I don't know if I'm the best person for the job. What if I'm not—"

"Perfect? What if I find out you might have a flaw here and there? God forbid either of us should have a weakness, Debra, but together, we can do anything we set our minds to."

She tipped her head back and squealed, "This is incredible! First we'll need to apply for the permits and have your land surveyed, and then—"

"Debra?" He tugged her close to his body, every luscious curve molding perfectly against him. "Shut up so I can ki—"

But she kissed him first. Their hats bumped together in their need to be as close to each other as possible. Her tongue delved deeply, searching with mastery. She tugged open the second and third snaps to his shirt, running her fingers over his chest.

He groaned and pressed her against the door of his truck. Her shirt had ridden out of her jeans and he slid his palms over the skin of her lower back, the hot slick surface about doing him in. "The hay," he muttered through her desperate kisses.

She only spread her legs, allowing him to slide his knee into the sweet spot between her thighs.

"The gate," he said next, feeling her pull him back toward the seat of his truck.

"You know," she said, feverishly kissing his cheek, sliding her mouth back to his ear. "I've never been in the backseat with a guy before."

He chuckled and cupped his palms over the roundness of her rump. "From previous conversations," he said through her kisses. "I'm guessing you've never been in the front seat with a guy either. But Debra . . ." Kiss, kiss, kiss. ". . . honey . . ." Kiss, moan, kiss. "I kind of wanted our first time . . . to be special. We could go over to my cozy little cabin . . . maybe share a shower first, you know. Go slow."

"Slow?" she said, delving her hands inside his shirt, gently scratching her fingernails over his skin, sliding up around his neck. She stood on his boots and planted her lips on his, reaching her tongue inside and teasing his. "How slow is slow?" she asked, thrusting her tongue in and out, mimicking the sex act.

Holy shit.

"What happened to innocent little Debbie Walker?" he asked, grabbing her rump and setting her on the end of the backseat.

She gave a seductive laugh. "She grew up," she said, pushing backwards. "So, is this what is referred to as the negotiation couch?"

He chuckled and grabbed her boots, sliding her back to him so she was lying flat on her back with her legs between his, dangling out the door. He gave a quick glance down at her knees, precariously situated below his male anatomy. "Uh, you're okay with this, right?" He arched his brows, slipping her a lopsided grin. "Your history with men has me a little nervous. You sure you wouldn't rather go to my cabin?"

"Do you have your cell phone?"

He patted his shirt then shook his head. "I think I set it on the counter when I filled up the water jug."

"Perfect. I definitely don't want to go back to your cabin. We won't have to worry about any phone calls out here." She reached up and curled her fists into his shirt and tugged him down on top of her. "Now shut up and start negotiating."

CHAPTER SIXTEEN

Joshua gave a sultry chuckle and pressed her down to the leather upholstery, lying completely on top of her without reserve. He quickly lowered to her lips and moaned into her mouth. "Sweet little Debbie." He massaged her lips for several seconds then drew away. "Mmm, you taste good. What is it? Something fruity."

She inched her hands down to her waist and he almost flinched away when she slid further between their jeans, brushing incredibly close to his zipper. He sucked air through his teeth. "Darlin', you sure you haven't done this before?"

She giggled. "I'm positive. In fact, I'm stuck. You're going to have to get off me if you want this."

He scratched the side of his head. "That's not really how it works, but for argument's sake, I'll give you the benefit of the doubt." He rolled off her until he was lying beside her. They both pushed clear over to the other door so their heads were practically resting on the armrest, their boots intertwined, hanging out the other side.

She turned on to her side, facing him with her back to the seat. Their thighs pressed full length against one another, demonstrating just how perfectly they fit together. The bench was surprisingly wide enough to accommodate both of them. Whoever invented quad cab pickups definitely had a couple's best interest in mind. Sliding his arm under her neck, he tucked her snuggly into the crook of his elbow.

When she slid her hand back to her pocket, he heard a crinkly sound and he had to tease. "I'm shocked, Miss Walker."

With her hand still in her pocket, she froze, her eyes widening with concern. "Why?"

"That you had the forethought to bring protection."

She gasped. "It's not . . ." she stopped midsentence, her face turning bright crimson. He couldn't help but let out a loud bellowing laugh. She yanked her hand from her pocket and held up a red, cellophane-covered candy disk. "You know, for a man who's got a woman lying next to him who's known for her knee-jerk reactions, you sure are pushing your luck."

He spoke through his laughter. "I know, but you should see your face. Priceless."

"For your information, this is the only thing I have in my pocket." She raised her head, her expression turning serious. "I figure you had—I'm not on the pill or anything. I never even thought . . . maybe this isn't—"

He covered her sweet pink lips with his mouth and pressed her head down into the crook of his elbow. When he felt her completely melt into his arms, he placed a soft kiss on the tip of her nose. "Don't worry," he murmured, next to her mouth. "I'm covered. Or at least I will be in a few minutes."

Looking down, he uncurled her fingers, now tightly clenched around the candy disk. "So, this is what you were going for." After unwrapping it, he slid it onto his tongue. "Good, but not the same. Your lips must add extra sweetness."

She reached up and swept off his hat then dumped it on the floorboard behind him. "Joshua, would you do me a favor?"

He squished in closer, sliding his knee between hers. "Anything. You name it."

She unabashedly draped her leg all the way over his waist. "Could we forget about Walson? Forget about the Nelsons." She unsnapped the remaining two snaps to his shirt. "Take me somewhere far away. Someplace I've never been before."

He smiled and pressed his leg firmly into the apex of her jeans. "Darlin', I'll take you wherever you want to go." He kissed her ear, drawing her perfect little lobe into his mouth, tasting salt and sweet perspiration. Her earthy scents of wildflowers and hay were better than any aphrodisiac money could buy. She shivered and arched her neck as he kissed down to the pulse point of her throat, beating almost as fast as his.

A gust of wind whirled through the cab. A distant thunder rumbled in the distance lasting several seconds. She wedged up on her elbows and glanced toward the sky behind them. It hadn't started raining yet, but the clouds were dark and heavy, looking like they could let loose at any moment.

She looked back at him with her brows arched in worried anticipation. "Do you think this is safe? Necking in the middle of a storm?"

He chuckled and tugged her back to the crook of his arms. "I can see I need to give you a few more lessons on the fine art of appreciating Mother Nature, and I ain't just talking about wind and rain."

"What about the gate? Shouldn't we go close it?"

"The horses were all up by the barn when I headed out. They'll stay under the overhangs if it starts to storm."

She relaxed her shoulders and traced her fingertips over his jaw, back to his ear. "I'm suddenly nervous."

"About the storm?"

She shook her head.

He smiled and thought she was undoubtedly the sweetest woman he'd ever known. His heart shouted for him to say those three little words to her. The same words he'd never been able to tell his father. But somewhere in the recesses of his mind, something told him to beware, that opening up too soon, too fast, might push her away. He'd professed his love openly and honestly to Michelle almost from their first date. He'd fallen hard and fast, and ended up losing her in the end. Now it seemed, he'd plunged headfirst down the same path.

The last things Michelle had said to him was that he was overbearing and that he'd suffocated her with all his affection. Said she'd needed her space, just like Debra had said a month ago. Now here he was, crowding her in the backseat of his pickup. Although he had absolutely no reservations about marrying her and making her his wife, was she ready for this?

He placed a kiss on her forehead. "Tell you what. Maybe we oughta go back to my cozy little love nest, talk about it, and make sure this is what you want."

"No, Joshua. I'm done talking. Please," she covered his mouth, speaking through devouring kisses. "This is what I want. *You* are what I want."

Her tongue slipped into the action, the tip barely touching his teeth. He closed his eyes and became still as she traced his lips with the tip of her tongue, first the top, then the bottom. She deepened her search, her breathing turning heavy while her fingers combed through his hair.

Her slow inquisition wreaked havoc with any self-control he might have had. He quickly drew her tongue into his mouth, devouring every sweet morsel she had to give. His hands roamed up and down her side, inching lower, pressing her firm hips into his jeans, suddenly made tighter with desire.

Another thunderclap rumbled around them. She didn't even flinch. Hopefully, this meant she was learning to trust him. She'd found her way into his heart as an eight-year-old little girl, and now he realized she'd been there all along. He loved Debra Walker to the depths of his soul and wanted to spend a lifetime with her.

A little moan escaped into his mouth as he continued to swirl his tongue with hers. He savored the sweet raspberry taste as her overflowing compassion filled his soul. He inched his hand higher, gently cupping her breast through her shirt with the palm of his hand. As right and perfect as this felt, he could only imagine how right everything else would feel.

The sounds of the rushing water from the stream nearby were mixed with sensual sighs of delight as she unleashed her untapped reservoir of passion. His hand slid over her firm stomach, fiery and hot to the touch. A sensual sheen of perspiration only heightened his desires to love her, to pleasure her. He traced his tongue over her lips then slid soft kisses along her jaw to her ear. She stroked her hands over his chest. Her fingers felt like prongs of fire as they kneaded his flexing muscles.

He gazed down at the voluptuous mounds that were her breasts, straining under her tight-knit tank top. He trailed his fingertip along the neckline of the low-scooped T-shirt, the tips of her breasts protruding through the thin material, begging to be suckled. But it was her mouth he wanted to concentrate on first, her lips shining and aching to be kissed.

She exhaled fully into his kiss, her long curling lashes fluttering over her eyes, brushing his cheekbones. He wanted to make this first time the most memorable one of her life.

Debra reveled in the strength and tenderness of this extraordinary man. Joshua had so much to give, so many years of hiding behind his barricade of fear and distrust. Had she finally succeeded in crumbling that wall?

Something drew her to meet his hips, something deep, something primitive. She'd never felt this overwhelming desire to be so close to another human being. Everything about him was hard and masculine, yet his kisses and the way he touched her was soft and tender. Her heart beat loudly in her ears, drowned out only by the distant rumbles of thunder. She thought of the little filly and hoped it would stay near her mother under the overhang of the barn.

She exhaled deeply into his mouth then arched her head back. "This is how I felt the other night at Jasmine's. I don't know what you do to me, but I feel like I'm on fire." With his leg between hers, she squeezed her legs together like a vice around his thigh. He slid his hand around her ribcage, his thumb sneaking under her bra and brushing against the lower swells of her breasts.

In one quick movement, he unhooked the clasp and lifted her shirt up to her neck. The tips of her breasts hardened as the warm summer breeze filtered through the opened cab door. Goosebumps covered her heated flesh.

He raised slightly and gazed down at her with dreamy desire. "Do you have any idea what you do to me? How beautiful you are?"

A little abashed at being exposed, she tugged him back to her lips, raising her hips, not wanting any separation between them. She dragged wet kisses back to his ear and whispered through heavy breaths. "I don't know if I'm doing this right."

He cupped his hand over her breast and tweaked the hardened tip between his fingers. "Darlin', you just follow your heart, and your body will do the rest naturally."

Soft moans escaped her throat as her fingers clenched his shirt. Dear God in heaven, every fiber of her being wanted to be with this man. She loved him so much. Was she ready for this? Was *he* ready for this? Was he serious about hiring her at the ranch? And if they were going through with what she thought they were going to do, did that mean he would marry her?

She felt a scorching flame shoot from her hips all the way to her breasts to the roots of her hair. She gasped and had to bite her lip. "Oh, Joshua." She tunneled her fingers into his hair, rocking her hips harder against his thigh.

Sliding his fingertips along the ridge of her jeans, he unfastened the top button with one simple movement then deftly tugged the zipper down. When his fingers slid into the soft tuft of curls at the juncture of her thighs, she grabbed his hands, stilling his movements. She'd never even allowed her mother to see her before, now here she was, with a man she loved with all her heart and soul, ready to bear it all.

"If you want me to stop," he murmured through his kisses. "I will." All the while the tips of his fingers cleverly kneaded the soft flesh of her secret lips.

She relaxed her grip on his hand and closed her eyes. "No," she sighed through a heavy breath, deciding to throw modesty out the window.

"No, you want me to stop?" he asked, delving deeper, hot, moist fluid from her body seeming to glide him into places she wasn't even aware she had.

"Or no, you want me to keep going."

"Yeah," she sighed. "It's . . . oh, yeah . . . I just . . ." she gasped as he stroked further back with the softest touch.

"It's just what?" he teased, slipping his finger deeper inside then pulling out in slow thrusting movements.

She gasped with every deep thrust. "You're very . . . good at this . . . nature stuff." She turned and spoke near his ear. "I . . . I've definitely never been here before."

"Hold on, darlin', 'cause we ain't there yet." He gave a throaty chuckle, tugging her jeans down over her hips. When his fingers delved quickly back between her legs and worked their magic, he trailed wet kisses up and down her neck and stopped at the hardened tip of her breast. He tugged it into his mouth, nipping at the tip with his teeth.

That was it. She let go of everything. Nothing else mattered now as she fell into a world where only two people existed. Her body shuddered. The feeling was like nothing she'd ever experienced before. *Heaven.* She must be in heaven as her very own guardian angel took her to a far distant galaxy.

His mouth covered hers as he brought her to the mountain top, a peak they'd both climbed together. She held her breath, her legs firmly wrapped around his hand, his fingers buried somewhere in the depths of her soul.

As if she'd just broke through the gates of heaven, her insides exploded and she arched her neck, blowing out a huge gust of air. The sound that came from her throat didn't even sound like her, but she didn't care. She wanted him all, she wanted him now.

"I love you, Joshua," she heard herself say through a whisper. "I love you so much."

As she slowly descended from the peak of ecstasy, he slid his hand up and over her exposed rump, pressing her against his belt buckle. She peered up at him through slitted lids, enough to see a sensual smile spreading from ear to ear.

Suddenly embarrassed, she groaned and turned her face into his chest, trying to hide the heated blush covering her cheekbones. "That's never happened to me before. It was absolutely incredible. I don't know what came over me."

He gave her rump a gentle caress. "What did you think happened after the prince kissed the princess in your storybooks?"

Through a dreamy smile she looked up and sighed. "They rode off on a horse, got married, then lived happily ever after."

"Okay," he said, arching his brows. "Is tonight soon enough?" He flicked a glance at his watch. "If we leave now, we could be in Reno by sunset. Even though a horse is more romantic, a jet might be more practical."

"What did you say?"

"Let's get married. It's got to be a heck of lot cheaper than hiring you, and that's not even discussing the benefits." He started unfastening his western belt buckle.

"Wait," she said, blinking. "Did you just propose?" She reached down and tugged her underwear back over her hips.

He arched his brows, watching as she wiggled into her jeans. "Uh, sweetheart. I'm not done with you."

Her face flamed red hot as she tugged her bra and her shirt down over her breasts. "I'm sorry, but this is just so overwhelming."

"Tell me about it," he said, sliding his hand back under her shirt. He cupped her breast, then pressed a bulging mass of desire against her thigh, groaning into the side of her neck. "Overwhelming doesn't describe the way I'm feeling right now."

She laughed and pulled his hand away. Lightning streaked across the sky stretching from one end of the horizon to the other, followed by a loud explosion of thunder. Glancing out the window, she hoped the foal she'd let out stayed by its mother.

In the next instant water poured from the heavens spraying into the opened door where their boots were hanging out. She jerked her feet inside and quickly reached over and yanked the door shut. Rain began to pummel the roof of his pickup.

Normally, she'd be freaked out by the storm, but right now, she was more freaked out by what was transpiring between her and Joshua—and she wasn't just talking about sex. She turned to face him, gripping his hands to keep them from roaming all over her body. "You're making this hard for me to think," she said, avoiding his lips as he dipped to her mouth. "Joshua, stop. As much as I want to continue on our, er, nature trip, I want to make sure I understand you correctly."

He cleared his throat and straightened, trying to look serious, but his gaze was heavy with desire. "What don't you understand?"

"Well, for starters, why now all of sudden? I mean, deciding to open an outreach camp for kids is a huge decision in itself. Now you're asking me to marry you?" She swept her hair back over her head and shoved his leg off hers. "I thought you never wanted to get married. Said it was too risky."

"Well," he said, resituating himself beside her, his belt buckle dangling unfastened. "For one thing, you're out of a job and need a place to stay. I need help with my ranch and someone to get the ball rolling on this outreach camp. It's perfect. We'll build a huge colonial house back here by the stream just like you've always wanted. It'll be everything you've ever dreamed."

Debra held her breath. *Love, Joshua. Please tell me you love me. Please tell me this isn't just a business transaction—a marriage of convenience. Please tell me you love me.*

He slid his hands around her waist and tugged her closer. "Marry me, Debra. Make me the happiest man on earth. Together we can do anything."

Tears welled in her eyes. "I love you, Joshua," she whispered, praying with all her heart he would return those three little words.

He kissed the tip of her nose. "Does that mean yes? Does that mean you'll be my wife? Maybe someday we can work on those two boys and two girls you've always wanted."

Say it, Joshua. Say you love me. Please tell me you love me. Blood pulsed loudly through her veins, drowned out by the heavy rain pounding on the roof of his pickup. As the seconds ticked by, she felt a thick lump in her throat and she thought she was suffocating.

Crushed, she closed her eyes and blew out the pent-up air in her lungs. Her heart shattered into a million tiny pieces at the stark reality staring her in the face. He couldn't say it. His heart would always be with his first true love . . . Michelle.

So what should she do? She loved this man with all her heart and soul. She couldn't imagine life without him. And she had absolutely no doubt that he had strong feelings for her. Maybe in time, he would come to love her, too.

"Debra?"

She opened her eyes.

"Marry me?"

She heard a voice say, "Yes," but it didn't sound like hers. A loud thunderclap shook the ground. He cupped her face and sealed their engagement with a deep devouring kiss. The rain turned to hail and she gasped.

"Come on," he said, hooking his belt buckle back together. "Let's get out of this storm. As much as I'd like to finish our nature study, I think I'd rather do it properly with you as my wife. We can be in Reno tomorrow night and get a fancy honeymoon suite with a large, king-sized bed where our feet won't hang off the end."

"What about the reunion?" She asked in a shaky voice, not entirely sure she was ready for something this fast. "We've already committed to Milten and Jasmine and Glen and Heather."

"Tell you what. Since we'll be dressed up anyway, we'll do it afterward. Glen owns a four-passenger Cessna, and I'll get him to file a flight plan to Reno. I'll get Mom and Brad to watch Heather's kids, and she can be your maid of honor. It'll be the perfect storybook ending." He climbed over the seat and slid behind the wheel.

Maybe not quite perfect. She followed, sliding down in the middle next to him, but she couldn't seem to focus on anything but the fact that Joshua didn't love her—not like he loved Michelle. His heart would always belong to another woman.

Debra swallowed hard. Could she accept that? Could she go through life knowing he didn't return the kind of love she felt for him?

He switched on the ignition and the windshield wipers, but she could barely make out the broad side of the old red barn. She just prayed Brandy had found cover. Her heart jumped out of her throat. "The little filly!" she almost screamed. She grabbed Joshua's arm. "I let her out in the paddock to play with the colt!"

He wrapped his arm around her shoulder. "Take it easy. She'll stay by her mama till we get her into the barn."

As he drove slowly toward the ranch yard, he tugged her closer, placing a kiss on the top of her head. "I know you've dreamed of the big wedding thing, but I kind of got soured on that the last time around. Are you okay with Reno?"

They hit a terrace and she grabbed the dash to steady herself. All she'd ever dreamed of since she was ten was the perfect storybook wedding. She wanted to be married in a church with a white runner down the aisle. She wanted bridesmaids and flower girls and a beautiful white gown with a train that trailed half the length of the church. She wanted to carry a bouquet of pink roses and have a three tier wedding cake with a little fountain of champagne in the middle. She wanted to dance with her husband under a canopy of stars as a band played their song.

Their song. They didn't even have a song.

She'd also dreamed of her father walking her down the aisle. She blinked back the sting of tears. Her father was gone now. All she had was her mother. Maybe a big wedding wasn't important. What was important was that Joshua was willing to make a commitment to her. He'd even said that maybe someday they'd work on having kids.

Maybe she repeated to herself. Did that mean he wasn't sure?

"Debra? You okay?" he asked, holding her secure as the truck bounced over the hayfield. "You don't look like a woman who just got everything she ever dreamed of as a little girl."

Not everything, she wanted to say. She slid her hand onto his thigh and gave him a forced smile. "Guess I'm a little uneasy about this storm. I hope the filly is okay."

A lightning bolt flashed, darting from one end of the universe to the other. In the next instant, another struck the cupola on top of the old red barn releasing an ear-shattering explosion that rocked their truck. A gulf of fire shot from the roof.

"Oh, my God!" she screamed.

Several horses that were huddled under the overhang stampeded away from the ball of fire toward the back paddock. She grabbed Joshua's arm. "The horses! They're stampeding toward the steep part of the ravine!"

Joshua gunned the accelerator till they came up to the gate. He slammed it into park and reached across her lap to grab a lariat off the floor of the cab. "Call nine-one-one," he ordered. "Find the filly and get her into the steel building with her mother. The horses know where to stay away from. It's Brandy I'm not sure about. I'm going after her."

Before she could make any objections, he was out of the truck and flagging her to drive through the gate. She slid over and dropped the gearshift into drive, gunning through the gate. She pulled up in front of Joshua's cabin and whipped the truck into park, then got out, and watched through the pouring rain as he ran over to the steel barn. He let out a loud whistle that was barely audible over the storm, but Evening Star pranced up beside him. He grabbed hold of the horse's mane and hoisted himself on top, bareback, then kicked his horse in the flanks. Evening Star galloped straight into the hail and wind.

Debra tipped her head back to the sky, letting heaven's floodwaters pour over her face. *Dear God, please don't let anything happen to Joshua.* If he got hurt because he'd gone after her horse, she'd never forgive herself.

Rain pummeled against Joshua's face as he crouched low next to Evening Star's head. He gripped his legs tighter and almost slid off when the horse angled to the right toward the steepest part of the ravine.

"Come on, boy, help me find her!" he yelled through a ragged breath. All he could see was his father's chestnut mare sprinting out into the road and being hit by the truck. He couldn't let anything happen to Brandy. He had to reach her before she got clear back by the ravine. She'd only been there once and didn't know the terrain like the other horses. If he didn't stop her in time, she could break through the electric fence, lose her footing on the shale and loose rock, and plunge head first down the steep incline, dropping into Elk Ridge Ravine. If the fall didn't kill her, the raging waters below would more than likely sweep her downstream to her death.

They were within a hundred yards of the ravine when he spotted a group of horses zigzagging back and forth, trying to find shelter from the pounding hail. Another lightning bolt struck a nearby tree. The horses reared up and whinnied then galloped away from the creek.

All but Brandy.

He veered in behind her. Mud clods spewed up into his face, kicked up from Brandy's hooves as she continued on a dead run toward the ravine. He grabbed the lariat from around his neck and gave several whistles, waving Brandy down.

"Yeeaaah!" he yelled, urging Evening Star faster.

When he was within ten feet of Brandy, he held the lasso out to his side and adjusted the loop. He made three warm-up swings over his head and knew he had one shot. If he missed . . .

He held his breath and let go of the rope. As if in slow motion, the lariat whipped through the rain and hail, slipping over Brandy's neck. He yanked hard and galloped alongside the mare, staying between Brandy and the edge of the cliff. Brandy started to slow as he eased Evening Star back to a canter. They rode parallel until their strides were down to an easy trot. Brandy snorted and tossed her head, and both horses wheezed for air.

He tipped his head back to the sky and let the rain soak his face. "I got her, Dad!" he shouted. "I got her!"

Keeping Brandy safely beside him, he urged Evening Star toward the ranch yard. Despite the heavy rain, a ball of fire engulfed the sky. He entered the ranch yard and jumped to the ground before the horses were even stopped.

"Debra!" he yelled, frantically searching the opening of the barn.

"Joshua!"

He swung around just as she bolted out of the steel building and jumped into his arms, fully knocking him backwards onto the ground. He couldn't help but give a whoop and a holler as he raised his head up out of the mud. "Whooeee, girl! You've put on a little weight since you were eight years-old."

"Joshua David Garrison, if you ever scare me like that again, I'll—" she stopped just as Brandy rubbed her head against Debra. She sat back, straddling his waist, and threw her arms around the mare's head. "Oh, baby. Thank God you're safe."

"Oh, sure. I get scolded and the horse gets a hug."

In the next second, she feverishly pressed her mouth over his, tasting of rain and tears and a hint of raspberry. He closed his eyes, holding her tighter than he'd ever held anyone before. He loved her so much and wanted to be her Prince Charming. Marry her and give her a hundred kids, if that's what she wanted.

He just prayed this storm and the barn catching fire hadn't scared her into changing her mind about ranching.

CHAPTER SEVENTEEN

Jasmine twirled around for her husband. "Do you remember when I wore this dress the first time?"

Milt's eyes glinted with a hint of mischief. "Homecoming," he murmured in a scratchy voice. He wheeled across the living room floor. "In fact, I remember . . . everything . . . about you." He touched her fingertips. "You're more beautiful . . . than I've ever seen you before. You're almost glowing."

"I promised I wouldn't cry tonight," she said, putting her fingers over her mouth. Tears streamed from the corners of her eyes, probably streaking her makeup.

Milten looked so debonair in his black tuxedo, complete with shiny black leather shoes. He was almost as handsome as the night of their wedding.

"Why is it just being near you lately makes me cry?"

He patted his thigh for her to sit on. She climbed onto his lap and wrapped her arms around his neck.

"You've been through . . . a lot, Jazzy." He kissed her neck. "It's time . . . you let me . . ." He paused and kissed her chin. ". . . take care of you." His hands trembled slightly as he trailed his fingers alongside her hair, swept tightly in a chignon at the base of her neck.

"How's your head?" he asked, referring to the headache she'd had all morning. Between that and her upset stomach that afternoon, she was afraid she was coming down with the flu. She'd debated on whether to go to the reunion at all. But then she remembered the last time she'd stayed home sick and Milten had gone on without her. She didn't ever want to leave his side again.

She gave him a reassuring kiss on the lips and smiled. "My head's a lot better. Just keep this lap open in case I get tired. I can barely keep my head up past eight o'clock these past few weeks."

"You're a wonderful wife, Jazzy. Thanks for all you've done for me. Now that I'm home and stronger, I promise I won't let anything happen to you."

"Nothing's going to happen to me, baby."

"I've been thinking, maybe I can put my computer engineering degree to use. There's lots of phone-support jobs I could do that make pretty good money. You could quit Walson and we could start that family we've always dreamed about."

"You've never liked me working there have you?" She wrapped her arms around his neck. "Truthfully, though, it all sounds wonderful, but I don't want to push you too fast."

He rubbed the skin of her bare arm, the spaghetti straps struggling to hold up her breasts. It had only been six years since she'd been crowned homecoming queen at Colorado State University, but she didn't remember having this much trouble holding all of herself in. From the loving glances she was getting from Milten, she had a feeling he liked the improvement.

The doorbell chimed. "That's probably J.D." She hopped off his lap and met J.D. at the door. He was dressed to the nines in his black tuxedo, and she smiled. "Hi, gorgeous," she said, holding the door open.

He whistled and took both her hands, scanning her from head to toe. "Wow, you look terrific. I bet this will get some new memories stirred for Milt." He winked and kissed her on the cheek.

"Did Debra tell you she was getting ready over at Heather's?"

"Yeah. I talked to her briefly this morning. She's borrowing one of Heather's dresses."

"I heard congratulations are in order. When's the big day?"

"Tonight, if I have anything to say about it," he said with a huge grin.

Jasmine couldn't help but smile. He and Debra were a match made in heaven.

He looked toward the street. "The limo's not here yet?"

"No, but maybe it will give you and Milten time to talk. I need to finish getting ready.

Milten wheeled his chair into the foyer and held up his hand in a fist. Joshua bopped his fist, then gripped his hand. "How's it going, buddy? Are you ready for tonight?"

"As ready as I'll ever be."

Jasmine hunched over and pressed a kiss to Milten's cheek and heard him whisper, "Love you, Jazzy."

Joshua slid his hands into the pockets of his black tuxedo trousers, enjoying this beautiful relationship between Milt and Jasmine. Even with everything that had happened to them in the last year, it seemed their love remained strong. Perhaps adversity had even strengthened it.

Neither of them knew it yet, but they were both going to play a big part in his new camp for kids.

"Glad you're here," Milten said as Jasmine trotted off toward the bedroom. "Would you like a drink?"

"Nah, I'm good." Joshua followed Milt into the living room over to the couch and sat near the end.

Watching the bedroom door close, Milt said, "I'm going to put a call in to Connelly Communications next week. See about finding a job there. I don't want Jazzy working for Walson any longer than she has to."

They obviously hadn't heard about Robbie shutting down

the Rocky Mountain division. Jasmine was going to be out of a job anyway. By Milt's worried expression, Joshua couldn't help but wonder if it was her working such long hours that had Milt wanting her to quit. "What's the rush all of a sudden?"

"Look," Milt said, making another wary glance toward their bedroom. "There's something you should know in case something happens."

Not liking where this was headed, Joshua ran a finger around the rim of his bowtie. "What's this all about, Milt?"

"The day I got sick this last time, I had a visitor." He gripped the armrests of his wheelchair. Speaking through clenched teeth, he added, "I remember what happened the night of my accident."

"It wasn't a deer like the police suspected, was it?"

He shook his head. "That note you found? It was a warning. I think Jazzy might be in danger."

"What's going on, man?"

Milt reached out and handed over an old newspaper clipping that was folded inside his yearbook. Joshua read the headline, not sure what Milt remembered. "This is the article on the state championship our senior year. What's this got to do with your accident?"

"I almost killed Hank," Milt ground out through gritted teeth.

Joshua reached over and gripped Milt's knee. "How many times do we gotta go over this? You didn't do anything wrong. It was a clean hit."

"Guess that makes us even, then," he said, not making any sense.

"What do you mean? What makes you even?"

His Adam's apple bobbing heavily, his throat working hard as he swallowed. "It was Hank. Hank ran me off the road."

"Are you sure? The police said there were no eyewitnesses."

"He was there, J.D. He pulled me out of a tangle of brush.

He'd been drinking. Made me promise not to tell the police because he was afraid to go to prison."

Joshua reached into his jacket pocket and pulled out his cell phone. "We have to call the police."

"No." Milt grabbed his arm. "Hank threatened to hurt Jazzy if I said anything to anyone."

"Is that what that note was about that I found? Was Hank your visitor?"

"Yeah. That's when I remembered him at the crash."

"Son of a bitch. We can't let him get away with this. He almost killed you."

"I can't risk hurting Jazz. I only told you in case Hank doesn't keep his word."

"And allow him to control your life? What about the next time he's out drinking?"

Milt closed his eyes.

"You gotta do the right thing, Milt. We can't risk him going out and causing another accident. I'll call Detective Dan Malone and have him meet us at the police station. At least he can pick up Hank's sorry ass and find out what he has to say."

"What about Glen and the girls?"

He glanced at his watch. "We've got an hour. How about if you call the limo company and have the driver head straight over to Heather's. I'll fill Glen in on the situation and have him bring the girls to the hotel. Hopefully, they'll have Hank brought in for questioning tonight and we can head over to the reunion. You, Glen, and me will be together again, just like old times."

"The Three Musketeers," Milt said, his expression relaxing into a smile.

Joshua held out a fist. "All for one?"

Milt bopped his fist then covered Joshua's hand with his. "And one for all."

★　★　★　★　★

Glittering lights illuminated the grand entrance of the Antler's Adam's Mark Hotel. The historic hotel was situated in downtown Colorado Springs in the shadow of Pikes Peak. A procession of cars and limos inched closer to the entrance as couples dressed in exquisite evening wear entered the hotel.

Staring out the tinted glass window of a stretch limousine, Debra couldn't seem to let herself get excited about the night ahead. So far her Cinderella evening hadn't gone exactly as she'd hoped. When Glen had arrived alone to pick her and Heather up, Debra thought maybe Joshua was having cold feet. Not just about the reunion, but about his proposal of marriage.

She hadn't seen him since Monday after the fire. She'd helped him clean up, then headed home to Denver to stay with her mom. Since Debra's wardrobe of jeans and flannel shirts wouldn't be appropriate for a night like tonight, she'd driven down this morning to borrow a dress from Heather.

Debra nervously clutched the borrowed black sequined purse that matched her floor-length evening gown, staring pensively out the window. She hoped Joshua was already there to meet them. Glen grabbed the bottle of champagne that was chilling in a sterling silver bucket of ice. He poured three glasses and handed one to her and one to Heather.

Although Debra didn't like to drink, she took it anyway. The coolness of the long-stemmed crystal goblet was a relief on her sweaty palms. "Joshua didn't give you any indication why he was running late? Was there something wrong at the ranch? One of his horses?" she asked, nervously bringing the glass to her lips.

Glen sipped his champagne before he finally answered, "Let's just say he's taking care of some overdue business. Hopefully, he won't be much longer."

The limo lurched to a stop at the red carpet stretching from the hotel to the curb. The chauffeur got out and strode around the passenger door of the stretch limousine.

Debra cast an anxious glance out the window. Several couples in elegant evening gowns and black tuxedoes filtered into the hotel. The chauffeur opened their door. Glen set their glasses aside, then stepped out to the sidewalk, extending his hand to Heather first. "If I haven't told you before, you look stunning tonight, Heather."

Heather stood next to Glen, gazing dreamily into his eyes. "Thank you. I'm afraid it's been a while since I've dated. I'm a little nervous."

He gave her hand a reassuring squeeze. "Don't be. We've been friends a long time, and you know almost every one here. Just have fun."

She smiled and pressed a kiss to his cheek. "You're a good friend, Glen. I can't remember the last time I was dressed up like this and didn't have macaroni and cheese smeared all over my front."

He laughed and touched her elbow. "Well, as long as I've known you, I don't think I've ever seen you looking more elegant. Thank you for coming with me." For a moment they both just stood there, gazing into each other's eyes.

Debra wanted to cry. Maybe it wasn't too late to have the limo driver take her back to Heather's. She peeked her head out the door. "Uh, guys? I'm not feeling too good. Would you mind if I just went back to Heather's?"

"Oh, no, you're not," Heather stepped closer and grabbed her hand.

Glen took hold of her other arm at the elbow. "Come on, Debra. We're not letting you out of our sight till J.D. gets here. And he *will* get here, I promise."

Without another protest, he helped her to the sidewalk then held out both of his elbows. With a grin that spread from ear to ear, he said, "Two beautiful women on my arms. Life doesn't get any better than this."

They followed several other couples down the red carpeting to the entrance of the famous historic hotel. Debra had spent the entire afternoon with Heather and Katie, primping, doing nails, eyebrows, hair and makeup. When Debra had stood back from the mirror and examined her reflection, the tall, pale-faced high school girl she remembered had been replaced with a mature, sophisticated woman.

Heather had swept Debra's hair into a loose bun with wisps of ebony tendrils framing her face. Curly locks of hair brushed the nape of her neck, and her shoulders were bare except for two thin straps holding up her gown. She felt like a glass of champagne, sparkling with elegance and grace. She wanted to pinch herself to make sure she wasn't dreaming.

She'd never attended her senior prom, or any of the dances for that matter, and now she wished she could take a picture for her mother.

As they entered the hotel, Glen rested his hand gently on her lower back, exposed by the scooped dress she'd chosen. The black floor-length evening gown with its see-through silver overlay shimmered in the iridescent lights of the hotel. With trembly fingers, she touched her throat, reassuring herself that the diamond teardrop necklace Heather had loaned her was still secured safely around her neck.

As Debra shuffled in with the throng of reuniongoers, a tingle of exhilaration coursed through her. The lobby greeted them with rich woodwork and massive wooden columns. The luxurious marble floor and the grandeur of the hotel swept her away on the most exquisite evening of her life.

After what seemed like an hour of introductions, she'd met every person in Glen's senior class of nearly six hundred. Heather seemed to know everyone and had flitted across the room with some old friends. Glen, bless his heart, had stayed with Debra the whole time, introducing her to wave after wave of classmates and their spouses.

Everyone except Joshua. It was almost seven, and there was still no sign of him. Glen handed her a glass of champagne and they toasted to an evening full of wonderful surprises. She clinked his glass and sipped the bubbly confection, the carbonation making her nose tickle.

An announcement drew everyone's attention toward the main ballroom. They filtered through the double wooden doors. The elegance and grandeur of the banquet room heightened Debra's sense of awe. Large round banquet tables surrounded a shiny marble dance floor, where a black grand piano was positioned in the corner.

Linen napkins, crystal goblets, and a full array of gold-embossed stemware exquisitely adorned each table. Glen led them to a table near the dance floor. He held out Debra's chair and waved to a friend across the room. He leaned close and spoke next to her ear. "Will you be okay here for a few minutes?"

"Sure, go have fun. I love watching everyone." Debra smiled, secretly hoping for a few minutes alone. She fingered Joshua's gold-embellished name card placed next to hers, then glanced around the room. A woman across the table gave her a nod and smiled. Debra returned the gesture, then eagerly, but carefully, picked up her water goblet and gulped down a huge drink. After all the smiling, the coolness of the ice water refreshed her parched lips.

Glen returned and held out Heather's chair, then took the seat on Debra's left. The table sat eight, with three empty chairs remaining. She figured two were for Milten and Jasmine, and then there was Joshua's.

Dinner arrived in style, with the choice of filet mignon or stuffed chicken breasts. She'd chosen the chicken along with sides of steamed carrots, broccoli, and a baked potato. With her stomach bunched in nerves, she merely moved her chicken around on her plate, taking a small bite every now and then to appease the casual observer.

The lights dimmed. A tall stout woman in a pale blue gown bellowed into the microphone and welcomed everyone to their ten-year high school class reunion.

Glen leaned close and whispered, "That's Shelly 'Belly' Whipstock. She was president of the debate club."

Debra gave a small laugh. "Go figure."

"Are you having fun? I hope this isn't too boring."

"I'm having a wonderful time," she reassured him. "I'm afraid I'm not very hungry though."

"Hey," he said, touching her chin. "J.D. will be here before they serve dessert. Who knows what'll happen before the stroke of midnight?"

Joshua practically squealed his tires as he pulled up to the curb in front of the hotel. Jasmine reached forward and grabbed the dash. "Take it easy, J.D. Nothing's going to happen to us here."

"As long as that scumbag is on the loose, no one's safe."

"We'll get him, J.D.," Milt assured him.

"Damned straight, we'll get him." Joshua whipped the gearshift into park and jumped out of his cab. Grabbing Milt's wheelchair out of the truck bed, he unfolded it and opened the front passenger door. As he scooped his best friend into his arms, J.D. swore under his breath and gently deposited him in the motorized chair. He straightened, setting his feet on the footpads.

Leaning his hands on the armrests, he stared into his good friend's eyes. "I'm going to nail him, Milt. He's going to pay for what he's done to you and to everyone else."

"You're a good friend, J.D. Just don't do anything that'll land your ass in jail."

"I don't know how I'm going to break the news to Debra. She'll be devastated."

Checking his watch, Milt said, "Let's just hope she's still speaking to us after we stood her up."

"Good point. I told Glen not to mention why we were late. I didn't want her to worry." Joshua stood and extended his hand to Jasmine, helping her step out of his truck. "If you hadn't noticed, Milt, your bride has never looked more beautiful than she does tonight."

"Thank you, J.D.," she said, carefully planting her high heels on the ground. "You have to promise Milt and me not to take things into your own hands. Don't go being a hero and wind up in prison, or worse, in the ground. You'll be of no use to any of us if that happens." Pressing a kiss to his cheek, she added, "I love you, by the way. You've been a true friend."

"I second that, you big lug," Milt said with a lopsided grin. "Now go in there and find that pretty lady of yours and tell her how much you love her."

Joshua reached into his coat pocket and pulled out a small maroon box. He flipped it open and gave a nervous smile. "Think she'll forgive me for sending Glen to pick her up?"

"Oh, J.D. It's stunning!" Jasmine gushed. "She'll be thrilled!"

Joshua tucked the ring box safely into his jacket near his heart and gave the valet his keys. "Shall we?" He offered his arm to Jasmine and pushed Milt down the red carpet to the lobby.

Shelly Whipstock's voice bellowed from the banquet room. Joshua groaned. "Think ol' Shelly Belly will just let us walk in without making a fuss?"

They pushed through the doors and Shelly about dropped the microphone. "As I live and breathe," she crooned. "I heard he was going to be making an appearance but I didn't believe them. Everybody? Would you please welcome our senior class president, Joshua David Garrison, and the man who helped us win two state football titles, Milten King. Come on, you two, come down here and start the dance with our high school fight song. Glen Frost?" she roared into the crowd, her hand shielding her eyes from the stage lights. "Where are you? You boys come down here and show this class you've still got spirit!"

The whole room stood as Joshua pushed Milt around the tables. Joshua leaned over the chair and spoke over the crowd so Milt could hear. "It was too much to ask, wasn't it?"

"Classmates and spouses?" Shelly interrupted as they made their way to the main ballroom floor. "We'll be holding a silent auction for Milten and Jasmine King. All the items that were donated are either placed as centerpieces on your tables or are on display throughout the room. Please be generous and help the Kings on their path to a full recovery."

Everyone applauded as they lined up next to Shelly. Joshua recognized several women who used to be cheerleaders. Glen made his way through the crowd and bopped Joshua's fist. "How'd it go down at the police station? Did they find Hank?"

"Yeah. You're never going to believe what he had to say. I need to find Debra. I don't want her left alone."

"Why? What's going on?"

Before he had a chance to explain, a group of women surrounded the three of them, chanting an old cheer they'd performed in high school. Joshua made eye contact with the one woman he'd been dreading to see all evening—or more like, for the past ten years.

Michelle Davis, or was it still Nelson? She'd been the captain of the cheerleaders, and now here she was, in all her glory, surrounded by several of her old cheerleading friends.

Michelle latched on to his arm, standing on tiptoe to speak near his ear. "Hey, J.D.," she drawled in a sickening southern twang. "It's good to see you. I was hoping you'd show up this year. I've been wanting to talk to you." Before she said another word, one of her friends flung her arms around Michelle and screamed.

He cringed. He'd forgotten how loud these women could be. He rubbed his ear and forced a smile at the other woman, recognizing her as one of the cheerleaders. For the life of him, he couldn't remember her name.

The band began to play their fight song just as Glen joined them, clapping Joshua on the shoulder. "You seen Debra yet?" he asked.

Thankful for the interruption, Joshua shook his head. "Not yet," he answered, practically yelling into Glen's ear. "Where is she?"

Glen motioned his head to the double doors in back. "Over there. She's been awfully nervous since I picked her up. I think she was worried you weren't going to show."

"Damn, I was afraid of that. What did you tell her?"

"What else? That you'd be here to sweep her off her feet any moment."

Joshua stared toward the back of the room and squinted through the maze of classmates, then he saw her and became transfixed in her gaze. She made her way through the maze of tables, holding her shoulders back, carrying herself with elegance and grace. Her hair was swept on top of her head with curly wisps framing her face and trailing softly down her long neck.

He couldn't help but notice heads turn as she glided by. She wore a black evening gown with some kind of a silver shell on top, and the dress molded her breathtakingly slender physique. She practically shimmered in the soft, iridescent lights.

"Dear God, she's beautiful," he said out loud.

"Go to her, J.D. And if you don't put a ring on her finger,

you're more a fool than I thought."

"Don't worry," he said patting his jacket. "By the stroke of midnight, we'll officially be engaged and if I have my way, we'll fly off to Reno tonight."

"I filed a flight plan like you asked. My Cessna's gassed up and ready to go whenever you say the word."

"Perfect. Wish me luck." Joshua approached the table and ran a finger under his collar. As she drew near, a pink blush covered her chest, working all the way up to her earlobes, sequined in a stunning pair of diamond earrings. Everything about her glittered. Her teardrop necklace, her shimmery black gown. All except her eyes; a trace of sadness flickered in their depths. He hadn't seen her since the fire at his ranch. She'd moved home to be with her mother in Denver.

Had she changed her mind about returning to the ranch? Had she decided to go back to Denver with her mother for good?

He warily approached and placed a protective arm around her waist, the low-scooped back of her dress exposing the creamy softness of her skin. Smooth, satiny skin that only he'd had the sheer pleasure of touching. She fluttered her long curling lashes and when she looked up, Joshua met her gaze. Neither of them turned away.

There was no way of escaping his feelings. He loved this woman to the very depths of his soul. He wanted her beside him every day working with the horses, making their ranch a success. She'd made him realize how much he ached for children, for a family to raise. He wanted to teach his kids all the things his father had taught him. He wanted the Garrison name to carry through to the next generation.

First, he had to tell her why he was late.

Debra held her breath, reveling in the softness of Joshua's heated palm on the skin of her exposed back. She gazed into his eyes and the rest of the room disappeared. He stood there in his black western cut tuxedo, wearing a white, button-down, ribbed shirt that strained against the width of his broad chest.

Her legs weakened. Her face flushed when she remembered how he'd touched her, giving her a glimpse of paradise. He'd moved her not only physically, but he'd taken the love she'd felt for him and had lifted it to a new height.

She closed her eyes briefly, wondering if she hadn't somehow been caught up in one of her fantasies. Was this all some weird dream? Was she going to wake up and be sitting on a smashed pumpkin?

His sexy baritone voice drifted into her ears. "You look astonishingly beautiful tonight, Debra. I want to whisk you away from here and devour you from head to toe right now."

As his warm minty breath fanned her face, she rubbed her cheek against his mouth, wanting to feel his lips devouring every part of her body and be whisked away to anywhere but here.

He kissed her temple then breathed deep in her hair. "Hmmmm, you smell sensational."

"So do you. I missed you," she murmured next to his ear. "Thought maybe you'd found another woman and were standing me up." She said that as a joke, but deep down, she couldn't help but wonder if he'd run into Michelle yet.

"There you are, J.D.!" A high southern twang about set Debra's nerves on fire.

A petite blond woman slithered up and possessively wrapped her hands around Joshua's arm. "You took off so fast, I didn't get a chance to tell you my news. It's so noisy in here I can hardly hear a thing. Can you believe how many people showed up this year?" She barely took a breath before she asked, scanning Debra from head to toe, "Oh, who's this?"

Debra dropped her hold on Joshua and edged backwards, bumping into a chair behind her. She had a sinking feeling in her stomach that she knew who this woman was.

Joshua cleared his throat, avoiding Debra's gaze. "This is Debra Walker. Debra?" he said, gesturing his hand toward the woman. "This is Michelle Nelson."

Debra squared her shoulders and extended her hand in greeting. "Nice to meet you. I've heard so much about you," she said, suddenly feeling like the ugly stepsister.

The woman was, in fact, everything Debra was not. Sophisticated, petite, carrying an air of wealth that shouted refinement and regal certainty. Her blond, silky hair, her radiant emerald eyes, and her dazzling white smile; all were attributes that were no doubt her lure for capturing men's hearts . . . including Joshua's.

Michelle's floor length red-sequined gown dipped so low in front, Debra fought herself from dropping her gaze to the voluptuous swells of her bosoms. She had the feeling that every man in this room would probably enjoy that view.

The only thing she really knew about this woman was that she'd miscarried Joshua's child and left him heartbroken the day before their wedding was to have taken place. From the way she was draped all over his arm, Debra deduced Michelle still had strong feelings for him.

The question was, of course, did Joshua still have feelings for Michelle?

Michelle squeezed Joshua's arm, giggling and nuzzling up to him. "J.D. and I go way back. How do you know him?"

"Actually, we go way back as well," she said, avoiding Joshua's gaze. "Our fathers were business acquaintances when we were kids."

Feedback from the speakers made a high-pitched squeal as Shelly "Belly" hollered into the microphone. "Since J.D. has decided to grace us with his presence this year, our prom queen suggested we kick off the dance portion of this evening with 'Stairway to Heaven,' the official theme song at our senior prom."

Everyone cheered. Joshua squeezed Debra's hand and whispered. "Don't worry. I'm not going to dance with her."

She turned and widened her eyes. "Why not? I hope it's not because of me."

"Of course it's because of you. I don't want to dance with anyone but you."

"Really, Joshua. The night is still young. Listen to everyone. They want to see you two together just for old time's sakes. Go. It's really not a problem." If there was something still lingering between them, Debra wanted to know now before she gave away any more of her heart, although the way it hurt right now, she didn't think she had much left to give.

"Come on, J.D. They're waiting for us," Michelle whined, tugging on his arm.

Joshua gave Debra's hand a squeeze before letting go. As they made their way to the floor, she heard Michelle say, "It's so good to be with you again, J.D. It feels like old times, doesn't it? Maybe they'll play our song for us next."

Joshua groaned as the lights dimmed and the traditional silver ball spun above them, creating rainbow flashes across the room. He strode in front of Michelle to the dance floor, took Michelle's fingers, and held her apart in a slow waltz.

Michelle wriggled closer, pressing her breasts against his stomach. "Come on, J.D. It's been ten years. Don't tell me you're still upset with me."

"Nope," he admitted off the cuff. "Like you said. It's been a long time."

"I know we left things a little, er, strained—"

"A little strained?" he repeated, his voice rising.

"Shhh," Michelle admonished, looking around. "I didn't come home to fight with you. In fact, I've been thinking a lot about you. You heard I'm divorced, didn't you?"

"What's the matter? Got bored with all Robbie's money?"

"No, J.D. I had to get out before he hurt Shelly Lyn."

He stiffened and stopped dancing. "What are you talking about? Who's Shelly Lyn?"

"She's my daughter."

"You have a daughter?" Although he had nothing but contempt for this woman, he wouldn't wish any physical harm on her or her daughter. Feeling a sudden protectiveness, he asked, "Tell me. Has Robbie hit you?"

"At first I thought he was just jealous."

"Jealous? Of what?"

"Of you."

"Why would he be jealous of me? I was the one you dumped, remember? He won."

"I think he knew I never really loved him, not like I loved you."

He shook his head. "If you loved me, then why did you run off with him?"

"Because the baby was his, J.D. I couldn't bear to lie to you and force you into marrying me, especially when you had your whole future ahead of you."

"Lied to me?"

She nodded. "I didn't lose the baby. I had a little girl. Her name is Shelly Lyn. She'll be ten next month."

Joshua's heart jumped to his throat. "Are you telling me, I've gone through the last ten years wondering whether our child was a girl or a boy, thinking about it every year on the anniversary of your supposed miscarriage, only to find out you never lost it? Son of a bitch," he swore, raking his fingers through his hair.

Robbie Nelson was the father?

"I'm sorry, J.D. I didn't know how to tell you. But it's over between Robert and me. I think he knew I would never love him like I loved you. That's probably why he started drinking. He's an alcoholic and abused me for most of our marriage. When he raised his hand to Shelly Lyn, I knew I had to leave him. That's when his father had his stroke and he moved back here to the Springs. But I'm worried. He called last week and said he's closing down the Rocky Mountain division and is moving back. He wants custody of Shelly Lyn."

Joshua gritted his teeth, trying to comprehend everything she was telling him. She didn't miscarry. She had a little girl. But the little girl wasn't his. Robbie had gotten Michelle pregnant, just as Joshua had suspected all those years ago.

Not sure what he felt, he stared down at her. "What do you want from me, Michelle? I'm not a lawyer."

Tears filled her eyes. "No, but you'd make a wonderful husband and father. Robert was right. I never stopped loving you. I was hoping you would give me another chance."

He started to pull away just as she pressed her fingers over his lips. "Please, don't say anything yet. I know you're angry with me, and you have every right. But I thought I was doing the right thing at the time. You had your whole future ahead of you and there was no way you would've been able to support us and go to college. I had the baby to think about. If I'd known how Robbie was going to treat us, I never would have left you."

She stood on tiptoes and slipped her hands around his neck. "Remember all the good times we used to have? I know we could get that back. My parents even said Shelly Lyn and I can stay with them until we get things arranged between us. Please, J.D., just think about what I said."

Joshua gazed down into her emerald green eyes, and as he

held her soft, voluptuous curves, breathed in her expensive perfume, nothing flowed between them. Certainly not love. He'd always love the memories they'd shared together. After his father had died, Michelle had been there for him at a lonely time in his life. But the love that he'd thought was real all seemed a distant memory now.

He set her apart and tried to keep his voice level. "I'm sorry, Michelle. I don't love you anymore. I've grown up since high school. As far as Robbie is concerned, I think staying with your folks is a good idea right now."

Especially in light of what he'd learned tonight.

Debra made her way through the mob of reuniongoers from the ladies' restroom. As the music got louder, so did everyone else. Women kicked off their shoes and danced stocking-footed. Men discarded their jackets and undid their bowties.

She didn't see anything of Joshua as she picked up a water goblet, taking a long drink before setting it back on the table. She almost choked when a large warm hand covered her arm, followed by fresh minty breath fanning her face. "Are you ready for that dance?"

Debra froze, breathing in Joshua's wonderful manly scents. The leather and horse smells that she'd come to love were replaced with a hint of musk and spearmint gum.

Without turning around, she spoke, but it was hard to get it out without shaking. "I've kind of got a headache. I was just going to call a cab and go home. Besides, I think Michelle is looking for you."

"I don't want to be with Michelle, Debra." His fingertips trailed down her arm, making her shiver. He interlaced his fingers with hers and spun her gently around. "Please, dance with me. I have to talk to you." He stood there, only inches from her face. His intoxicating scents were more than she could take right now.

She closed her eyes so she wouldn't have to look into his deep brown eyes. The eyes she'd fallen in love with. The eyes she'd pictured on her little boy. "I need to go," she barely whispered over her beating heart.

"Nope." He leaned closer and squeezed her hand. "Not until you dance with me. I even wore my shoes with the bricks in the ends."

She opened her eyes and found his gorgeous smile, his dimple giving her that little wink. His eyes almost twinkled. She stood back and tipped her head to the side. He, in fact, looked ornery. "What is that smile all about?" she asked through her tears.

"You don't look like you're having a very good time. Come on, we need to have some fun." He twirled her hand above her head, swinging her out onto the dance floor.

It was a fast swing song and she laughed as he began to jitterbug to the beat. "Are you drunk?" she yelled over the music.

"Only on you, darlin'!" he yelled back. "Only on you!" He twirled her around again and she couldn't help but laugh and follow his lead. His bow tie hung loosely around his collar and his shirt spread open, unbuttoned at the neck. It revealed a few dark wispy hairs from his chest, the chest she yearned to touch and feel pressed up against her again.

A wide black cummerbund fit snuggly around his firm, trim waist. His black jacket with tails made him look like the prince she'd fantasized about in all her storybooks. He hadn't taken his eyes off her from the moment they'd started dancing. She tipped her head back and let out a fit of delirious laughter, enjoying the close bond of friendship with this extraordinary man.

Friends. If that's all their relationship ever turned out to be, that was fine by her. She couldn't imagine life without a friend like Joshua Garrison.

She let out a little scream as he whipped her around again and twirled her into the hardness of his body. He encircled her with his muscular arms, swaying into her from behind. With his cheek pressed next to hers, she looked at him out of the corner of her eye. "Joshua David Garrison, what's gotten into you?"

His wonderful sexy laugh made her shudder. "You sound like my mother." Kissing her earlobe, he lowered his voice to a sensual murmur. "But you certainly don't look like her. You are the most beautiful woman here tonight, in case you didn't know."

"You must be drunk." She giggled and tried to pull away.

"No way. I haven't touched the stuff since high school." He whisked a strand of hair out of her neck and kissed her nape. She reveled in the softness of his lips as he squeezed her tighter from behind, cocooning her into his embrace.

Swaying with the fast rhythm of the music, she closed her eyes and blocked out everyone else. A sensual shiver ran all through her body down to her toes. She rubbed her face against his smooth, fresh-shaven skin, then stroked his forearms with her fingernails. "I don't know what you ate, but I hope you have more before the night's over."

"Believe me, it's nothing I ate . . . yet." He nibbled her earlobe and slid kisses down her throat.

She couldn't help but arch her head back against his chest. "What about Michelle?"

"I don't love Michelle, Debra. I don't think I ever did." Her heart swelled with joy to hear those words, but it was the other three words she wanted to hear the most.

The tempo switched to a slow ballad. The floor was packed with couples dancing under the silver ball. His large palm flattened against her stomach, his thumb brushing the lower swells of her breasts. He slowly spun her around to face him, brushing a whisper-soft kiss across her lips that made her legs about as sturdy as overcooked noodles.

She leaned her forehead against his chin. "How do you do that?"

"Do what?"

"Kiss me and turn my brain into soggy oatmeal. I think I need to get some air." She started to pull away, but he covered her lips again, this time with more mastery, more passion than she'd ever felt. Her arms curled against his stomach, rock hard and radiating with heat as his hand gripped her lower back to hold her up.

She closed her eyes and leaned her head onto his shoulder as he trailed the back of his fingers over the nape of her neck. "How's your headache?" he murmured into her ear.

"Hmmm," she moaned. "What headache?" She peeked at him through half ruised lids then took a quick intake of air, surprised when he brushed his lips across hers. She didn't hesitate a moment to respond by parting her lips and drifting away on a succulent journey into his soul.

Never had she tasted anything so warm and giving. His tongue traced her teeth, taunting her, teasing her into leaning into him. His hand dipped lower in her gown, the flesh of his palm burning against her skin. It seemed nothing could put out the flame that he'd ignited in her soul.

She didn't know of anywhere she'd rather be than right here. The slow, steady tempo and the darkened dance floor transported her into her very own fantasy storybook. Dancing with the man she loved, dressed in all of his finery, fulfilled every dream, every wish she'd ever made as a little girl.

But she wasn't a little girl, and this wasn't a dream. It was real. Joshua was real. The hardness of his shoulders and his stomach pressed to hers were real. He slid his thigh between her legs, pressing his hardened midsection into the apex of her legs.

She groaned into his ear. "I don't think you should do that," she whispered, making no attempt to push him away. "I'd hate to embarrass you in front of all your friends."

He slid his hand further inside her dress, pressing her closer with his arms of steel. "I want to make love to you so desperately, Debra." His voice was a husky murmur next to her ear. "To-night."

"I'd kind of hoped the first time would be a little more private," she teased, stroking her fingernails across the nape of his neck. All too soon the music switched to a fast tempo. She wrapped her arms around him, afraid to let him go, afraid that at the stroke of midnight her fairytale would end.

He gazed lovingly into her eyes, his lips forming that delectable smile that always made her toes curl. Dear God, she loved this man so much.

Lowering his head, he gave her the same sweet kiss he'd given her at his parents' house during the thunderstorm. When he drew away, she was speechless. A tear dripped from the corner of her eye as she gazed up at him through heavy lids.

He kissed the corner of her eye. "I'm going to take it as a compliment when you cry after I kiss you."

Her shoulders shook as she let out a quiet sob. "I'm sorry. I don't know what's wrong with me."

Tugging her even closer, he murmured, "I'm sure everything that's happened in the last several months has a lot to do with it. I'm afraid I've got some bad news, though."

She stiffened, bracing herself. "What is it? Did something happen at your ranch?"

"No. Everything's fine at the ranch. I've even talked to a builder about putting up another steel building to match the other one."

"That's great. What's the bad news?"

"Milt remembered what happened the night of his accident.

That's why we were so late. We had to go down to the police station."

"The police?"

He nodded. The band started playing a fast-tempo song, but they remained in the middle of the floor, swaying slowly as he explained the whole story about Hank's injury in high school.

"Nadine said he got addicted to painkillers," Debra added. "Now he can't get his prescriptions renewed."

"The night of the rodeo, Milt dropped Glen off at his mom's condo. Glen had been drinking and didn't want to be on the roads. His mom lives in the same complex as Robbie Nelson, and when Milt was driving out, he saw Hank giving money to Robbie in exchange for some kind of drugs. Come to find out, Hank and Robbie had a little arrangement. Robbie was selling Hank his father's pain pills. More specifically, Vicodin."

"That's a narcotic. Why would Robbie get involved in something like that?"

"Hank admitted he was blackmailing Robbie."

"Blackmail? For what?"

"Extortion. He was skimming money from the books wherever he could; exaggerated travel expenses, bogus office supplies, used, low-quality computer equipment but was charging the customers full cost."

"Do the police know?"

Motioning his head to their table, he said, "I think we ought to sit down."

She remained in the middle of the dance floor. "Tell me what's going on, Joshua. You're starting to scare me."

Gripping her shoulders, he said, "At first, Milt thought Hank had run him off the road."

"Hank, why?"

"Let me start at the beginning. Like I said, Milt saw Robbie giving him the drugs, but it's what he heard that was the incriminating part. According to Hank, Robbie and his ex-girlfriend, Carolyn Strome, had been extorting funds from the company for months. He was doing it at their Boston division, as well. Hank found them in Robbie's office late one night, drinking, and learned all about their plans to shut down the Rocky Mountain division. Hank threatened to go to the police, and since Robbie knew about Hank's addiction, he bought Hank's silence with pain pills. The police found Carolyn and brought her in tonight as well. She was fully cooperative and agreed to testify against Robbie in exchange for a lesser charge."

"So, what happened the night of the rodeo?"

"After Milt dropped Glen off, Milt heard Robbie and Hank arguing about what Robbie was doing at Walson. Milt took off down Pikes Peak to go to the police—"

"But Robbie took chase and ran him off the road," Debra finished. "Not Hank."

"I'm afraid so. Hank followed and actually saved Milt's life, but with a DUI already on his record, he fled the scene and made an anonymous call to nine-one-one. When Milt started to get his memory back, Robbie sent Hank to give Milt a little warning. Said he'd hurt Jasmine if either of them thought about going to the police."

Suddenly frantic for Jasmine's safety, Debra grabbed Joshua's shirtsleeves. "Where's Robbie now? Did the police arrest him?"

Joshua's eyes narrowed. Muscles in his jaw ticked as he clenched his jaw together, but he only shook his head no. "They've got an APB out on him, but they can't locate him. He's not at Walson, his condo, and even his parents don't know where he is. Since Stan's stroke, they've been pretty much out of the loop, giving Robbie full access to everything. Robbie even has power of attorney for his dad." Joshua gave a cynical shake of his head. "He's been stealing money from his own father."

"So, what do we do now?" Debra made a frantic search

around the nearby tables. "Milt and Jasmine. They're not safe."

He motioned his head to the other side of the dance floor. Jasmine was curled on Milt's lap as they swayed to a slow love ballad. "Relax, honey. Nothing's going to happen tonight. Between Hank and Carolyn's testimony and a complete audit of Walson's records, Robbie's ass is grass. He won't be able to hurt anyone ever again."

"Thank goodness," Debra said through a loud sigh. She slipped her arms around the security of Joshua's waist and leaned her head against his chest. "Money can sure do strange things to people."

Joshua tightened his hold on her and pressed a kiss to the side of her face. "Debra? I haven't told you the worst part."

She froze.

"Come on, we need to sit down."

This time, he wrapped his arm around her waist and led her across the dance floor. He pulled out a chair and waited until she was sitting before he pulled up a chair for himself. As if gathering courage to tell her something, he filled her water goblet and offered her the drink. She took it, but only so she had something to hold on to as she tried to prepare herself mentally for whatever it was he was about to say. It had to be bad for Joshua to be so nervous.

When he finally finished off a full glass of water, Debra couldn't stand it any longer. She set her glass down and gripped his knee. "Joshua, whatever it is, just tell me. Straight out. You don't have to baby me. I'm not going to break. What is so bad that it has you sweating bullets right now?"

His throat worked hard as he swallowed. Taking both her hands, he gave them a reassuring squeeze. Lowering his voice, he said, "Your father's death wasn't an accident."

Confused, she drew her head back. "What are you talking about? I was there. I saw it happen."

"You told me you thought you saw taillights."

"It was lightning," she quickly interjected.

"Robbie was there, Debra. He wanted his money. When your father told him he didn't have it, Robbie killed him, bashing him in the head with a wooden post. He dumped him in the cattle pen and let the steers loose to make it look like an accident. Your dad didn't have a chance. After what you told me, Robbie obviously thought he could get the life insurance money from you, only there was no policy."

"Oh, God," she said, covering her mouth. "H-how do you know this? You said Hank was blackmailing him. Was he there, too?"

"No, but Carolyn Strome was. She saw the whole thing. Said he'd been drinking and threatened to kill her if she said anything."

"I think I'm going to be sick." Her breathing turned rapid. She pushed away from him, tears filling her eyes. "Robbie killed Daddy?" Still not quite believing everything, she blinked, trying to clear her eyes. "I saw the steer. There was so much blood!"

He gripped her shoulders and crushed her to his chest. "Shhh, it's over now. The police won't let Robbie get away with it. He's going to be spending the rest of his life regretting he ever laid a hand on you or your father."

Debra flung her arms around his neck. "Oh, Joshua. This is all so overwhelming." It wasn't her fault. She hadn't let her father down. It was Robbie. He'd killed her father.

Joshua pulled her close and squeezed her tighter, his fingers dipping below the material on her lower back. "Who knows? Maybe they have Robbie's ass behind bars as we speak. I promise, Debra. He'll never hurt anyone ever again."

"Oh, God, Joshua," she cried. "How can one person be so vicious?"

He blew out a heavy breath and shook his head. "I don't

know, honey. I don't know."

As she let the devastating news sink in, she clung to him for several minutes, feeling secure in his arms. She loosened her hold and let out a deep, calming breath into the side of his big brawny neck. She was safe here. *Robbie will never hurt anyone ever again.*

She gave a small shudder when Joshua pressed his mouth to her ear and spoke in a husky murmur. "How about we just forget about all this for awhile and concentrate on us for a change. Did I tell you how extremely beautiful you are tonight?"

"Several times, as a matter of fact." She snuggled closer. "But a girl can't hear that too many times."

He dragged his fingers over the smoothness of her arms and interlaced their fingers together. "Come on, darlin'. Let's get out of here." He pulled her snugly into his side, his hand cupping her hip, squeezing gently. "I'll tell everyone we're leaving."

They'd just exited the ballroom when they saw Glen jogging toward them, almost knocking over one of the waiters. "We got a message at the front desk that someone broke into Heather's condo. We called the police and they're on their way. We gotta get over there."

"Shit," Joshua swore, not even trying to hide his anger. "What else could go wrong tonight?" He gripped Debra's shoulders. "Listen, honey. I want you to go with Milten and Jasmine and make sure they get home all right. I'll get my truck and take Glen and Heather and check things out. I'll pick you up from the Kings', okay?"

Debra nodded in agreement, her eyes filled with fear and disappointment. He cursed again and shook his head, looking at Glen. "I don't want them going back to Milt's. Until we know for sure they have Robbie, I don't think Milt or Debra are safe."

"I agree," Glen said. "What do you want to do?"

"My ranch. I'll have the limo take them there. They'll be safe with my folks tonight. I'll go get the truck and take you and Heather with me to find out what's going on."

Glen handed him a set of keys. "I got these from the valet."

He slid off a key and pressed it into Debra's palm. "This will get you into the main house, honey. I'll get Heather and the kids and bring them out with me. I think for now, the ranch will be the safest place for everyone." With love in his eyes, he kissed her and spoke next to her mouth. "I'm sorry. I promise, when this is all over, I'll make it up to you."

She threw her arms around Joshua's shoulders and squeezed. "Be careful, cowboy. Let the police earn their badges."

Without another word he dipped his face to hers and gave her one last kiss. She almost clung to him when he pulled away, his gaze burning into hers. For a moment, she thought he might actually say it. Tell her that he loved her.

But he only touched her cheek with the backs of his fingers before he turned and fled the hotel. All she saw were the tails of his tux flying up as he jogged across the parking lot toward his truck. Glen took Heather's elbow and escorted her out to the curb to wait for Joshua.

She met Milt and Jasmine near the door. Jasmine's eyes were bloodshot and she was carrying her shoes, trying to push Milten across the front of the hotel. Debra wedged in front of Jasmine and took hold of the wheelchair. "Allow me to do the honors," she said. "Where's the limo? Is it here yet?"

"I think it's still parked over there," Milt said pointing to the white stretch limo near the back of the parking lot."

"Maybe the driver fell asleep. Come on. Let's hike over. It you want, you can hop on Milt's lap, Jasmine. I'll be your personal chauffeur."

Joshua jogged up to the driver's side of his truck, catching a glimpse of Debra as she steered Milten's wheelchair toward the limo. Jasmine had even climbed on, resting her head on Milt's shoulder. Joshua started his vehicle, catching another glimpse of the lady who'd showed him how to live, how to love.

Why didn't they wait for the limo to pull up to the curb?

An eerie sensation needled his gut. He drove up to where Glen and Heather stood and rolled down his window. "Who called you about Heather's condo?"

"Heather got the message from the front desk clerk."

"So you never actually talked to the babysitter or the police?"

"No. When we tried to call Heather's, the number was busy."

A set of headlights popped on from the limo. It started moving toward Milt, Debra, and Jasmine as they walked across the lot.

It sped faster, barreling straight toward all of them.

Before Joshua could comprehend what was happening, Jasmine screamed. Debra shoved Milten's wheelchair out of the way.

In the next horrifying instant, the limo rammed into Debra, flipping her body into the windshield, and sending her flying over the top of the limo, landing hard on the pavement. She rolled several times before she came to a stop.

The limo swerved, then made a U-turn—intent on taking another run at Milt and Jasmine.

"God damn that son of a bitch!" Joshua roared, and he had never meant it more in his life. Dropping his truck into drive, he floored the accelerator, his tires squealing as he veered his truck on a head-on collision course with the limousine.

With his foot all the way to the floor, his four-by-four tonner pickup truck slammed into the hood of the limo. Airbags deployed, but he kept his foot on the gas, shoving the limo into several parked vehicles, caging the driver in a mass of crumpled metal.

As the air bags slowly deflated, Joshua stared through the

windshield and saw Robbie slumped over the steering wheel, motionless, blood dripping down the side of his face. The engine of Joshua's truck was still revved as his foot was practically frozen to the floorboard.

Then he saw her.

Debra. Her crumpled body was lying on the ground just yards away. Glen and Heather sprinted over to where she lay.

Prying his foot off the accelerator, Joshua switched off the ignition and shoved against the driver's side door, jammed from the impact of the crash. He let out a thunderous roar, releasing a volcano of anguish before he crawled over to the passenger side and pushed the door open. His chest heaved for air. He staggered as pain seared through his leg.

He shoved a bystander out of the way as he bolted to Debra's side, falling to his knees and taking her hand. "Sweet Jesus."

"We called nine-one-one," Heather whispered, stooping over Debra on the other side.

Debra struggled to breathe. Her whole body trembled. Joshua whipped off his tuxedo jacket, draping it over her shoulders and midsection. Her skin looked ghostlike next to the crimson liquid oozing onto the pavement.

She gasped, then tried to speak. Her eyelids opened halfway.

He leaned over her face, carefully stroking her hair. "Hang on, darlin'," he whispered in her ear. "Help's on the way."

"Joshua?" She swallowed. A tear dripped from the corner of her eye.

"Shhhh, don't try to talk, baby." He gently squeezed her hand and pressed his cheek next to hers. Tears stung his eyes.

Her grip loosened as her eyes slowly drifted shut. "I love you."

"Oh, God," he cried. "I love you, too, Debra. I love you so much. Please don't leave me. Please, darlin'. Stay with me."

CHAPTER EIGHTEEN

Debra licked her parched lips. She tried to open her eyes. Bright lights pierced through her slitted lids. She clamped them shut. Voices. What were they saying? She couldn't understand. Where was she?

In desperation, she forced a small sound from her throat. Someone took her hand. Warm minty breath mixed with an odd smell that reminded her of a doctor's office.

"Debra? It's Joshua. Can you hear me, darlin'?"

A soft kiss on her lips encouraged Debra to open her eyes. A vision of a handsome man wearing a familiar blue denim work shirt filled her eyesight. "Am I in heaven?" Her voice sounded hoarse and scratchy.

He smiled and placed a tender kiss over her lips. "No, thank God. You're in the hospital. How do you feel? Can I get you anything?" He started straightening the blanket and resituating her pillow.

"I'm thirsty," she choked out, trying to get her tongue to function.

"Here. You can have some ice chips," he said, scooping a few chunks into her mouth.

She savored the coolness on her tongue and licked her lips. "What time is it?" she asked, in a voice that could barely be heard over the sound of several machines beeping.

"First, I think you should know what day it is. It's Tuesday afternoon, around four-thirty. You've been going in and out of consciousness for three days. Do you remember the accident?"

"Accident?" she repeated. She felt like she was floating. Monitors beeped in a steady rhythm near her head. The smell of disinfectant combined with medicine swirled through her senses. She tried to lift her arm but was hindered by an IV line taped to her wrist. Her head throbbed, every facet of her body ached, and she felt as if she'd been run over by a Mack truck.

Then she remembered bright lights . . . running. *Milten.*

"Oh, God, Joshua, Milten. Is he all right?"

"He's fine and so is Jasmine. You saved their lives." Joshua pulled up a chair and sat next to her, kissing her fingertips. "Do you remember the car hitting you?"

She closed her eyes and gave a slow shake of her head. "It happened so fast."

Joshua exhaled loudly and pressed her hand to his cheek. "It's a miracle you survived. It's been pretty touch and go."

"Who was it?" Her heart sped up, beating loudly in her ears.

"It was Robbie."

She closed her eyes. "Did he get away?"

"Not this time. He took another pass at Milt and Jasmine, but I rammed him with my truck. I'm afraid he's meeting his judgment down under as we speak."

"So he's . . ." she swallowed hard.

"Yes, Debra. He'll never hurt anyone again."

"Oh, Joshua. What's going to happen to you?"

He reached up and stroked wisps of hair out of her face. "Calm down, honey. I've been cleared of any charges."

A tear trickled down her cheek. "Thank you," she managed to say barely over a whisper.

He brushed a kiss over her lips. "All part of a pickup man's line of duty, ma'am."

She smiled and tried to move her legs, but couldn't feel anything. "My legs. I can't move." She clenched Joshua's hand, her breathing turning short and ragged. "Joshua. I can't move!"

"Shhh, don't worry. The doctors said it's too soon to tell how much damage has been done. You suffered severe internal injuries and a broken leg, and there's still a lot of swelling."

She breathed heavily, the exertion of trying to move exhausting her. "Did I hear my mom? Is she here?"

Joshua's jaw tightened as he gripped her hand. "Oh, yeah. She's been here since they brought you in. She's out with the doctors now. They'll be in to talk with you in a little bit. They want to make sure you're coherent."

She started to laugh, then grimaced. "I don't feel very coherent right now."

He cupped her face with both hands, the warmth sealing her into his loving embrace. "God, I thought I lost you. There's something I have to say to you. I can't let it go another second." A tear fell from his eye, sliding down his cheek. "I love you, Debra Walker."

A sob tore through her chest, but it was a cry of happiness. He said it. He actually said those three little words.

"I love you, too," she mouthed, finding it hard to make a sound come out of her throat.

"I want us to get married right away so I can take you out to the ranch and help you recuperate." He kissed her nose, then rested his large palm over her abdomen. "As soon as you're stronger, I want to start on that huge family you've always wanted. I want to watch our kids grow up, watch you love them and nurture them just like I know you'll do."

"Oh, Joshua," she barely managed through a choked voice. "Do you know how good it is to hear those three little words?"

He brushed a tear off her cheek with the pad of his thumb. "I want to make my father proud, honey. I want to carry on his name, keep the Garrison legacy going into the next generation." He kissed her forehead. "I love you so much."

"Are you sure? I know how you feel about marriage and kids."

"I admit, I was scared, but tell me one person who isn't when taking on that kind of responsibility. But together, we can do anything, honey." He reached into his shirt pocket and pulled out a small box. "I wanted to give this to you after the reunion."

He tugged out a sparkling diamond solitaire and took hold of her hand. His eyes misted over as he slid it onto her finger. "I love you, Debra Walker. I want to make you my wife and live with you happily ever after."

He placed a kiss over her finger then sealed his love with a kiss on her lips. All she could do was cry. "Oh, Joshua, I love you, too."

Several people filtered into the room. "Debbie? Honey? It's Mother. Can you hear me?"

Debra smiled through her tears. "Yes, Mother. Loud and clear."

"I've been going out of my mind worrying about you," Mrs. Walker said, grabbing her other hand.

"I'm fine, Moth—" She winced as searing pain jolted up her leg into her hips. "I think."

Several doctors in white coats and nurses dressed in scrubs surrounded her bed. A doctor leaned over her, flashing a light into her eyes. "Miss Walker? I'm Doctor Ramsey. I'd like to fill you in on your injuries."

"Will I be able to walk again?"

Her mother squeezed her hand and spoke to the doctor. "I think it'd be best if just you and I spoke with Debra right now."

Joshua shook his head and squeezed her other hand tighter. "I'm not leaving, Mrs. Walker."

"Are you Debra's husband?" the doctor asked.

Raking his fingers through his hair, Joshua let out a heavy sigh. "No, not yet, exactly."

"Then, I'm afraid you'll have to leave. If Debra wants to fill you in on the details, that's up to her, but right now I think it'd be best if I spoke with Debra and her mother alone."

Joshua searched Debra's eyes. "Will you be okay?"

Debra smiled reassuringly. "I'll be fine. I'll see you in a little bit."

Grudgingly, Joshua left Debra alone with her mother and the doctor. He slid several quarters into a coffee machine and abruptly hit the button. What were they saying? What could they be telling her that he couldn't hear?

After several minutes, the doors to Debra's room flew open and the doctor and her mother both converged over near the nurse's station. Joshua hurried back into her room. Debra's eyes appeared glazed over as she stared up at the ceiling. Tears coursed down her cheeks.

Sweet Jesus. He threw his cup in the trash and took her hand. "I'm here, darlin'. You're going to be okay." She didn't respond to his touch. She wouldn't even look at him. His heart gave a hard kick in his chest when he noticed her ring finger. There was no ring. The box was sitting near her on the table.

"What is it, Debra? What's wrong?"

She rolled her head away from him and closed her eyes. "Go away, Joshua. I want to be alone."

He leaned closer, bracing his hands beside her shoulders. "Did the doctors say something to upset you?"

"I'm going home to Denver with my mother as soon as everything is arranged."

He swept her hair from her neck and huddled near her. "I don't understand. I thought you'd want to stay with me. You don't have to listen to your mother. Is it your legs? What did they say? No matter what happened, it doesn't matter. As long as you're alive and smiling, that's enough for me. We'll make this work. Please. Let me take care of you."

She turned her head. "No. You deserve a whole woman. I don't want to be a burden on you. I'll only be a hindrance to your ranch."

"No, sweetheart. You'll never be a burden. We'll get through this together, just like Jasmine and Milt. I'll build ramps and we'll get special equipment installed." He swallowed and cupped both hands over the delicate skin of her face. "Please, honey. I need you to stay." Tears filled his eyes. "I love you so much," he murmured barely over a whisper.

She reached for the nurse's call button and punched it frantically. "I've made up my mind. You deserve a whole woman. I can't . . . I won't do this to you. Please. If you really love me, you'll let me go."

CHAPTER NINETEEN

Debra grimaced as the morning stiffness worked its way out of her legs. The mornings were the hardest, on her body and her spirit. Her survival of the attempted murder had been a miracle in itself.

She'd suffered massive internal injuries, the surgery adding a lovely new scar across her lower abdomen to her already long list of injuries to her body. She'd also sustained a broken leg, several torn ligaments, and twisted tendons. After six months of rehabilitation and therapy, she'd regained most of her strength and could walk without the aid of crutches.

Now if she could only wrap a cast around her wounded soul, she might even heal.

She ached every day as she forced herself out of bed. But each day that dragged by was one more day without Joshua. He'd pleaded to take her out to the ranch, to tend to her, to take care of her. That'd be a riot. There was no way she'd force her crippled body on a young, virile man in the prime of his life.

She grabbed her cane and slowly stood, her legs trembling with the effort. It didn't matter anymore. As much as it hurt emotionally, she had to let go of Joshua. She hadn't even spoken to him in almost two months—not that he hadn't tried to communicate with her. She'd even gotten an unlisted phone number, but of course that just meant he drove up here every chance he could get. When she still wouldn't see him, he finally gave up and resorted to letter writing.

A stack of mail sat unopened on her dresser. Dozens of glass vases and dried flowers had been boxed and given to charity. Christmas had been incredibly difficult, not only because she missed Joshua, but because it was the first Christmas without her father.

Mother had surrounded her with gifts and food, lots of food, especially cookies. Debra was amazed she could still fit into her jeans. She'd even eased back into the workforce and taken a job in Denver, working half-days. They'd promised her full-time employment whenever she was ready. She just had to say the word.

Debra hobbled to the bathroom, grimacing with each step, then adjusted the shower head to a pulsating jet spray. The heat of the water helped work out some of the morning kinks in her hips and knees. She stretched while the water heated. Even the simplest tasks like taking a shower and getting dressed still took her over an hour.

Stan Nelson had been incredibly supportive throughout her recovery. Although he'd lost his son, Stan had stepped forward and had taken full responsibility for his son's actions, helping her to get into one of the best therapy centers and covering all the costs. He wouldn't even hear of her paying off her father's debt. Money had been the root of all their problems from the beginning, and he didn't want to hear about the loan ever again.

Walson Technology shut down the Rocky Mountain division in Colorado Springs, but Stan was through with the corporate world. He'd sold his portion of the company and was traveling with his wife now.

And so, it would seem, life goes on.

Debra limped back to her bedroom, feeling like she'd just run a marathon. She twisted her wet hair into a French braid and flipped it over her shoulder. Wearing a long blue denim skirt, she slipped a white angora sweater over her head before slumping to the edge of her bed, breathing heavily.

She tugged on a pair of low-heeled, black Roper boots and tied the laces. Perspiration beaded her upper lip, testimony to the effort it took to do the most mundane of tasks. She blotted her face with a towel and took slow, even breaths as her pain waned to a dull throb. The doctor had prescribed pain medication, but not wanting to fall into addiction, she only resorted to those if she absolutely couldn't tolerate the agony any more.

As she headed downstairs, her mother called out from the kitchen. "What would you like for breakfast, dear?"

"Cereal's fine, Mom, but I can get it myself." She made it to the bottom of the steps and clutched the wooden banister. Her mother set a box of corn flakes, a pitcher of milk, and a bowl on the table along with a plate of cantaloupe cut into bite-sized cubes.

Debra smiled. "I appreciate all you've done for me, but seriously, you don't have to wait on me anymore."

"It's your birthday, Debra. The least I can do is make you a bowl of cereal. In fact, I would love nothing more than to wait on you another six more months."

Debra gave a short laugh. "I don't think my hips could take six more months. And besides, I'm planning on finding my own place this weekend. It's time I quit moping around here and got on with my life." She limped to the kitchen table and scanned her mother approvingly. "Wow, you look pretty today. Is that a new jacket?"

Her mother smoothed down a spring pantsuit of mint greens and mauves. Her shoulder-length, silver-blond hair was gathered in a matching chiffon scarf. "I bought it this week. Do you like it?"

"Very nice. Are you meeting with your book club today?"

"No, but I'll be out most of the day. I've got some errands to run." Her mother hurried off to the kitchen and quickly returned with a small cake. Two candles in the shape of the number two and the number five flamed brightly on top. "Happy birthday, Debra." She set the cake in front of her.

Debra took hold of her mother's hand. "Do you know that no matter how bad things got at the ranch, you always made my birthdays special? Thank you."

Her mother swiped at a tear. "Now look what you've done. Quit talking and make a wish."

Rolling her eyes, Debra stared at the flickering flames. "I think I'm done wishing for things in this lifetime. Wishing only leads to disappointment when my dreams don't come true."

"Now Debra. Life is just full of surprises. Never give up on your dreams. Blow out the candles before wax drips all over the icing."

Debra smiled and made a wish, but it wasn't for her. She wished that Joshua could find a woman who could give him a lifetime of happiness and fulfill all his dreams of ranching and raising kids. She felt tears sting her eyes and blew out the candles.

Her mother handed her a gift.

"Presents, too? What is it?"

"This is just something small for now. I'll give you the rest later. Now go on, open it."

Debra slid her finger under the silver foil wrap and revealed a small rectangular box. She flipped open the lid. "It's a locket."

"Open it."

As soon as she flipped it open, her eyes teared over. "It's a picture of you and Daddy."

"I wanted you to know that no matter what, we'll always be close to your heart, sweetheart. Even when things seem like they'll never get better."

With shaky fingers, she held the locket to her neck. "Would

you help me put it on?"

"Of course."

Debra tugged her braid to the side as her mother draped the locket around her neck. As soon as it lay against her skin, Debra felt a certain peace wash through her. It was reassuring to know her parents would always be there to help her through all of life's trials.

"Thank you, Mom. You'll never know how much this means to me."

After a soulful embrace, her mother pulled back. "Joshua called again this morning."

"He did? I mean, he did?" she stammered, trying to hide her enthusiasm. "What did he want?"

"He wants to see you, Debra."

She jerked her head up. "You didn't tell him did you?"

"No, of course not. But he needs to understand why you're shutting him out."

"Mother," she said with a grimace as she stood and hobbled over to the counter. She grabbed her cane and leaned on it for support. "We've been over this a million times. You heard what the doctors said."

"Debra, you're healing. The doctors are amazed at how quickly you're bouncing back. They assured you that in all likelihood, you'll have a full recovery." Her mother approached and cupped Debra's shoulders. "You've been so strong throughout this whole ordeal, but it's time to let Joshua back into your life again. He needs you, honey. I can hear it every time he calls. You can't reject him because of what might or might not happen."

She closed her eyes, remembering how she'd said those exact same words to Joshua last summer. "Our lives have taken the exact opposite directions, Mother. You of all people should understand why I can't see him anymore. It would never work.

We'd both be miserable after time. I will never be the kind of wife he deserves."

She looked down and flattened her palm over her abdomen. "Do you know that he'd finally admitted how much he wanted children? He said he wanted to carry on his father's legacy and continue the Garrison name into the next generation."

She lowered her head and asked the same question she'd been asking since the doctors had told her. "Why Mother? Why would God change Joshua's mind about wanting children, then take away my ability to have children, all in the same breath?" She shook her head and closed her eyes. "God, this is killing me."

Her mother's fragile hands gripped her shoulders. "Debra, the doctors didn't rule out children entirely, and even if, and I stress *if,* you never bear your own child, there's always adoption. But you can't keep yourself from loving Joshua."

Debra pulled away and paced the kitchen, every step sending a jarring pain through her body, although she didn't know if it was the physical pain or the emotional pain that cut into her heart. She closed her eyes briefly, forcing back the tears she'd not allowed to fall since she moved back with her mother. "I couldn't live with myself knowing I'd denied him a future with his own children. He'd eventually grow to resent me."

Her mother stroked her delicate fingers over Debra's cheek. "As long as you love each other, everything else will work out. You know Joshua's heart and soul. You share the same dreams. You love horses and ranching, and if you can't have your own children, you can adopt. But please, Debra, don't let your fears come between you and your dreams."

Debra stared out the front kitchen window. Fresh green grass replaced the browned winter lawn down in the atrium. Dormant tulips peeked through the earth as winter's death conformed to spring's new birth.

Could Mother be right? Could she and Joshua have a life together even without children?

Wiping her eyes, Debra squared her shoulders and limped to the hall closet to retrieve her spring jacket.

"Debra? Are you okay?"

She turned and met her mother's saddened eyes and nodded. "I'm fine, Mom."

Her mother held the door open and brushed a wisp of hair out of Debra's collar. "Just keep an open mind where Joshua is concerned. He loves you. You have to trust him and give him a chance."

Debra stepped outside then hesitated for a long moment before she turned and faced her mother. "In case I've never told you, I love you and I'm glad you're my mother."

Her mother smiled and tenderly touched her cheek. "My sweet little Debbie." Her voice choked. "I love you, too."

Debra hobbled down the long corridor to her desk and eased her sore body into her chair. Although she still resided in a small corner cubicle, she had a window view of the distant Rocky Mountains in the west. The snow-covered peaks glistened in the midmorning sun against a canvas of dark blue sky.

After everything she'd lived through, she realized that she couldn't control her destiny. She understood that somewhere, all around her, there was a divine Power at work and she had to accept the life she'd been dealt.

She cupped her hands around a hot mug of coffee and inhaled the rich aroma of hazelnut. A photograph of her and Brandy taken a year ago caught her attention. She pulled it down and traced Brandy's white blaze running down her face. "I miss you, girl. I hope Joshua is taking good care of you." Debra kissed the picture then hung it on the wall just as her phone rang.

She swiveled around and answered, "Hello, this is Debra."

"Hey, darlin'."

Debra's heart skipped a beat. As she tried to breathe, she wondered if it had actually gone into cardiac arrest. "Joshua?" she finally managed.

"I'm here to whisk a sweet young damsel off her feet."

She closed her eyes, knowing she should just hang up. But then something he said suddenly clicked. "Wait. What do you mean? You're here. Now?" Voices outside her cubicle became louder. Forcing air into her lungs, she shoved herself up and peered over the partition. The phone dropped from her hand, making a loud thud as it clanked to the floor.

There, at the end of the corridor, stood that same ruggedly sexy cowboy she'd fallen in love with so many months ago. As soon as their eyes locked, he closed his cellular phone and his smile broadened, deepening that adorable dimple in his cheek. It was the same melt-in-your-boots kind of smile he'd given her at the auction barn last summer.

His black Resistol cowboy hat was pulled low over his forehead as his gaze, fixed and unwavering, narrowed on hers. Debra Walker. She'd only seen that look one other time in her life!

Dressed in his star-spangled western shirt and black denim jeans, his large powerful thighs carried him toward her in long, purposeful strides.

She gulped, her feet seemingly super-glued to the floor. By now, everyone within earshot had stepped out of their cubicles as he stopped in front of the opening of her cubby, holding her gaze captive with his.

He swept off his hat and smoothed his dusky brown hair over the sides. "Did your mother give you the message?" His voice was even and low, demanding a response.

Her chest rose heavily, and she gasped for air as he stepped closer, boxing her against the wall. "Sh-she," Debra stammered as she cleared her throat and nudged against her desk, her hands searching for the edge. "She said you called a few times."

"A few times?" he repeated with incredulity. "Did you read any of my letters?"

She nervously bit her bottom lip.

"I didn't think so." He arched one eyebrow then glanced over the partition at all the people watching. "Which one's your boss?"

Debra made eye contact with Ms. Gurnish, a short woman, early fifties, who could easily pass for forty the way her jet black hair hung loosely around her shoulders. Her business suit clung tightly to her petite, five-foot frame.

She stepped forward and held her hand out in greeting. "I'm Ms. Gurnish, Debra's boss. Can I help you?"

"Yes, ma'am." Twisting his hat in his hands, Joshua returned his gaze to Debra. "Miss Walker needs the rest of the day off. Can that be arranged?"

Ms. Gurnish arched her perfectly shaped brows and gave a worried glance toward Debra. "Do you know this man, Debra?"

Joshua's eyes narrowed, giving Debra a subtle warning. She had to stifle a laugh. "Uh, yeah, I definitely know this man."

"Well then, I have no problem with you taking the rest of the day off. You've been working too hard as it is." She openly scanned Joshua from his gorgeous head down to his shiny booted toes. "Go—and if you won't, I will," she added with a wink.

Joshua slid his hat back on and grinned. It was an evil smile, his lips thinning into a flat line, flickering a warning that he wasn't going to take "no" for an answer. Ms. Gurnish shooed everyone back to their cubicles and Debra suddenly found herself alone with this overbearing, overprotective, bullheaded cowboy.

Placing a hand on the wall by her shoulder, he moved closer, lowering his gaze to her lips then back to her eyes. Her knees trembled. She traced her lips with the tip of her tongue and swallowed. "Joshua? What are you going to do?" Her face warmed under the heated glow of his eyes, burning like wildfire. She scooted against the wall and braced her hand on the edge of her desk to keep her knees from buckling.

"Are you going peaceably? Or do I have to throw you over my shoulder and carry you out of here kicking and screaming?"

She nervously shook her head. "You wouldn't."

"Wouldn't I?" He dipped his head to hers and brushed a long, lingering kiss over her lips. Lips that seared an imprint on her soul. God, she missed these lips. Tears formed in her eyes, the pain in her hips and legs intensifying with each delicious, lingering moment she tried to stand.

She grabbed his shirt, clenching it in her hands, grimacing through his kiss. "Joshua, I can't . . ." Her entire body gave way as her knees mercilessly buckled beneath her.

He mumbled a low curse and in one easy movement, swept her into his arms. "I'm sorry, honey. Are you all right?"

She wrapped her arms around his neck, grimacing as another pain shot through her hips. But she didn't care. She buried her face in his shoulder, feeling his warmth wrapped around her.

"Take it easy, darlin'." He spoke softly into her hair. "Did I hurt you?"

"No," she cried. "You just kissed me."

He chuckled and pressed his mouth against her cheek. "So I haven't lost my touch?"

"No, you definitely haven't lost your touch." Her lips tipped into a smile before she kissed him this time. It'd been so long since she'd felt his warm breath mingle with hers, tasted his love, enjoyed his big, teddy-bear hugs.

He breathed deeply then pulled back, looking into her eyes.

Unabashed tears fell from his eyes. "I don't think I could've gone another day without seeing you. I've missed you so much."

She held his cheeks in the palms of her hands. "I've missed you too. But, Joshua, this will never—"

He hushed her with another kiss, then spoke next to her mouth. "Please, don't say anything. I want to show you something."

She stroked his cheek, trailing her fingers down to the soft whiskers of his bearded chin, losing her heart in the depths of his compassionate brown eyes. Nothing was going to tear her away from this man right now.

He dipped her down so she could grab her cane, her purse, and her jacket. Her co-workers applauded and cleared the aisle as he carried her, blushing face and all, to the parking lot. Carefully, he slid her into the passenger side of a brand-new shiny red pickup.

"New truck?" she inquired, admiring the rich leather interior.

He spoke as he strapped the seatbelt around her. "Yeah. My other one kind of got totaled." He reached up and stroked the side of her face, his roughened hands warm and gentle. He ran his thumb over her bottom lip, swept off his hat, and ducked clear inside the cab, placing another delicious, wet kiss over her mouth. The weight of her head forced her to the back of the seat.

"I've missed you so much," he whispered through his kisses . . . and his tears.

She rubbed her thumb over the corner of his eye. "I see I'm not the only one affected by a kiss."

"Darlin', you have no idea how you affect me."

"Where are you taking me, Joshua David Garrison? That look has me a little concerned."

He stood, settled his hat over his head, and rubbed his hands together. "That's a surprise." He shut the door then strode to the driver's side and slid in, whistling.

She tipped her head back and couldn't help but laugh. "You're worse than a kid at Christmas."

"Oh, this is much better than Christmas."

"Aren't you going to give me a little hint?"

"Nope."

Debra couldn't help but stare at the wonderful man she'd come to love with all her heart. His dimple, the way it deepened when he smiled, and his eyes, how they twinkled with mischief. Maybe *he* was Santa Claus. A modern-day Santa who drove a big shiny red truck, played pickup man at rodeos, and could kiss her to tears.

"So, how's Brandy?" she asked, trying to keep from sounding too anxious.

He slid her a crooked grin. "Oh, she's been worth every penny I paid for her. I think she misses you, though."

Debra sighed. "I miss her, too." She stared out the window. Piles of dirty slush were still heaped along the interstate from the last snowfall, but for the most part, the snow had melted.

Joshua stroked her hair out of her face, then rubbed her shoulder. "You okay? Any more nightmares?"

She shrugged. "I have them occasionally. Sometimes it's my dad in the pen of steers. And other times, I see the headlights from the limo just before it ran over me. My feet feel frozen in both dreams, and then I wake up. But I'm healing. It's been a blessing staying with my mom. Having her tend to my every need for a change has actually been pretty nice."

Feeling her necklace between her fingers was a reassuring reminder of how much her parents loved her. Joshua caressed the side of her face with the backs of his fingers. She closed her eyes and leaned into his hand. This was why she'd resisted him all these months. Even now, she didn't know how she would ever be able to leave him again.

Hoping to divert her attention away from Joshua, she straightened up. "So, how's Dillan? Is his heart doing okay?"

He gave a proud grin. "More than okay. He's been out riding Evening Star every day his mom lets him. He'll be on the pro rodeo circuit for team roping by high school."

"That's wonderful. And what about Kyle and Katie? I really miss them. I bet they've grown."

"Faster than giant sunflowers. They ask about you now and then. They want to know where the tall lady is with the pretty smile."

"They still remember me, huh?" Melancholy swept over her, as she pictured Heather's kids. Remembering Joshua with them and knowing she might never have kids still hurt like an aggravated ulcer.

"Hank's out of the rehub center," he said, easing into the passing lane. "He's been off painkillers for three months now."

"That's good to hear. How are Nadine and the kids?"

"Good. She's still shuttling them all to soccer."

He trailed his fingers down her arm and slid them over her hand, squeezing gently. "We're almost there." He stopped his truck at the end of the road leading to his ranch. Her stomach tightened. She hadn't even realized where they'd headed. How could she possibly step foot on his ranch, knowing she would never be able to return to it?

"Joshua, I don't think this is a good idea."

"It's not what you think. Just trust me one more time." He reached behind the seat and pulled out a red bandanna.

"What's that for?"

"You." He slid over and proceeded to blindfold her, tying a secure knot at the back of her head. "How's that? Can you see?"

"No." She laughed, then gasped when he lowered his mouth over hers, taking full advantage of her weakened state of mind.

Her head drifted to the back of the seat as his tongue delved between her lips, searching for more, tasting and swirling, sending her to a destination she never wanted to leave.

All too soon, he drew away, but she could still feel his warm breath wash over her face as he hovered in front of her. When she finally found her voice, she sounded breathless and winded. "You didn't have to blindfold me to do that, you know."

"No, but I did for your surprise." He shifted into drive and pulled ahead for what seemed to be a very short distance. Stopping, he slid his hand behind her head and pulled off the blindfold. After adjusting to the midafternoon sun, she looked up and found two wooden wagon wheels hung at the corners of two telephone poles with a cross pole connecting the two. Big wooden letters across the top beam read, "J Bar D Ranch For Kids".

Debra's mouth gaped open. Tears formed in her eyes. "Oh, Joshua. It's beautiful. Is the D for your dad, David?"

"Nope." He reached across and squeezed her hand. "Stands for Joshua and Debra." He slowly pulled under the cross beams on a newly asphalted lane leading up to a parking lot. Several cars were parked diagonally as Joshua pulled into the front space near his parents' ranch house.

A wooden hand-carved shingle hung above the door, reading, "J Bar D Ranch for Kids".

Her heart swelled. It felt like a balloon inflated inside her chest as the impact of what he'd done filled her with happiness. "Oh, Joshua," she whispered. "You did it."

Four small log cabins nestled at the base of the hill behind the house. An asphalt drive ran all the way to the barn and corrals. A little pen held various small animals set up as a petting zoo. A baby goat, a potbelly pig, and a miniature pony grazed on a bale of hay.

"You've even put in a petting zoo?"

"Darlin', you ain't seen nothin' yet. Wait till you see the playground out back. It's big enough for a whole slew of kids to play on."

"But, Joshua—"

"Don't say anything yet. Wait a minute and I'll help you out."

She wiped a tear that trailed down her cheek and met Joshua's warm smile as he opened her door. Any pain she may have felt as she put pressure on her hips vanished as soon as his arms wrapped around her.

Several people poured out of the office. Her mother, smiling from ear to ear, stood next to Joshua's mom and Brad. Jared held Kyle's hand as Heather and Katie tagged along behind. Her eyes widened as Milten *walked* out the door.

"Milten?" she almost squealed. "You're walking!" When Jasmine waddled out behind him, holding a burgeoning waistline, Debra's hand flew to her mouth to stifle a scream. "Oh, my gosh! You're pregnant?"

Jasmine looked down and snuggled closely to Milt. "I thought J.D. would have told you."

She gave a sideways glance, finding Joshua's narrowed gaze. He cleared his throat. "Uh, she hasn't exactly been too receptive when I've tried to talk to her."

Hoping to keep the mood happy, Debra asked, "So, when are you due?"

"Any day now. And the way he's kicking, I think the baby is definitely taking after Milten's side of the family."

Debra wrapped her arms around Jasmine's shoulder, pressing into her hard belly, filling Debra with longing and with love.

Her mother interrupted and wrapped her arms around Debra's neck. "Happy birthday, Debra. Welcome to your new home."

Debra pulled back and whispered, "But I don't understand, Mom. You've known all about this?" Everyone laughed, making her feel like she was on the outside of a very private inside joke.

Only the joke wasn't on her anymore.

Everyone gathered around her, taking turns hugging her and wishing her a happy birthday. She kept her gaze on Joshua the whole time. He'd stepped back, but he hadn't taken his eyes off her either. How was she going to tell him he'd done this all for nothing?

She had to say something. But how? Joshua's smile melted all her resolve like snow in the middle of July. She should have been ecstatic. She should have been happy for all of Joshua's accomplishments.

Instead she ached, knowing the storybook ending she'd dreamed of all these years was going to end unhappily ever after. How could she commit to someone, anyone, knowing she might never be able to have children? It wouldn't be fair. Joshua needed someone stronger, someone who could work beside him on the ranch and help him achieve his goals.

Someone who wouldn't be a burden.

She wiped her eyes, from joy . . . from sorrow.

Joshua approached her again and took her hand. "Come on, I've got another surprise." With her cane in the other hand, she slowly strolled along with him down to the corrals. She searched for Brandy, but she wasn't among the throng of milling horses.

"Where's Brandy? Is she okay?"

Joshua's smile broadened. They rounded the corner of the barn, and she stopped in her tracks. There before her was the most beautiful sight she'd ever beheld. A long-legged, chestnut colt with four white socks nuzzled against Brandy.

Debra covered her mouth and gasped. "Brandy's a mommy? How did this happen?"

Joshua's deep laughter made her knees tremble.

"Turns out you sold her to me three months in-foal."

She threw her cane down and hobbled to the fence. "Hey,

Brandy. Did you have a baby?"

Brandy loped over and sniffed Debra's outstretched hand. Debra wrapped her arms around the mare's head and kissed the blaze running down her face. "Oh, Joshua," she cried, letting her emotions flow as this bittersweet day continued to tear at her heart and soul. Her shoulders shook and her stomach tightened.

Joshua encircled Debra from behind, snuggling his face into her neck. "I love you so much, Debra. I'm never going to let you go again."

"Oh, Joshua." Debra let out a quiet sob, closing her eyes.

Joshua turned her around and cradled her in his arms, stroking her back, bringing her closer. He slid kisses down her face, to her ear. When he dragged his mouth along her jaw, she breathed in his love and compassion as he devoured her lips, forcing her into the corral fence. Her legs weakened.

She brought her hands to his chest and pushed him back. "Don't," she implored in a breathless whisper. "Stop, please. I have to tell you something." She turned around, bracing her hands on the top rail of Brandy's pen.

"What is it, honey?"

She closed her eyes. Her voice was hoarse and ragged when she spoke. "I can't do this. I can't marry you."

Silence stretched between them. Brandy snorted as she nudged against her young colt. Bracing his arms on the fence rail, Joshua caged Debra with his arms, boxing her in from behind. He spoke softly into her hair. "I understand that you didn't want to be a burden on me when you got hurt, but I'd have loved you even if you never walked again. Please, Debra, don't turn me away. I know we can make this ranch a success. Together we can do anything. I'm not going to end up like your father. I want you here beside me every day, making our dreams come true together."

The torment in his voice was almost unbearable. She lowered her head. "It's more than just making the ranch a success."

"What then? Why won't you marry me? Is it about kids? I told you, I want children now. I want as many as you're willing to bear. I've never wanted anything more in my life. But I can't do it without you. I want you to be the mother of my children. I want to watch you push them on the swings and hold them when they're sick. Please, honey, you have to believe me. I know we could be happy together. I've never loved anyone so much in my life."

"Stop!" she cried, turning around in his arms, looking into his eyes. She clenched the poplin material of his western shirt in her fingers. "The doctors said I might never be able to have children!" Her body trembled, almost quaked, as she sobbed openly. Lowering her forehead to his chest, she spoke through a heavy sob. "The doctors said I had so much internal damage that the scar tissue from my injuries may prevent me from ever having kids. That's why I can't marry you. It would eventually tear us apart. I couldn't live knowing I'd deprived you of your family legacy."

She closed her eyes and slumped to the ground. Curling her head into her arms. "I'm sorry, Joshua. That's why I haven't wanted to see you. Oh, God, I'm so sorry."

Joshua gripped the top rung of the fence, looking down at this broken lady as she rocked back and forth. Her shoulders shook. Her sobs wrenched a hole clear through his gut. She looked physically and emotionally beaten.

What could he say to her? For the past six months, she'd shut him out of her life. He thought it was because of her legs.

He clenched his eyes shut, chastising himself inwardly for everything he'd just said. He couldn't deny that he wanted children. That he wanted to carry on his family legacy, but only with Debra. Without her, nothing else mattered. How could he ever get her to see that?

Cautiously, he hunkered down in front of her. Her sobs had eased to quiet hiccups. He cupped his hands on her shoulders, then rested his forehead against hers, praying he'd say the right words. Sliding his palms to her tear-soaked cheeks, he lifted her face and whispered, "It doesn't matter." Kissing the tip of her reddened nose, he added, "All that matters is you're alive and you're here where you belong. This *is* your home now, Debra."

She pulled her head back and started to speak. He placed two fingers over her lips. "Listen to me. There will be so many children here throughout the year. We'll give them all the love as if they were our own."

She vehemently shook her head. "It won't be the same. They won't have your name."

He crouched down in front of her. His hands gently caressed her back through the softness of her white sweater. His gaze captured hers and for a moment, he drifted away in her eyes. Dear God in heaven, he loved her so much. He said a small prayer that he would have the right things to say, give her the same hope she'd given him. Another tear streamed down her cheek. He brushed it away with his thumb. His own eyes burned as moisture threatened to spill over.

"Remember your speech about seeing the positive things in life? That's what you need to do now. Take this opportunity and turn it into a blessing. You're so loving and nurturing. There are going to be needy kids here all year long. Give your love to those kids whose lives are filled with pain and suffering. Take them and show them love and happiness."

His voice choked with emotion. "*You* are why I opened this place, Debra. My name isn't important. We'll adopt if we have to, but this is *our* dream. This is our storybook ending. Please, make it real." He pulled her into an embrace. "All you have to

355

do is say one tiny word and our lives have just begun." He whispered in her ear. "Please, darlin'. Please say you'll marry me. I love you so much it makes my teeth ache."

Debra's heart throbbed at the decision she had to make. Could they have a life together? Every power within told her to say it, just one little word. As he stroked her back, breathed his love into her soul, she knew there was only one answer.

She pulled her head back, and swallowed. "When did you get so wise?"

He kissed the tip of her nose. "I'm in love with a very wise woman."

"You're going to regret this."

"Say it, Debra." He leaned his forehead against hers. "I promise, neither of us will ever regret it."

"Yes," she finally said with tears streaming down her cheeks.

"Yes, I'll regret it? Or yes you'll marry me."

"Both," she said with conviction.

He shook his head. "Uh-uh, there's no way I'll ever regret sharing anything with you, darlin'."

Without hesitation, his lips descended upon hers. The euphoria she felt numbed any pain that might have been there before, in her hips, but mostly in her heart. She couldn't deny their love any longer. She clung to him, vowing never to let him go again.

Touching his face, she smiled through her tears. "I love you Joshua David Garrison. I think I've loved you since I was eight years old."

"Oh, baby. You've made me the happiest man alive." He tipped his head back and gave an ear-piercing whistle.

Jingling reins and the snorting of a horse sounded as Evening Star rounded the corner of the barn. Debra gasped as Joshua's big black gelding pranced toward them all saddled and ready to ride.

"You don't think I'd let my princess just walk off into the sunset do you? I checked with your doctor and she said if you took it slow, it was okay to ride." He scooped Debra into his arms and stood. "It's a special saddle so I can secure your legs until you get stronger."

She wrapped her arm around his shoulders. "You've thought of everything."

"Yeah, I've kind of been going out of my mind these past few months. I couldn't wait another day."

He led her to a stoop and helped her stand. With his hands secured around her waist, she shoved her foot into the left stirrup then slowly swung her leg over the horse. Sharp, needling pains seared into her hips and lower back. She bit down on her bottom lip and grimaced as she eased into the saddle.

He tenderly massaged her leg. "Are you okay? Maybe we should hold off on this till you're feeling stronger."

She took a deep breath and relaxed. "No, it's okay. I think my legs have to get used to this again. Just don't go jumping any fences."

He buckled leather straps around her calves then hoisted himself on the back of Evening Star. Wrapping his arms around her, he took the reins and nudged his horse slowly from the barn.

A purple-orange haze painted the backdrop of the clear blue Colorado skies. The smells of the barnyard and the fresh outdoors filled her with a sense of home, as if she really was home. They took the trail that led to the back of Joshua's property toward Elk Ridge Ravine. Her eyes widened as this day unfolded yet another wonderful surprise.

"I don't know what to say."

She stared up at a massive colonial two-story home, complete with a wraparound porch and swing in front.

He nestled closer to her ear. "Is there anything I forgot in your storybook fantasy?"

She smiled and looked at him out of the corner of her eye. "Yep."

He chuckled. "What's that?"

"A kiss."

Shifting in the saddle, he planted an absolutely sumptuous kiss on her lips. A kiss that put all of her fantasies to shame. She leaned her head back against his chest and heard his heart beating in a fast cadence with hers.

As his arms surrounded her with love, she realized that all her dreams had come true. Soon she'd be living in this grand two-story home with the man she loved. Horses would be grazing in the pasture, and when the camp opened, she'd be surrounded by children . . . lots of children.

Yes, this was a storybook ending.

Joshua slid off Evening Star and unstrapped her legs. She lowered herself into his arms, wrapped her arms around his neck, and gave a loud, wistful sigh.

"Don't tell me I forgot something?" he said, looking from her to the house.

She tipped his hat back on his forehead and quirked him a little grin. "Have I ever told you about my storybook wedding? The surrey with the fringe on top, the six white steeds leading me down a tree-lined lane. Oh, and bridesmaids. I want at least four. Of course Kyle and Katie would be in it, and—"

He hushed her with a kiss that left her breathless. He didn't stop kissing her till he'd climbed the stairs and opened the front door.

She clung to her ruggedly handsome pickup man as he carried her through each room, empty and waiting for her finishing touches. When he whisked her over the threshold of their new bedroom, they stepped into their new life.

As he laid her on a massive king-sized captain's bed, he

arched his brows and spoke with heavy seductiveness. "Now, have I ever told you about my fantasy honeymoon?"

She laughed and started scooting backwards. "Does it have anything to do with a damsel in distress?"

He threw his hat on a chair behind him then crawled in beside her, boots and all. "Define distress."

With love in his eyes and compassion in his heart, Joshua lowered and gave Debra a kiss that placed her safely in his heart forever.

ABOUT THE AUTHOR

Jacquie Greenfield lives on a small horse ranch in a little part of heaven known as Iowa. She is married, has four teenage children, and spends most of her free time at school sporting events and weekend horse shows. Check out her Web site at www.jacquiegreenfield.com.